New York Times and *USA* Barbara Dunlop has written Mills & Boon, including the a series for Mills & Boon Desire. Her flirty, lighthearted stories regularly hit bestseller lists, with one of her novels made into a TV film. Barbara is a four-time finalist for the Romance Writers of America's *RITA*® Award.

Katie Frey has spent the better part of her adult life in pursuit of her own happily-ever-after. Said pursuit involved international travel and a few red herrings before she moved from Canada to Switzerland to marry her own mountain man. She is a member of a tight-knit critique group and an avid writer, and *Bad Boy Gone Good* is her fourth novel for Mills & Boon Desire. She wrote the bulk of the book in a local coffee shop... Any excuse to stay near the fresh croissants! You can join her newsletter here: bit.ly/3COLHoP. Visit her author website: romanceinthealps.com

Also by Barbara Dunlop

High Country Hawkes
Breakaway Cowboy

Gambling Men
The Twin Switch
The Dating Dare
Midnight Son
Husband in Name Only

Also by Katie Frey

Hartmann Heirs
How to Catch a Cowboy
Fake Dating, Twin Style

Montana Legacy

Discover more at millsandboon.co.uk

FROM HIGHRISE TO HIGH COUNTRY

BARBARA DUNLOP

BAD BOY GONE GOOD

KATIE FREY

MILLS & BOON

First Published in Great Britain 2023
by Mills & Boon, an imprint of HarperCollins*Publishers* Ltd
1 London Bridge Street, London, SE1 9GF

www.harpercollins.co.uk

HarperCollins*Publishers*
Macken House, 39/40 Mayor Street Upper,
Dublin 1, D01 C9W8, Ireland

From Highrise to High Country © 2023 Barbara Dunlop
Bad Boy Gone Good © 2023 Kaitlin Muddiman Frey

ISBN: 978-0-263-31764-0

0723

FROM HIGHRISE TO HIGH COUNTRY

BARBARA DUNLOP

For my mom. Happy ninetieth!

One

Colorado rancher Austin Hawkes wasn't a suit-and-tie kind of guy, but he'd made an exception as best man at his brother's backyard wedding.

A cattleman through and through, while the preacher intoned about the joy and sanctity of marriage, Austin's gaze strayed past his brother Dallas and bride, Sierra Armstrong, to the rolling meadows and mountains of the vast Hawkes Cattle Ranch.

It was early October. The drought had broken late in the summer, and the grass was knee-high now on the home fields. The aspen leaves were golden, the cottonwoods russet, and the annual roundup would start just as soon as Dallas was happily married off.

Fall was always a frantic time on the Hawkes' eighty-thousand-acre ranch, but Dallas and Sierra had been impatient to tie the knot. So, a small group of family and friends had gathered for a low-key wedding in the picturesque gazebo above the waterfall feature of the main ranch house overlooking the western valley.

It was a cloudy day and the wind lifted stray wisps of Sierra's braided, upswept blond hair. But the rain held off. The clouds parted and a rainbow appeared above the distant mountains as the couple began reciting their vows.

Sierra was a beautiful bride. Her dress was flat white lace, fitted to her slim waist, with drop-capped sleeves and a slightly flared knee-length skirt. The crown of tiny blue wildflowers set off her shining eyes. Since she mostly wore blue jeans and flannel shirts these days, the transformation was quite striking.

Austin wasn't completely sure his brother deserved her. But

who was he to question such an intelligent woman's taste in men? And Dallas was improving with age. The reckless, foot-loose rodeo cowboy had finally come home for good.

As the vows finished, the preacher looked Austin's way. Austin stepped up with his grandmother's wedding ring, overjoyed to be getting another sister. The family was more than ready for a new generation to start running through the rambling main house.

The preacher pronounced the couple married, and they shared a grinning kiss that had the small crowd clapping and hooting with approval.

After a round of congratulations and plenty of photographs, the bride and groom led the way along the cobblestone path, over the footbridge that crossed the brook, to the back patio where ranch cooks Victor and Mrs. Innish presided over an outdoor feast.

Austin hung back for a moment, enjoying the sight of his brother and father engaged in friendly conversation. That had been a long time coming. Sierra was laughing with Austin's sister, McKinney, who looked almost as pretty as the bride in azure blue with a little bit of lace. The two were friends from college, and McKinney was the maid of honor today.

A huge prime rib roast was turning on the spit. Round ta-bles were covered in white cloths, six chairs at each, with pro-pane heaters dotted in between. The wildflowers on the tables echoed the colors in Sierra's bouquet. Champagne was on ice, with flutes and fine silver set out and waiting.

Austin glanced at the sun, gauging its arc. If he was lucky, the formal lunch would wrap up in time for him to get out of these impractical clothes and meet Hardy Rawlings at the head of the Golden Ridge range. The hands should have the central herd bunched up there by now, ready to drive them down to the home corral in the morning.

A movement caught his eye at the far corner of the house.

At first, he thought it was a cowboy, but there was a flash of purple—bright metallic purple. He focused in on a woman who looked like she belonged on a fashion show runway. Her silver-and-purple blouse flowed in long lines over a pair of snug gray slacks and impractically spike-heeled ankle boots. She wore dangling earrings and jaunty sunglasses with a wispy scarf around her neck.

She looked hesitant and uncertain standing there on the cobblestone path peering at the wedding party.

He didn't blame her. If she was a friend of Sierra's from California, she'd completely missed the ceremony. She should be embarrassed.

He looked to see if Sierra had noticed the arrival. But she was surrounded by well-wishers.

Instead of interrupting, Austin started for the woman. Late or not, she was entitled to hospitality.

"Afternoon," he said as he approached.

"Hi." She popped her sunglasses up on her long, dark brown hair to look at him. If anything, the uncertainty seemed to grow in her pretty eyes.

"I'm Austin, brother of the groom, best man." He offered his hand.

She reached out to shake, revealing a slim, supple hand.

He took it gently, afraid he'd scratch her delicate skin with his calluses alone.

"Ruby Monaco," she said, her skin cool against his palm. "I've clearly come at a bad time."

"I'd say so." Now that he had her hand in his, he was reluctant to let go. He found himself gazing into her wide-set, expresso-dark eyes. Her lashes were long and lovely, balancing a pert nose and full lips.

He cocked his head sideways. "We're all down on the patio." Although that was obvious.

She nodded and withdrew her hand.

"I'll walk you down," he said and turned.

She stayed put. "Are you sure?"

He sent her a puzzled look. "Sure, I'm sure."

She gave a little shrug and fell into step with him.

"From California?" he asked.

Sierra was originally from Carmel. Although she'd mentioned having some close friends living in LA.

"Boston," the woman answered.

"Really?"

Sierra hadn't talked about anyone from Boston.

"I teach at U Ainsworth."

"Good for you."

"History."

"That must be interesting." He only needed about forty-five seconds of small talk to get them there, and this woman seemed more than capable of holding up her end.

"I'm researching a book right now."

"I see."

Her steps slowed. "Are you sure about this?"

He paused as she stopped.

"I can always come back," she said.

"Why?" He didn't know what she meant by that. Missing the ceremony wasn't the end of the world. If her plane was late or something, Sierra was going to understand.

"I'm intruding."

"Being late isn't intruding."

Something akin to panic came into her eyes.

"Austin?" Sierra approached him from behind.

He turned, smiled, and gave her a quick hug. "Welcome to the family."

She drew back with a bright smile of her own. "Thanks."

"And look who's here," he said, gesturing. "Ruby made it."

Sierra's gaze narrowed in puzzlement on the woman.

"Are you surprised?" he asked, wondering if Ruby hadn't been expected.

Sierra hit him with another fleeting glance before returning her attention to Ruby. "Hi." She paused. "I didn't know Austin had a girlfriend."

Ruby Monaco was instantly mortified.

She'd crashed a wedding reception. It was entirely accidental. But yikes. This wasn't the way she'd wanted to introduce herself to the Hawkes family.

"Girlfriend?" Austin choked out, sounding stupefied.

The bride held out her hand and smiled. "I'm Sierra. Bride." She laughed as she gestured to her lovely white dress.

"She's not—" Austin started.

"You live in Jagged Creek?" Sierra asked, looking like she was trying to place Ruby while ignoring Austin as they shook.

"Boston," Ruby automatically answered. "I'm afraid there's been a mix-up."

"Is *that* what you'd call it?" Austin demanded.

Concern pinched Sierra's face. "Did I interrupt something? I'm so sorry." She took a step back.

The groom arrived then, his arm going lightly around Sierra's narrow waist. "What's up, guys?"

Ruby guessed this was another of the Hawkes brothers. He was a near carbon copy of Austin, maybe an inch shorter, with slightly darker hair.

Sierra canted her head to look up at him. "Did you know Austin had a girlfriend?"

The groom's brow lifted in obvious surprise. "Say what?"

"At least I'm not the only one," Sierra said, pursing her lips.

"She's not—" Austin tried again.

"I think they're having a tiff," Sierra said, blowing past Austin's efforts to explain.

"Do you have to do that here?" the groom asked Austin, sounding annoyed.

Ruby put her palms face out and took a step back. It was well past time for her to have made a graceful exit. "Listen, I'll just get out of your way."

The last thing she wanted to do was disturb someone's wedding day.

"What's all this then?" An older man, imposing and quite clearly the two Hawkes men's father, strode up.

"Austin's girlfriend," the groom said.

"Will you *stop*," Austin demanded.

"I think they're fighting," Sierra said.

"I should leave," Ruby said, taking another cautious step backward. The heels of her boots were precarious on the cobblestone walkway.

"Dallas?" Sierra said to the groom, sounding worried.

"You're going to just let her walk away?" Dallas asked Austin.

"There's been a huge misunderstanding," Ruby said, wanting desperately to get out of there, regroup and figure out how to salvage the situation. "I showed up unannounced, and Austin was kind enough to—"

"You didn't *invite* her?" Sierra asked Austin, seeming incredulous.

"What is wrong with you?" the older man demanded.

"We should let them talk," Dallas said, giving Austin a nod of understanding.

"Make it quick," the older man admonished.

"Take your time," Sierra said with a compassionate smile. "But lunch will be served in about ten minutes."

Before Ruby could get away, all three withdrew to join the small joyful-looking crowd sipping champagne on the festively decorated patio.

There was no denying it was one of the most beautiful houses and beautiful locations she'd ever seen. What kind of a ranch had a babbling brook and a waterfall in their landscaped backyard? She'd been looking for a Colorado high-country ranch that was both historic and successful. She'd hit the jackpot here.

"Leave." Austin scowled, his tone grim. "Just leave."

Ruby scrambled for a way to recover from such a disastrous start. She desperately wanted to be in his good graces. "I'm sorry that went so far sideways. I only wanted to introduce myself."

"Who interrupts a wedding to introduce themselves?"

"I didn't *know* it was a wedding."

"The white dress and all the flowers didn't give it away?"

"It took me a minute." At first, she'd thought it was a picnic. It would have had to have been a very elaborate picnic, sure. But before she'd worked it out in her mind and decided on a course of action, Austin had walked up and started talking.

"Pretty slow deduction, *Professor.*" His sarcasm grated on her.

"You were the one who invited me to come on down."

"I thought you were Sierra's friend from California."

"I never said that."

"Why else would you be here all dressed up?" He gestured up and down her outfit.

"I wouldn't wear this to a wedding." The outfit was several notches too casual for a wedding.

"It's a ranch yard wedding."

"Still. Slacks and boots?"

He paused, seeming to realize they'd gotten off topic. But at least his scowl was gone.

"I'll get out of your way," she said. "Maybe we can pick a time in the next few days."

"To what?"

"To meet and talk. As I said, I'm doing research. The Hawkes ranch is noteworthy from a historical perspective. Your family captures the very essence of cattle ranching, hard work, initiative and perseverance. The mere fact you've survived to this day, never mind survived this well…" She gestured to the reception on the patio, the landscaping and the rich hills beyond, knowing she'd lucked out and feeling a deep shiver of excitement at the opportunity both the family and the ranch presented. "It's worth exploring," she finished.

"No," he said without elaboration.

She wasn't about to accept that answer. "I haven't even asked you for anything." What kind of a grouch said no to a preliminary meeting?

"You want to pick my brain."

She tried to reassure him she'd be respectful of his time. "I've done weeks of research on the region, the town, ranching, and the Hawkes. I'm not starting from scratch or anything."

"No," he repeated.

Ruby searched for the words to change his mind. She desperately needed this project to salvage her career, and Austin was her first choice as a contact.

As the eldest son, he'd been a constant presence on the ranch for three decades—unlike his two brothers, one of whom spent much of the year riding rodeo, the other a navel officer, presumably away from home for months at a time. He also had a sister, not that Ruby had a gender bias in this. But McKinney was considerably younger than her brothers.

Ruby hated losing the chance at Austin. Still, she was a realist. Her attention strayed to the others at the reception. "I suppose I could talk to someone else."

"Oh, no you won't." His tone was clipped. "I speak for the family."

Well, that was presumptuous since he hadn't even asked them. People were generally thrilled to have their family history documented in a scholarly work.

"You can't know that," she challenged.

"I can, and I do."

"Are you that annoyed? Really? An unfortunate mix-up about who I was, and you're going to hold it against me?"

"I'm not holding anything against you."

She didn't believe that for a moment. "Ha!" It wasn't her finest retort, but it had jumped out before she could come up with something better.

He moved a little closer and lowered his voice. Odd, since the others were a good thirty feet away and talking among themselves. It wasn't like he'd be overheard.

"We're a working ranch, and it's fall roundup. Nobody has time to waste writing a book."

"I'm the one doing the writing."

"You know what I mean."

She did. Her instincts told her to walk away. But she couldn't afford to take no for an answer. Too much was at stake.

She took a cleansing breath, schooled her expression and moderated her tone of voice. "It's just a few questions."

"What part of no don't you understand?"

"I think we got off on the wrong foot."

"Austin?" a voice called from the crowd.

He looked up.

"You two coming?"

Everyone was seated. Austin likely had a speech or a toast to the bride to make.

Ruby knew she had only seconds left to get him to soften his stance, or at least moderate his opinion of her so she could approach him another day. "I really am sorry, Austin. This isn't how I wanted it to go."

He gave a cool smirk and an eyeroll. "No kidding."

And then he turned his back, walking toward the beautifully decorated lunch tables for the reception.

Ruby caught Sierra's look of confusion and quickly turned herself, hustling back along the pathway to where she'd parked her rental car.

She climbed into the driver's seat and squeezed her eyes shut, clamping her jaw. This couldn't be how it ended.

Lunch over and the cake cut, Austin drifted to the edge of the festivities and paused at the gas fireplace that stood alongside the babbling brook. He had no intention of ducking out early, but he couldn't help noticing the sun sinking toward the western horizon. He'd hoped to check on Hardy and the state of the herd before dark. Too bad nobody seemed in a hurry to wrap this up.

Dallas saw him and started his way, leaving Sierra, McKinney, and a few other women, chatting around one of the tables. His brother's tie was loosened now that the formalities were over and people were starting to kick back.

"Why did Ruby leave like that?" Dallas asked, coming to a halt next to Austin.

"She's not my girlfriend." Austin had been waiting a couple of hours now to make that very point.

"Too soon, huh?"

"No. Not too soon. I'd never even met the woman before today."

"Really?"

"Yes, really."

"So why'd you invite her to the wedding?"

Austin scowled at his brother. "You're such a comedian."

"You were bringing her down to the reception."

"I thought she was a friend of Sierra's."

"Why did you think that?"

"Did you get a look at her?"

The woman was poised and stylish. Beautiful, sure, but she'd also had an air about her. She was big city through and through. Boston, as he'd learned. And it wasn't like Dallas had a lot of fancy city friends he'd invite to his wedding—especially not stunning women.

"I did get a look." Dallas arched a brow. "You sure you don't want to date her?"

"Give me a break. And shouldn't you pay attention to your bride right now?"

Dallas waved a dismissive hand. "She's fine. They're having fun. They don't need me."

"Need's not the point. You should act like a gentleman."

Dallas had spent the past ten years hanging out with rangy cowboys on the rodeo circuit. It was clear he adored Sierra, but he'd come back a little rough around the edges.

"You're itching to get out of here, aren't you?" Dallas asked.

"Not so much."

Dallas coughed out a laugh. "Which herd are you bringing down tomorrow?"

"Central. Hardy's with them at the head of Golden Ridge. With all the nitrates in the new growth up high, I won't be happy until I get eyes on them." Austin never took the health of his cattle for granted.

"You can leave, you know."

"I'm not leaving." Austin would get a call from Hardy if there was anything serious to worry about. That was assuming the new signal booster was working out there today.

Dallas nodded as his gaze scanned the reception guests, stopping to rest on Sierra.

"I can't believe she said yes," Austin teased his brother.

"What did she want?" Dallas asked.

It was an odd question. "Sierra?"

"Ruby. Who was she?"

Austin's jaw tightened as he was reminded of the unsettling conversation. "She wants to interview the family."

Dallas drew back in obvious surprise. "She's a reporter?"

"Worse." At least a media article would be short-lived. "She's writing a book."

"On what?"

"Us, apparently."

"For the tourist market? Hey, did I tell you that new trinket boutique wanted to put a picture of me bronc riding on a mug? They seemed shocked when I said no. Told me I could make twenty-five cents per mug in royalties."

Austin cracked a grin at the disgust on Dallas's face. "You don't need the money?"

"I don't need the infamy."

"It's not a tourist book," Austin said. "She said she teaches history at U Ainsworth."

"A history book?"

"I think so."

"On us?"

"Grampa Clem, I'm guessing." Austin assumed Ruby would want to go back to the beginnings of the ranch and their four-times-great-grandfather who'd started it all.

"Hmm." Dallas seemed unconcerned by the intrusion on their privacy.

Austin knew better than to be blasé. They didn't need anyone poking around, looking for secrets and scandals. "I don't have time for it."

"I suppose. I know I sure don't. The construction crew is racing to have the new house clad to weather by the end of the month. Then we can finish the interior once the snow flies. And we're heading for the bucking horse sale in Wichita Falls next week."

"Still planning to put your money in rough stock?" Austin wasn't a huge fan of the idea.

"It's what I know. There's money to be made there."

"And it keeps you out on the rodeo circuit." Austin guessed at his brother's true motive.

"But pain free." Dallas flexed the shoulder he'd injured in a fall from a bronco earlier in the year.

"It's a gamble," Austin couldn't help noting.

Austin would have liked to see his brother join with the rest of the family raising cattle. Just like he hoped his brother Tyler would retire from the military soon and come back home.

But Dallas had decided to use his share of the Hawkes' family acreage to raise bucking horses. Dallas was dogged and stubborn, and nothing was going to change his mind.

"It's what I know," Dallas repeated, all traces of amusement leaving his expression.

The two men had had this argument many times before.

"Up to you," Austin conceded this time, not wanting anything to mar Dallas's wedding day. And it was completely up to Dallas what he did with his land and his own future.

Austin didn't have to like it.

"You should call her," Dallas said after a moment of silence.

"Call who?"

"Ruby."

"Why would I do that?"

"Tell her about Grampa Clem, the cattle drives, the winters, the wolves. You know, all that exciting adventure stuff. Maybe she'll go out with you."

Austin didn't answer. He was too busy gaping at his brother's preposterous suggestion.

"You need to find someone special, Austin. You never date."

"What is this? Misery loves company?" As soon as the words were out, Austin deeply regretted them. His gaze flicked to Sierra. "Sorry. That was a vile thing to say. Sierra's wonderful. We all love her, and you're a very lucky man."

Dallas seemed more amused than perturbed. "I know I'm a lucky man. And you can be lucky, too. Just find yourself a good woman."

Austin frowned. "I've got a herd to bring in." He wasn't going to discuss his personal life with his starry-eyed brother. And he wasn't going anywhere near Ruby and her plans to ransack his family's privacy for profit and entertainment.

Two

Ruby was surprised to find anything like the Oberfeld Hotel in the small town of Jagged Creek. She'd been convinced the website had overstated the opulence of the resort. But here she was, upgraded to a suite no less, in a brand-new, five-star hotel overlooking cattle country in the Colorado mountains.

She was on sabbatical from the university this term—having just lost out on a permanent position to Dr. Bert Bartholomew, a tall, snooty, Briton with an impeccable dress code. She was taking a breather, recentering herself and her career.

Still, she gave in to an urge to scroll through the faculty email.

When she saw his name on a message, she affected a British accent. "'It is difficult, Dr. Monaco, to overstate the impact of Westminster parliamentary governance on democracy and European social history.'"

Then she made a raspberry with her tongue.

Ruby didn't have anything against the British monarchy or parliamentary democracy. And she had no doubt it impacted European social classes. But she sure hadn't enjoyed his prolonged supercilious lecture on the subject at her final faculty event in August.

She closed her laptop on the rest of the messages and took a last longing look at the oversized soaker tub through the doorway of the grandiose bathroom. It had been tempting this morning, but she'd opted for the shower so she could get straight to work.

She might have had a setback with Austin yesterday, but she was a long way from giving up on the project. A rational person acknowledged their own weaknesses, analyzed the situation then did something about it. The best way for her to beat the next Bert Bartholomew in a succeeding job competition was to beef up her publishing credits with an influential history book on a compelling and unique subject.

Enter the Hawkes family. They were her opportunity to do just that.

Her makeup done, her long hair twisted into a neat French braid, and the rest of her wrapped in a fluffy white bathrobe, she carried the laptop from the bedroom to the four-person table in the bay window alcove. There, she gave in to temptation and took a bite of the giant complimentary cookie left for her yesterday, along with a welcome floral arrangement and a bottle of chardonnay. Depending on how her day went, she might crack open the wine later.

For now, the buttery oatmeal chocolate-chip cookie was to die for. Who needed a proper breakfast anyway?

Appreciative of the fast hotel WiFi connection, she searched her way through local businesses, looking for long-standing stores or restaurants where cowboys might hang out and where employees might know the town stories and history.

She came across a seniors' residence called Topaz House and sat straighter in her chair. Seniors who retired locally had likely lived in the area for decades. After all, who moved *to* a place like Jagged Creek for their golden years? These were exactly the kinds of people she wanted to meet.

The Topaz House home page described thirty-six spacious suites, a central dining room, lounges and scheduled activities. It looked like a very nice place to live along with being a potential goldmine of information.

She took another bite of the cookie as she scrolled further through the site, wondering if they'd be open to her stopping by and asking questions. If she was lucky, she might even come across an old ranch hand who liked to recount the past.

She saved the building's address on her phone and pulled up a map of the town to orient herself, discovering Topaz House was only a few blocks from the hotel at the end of Lister Lane.

She hummed as she got dressed, feeling a renewed sense of purpose. She'd take another run at the Hawkes family for sure, since their ranch would be the perfect centerpiece for her book. But there were plenty other leads to chase down while she gave Mr. Austin Hawkes a bit of time and space to cool off.

Not wanting to arrive at the seniors' residence empty-handed, Ruby took a recommendation from the hotel concierge and stopped by Maggie's Bakeshop to pick up two dozen doughnuts. They were still warm, fragrant with yeast and sugar as she carried them along the sidewalk.

Topaz House was a decades-old building made of smooth gray stone with four white pillars across the concrete front porch and a clock tower rising out of the peaked roof. It looked like it might have been a town hall in a past life. The hands were set at five minutes to two. Since it was barely ten in the morning, Ruby guessed the clock had stopped working at some point in the past.

It was a marvelous old building and looked very well kept. The lawn was trimmed, the loamy soil of the gardens well weeded. Inside was warm and welcoming. The lobby was decorated in soothing shades of burgundy and cream with hammered-copper art on the wall above a long gas fireplace, flickering now with orange flames. Sofas and armchairs dotted the airy room, and she could see a dining room off the back and a sitting room on the north side.

"Can I help you?" a pleasant female voice asked, the twentysomething woman walking Ruby's way.

Ruby gave the woman a friendly smile. "I'm not sure who I should talk to."

"About what to do with the doughnuts?" the woman asked, humor in her voice as she looked appreciatively at the box.

Ruby laughed. "Yes."

"I'm happy to take them off your hands." The woman reached out. "I'm Kiera Brooks, by the way, recreation coordinator for the Topaz residents."

Ruby handed over the box. "Ruby Monaco."

Kiera took an appreciative sniff and set the doughnuts on a nearby table. "How can I help you?"

"I'm a history professor at U Ainsworth in Boston." Ruby offered a business card. "I'm doing some research on the historic cattle ranches in the Colorado high country, especially those that have survived to this day."

Kiera took the card, looking both intrigued and curious.

Ruby took that as a good sign. "I'm staying in town for a while," she continued. "Hoping to talk to people who were involved in the ranching community."

"You've sure come to the right place for that."

Ruby's optimism took another leap. "That's great to hear."

"Are the doughnuts a bribe?"

Ruby was happy to use them as a bribe if it was going to work. "I didn't want to arrive empty-handed."

"Maggie's are legendary around here. Any cinnamon twists in there?"

"Sure are. Help yourself."

With a grin, Kiera opened the box. She snagged a cinnamon twist then set it on a napkin. "We can take the rest into the lounge. I'm sure they'll attract attention."

"Thank you." Ruby was delighted with her good fortune so far. "Do you think people will mind me asking them questions? Do you have any rules against that?"

"Rules against visitors and conversation?" Kiera shook her head as she headed for the sitting room. "We encourage visitors. The local playschool comes by Tuesday morning for games, and the church choir rehearses here on Thursday evenings. The more community involvement, the better."

"I'm not a community member." Ruby didn't want to mislead her.

They entered the lounge and Ruby took in three round tables at the center of the room, along with clusters of butter-yellow armchairs in the corners. There was a wide-screen television on one wall. The two-sided fireplace that backed onto the lobby was on another. Opposite was a wall of glass that opened into a fenced garden. The brick flower gardens were fallow now, but the cherry and maple tree leaves were bright red, and the grass was green and lush.

Three women were sitting quietly in one of the armchair groupings near the window. Two men were playing cribbage at one of the tables.

"Let's set you up right here," Kiera said, putting the doughnut box down on a table. She set the small stack of napkins to the side. "Mimi over there. The one in the green blouse. She grew up in Jagged Creek. Worked on one of the ranches when she was young, cooking for the hands. And she loves to talk. And Cloris, next to her, the one knitting, her father was a ranch hand on the Hawkes Cattle Ranch."

Excitement and anticipation surged in Ruby's chest.

"I don't know if you've heard of it," Kiera continued. "But it's one of the big outfits in the area."

"I've heard of it. Do you think Cloris would be willing to chat?"

"Let's ask her."

"Are those Maggie's?" one of the gray-haired men asked, slowly rising from his chair to stand stooped over. He retrieved a cane that was leaning on the next chair.

"They sure are, Fred," Kiera answered.

Ruby gestured to the large box. "Please help yourself."

As Fred started slowly toward them, the other man grinned and came to his feet. He was balding, just a fringe of pale gray hair across the back of his head. His face was mottled with age spots, but his pale blue eyes were alight and his smile was infectious.

"This is Ruby," Kiera introduced her. "She's come to talk about our ranching history."

Fred chose a custard cream. "Haven't ridden a horse in years," he told Kiera.

"Would you like to sit down?" Ruby gestured to one of the six chairs surrounding the table.

"You don't have a horse," the other man admonished Fred.

"This is Oscar," Kiera told Ruby.

"Horse," Oscar scoffed as he peered into the box. "As if. Any chocolate?"

"Chocolate dipped," Ruby quickly told him, pointing.

Oscar squinted then lifted a chocolate-dipped doughnut.

"Here's a napkin," Kiera offered.

Oscar sat down heavily in one of the other chairs.

Ruby took the chair between the two men. "Were either of you cowboys?"

Fred swallowed his first bite. "Everyone was a cowboy back then. Mighty fine doughnuts. I thank you for them."

"I'd love to hear your stories," Ruby said. "I work at University of Ainsworth in Boston, and I'm doing some research here in Colorado."

Oscar cupped his ear. "Where did she say?"

"Boston," Fred said loudly.

Oscar harrumphed. "City folks."

"Guilty," Ruby said good-naturedly. "Did you grow up in Jagged Creek?" she asked Oscar.

"Born and raised," he said. "Didn't have a hospital back then."

"You were born at home?" Ruby did a quick calculation in her head and considered the dangers of giving birth that many years ago in a place so remote.

Fred laughed. "Back then we just called it being born. You didn't do nothing special," he said to Oscar.

"She asked," Oscar retorted.

"What was the town like back then?" Ruby asked them both. "I assume quiet and small?"

"Small, yeah," Oscar said. "Quiet, no."

"Place was full of rangy cowboys," Fred said.

"Remember Lucky Luke Scranton?" Oscar asked.

Fred grinned. "The man could stand up on his saddle."

"Slept in his own hayloft for years. Until he brought a wife home from Denver."

Both men guffawed.

"Chased him out of the Spur with a broom in her hand when she found out about the loft. Sent him home to build her a proper house," Oscar said.

Fred shook his head. "Don't make 'em like that anymore."

"She was one skookum woman."

"I meant Lucky Luke."

"Him, too."

Ruby caught Kiera's gaze and the two women shared a smile.

As the men kept talking, Ruby committed as much as she could to memory. She hoped to jot down notes at some point. But, for now, she didn't want to interrupt their flow by asking to record them or typing into her phone. She'd found people were often intimidated by electronic devices.

Through the open window of his office on the main floor of the Hawkes' ranch house, Austin recognized Ruby Monaco's voice. The sound gave his mood an unexpected and unwelcomed lift. Half of him had thought she wouldn't come back at all. The other half had expected her long before this.

It had been more than a week since she'd interrupted Dallas and Sierra's wedding reception. And Austin had wondered about her over the following days, even searching her name on social media—just to assure himself she was who she said she was and he wasn't missing anything nefarious. You never could tell these days.

All he found was what she'd claimed.

"I'm happy to wait until he's available," Ruby said from the porch.

Austin came to his feet, knowing he should settle the matter for good this time. He'd restate his message that the Hawkes family wasn't a specimen under a microscope and send her packing.

The fact that he'd like to have her stick around awhile didn't matter. She might be gorgeous and intriguing, with a quick, incisive mind... And his brother Dallas might not have been completely wrong-headed when he'd suggested Austin should ask her out. But he wouldn't, not under these circumstances.

He strode along the south hallway to cut through the great room and horseshoe into the foyer.

His sister McKinney met him halfway.

"The reporter from Boston is here for you," she said as they both stopped and faced each other.

"She's not a reporter."

"Ruby Monaco."

"I know her name."

McKinney cocked her head. "What happened between you two anyway?"

"Nothing."

"Dallas said you were going to ask her out."

Austin clamped his jaw in frustration. "That was his fantasy, not mine."

"Why not? She's sure pretty."

"You think I'm shallow?" Austin didn't date women based on looks. Sure, he appreciated beauty as much as the next guy. But Ruby had intrigued him on a completely different level.

"Well, she's here. So, I hope you weren't too much of a jerk to her last time."

Austin stepped around his sister. "I wasn't a jerk. Where are you getting this stuff?"

McKinney fell into step with him. "From Dallas. She looks nervous."

That didn't surprise Austin. Ruby had to know she wouldn't be welcome.

The thought of his behavior gave him pause then. Looking at it that way, he had to admire her for coming back. She'd struck him as tenacious on the wedding day. That much had proved right.

"I'll see what she wants," he said, cutting away from McKinney.

"It's not too late," McKinney called to his back.

Austin paced through the great room, coming out at the foyer, and Ruby spun to meet him.

His felt a jolt at the sight of her and sucked in an involuntary breath.

He thought he'd remembered her perfectly. But his memory didn't do her justice.

Her eyes were just as darkly compelling. But her face was softer, more finely drawn, an innate sophistication and intelligence in her expression. Fit and trim, she was wearing a cream-colored sweater over a pair of slim designer jeans.

He remembered her being taller then took note of her boots. They were low-heeled, ankle-high, Western-styled, brown-tooled leather with crisscross lacing along the outer ankles. They were cute, but they were also brand-new. She looked like she was trying a little bit too hard to blend.

"Ms. Monaco?" he intoned as he came to a halt, letting the greeting turn into a question.

"You can call me Ruby."

"You can call me Austin."

A glint of humor came into her eyes. "I was planning to do just that." Her musical voice was affecting him almost as much as her looks.

He squelched the reaction. "Can I help you with something?"

She pulled a little notebook from a mottled leather tote bag decorated with tiny studs and lines of braiding.

"You pick that up in town, too?"

She looked puzzled.

He glanced meaningfully to her boots. "Boots and Blues?" He named the popular local Western wear shop.

She smiled self-consciously and he knew he'd hit the mark. "Kiera told me about it."

"Kiera?"

"Over at Topaz House."

Austin digested that information with suspicion and a frown. "What were you doing at Topaz House?"

"Talking." She opened the notebook and clicked the top of her ballpoint pen.

"About what?"

"Stuff."

He didn't like where this was going. There were people at Topaz House who knew a lot about his ancestors—maybe even more than Austin knew himself. "What stuff?"

She flipped a couple of pages. "Stuff that I'm here to confirm." She paused. "Or you can deny, of course."

Austin didn't like the sound of that. Why was she expecting a denial? What had she discovered?

"Who've you been talking to?" he asked.

"Mimi Richardson, Fred Wylie, Oscar Maddock and some others."

Austin could have kicked himself for not seeing this coming. When he'd turned her down, he should have guessed she'd go looking for other sources. And there were other sources out there, that was for sure.

He braced himself. "What did they tell you?"

"That your great-great-grandfather Winston won his wife, Lillian, in a poker game."

Austin clamped his jaw. That wasn't strictly true, but it wasn't exactly false either. There had been a poker game, and an introduction to Lillian—new to town and a more glamorous woman than any cowboy in these parts had ever seen—had been part of the pot in a roundabout way. "It was a different time."

Ruby waited. Then her brow rose. "That's it? Wow. I thought I'd get a denial on that one."

Austin could see he'd played this all wrong. He shouldn't have been so quick to send her away. If she was here, at least he'd know what she was asking and who was answering. He should keep control of the narrative, not leave it all to chance.

"You plan to publish gossip?" he challenged her.

"I plan to publish recollections."

"Those old cowboys famously embellish their stories."

"They weren't my first choice. *You* were my first choice."

"I'm a busy man."

She didn't answer, just leveled a gaze at him.

She was clearly assessing his expression, looking for weaknesses. He tried not to give anything away, but they both knew she had him beat. His best choice here was to cooperate with her.

A muscle tightened in his jaw as the seconds ticked past.

"What is it you're looking for?" he finally asked.

To her credit, she didn't look triumphant. "I'm a history professor. I'm looking for history. Good, bad, exciting or boring, I want to know what happened in the past."

"But you'd prefer exciting."

She cracked an impish half smile, looking way too sexy for his peace of mind. "Exciting would sell more books."

"See. That's my problem with you." He was in the middle of a vast modernization of the cattle ranch that wasn't going particularly well and was opposed by his father. The work needed his undivided attention, and he didn't have time for this. "I don't need my family secrets twisted for dramatic effect and book sales."

She looked intrigued now. Intrigued and still sexy. "Secrets?"

"We weren't murderers and thieves, if that's what you're hoping."

"That would have been great."

He scowled.

"From the excitement perspective," she said. "But that's not what I'm anticipating."

"What are you anticipating?"

"You're the one who said there were secrets."

"I exaggerated. There are marriages, children, disease and death, droughts, and up and down cattle markets."

"That's all I'm looking for."

He seriously doubted that. "I really don't have time for this."

"It won't be so bad. I'll follow you around while you work and ask questions. I'll get in the way as little as possible."

"You want to follow me around while I work? All day?" He hated the idea even while he liked it. He also had to admit it was the best way to control what she learned.

She gave a shrug. "Why not?"

"I start at six a.m."

She didn't flinch. "Okay."

"I work late."

"So do I."

"You ride?"

"Horses?"

"No, motorcycles."

Her eyes narrowed at his admittedly lame joke. "I'm game."

"You might regret that."

"I said I'm game. I'll do whatever it takes."

"You'd move to the ranch."

The statement obviously took her by surprise. But she rallied quickly. "Absolutely."

He schooled his features, not wanting her to know she'd given him exactly what he wanted.

So long as she was here with him, she couldn't tackle the residents of Topaz House or anyone else in Jagged Creek for information. Given the choices in front of him, he'd settle for that.

Ruby stood back and gazed at the huge, detailed map on the ranch office wall. The spacious room was at the front of the house with big windows overlooking gardens, rockwork and a picturesque pond across the concrete driveway.

"Your ranch is massive," she couldn't help noting.

She'd read the place was eighty-thousand acres, and she'd seen a smaller map on a website. But she was awestruck now looking at this level of detail—the rivers, lakes, mountains and rangeland across two separate valleys.

It was an east-west triangle with two distinct arms stretching to the north and northwest. She looked out the windows to the closest mountains then compared their real-life distance to their position on the map. It left her feeling tiny and insignificant.

"We're running thirty-thousand head right now," Austin said. "But that'll go down over the winter."

Sierra wrote the figure down in her notebook. "How long did it take you to build it up to this size?"

"Seven generations." He used his index finger to draw a line across the eastern point of the map.

"Do you have the original deeds or bills of sale?" Ruby would love to get her hands on those original documents, the dates, the land descriptions, the historical signatures.

Austin took a beat. "I'll see what I can find."

"I don't mind hunting them down myself. Just point me to the file drawers or boxes or whatever."

He gave a chopped laugh at that. "Sure. Why don't I just open the company's books, too?"

"I'm not from the IRS, and I'm not looking for a corporate advantage."

He looked affronted. "Who says we're afraid of the IRS?"

"You sounded defensive there."

"I'm not defensive."

"Okay." She didn't believe him, but she wasn't about to argue the point. "I was trying to be respectful of your time."

"Then let's go."

The abrupt statement took her by surprise. "Where?"

"To work. The main barn, to start. You don't think I stand around the office all day."

"Of course not." She hadn't thought that.

She wasn't sure what she'd pictured his day looking like, maybe fixing a fence, or counting cattle, or dumping bales of hay from the back of a pickup box. Hopefully, they wouldn't be roping and riding out on the range.

He started for the door.

"Can you wait just a second?" she called.

He paused and pivoted, looking impatient.

"Okay to take a picture?" She pointed to the map.

He extended his palm in a gesture she took to mean yes.

She quickly pulled her phone from her shoulder bag and snapped a few photos of the big map.

"Thanks," she said, tucking her phone back as she moved his way.

"You'll have to ditch the bag," he said as they made their way down the hall to the great room and the big dining room. They'd had breakfast there this morning, along with Austin's father, Garrett, who seemed to be a mostly silent man—at least he was at breakfast while browsing some news sites.

"Why?" she asked.

"It's too big."

"How much can I bring?" She couldn't leave her notebook behind.

"Whatever you can fit in your pockets. You'll want a warm jacket." He stopped at the edge of the dining room.

"For the barn?"

"It's not all that warm in the barn." He looked down at her feet. "You have some sensible shoes?"

She'd thought her low-heeled boots were sensible. "These are quite comfortable."

"There's a whole lot of mud and manure where we're going."

"Oh." That put a different spin on it. She didn't want to ruin her new Western boots. They hadn't been cheap.

She'd brought along a pair of soft hikers, not that she was keen on ruining them.

"Do you need to borrow something?" he asked, looking resigned to her costing him more time.

"No, no." She hated looking so unprepared. "Can you give me a minute?" She pointed to the main staircase that led up to the guest room.

He didn't look thrilled by the question, didn't sound thrilled either. "Sure."

She trotted up the stairs to the spacious and lavish room she'd been assigned, pulled off her boots, changed into her most worn pair of jeans, stuffed the pockets of her waist-length quilted jacket with her phone and a mini notebook and pen set, then laced up her hikers.

She was back downstairs in under five minutes, putting her hair into a high ponytail along the way, but Austin still looked impatient with the wait.

He also looked sexy—ruggedly and unnervingly sexy.

She did an inventory of his appearance, trying to guess what had changed in the past five minutes.

He was clearly ready for work now—the kind of hard, sweaty work that put a man on the cover of a magazine.

He wore a thick, tan-canvas jacket, open at the front, that accentuated the breath of his shoulders. There was a Stetson in his hand and a pair of leather gloves tucked into his belt. She couldn't help noting the way his well-worn jeans molded to his thighs atop boots that looked like they'd seen hundreds of hours of range work.

His square chin helped, too, as did his smooth coffee eyes gazing intently her way.

She swallowed.

"Ready?" he asked—nothing sexy about the chopped question.

She nodded, feeling inadequate as she came up to him. She told herself she wasn't expected to herd cattle. She was coming along to take notes. Ranching might be Austin's area of expertise, but research and writing were hers. She wasn't inferior, just different.

He gestured to the front door.

Ruby walked across the porch, struck again by the beauty of the landscaping around the house. The brook and waterfall were off the patio at the back. Out front was a wide concrete porch that led to the garden-lined driveway. The lovely pond was bordered in the distance by a fringe of aspen trees. The driveway was clean, white concrete leading to packed dirt roads that took off in three directions, each gently sloping downhill.

"We'll take the blue one," Austin said, gesturing to a trio of clean, new-model pickup trucks parked on a widened area of the driveway. Each had the Hawkes ranch logo on the front doors.

Ruby headed that way and climbed into the passenger seat, hoisting herself up with the door handle. She was glad Austin didn't open the door or try to help her in. She wanted to show him she was a professional independent woman. Besides, they weren't on a date.

"Is it far?" she asked.

"Not far." He started the engine and pulled away.

Curiosity made her want to ask how far *not far* might be around here. But she didn't want to hit him with a question every second. She'd find out soon enough.

They took the middle of the three roads, rounded a corner, and the barn rose in front of them. It was all of a three-minute drive between two fenced paddocks where they parked outside a big open door.

"We couldn't have walked?" she asked, hoping he didn't think she'd needed a lift for such a short distance. She might not be a cowgirl, but she wasn't frail either.

"We could have," he answered.

He left the keys inside the pickup and got out.

She followed.

"Did you think I couldn't walk that far?" She wanted to assure him she was in reasonably good shape.

"No. I thought someone here might need a pickup at some point today. Makes no sense to have them all sitting in a row up at the house."

"That makes sense." She hadn't thought of it that way.

"Why, thank you."

"Are you mocking me?"

"I'm not mocking you." But there was amusement in his mocha-colored eyes. "I'm thanking you for supporting my decision to move the pickup."

"I was only curious."

"And I answered your question."

"Mockingly."

"You're too sensitive."

She didn't think she was, but she'd try harder. "I'm trying to be unobtrusive."

He angled toward the open barn doors. "Well, you're pretty bad at it."

"How am I bad?" She'd done everything he'd asked. She'd beat him to the breakfast table this morning. And he was the one who'd offered to stop by the office and show her the map.

"You're..." He paused. "Here."

"You invited me to stay." She was grateful, but it hadn't been her idea.

"I don't mean here on the ranch. I mean that you—"

"Exist?" She arched her brow.

"If you exist somewhere else, that'd work for me."

They crossed the threshold onto a concrete floor covered in the center by a rubber mat runner. The place felt huge and hollow around her. The sweet scent of meadow grass on the breeze outside turned to the earthy aroma of livestock in the still air.

"Maybe in Boston," he continued, his voice changing timbre in the echoing high-ceilinged building.

"You can help speed up my getting back there," she offered pragmatically as she glanced around at the rows of horse stalls on either side of the main aisle where they walked. It had been years since she'd been inside the much smaller stable at the riding academy where she'd taken a few lessons as a girl.

Most of the stalls looked to be empty, but a pretty brown horse and a pale-colored one both stuck their heads out of their stalls as if they were curious about Austin and Ruby.

A couple of voices sounded in the distance, giving her an even better sense of the vastness of the barn.

"Do tell," Austin prompted.

In her mind, it was quite straightforward. "Give me the goods. Don't hold anything back, and I'll get out of your hair."

He hesitated a moment then answered unconvincingly. "Sure."

She mentally rolled her eyes.

He looked her way. "What?"

"That sounded a whole lot less than sincere."

His gaze was penetrating. "Tell me what you want to know."

She was honest with him. "The secrets, Austin. I want you to tell me all your family secrets."

Three

Austin hadn't expected the house to be so deathly quiet.

Dallas and Sierra were staying in a trailer on their house building site near White Foam Falls. His father and McKinney had headed down to Denver for a couple of days. And the family cook, Victor, had a new grandchild on the way in Boulder and had left this afternoon.

Austin had alternated between putting Ruby through her paces today then backing off when she'd looked tired and it made him feel guilty. He was sure she'd want to be treated like anyone else on the ranch. She was in good shape. And she didn't seem to mind getting her hands dirty. He hadn't expected that.

He'd expected her to shriek out in consternation when that yearling had kicked mud in her face. She hadn't. She'd looked disgusted and wiped it off with the rag he'd offered. And when a bull had made a mock charge at the fence where they'd been standing, she hadn't jumped back in fear. She'd trusted the fence.

Later, she'd seemed fascinated by the medical checkup of the animal, asking the vet reams of questions about the herd's bloodlines. Austin hadn't exactly been jealous of the interaction. But it had occurred to him that Dr. Miller was single and more like the kind of guy who'd interest Ruby.

"I feel completely refreshed," she said now as she came to the bottom of the main staircase. She wore a pair of snug black slacks, a cropped, multicolored pullover sweater with the sleeves pushed up, and a pair of burgundy flats. Her cheeks were flushed, her lips full and deep pink, and her hair was damp and loose around her face.

She looked terrific, especially considering how quickly she'd showered and changed.

He hadn't beat her by much.

She glanced around the great room and the adjoining dining room, lowering her voice as she glided toward him. "Pretty quiet around here, huh?"

He was at the wet bar across the great room, pouring himself a bourbon. "It is tonight. Family's away and our cook had to go down to Boulder. Drink?"

"Sure. What 've you got?" She came to stand beside him, checking out the liquor bottles lined up along the bar.

He was surprised that she seemed chipper instead of tired.

"Any of these," he said, gesturing. "More choices in the cupboard underneath. Or there's wine in the cellar."

Her expression perked up. "You have wine?"

"Oh, we have wine." It was the understatement of the decade. He cocked his head toward the south hallway. "Want to check it out?"

"You bet."

He gestured for her to go first, watching the way she walked, wondering if she was sore from the riding they'd done today. It hadn't been far, just down to the cattle pens and the ancillary barns. But it was enough for a beginner. Maybe too much for a beginner. He felt a new twinge of guilt for having pushed her.

But her gait was smooth now, her thighs firm and trim, and her butt was sexy and shapely in the formfitting slacks. He let his gaze rest there for a moment, telling himself his interest was medicinal. The lie lasted about ten seconds before he forced himself to stop staring.

"How are you feeling?" he asked, refocusing his thoughts. "Stiff or sore?"

"Not too bad," she called over her shoulder.

He was surprised to hear that. She claimed to have only ridden a few times in the past. She had an unusually good seat for someone with so little practice.

Either she was a natural or she'd downplayed her experience. He had to wonder why she might do that.

"Wow," she said, stopping as she came to the wine tasting bar.

It was horseshoe-shaped, built of local stone, with a mottled cream-colored marble top. Eight wood and leather chairs surrounded the front, while the arched stone entry to the wine cellar stood behind.

"This is…" She paused, gazing around.

"Overkill," he finished for her. His father was a connoisseur and collector.

"*Quite* the selection," she said, peering through the glass-paned door into the cellar.

Austin rounded the end of the bar and opened the door, standing aside. "Come on in. Pick yourself out a bottle."

She slowed. "I wouldn't have the slightest idea where to start."

"Red or white?" he asked, gesturing for her to enter.

The cellar was rectangular, sixteen feet by twenty-four, with racks all around and more in the middle. There was a narrow, high, tasting table with four wooden stools near the back.

Ruby gazed up and down as she walked the perimeter.

"Old World wines on the left, North American on the right, with some Australian and South American vintages at the back."

"I like chardonnay," she offered absently, still scanning the racks.

Austin was both amused and sympathetic. The place could definitely be overwhelming.

"How about a white burgundy?" he asked.

"I've never tried one."

He gestured to a section of the cellar. "Here's your chance."

She moved in beside him as he withdrew a bottle.

She leaned in to read the label. "Is this one that you like?"

He shrugged. "I'm not fussy." His father's cellar contained nothing but fine wines. Depending on what they were paired with, he enjoyed almost all of them.

She slid a different bottle from the rack and read the flowing script on the plain white background. A gold crest above the lettering was the only decoration.

Austin recognized the vineyard and knew it had an outstanding reputation. "You have good taste."

"That sounds expensive." She put it back.

"Don't worry about it," he said with a smile.

She tipped her head. "I don't want to take advantage."

Their gazes caught and held.

She was beautiful, beyond beautiful. There was a glow in her dark eyes, a sheen to her smooth skin. Her lips were full, her chin perfectly shaped, her neck slender and graceful above the scoop of her sweater's collar that only hinted at the cleavage below.

He was shot through with desire, struck with an urgent need to draw her into his arms, cradle her, whisper in her ear, and kiss those tender lips.

Her thick lashes fluttered as she blinked, amping up his desire.

A wayward wisp of hair had crossed her forehead and he was overcome with an urge to brush it back.

He steeled himself.

She gazed into his eyes. The scent of her freshly washed hair invaded his nostrils. The hazy heat of her body curled out to tease him.

She touched the wine rack, seeming to steady herself.

Without thinking, he cupped her elbow. A surge of warmth flowed through his palm, up his arm, tingling, raising goose bumps and racing straight to his chest.

Her breasts rose with an indrawn breath, her lips parting ever so slightly.

He gave in to the urge and brushed the hair from her forehead.

Her skin was tender smooth against the rough pads of his fingertips.

He wanted to apologize for that.

But she tilted her head, swaying ever so slightly his way.

His subconscious took over and he leaned down, bringing his lips to hers, kissing her gently and reveling in the taste of her sweetness.

Her lips softened and parted as she took a step forward.

He closed the rest of the distance, sliding an arm around her waist and settling her close, chest to chest, thigh to thigh. He widened his stand, savoring the feel of her supple body against his.

Their kiss deepened. He cupped her cheek, spreading his fingers into her flowing hair.

She grasped his arms, her hands curling around his biceps then sliding to his shoulders and around his neck.

He wanted to scoop her into his arms, rush up the stairs, carry her to his bed.

His mind galloped ahead to making sweet, satisfying love.

He was about to do it when she dropped her arms and pulled back.

He opened his eyes to see her flushed cheeks and swollen lips.

"Whoa," she said, blinking in bewilderment.

He quickly shook some sense into himself. "Did I misread?" He wondered if he should apologize.

"No." She shook her head. "That was both of us."

"Okay." He nodded, not exactly sure where to go with the conversation. "How did you feel about it?"

"Unprofessional. You?"

If he was honest, he'd say turned on, excruciatingly turned on. Luckily, he wasn't that honest. "It took me by surprise."

"Me, too. So, whoops." She raised her palms and took another step back. "Can't let that happen again. I'm here for research, not for…you know."

He understood, even though he was sorry to have her spell it out so categorically.

He forced his attention back to the wine racks. "Chateau Mormont Grand Cru?" He removed a bottle.

She checked out the label. "So long as it's not too expensive."

"It's on par with a lot of the wines in here." He said, covering his stubborn breathlessness as his heart rate reluctantly slowed back to normal.

"I don't know what that means."

He inhaled deeply, struggling to shake his desire and accept the disappointment. "You don't need to worry about what it means. The point is, I think you'll like this."

"So long as you're sure about us drinking it." She seemed less affected by their kiss than him. It was an ego blow for sure.

"I'm positive." Having no choice but to move on from the moment, he gestured to the hundreds of bottles in the cellar. "We can drink wine all week and not make a dent in the supply."

She frowned. "I'm not here to get drunk."

"I was exaggerating for effect. Come on, let's have some wine."

As Austin topped up her glass with some more of the amazing white burgundy, Ruby realized she'd better eat something if she was going to keep enjoying the wine.

They'd returned to the great room and settled on a large sofa next to the huge stone fireplace. She'd clamped down on her arousal as they'd kept an inconsequential conversation going about the layout of the ranch and today's horseback ride. But the memory of Austin's kiss lingered in her veins, tingled through her chest and sang along her synapses, leaving behind a rosy glow.

The ceilings in the room were beamed and high, with soft yellow light bouncing off the polished logs. Austin had effortlessly started a wood fire in the fireplace, the crackle and warmth of the flames made the enormous room feel cozy.

She hadn't been kissed in a while, maybe that was the thing. Then again, there was no denying it was a fantastic kiss. An extraordinary kiss. The kind of kiss that made a woman forget all the kisses that had come before it.

As it built up to almost mythical status in her mind, she gave herself a stern shake. It was just a kiss. A kiss followed by a glass of fabulous wine that she'd sipped way too fast and had gone to her head.

He set the bottle down on the low square table between them and returned to the other brown leather armchair.

"Not to be presumptuous," she ventured, knowing she should at least do something about the wine buzz.

"Presume away," he said easily.

"I should probably eat something before this goes to my head."

He looked instantly guilty, which wasn't what she wanted.

"I'm not criticizing," she quickly added.

"The cook's off tonight." He rocked to his feet.

"It's not an emergency," she said, unsettled by his instantaneous reaction.

"We can hit the kitchen and see what's there." He tipped his chin toward a door on the far side of the dining room.

"I'm in," she said, standing herself.

He scooped up the half bottle of wine, and she picked up her glass.

"You don't mind if we make it ourselves?" he asked as they walked together through the great room, cutting the corner of the formal dining room and its huge twelve-person rectangular table to push open a swinging door that led to a magnificent kitchen.

"I cook pretty much every night of my life," she answered, glancing around the kitchen that was both beautiful and practical.

Like all the rooms in the ranch house, it was immense. Cream-colored marble countertops ran around the perimeter with a large island set in the middle and plenty of walking space between. There was a double gas range, two refrigerators side by side, a double sink set between the appliances and an extra-deep sink in the island. There were endless cabinets and drawers, and a sunshine ceiling that lit up every corner.

"We can keep it simple." Austin opened the door of one of the stainless-steel refrigerators. "There's usually some cold roast beef in here." He looked around but didn't seem to find it.

Ruby set her wine down and looked past him to see inside. "You have eggs."

He pulled a face. "Eggs for dinner?"

"And Swiss cheese." She wormed her way in and opened a crisper drawer. "Fresh spinach and tomatoes. What about a quiche?"

His frown deepened. "That doesn't sound particularly filling."

Ignoring his objections, she lifted the spinach and tomatoes then pulled out a tray of eggs. "I'll make us a big one."

He watched in what looked like skeptical silence as she set the items from the fridge on the island and hunted down a few more.

"Have a seat," she told him, gesturing to one of the high

stools on the opposite side. "Entertain me with tales of cowboy bravery if it'll make you feel more manly."

Her joke got a smile out of him. "My masculinity's not at risk, just my stomach."

But he sat down with his glass of wine.

She hoped to get him sipping and talkative. "You told me the original cabin burned down early on?" She gave him the opening and went silent.

"It was only two rooms, but a huge loss back then," he said. "When it burned down, they moved into the chicken coop."

She wrinkled her nose at the thought. "They *lived* in a chicken coop?"

Austin smiled. "It was brand-new, so the chickens hadn't move in yet—luckily. Granny Alice, that was my four-times-great-grandparent, wasn't too thrilled about the arrangement. The fire happened a week before the wedding and Grampa Clem didn't tell her about it. He was afraid she'd refuse to marry him."

Ruby smiled as she cut cold butter into a bowl of flour for the pastry. "I wouldn't have blamed Granny Alice. Then again, I have to admire Grampa Clem's moxie."

"He wasn't letting anything stand in the way of that marriage. She was the love of his life, or so he claimed."

Reminded, Ruby took a sip from her own glass before plunging her hands into the bowl to mix the pastry. "But she stayed."

"She stayed. Though I think they heard the fight all the way down in Jagged Creek."

His statement prompted another line of her curiosity.

"What was it like back then?" she asked. "I mean the town?"

"Wide spot on the road. A few houses. A store. A post office, bank and a one-room schoolhouse. Also, a saloon and plenty of mud most of the year."

Ruby was intrigued, especially by the schoolhouse. "Are any of the buildings still standing?"

"Not now. The center of town was rebuilt in the 1940s."

She squelched her disappointment as she floured the countertop and set the ball of dough in the middle. "Where do you keep the rolling pin?"

His brow rose in amusement. "I don't keep it anywhere."

Ruby had forgotten for a moment that Austin lived in a house staffed with cooks and cleaners. "Have you ever *seen* a rolling pin?"

"Only in pictures," he joked.

She glanced around, trying to guess where it might be stored. She began opening doors and drawers. "Do you know anything at all about this kitchen?" She found flatware then chopping knives then plastic storage containers.

"Only where they usually keep the cold roast beef and baked goods."

"Baked goods?" That gave her hope.

"Victor's sourdough bread is legendary."

"If he's a baker, he must have a rolling pin." She opened another drawer. "Aha!"

"Jackpot?"

"Yes." Victor had three rolling pins.

She chose one made of marble, curious to see if it worked better than the wooden ones she'd always used. Brandishing it like a victory trophy, she returned to the island.

"You just threw that together," Austin said as he watched her rolling out the pastry. "No recipe, no nothing."

"There are only four ingredients in pastry."

"And the filling?"

She chuckled. "Winging that one, too."

"You're very handy in the kitchen."

"Why, thank you. Tell me more about Granny Alice."

"I don't know anything more."

"You must know something. How many kids did they have?"

"Two." He paused. "No. Three. One of their sons died as a child."

"That's so sad." Ruby paused for a moment to reflect on how it might feel to lose a child. She knew expectations had been different back then, life harder, but she couldn't imagine the grief. "Do you know his name?"

Austin shook his head. "My great-great-great-grandfather was the surviving son. They called him Gunner. The sister was

Franny. I know she moved east in her teens. She was one of the first women to attend Boston university."

"Go, Franny." Ruby was liking the female side of Austin's lineage.

A moment later, it occurred to her they could provide a focus of her book. Maybe it wasn't the cowboys and the cattle that were the story here. Maybe it was the women who'd empowered them.

Austin grew quiet as she rolled the dough into a circle and pondered generations of Hawkes women who'd cooked and cleaned on this ranch, especially those who had given birth and raised children in the lonely wilds of nineteenth-century Colorado.

As she folded and transferred the sheet of pastry into a pan, she glanced his way. His gaze had dropped and was focused on her hands, watching as she shaped the pastry.

There was something sensual about his intensity.

Her skin began to heat, rushes of awareness pulsating through her all over again.

"Do you have any pictures?" she asked to distract herself. "Photos of the family?"

"No."

He kept watching her hands, and her heartbeat deepened to a firm thud.

"Are you sure?" she asked, her voice slightly strangled.

He finally lifted his gaze. "It was the 1800s."

"Some people sat for portraits back then."

She ordered herself to settle down. But he was just as sexy here in the kitchen as he'd been back in the wine cellar. She couldn't erase the memory of their kiss.

She moved determinedly to the sink to rinse her hands, using cold water to shock herself back to reality.

"Austin?" a man's voice called out. "You in here?" There was a muffled thump on the swinging door then a whoosh as it opened. "*There* you are."

"Here I am," Austin said, turning.

The man looked at Ruby and came to a stop. "Oh. Sorry."

"Ethan, this is Ruby Monaco. Ruby, Ethan Douglas."

"Sorry to interrupt," Ethan said, looking regretful.

She put him in his late twenties. He was shorter than Austin, wiry and good-looking in a fresh-faced sort of way.

"You're not interrupting," Ruby said. She briskly transferred the pie pan to the oven to partially cook it, demonstrating to herself and to Ethan that she was occupied with cooking. She wasn't standing around flirting with Austin—not at all.

"What's up?" Austin asked Ethan.

"The White Ridge booster went down again. Hardy and the boys are up in the high country without a signal."

"Technically down or physically down?" Austin asked.

"I've rebooted and double-checked everything from this end."

A look of concern crossed Austin's face. "Don't tell me it fell over again."

"I hate to say it, but maybe…probably."

Austin pushed his wineglass away and came to his feet, looking Ruby's way. "Sorry, but we have to check this out."

"No problem," she said, sympathetic to what seemed like a serious problem.

"I might be a while."

"That's okay." She waved him away. "Quiche is perfectly good lukewarm."

The two men left and she set the oven timer.

It wasn't until the silence settled around her that she realized she was all alone in the big house—all alone in what could be a treasure trove of Hawkes' family history.

As she blended the eggs and milk, she couldn't help pondering the possibilities.

She wouldn't snoop in closets or cupboards. But she recalled the big map on the wall of the office. What other communal rooms in this sprawling place might have family history sitting right out there in the open on display?

"Sorry to interrupt your date," Ethan said as they bounced along, the pickup's headlights illuminating the rutted track in front of them.

"It wasn't a date." Austin's memory flashed to kissing Ruby.

"No?" Ethan sounded surprised. "You two looked pretty cozy."

"She's here doing research."

"And you're not the subject?" Ethan asked with a salacious lilt.

Austin grimaced at the thought of gossip starting up. "The ranch is the subject."

"What about it?"

"Our illustrious history."

Austin made his way to the top of the rise then turned and the headlights flashed onto the collapsed and twisted twenty-foot signal booster tower.

"What the—" Ethan whistled under his breath.

Austin came to a halt and hopped out of the cab, adding a floodlight to the illuminated field.

Ethan slammed the passenger door behind himself, marched forward and crouched in front of the damaged antenna array. "We're definitely going to need parts for this."

"This doesn't look like the wind," Austin said.

The weather had been clear and still for the past few days. The tower hadn't simply tipped over. It looked like it had been torn down in anger.

Ethan rose and looked around at the debris.

"Sabotage?" Austin asked, scanning with the light.

"Way up here? Who'd do that?"

"Good question." It wouldn't have been any of the cowboys on the Hawkes ranch. Never mind that they'd never pull a stunt like this, they were all in support of the effort at modernization. It made their lives easier.

That left the neighboring ranches. But that didn't make sense either. There was a healthy sense of competition, and the occasional cowboy skirmish from ranch to ranch, but nobody was openly hostile.

Then his light picked up something strange.

Austin squinted, ambling forward to crouch down.

"Look at that," he muttered.

"What?" Ethan turned his attention.

"Bear," Austin said, running his fingers over the tufted of black fur left behind. "Must have been a big one." He rose and scanned the ground, looking closely at the grass and mud until he spotted a paw print.

"Are you serious?" Ethan asked, coming over to look.

"See there." Austin pointed.

"You sure that's a bear?"

"I'm sure.

Ethan looked around in obvious confusion. "Why would a bear care about the signal tower?"

"Beats me," Austin said. "It's not like there was food on it."

Bears had occasionally ransacked the outer ranch cabins if food was accidentally left behind. But once they'd finished anything edible, they generally ambled on their way.

"What now?" Ethan asked.

"We'll have to rebuild it."

"Again." Ethan sounded weary.

Austin didn't blame him. "Yeah. And reinforce it even more this time."

"This is getting old. Wind-proofing was one thing."

"The installation manual didn't mention bear-proofing?" Austin asked, searching for a scrap of humor in the situation.

"I didn't specifically look for it," Ethan managed to joke back.

"Probably a disclaimer buried in the fine print."

Ethan paused to survey the mangled metal. "This is a mess."

It was a mess. A huge one. And Austin didn't look forward to explaining this latest problem to his father. They'd already had glitches in some of the cattle's ear-tag chips, errors in the health data compilation, along with the communications disruptions.

Ethan pulled a multitool from his belt—everyone on the ranch carried one—and began unbolting the brackets holding the antenna array to the broken tower.

Austin pitched in to help, and together they carried the electronics to the pickup truck.

"Nothing more we can do here tonight," Austin said, taking a final look around and tucking his own multitool back into its case.

"I'll see what's what back at the workshop," Ethan said as he opened the passenger door to climb in. "I might run down to Denver myself to get the parts here sooner."

Ethan had been a witness to Austin's father Garrett's blow-ups over the cost and malfunctions of all the new technology, so he had a sense of what was at stake. It was better all around if they fixed the problem before Garrett even got wind of it.

"Good idea," Austin answered, staring the pickup. In the meantime, he'd ride out to meet Hardy and shift the cattle to where they could be within communications range.

It wasn't essential to maintain the new ear-tag tracking and communications with the cowboys. They'd certainly spent years without either of those. But now that it was possible, Austin liked the peace of mind it gave them all.

They drove back mostly in silence.

After dropping Ethan, Austin pulled back up to the house. He wondered if Ruby was still awake. It was close to midnight, but a guy could hope.

Not that he had any right to hope. And not that he had any business wanting more of her company. His best bet, his only bet, was to keep her at arm's length and to give her the basic facts about his family history as quickly as possible and send her on her way.

Still, as he closed the door behind him, he listened closely, waited a moment, then admitted there was nothing greeting him but silence. He hung his hat and jacket, brushed the dirt from his boots then washed his hands.

Much hungrier now than when he'd left, he went straight for the kitchen.

He smiled when he saw the quiche sitting out on the island with a single wedge missing. There was a clean plate, flatware, a napkin, and a colorful fruit salad waiting for him along with his wineglass and the remaining half of the bottle.

He silently thanked Ruby for the consideration.

He sat at the island and sliced off a large serving of the quiche.

The first bite surprised him. He'd expected something bland. But it was flavorful and substantial. The pastry was tender but hearty, while the filling was full of rich flavorful cheese, fish—he was guessing she'd found some leftover rainbow trout in the fridge—spinach and mushrooms, all blended with enough spice to entertain his taste buds.

He took another bite, nodding to himself, thinking it was a better dinner than he'd expected.

"You're back." Ruby's voice surprised him as she opened the door from behind.

"You're up," he countered, swiveling.

"I was restless. I took another look at the map. I hope you don't mind."

"I don't mind." Truth was, he'd be relieved if she focused her book on the geography of the ranch. "I'll track down those deeds for you."

"Thanks." She took a stool next to him. "Everything okay out there?"

"Not exactly. But that's ranching. We'll handle it."

She waited a minute, but he didn't plan to elaborate. The fewer people who knew about the technical problems, the better.

He took another bite.

"What do you think?" she asked as he swallowed.

"It's good."

"You sound surprised."

"I was expecting something more—"

She waited.

"Mild." He settled for the word. Then he took another bite and smiled, nodding his appreciation.

"It's the chili powder that livens it up. Just a pinch."

He recognized the taste now. "Secret ingredient?"

"I like to experiment."

He almost coughed, swallowing hard at the visual her words brought to him. "Good," he managed on a wheeze.

As if a switch had been flipped inside his head, he was sud-

denly more aware of her lips than her smile, the rise and fall of
her chest against the softness of her sweater, the swish of her
hair as it brushed her shoulders, looking like it would feel soft
as eiderdown under his touch.

"I should *not* have kissed you," he whispered under his breath.

Her sudden stillness told him she'd heard.

"You can't exactly take it back," she said.

He met her gaze, sorry but not sorry he'd said it that loud.
Now he could throw his worry out on the table. "We don't need
it hanging between us."

"I agree with you on that. Is there another wineglass around
here? I loaded mine in the dishwasher."

He started to rise.

"Just point," she said. "It's not like I haven't been snooping
around while you were gone."

He didn't like the sound of that and his tone went sharp.
"What?"

"For the chili powder and the fish and the rolling pin."

"Oh." He told himself to settle down already. "Try the top
corner cabinet at the end of the counter."

"And in the office again," she said as she went for a wineglass. "And that little alcove at the far end of the great room. I
couldn't help noticing the photos on the wall. Who are they?"

"I can't remember." It had likely been years since he'd looked
closely at those photos.

"They're hanging on your wall." She sounded skeptical.

"Fine. I know there are some wedding pictures. Starting with
Winston and Lillian, I think. Those are my great-great-grand-
parents." He took another bite of the quiche.

Ruby sat down and poured herself some wine. Then she held
the bottle toward his glass.

He nodded.

"What's notable about them?" she asked.

"They picked this building site," he answered, looking
around. "Got a start on the house—a smaller version of it.
Mostly, Winston expanded the land. He went from five-thou-

sand to fifty-thousand acres. He got most of it from the government. By all accounts, he was quite a negotiator."

"What about Lillian?"

He drew a blank on that. "I don't know much about her, beyond her being too glamorous for the town. They had two sons and twin daughters. The girls died before their first birthday, a fever of some kind."

"That's tragic." Ruby's eyes dimmed with sadness, giving her a vulnerable look that pulled at his emotions.

He wanted to enfold her in his arms and comfort her. Instead, he took another slice of quiche and stayed silent.

"What about the sons?" she asked after a moment.

"The oldest, Roy, never married. He worked as a cowboy into his eighties. TJ was my great-grandfather."

"Will you come and look at the photos with me?" she asked. "Maybe you'll remember something more."

The simple phrase *with me* teased his senses and heightened his desire.

"Sure," he said.

This was simple expediency, he told himself, tamping down his emotions. The sooner she collected enough stories, the sooner his life could go back to normal. He needed to be thinking about microchips, booster towers and the roundup, not about the taste of Ruby's lips, the scent of her hair and the softness of her skin.

He met her gaze once more and the soft glow of her irises tested his resolve.

"Don't look at me like that," he rasped.

"I'm not."

"You are."

She slowly blinked. "Okay, I am. But it's not on purpose."

"By accident?" He didn't believe her, but he didn't look away. A charged silence passed between them.

"We really shouldn't have kissed," she said.

He agreed with that. He had his own long list of reasons. Still, he couldn't help wondering about hers. "Why not?"

"It complicates…things."

"Your exploitation of my family?"

She gave a half smile. "My objectivity."

"And you need that." He found himself leaning forward, his own qualms dissolving into thin air. It wasn't like he'd blurt out family secrets in a moment of passion.

"I do." She was close now, very close.

"The damage is done," he said, still easing toward her.

"We can always make it worse," she cautioned.

"I'm willing to risk it."

"It's not your career." But she didn't back off.

"It's my life."

"So, we're agreed."

He was puzzled; did she mean to kiss again or to regret it? "On what?"

She gave that same sexy little half smile. "Your call."

So, he kissed her. He kissed her deeply and thoroughly while half his brain yelled *Stop* and the other half cheered him on.

It was as good as the first kiss, better, if that was possible. He rose, and she rose, too. He framed her face with his palms, reveling in the softness of her cheeks, her hair, and the intimacy of touching her neck and shoulders.

Her arms wound around his neck and she settled into the vee of his thighs, molding her breasts to his chest as her lips parted, inviting him in.

As the kiss went on, he drew her fully into his arms, basking in her sweet taste, the hint of wine, the heated tenderness of her lips. He bracketed her hips, lifting her to the counter, easing between her knees, skimming his knuckles beneath her sweater, brushing her bare back.

She took in a deep breath and drew away, pressing the front of his shoulders for leverage.

He blinked to meet her gaze.

Mussed hair framed her face. Her suntanned cheeks were darkly flushed in a way he loved, and her lips were swollen from his kisses.

"I think that made it worse," she said, sounding slightly breathless.

"Maybe we worked it out of our systems," he offered, knowing it was a big fat lie—at least, it was for him.

"That seems overly optimistic. But sure." She nodded. "Let's go with that."

He couldn't help but smile. Then he couldn't help brushing a wayward strand of hair from her cheek.

She caught his wrist and steered his hand away. "We need to redirect our energy."

"Do I get to vote on where?"

"*Re*direct," she emphasized.

He smiled again, liking her slightly offbeat sense of humor. He took a step back, breaking the last contact between them. "Understood."

She shifted to the edge of the counter.

His instinct was to reach out and help her down, but he kept his hands to himself.

"You run your ranch," she said as her feet touched the floor.

"And you write your book." He didn't like the arrangement, but he had to respect it.

"Deal."

Four

After range manager Newt Candor hustled Austin away from the breakfast table, Ruby had waited for Austin to come back. But after an hour had passed, and recalling the tense expression on Newt's face, she concluded Austin might be busy for a long time.

She told herself to be philosophical about it. She couldn't expect to have him as a tour guide everyday. Plus, after what had happened between them last night, it was probably better to have some time apart to let things cool down. She still felt a serious hormonal rush when she recalled their passionate kiss.

In that moment last night, it would have been the easiest thing in the world to give in and make love with him right there on the kitchen countertop. Her instincts told her it would have been fantastic.

But she wasn't here for fantastic sex. Lusting after Austin was a colossally bad idea. She knew it was, and she'd have stopped herself if she could. Short of that, she could at least put a little distance between them and catch her breath.

So she changed into a pair of nice shoes, shrugged into a more stylish jacket, and drove her rental car to Jagged Creek. She hoped Kiera wouldn't mind her dropping by unannounced again. Ruby had enjoyed chatting with the residents of Topaz House, and she suspected they had many more stories to tell.

Kiera was in the reception area when Ruby arrived.

"I wondered if we'd see you again." Kiera's smile was bright as she came forward.

The warm welcome contrasted with the cloudy day outside, cold rain beginning to tap against the window. The Topaz House lobby was cozy and cheerful, flames in the gas fireplace flickering, orange light dancing against the copper sculptures.

"I've been visiting out at the Hawkes ranch. I hope you don't mind me dropping in."

"We're happy to have you." Kiera's brow rose then in what looked like incredulity. "You visited the Hawkes ranch?"

"Yes."

"And they visited back?"

"Does that seem odd?"

Kiera pulled a face. "That family is not particularly hospitable."

Ruby was curious to hear more. Sure, Austin had his moments, and everyone else seemed busy and preoccupied. But they had invited her to stay with them. That seemed more hospitable than most.

"What makes you say that?" she asked Kiera.

"They're private people. Sure, they come out and support the community, at events, but mostly they stick to themselves." Kiera's expression was serious.

"Oh?" Ruby had found the Hawkes family to be agreeable, although now that she thought about it… Austin's father wasn't the friendliest, exactly. "It was Austin who invited me to stay."

She wondered if Kiera was focused on Garrett. He was the most standoffish.

"You *stayed* out there?" Kiera asked as they started toward the lounge. "As in overnight? Like a guest?"

"They have a guest room." Given the monstrous size of the house, Ruby guessed they had more than one.

"Curiouser and curiouser," Kiera said as they entered the lounge.

There were a dozen residents in the room today. Some were watching an old musical on the big screen, while others were dozing in reclining lounge chairs. Cloris was asleep at a table, her neck canted to one side, knitting still held loosely in her hands.

Ruby looked for more familiar faces, hoping to find someone

who was awake and willing to talk. She wondered if she should have brought doughnuts again.

"It didn't seem to be a huge deal," she said to Kiera. "I told Austin what I was doing, and he offered to show me around the place." She gestured to Cloris. "Does she usually sleep a long time?"

"She should stir in a few minutes. What exactly did you tell him?" Kiera gestured to a chair at an empty table then took one herself, positioning it so she could see into the lobby.

Ruby sat. "That I was researching a book."

"Hmm." Kiera drummed her fingertips on the table.

"What 'hmm'?"

"I went to school with the Hawkes boys. Austin was two grades ahead, Dallas after him. Then I'm the same age as Tyler."

"So, you know them all?" Ruby hadn't thought of Kiera as a source of information on the family, but it seemed like she might be a good one.

"Mostly from a distance. Like I said, they didn't mix and mingle with many of us."

"Even as kids? Why not?"

Kiera was a smart, friendly, pretty woman, and Jagged Creek was a very small town. Surely the teenage Hawkes boys would have been interested in her.

"I wasn't into horses. Or the rodeo. Or sports, for that matter. But you get the idea," Kiera ended.

Ruby didn't want to pry about Kiera's personal life. She switched the topic. "Is there anything you can tell me about their mother? Or their grandmother? She died at eighty-three if my research is right."

"You mean Peggy-Lyn."

Ruby nodded.

Kiera pursed her lips. "Imperious old biddy."

"Was she?" Now that was interesting.

"I remember her striding around town with a frown on her face, a ramrod spine, and her nose so high in the air I hoped she'd trip. She wore these bright-colored tailored coats with matching cloche hats, like she wanted to be sure everyone would see her from a mile away." Kiera paused for a breath. "She spoke her mind to anyone who would listen, up to and including the mayor. I swear, we all thought she'd live forever."

"She was tough?" Ruby couldn't help wondering why that would be. More and more, she was liking the idea of coming at her book from the perspective of the Hawkes wives.

"As nails," Kiera said with a nod.

"I'd imagine you'd have to be tough, stuck out on a ranch like that, way back when."

"Are you thinking she suffered actual hardship?"

"She must have." Ruby knew from Austin that the Hawkes family had started small and worked their way up to the spread they enjoyed today.

"It was the generation before her who built the big fancy house. Peggy-Lyn moved right into it after her wedding."

"Do you mind if I take notes?" Ruby reached for her bag.

"I really don't know much about them."

"You know more than me."

Kiera gave a playful grin. "Bring more doughnuts next time?"

"Absolutely." Ruby gathered her notebook and pen.

She wished she had a better memory. But she found it tough to recall everything that people told her.

She'd discovered people were less intimidated by a notebook than an electronic device. She'd transpose the notes tonight onto her laptop.

Kiera paused. "Well, now I'm drawing a blank. It was easier when we were just talking."

"Then we'll just keep talking." Ruby lowered the notebook to her lap where it was out of sight. "Did you ever talk to the parents? Garrett and Jessica?"

"Their mom, yes. She came into the school sometimes to watch our sports games and for fundraisers, things like that. She was very pretty."

"I saw her picture on the wall."

Kiera's expression seemed to tighten for a split second.

Ruby waited a moment, thinking Kiera might say something. But she didn't.

"It was from their wedding," Ruby finished, hoping to prompt a response.

"Oh. That makes sense. You know she died, right?"

"I read that in an old newspaper article. A car accident."

"Truck, but yes. A stormy night, a muddy road. She was driving by herself."

"That must have been tough on the family." Ruby knew the boys had been teenagers when their mother died. Their sister McKinney only a child.

"Lots of people went to the funeral, that was for sure."

"Did you go?"

Kiera shook her head. "Like I said, we didn't run in the same circles. A lot of people were nosy, so they went anyway. But it was none of my business."

Ruby picked up on the strange turn of phrase. "Not your business?"

"There were rumors. Nobody knew anything for sure. I don't know what they thought they'd find out at a funeral."

"What were the rumors?"

"That all was not well between Mr. Hawkes and his wife."

"How solid were the rumors?"

"They seemed believable. But I was only fifteen."

Ruby was intrigued. Births, deaths, marriages, even divorces, were important milestones. Family businesses often succeeded or failed based on the strength of family bonds. But she wasn't sure if she should follow up on a mere rumor. She couldn't even imagine Austin's reaction if she asked him about the state of his parents' marriage.

"Some people said she was leaving him," Kiera continued. "She didn't. I mean she died, so—" Kiera's attention suddenly shifted. "Oh, look. Cloris is waking up."

Austin's gaze shot to the front foyer when Ruby appeared.

She looked chic and confident dressed in a steel-gray blazer over a clingy white top trimmed with just enough lace to look extraordinarily sexy. Her thick dark hair was piled loosely on her head, framing her wide-set eyes and beautifully shaped face.

It was well into the evening, and she paused when she caught sight of him in the great room with his father and sister. She looked startled, or maybe that was guilt written on her face.

He was beyond curious to know where she'd been. He couldn't exactly grill her in front of his father and McKinney, but he'd get her alone as soon as he could.

"It's a whole lot of capital tied up on something that doesn't even work," his father was saying, his frustration clearly growing as Austin navigated his way through the explanation of the ruined signal tower.

Ethan was still making his way back from Denver with the parts, so their plan to gloss over the problem had failed. Now Garrett was asking about the entire monitoring system.

"We expected some hiccups." Austin tried not to be too obvious about watching Ruby.

"I hope you expected some successes along with your failures," his father continued, his tone clipped and caustic.

"Hi, Ruby," McKinney put in from where she sat on a sofa.

"I must be interrupting," Ruby said, moving haltingly forward.

When no one immediately reassured her, she gestured to the staircase beyond them. "I'll just get out of—"

"No need to rush off," McKinney said. "You were in town?"

"I was." Ruby nodded, still glancing at the staircase that was her way out.

"We made it back from Denver," McKinney offered cheerfully.

"Was it a good trip?" Ruby edged toward her goal as she spoke.

"Up and down. We paid too much, but we've got a new yearling bull."

"We paid fair market value," their father said with a frown. "That's how an auction works."

"Congratulations." Ruby sounded a little hesitant as she took one more step, her gaze darting from McKinney to Garrett and back again. It was clear she didn't want to get into the middle of anything.

"Exactly how long until we see some value from all this?" Austin's father asked him, apparently done with McKinney and Ruby.

"Ethan's working as fast as he can."

"That's not an answer."

"He's got a crew repairing the tower, and he's personally picking up the replacement components. He'll fix the booster, update the ear-tag software and get everything back online." Austin watched Ruby ease her way past his chair. He wanted to stop her, but there was no obvious reason for him to ask her to stay. And he sure didn't blame her for leaving.

"You bought obsolete software?" his father demanded.

"It's not obsolete. They update software all the time. It's regular maintenance." Austin was trying his best to stay patient.

He was also trying to stay positive, since they weren't certain the software update would fix all the glitches. He dreaded having this conversation all over again next week.

He was relieved when his father rose to his feet and brought the grilling to a halt.

"Morning comes early," Garrett said.

Ruby eased back to stay well out of his way.

"Night, Dad," McKinney offered with a loving smile, and he gave her a squeeze on the shoulder as he passed.

"Night," Austin echoed.

"Ruby." Garrett gave her a reserved nod of acknowledgment.

"Good night, Mr. Hawkes," Ruby answered.

As his father mounted the staircase, Austin held his breath, hoping McKinney would head up before Ruby.

"I hope you have a good plan for all that," McKinney muttered instead, hitting him with a look of skepticism.

"My plans haven't changed a bit," he answered. The technology rollout might not be going as smoothly as he'd hoped, but modernizing was still the right move. They'd work out the problems along the way.

"So, what happened? Too much too soon?" she asked.

"I never said that."

Ruby started for the stairs again. "I think I'll head—"

"It's early," he interjected.

"We didn't mean to be rude." McKinney backed Austin up, putting on a smile. "Have a seat. Have a drink. We should all have a drink."

Austin didn't echo the suggestion of everyone having a drink. He wanted McKinney to call it a night and leave him alone with Ruby.

"What's your pleasure?" McKinney asked Ruby, rolling to her feet. "Whiskey, wine, something warm and sweet?"

"What's warm and sweet?" Ruby asked.

"Decaf with…whatever." McKinney gestured to the kitchen.

"That sounds really nice."

"Let's do it."

Resigned, Austin trailed after the two women.

McKinney started a pot of decaf and Ruby jumped right in to help. She began sugaring the rims of three tall glass mugs while discussing with his sister the merits of various liqueurs.

One sweet drink and an hour of inconsequential chatter later, McKinney finally made a move for her room.

Ruby rinsed her mug in the kitchen sink.

"Will you be busy again tomorrow?" she asked Austin as the door swung shut behind McKinney.

"I wasn't busy today," he answered, coming up behind her with his own mug. "What were you doing in town?"

"Mostly talking."

"About?"

"The ranches, the area, same as usual."

"You were gone a long time."

She turned and smiled. "There are a lot of people in Jagged Creek."

The expression distracted him and softened his mood just a little bit. "First time I've ever heard that."

"You know what I mean."

"Name some names."

"Cloris, Fred and some others at the Topaz House."

Austin's edgy mood returned. Over the years, some of the town residents had come to resent the Hawkes family. It was impossible to amass a spread so large without ruffling a few feathers. He didn't want to read about their grievances in Ruby's book.

"What did they have to say?" he asked, taking a step back to keep both his focus and his equilibrium.

"That your grandmother was a force of nature, for one thing." Ruby sounded amused.

"Peggy-Lyn?"

She nodded.

"What did you hear about her?"

"It sounds like she ran the town with an iron fist."

"The woman had a heart of gold." He remembered that much about his granny.

Ruby lifted her brow. "Hidden under a gruff exterior?"

"Who said she was gruff?"

There was a teasing note in Ruby's voice. "You don't really expect me to reveal my sources."

In fact, he did. He wanted to know who was out there bad-mouthing his family. "She chaired the town council, first woman who ever did."

"Good for her. You know, there's something about the women in your family." Her smile faded.

"What?" he prompted.

She seemed to hesitate.

"What is it?" he prompted again.

"There was also talk about your mother."

Austin's spine stiffened and his shoulders went square. Defensiveness reared up inside him. "Talk?" he asked quietly and calmly.

"The accident," Ruby clarified, watching him closely, as if she was trying to gauge his reaction.

She'd heard about more than just the accident. That much was obvious. But she wasn't tipping her hand. Well, he sure wasn't about to tip his either.

"Yes," he answered shortly. "It was a terrible tragedy."

"I understand if you don't want to talk about that night."

"I don't want to talk about that night." It had haunted his family for over a decade.

"Maybe you could tell me something else about her."

It couldn't be more obvious that Ruby was fishing.

There'd been gossip about where his mother might have gone that night and if she'd fought with his father beforehand. Austin knew they'd fought—on that night and on many others as well.

"What do you want to know?" he asked tersely.

Ruby looked surprised by his tone. "If this isn't a good time..." she ventured, lifting his mug from his hand and turning to rinse it.

"No. It's fine," he lied. "What's your question?"

"Nothing specific."

He doubted that.

"Maybe it's better if we talk tomorrow," she continued, shutting off the tap and turning back.

"Why not now?" He didn't know why he was pressing. The last thing he wanted to do here was answer questions about his mother.

"Okay." She dried her hands and pulled up onto one of the stools, propping her shoes on the crossbar. "I heard she was sad."

"Sad about what?"

Ruby shrugged. "It was kind of a general comment. Like maybe she wasn't completely happy with her life here."

Austin didn't want to lie, but he wasn't getting into his mother's state of mind either. He took a stool one down from Ruby. "That's quite the accusation."

She looked guilty, as well she should. Then she shifted and seemed to regroup. "Right. Uh. Maybe... Was she by any chance a city girl?"

He was relieved to move to a safer question. "She grew up in Austin."

Ruby seemed to ponder the answer. "Texas? Is that where you got your name?"

He nodded. "It wasn't exactly a bustling city back then."

She squinted. "So, Dallas and Tyler, too?"

"All of us."

"What about McKinney?"

"It's less well known—a small city near Dallas."

"I suppose it would be harder to find girls' names."

"I suppose it would be."

Ruby traced the marble pattern on the countertop, connecting the lines into shapes. "Did she miss it, do you think? I mean, Austin is a fair size, especially compared to Jagged Creek."

"Not that I noticed." He followed the somehow sexy pattern of Ruby's fingers.

She paused, looking thoughtful for a moment. "Did your mom have family in Austin?"

"Her parents died before McKinney was born. She has a sister, Harmony, but we only ever met her once, back when we were kids. She lives in New York City. At least, she did then." It was so long ago that he could barely picture the woman who was his aunt, but he did remember her fancy clothes and shoes.

"She didn't come to the funeral?" Ruby asked with obvious bewilderment.

"It's a long way to travel."

"New York to Colorado? For your own sister's funeral?"

"They weren't close." His mother had never talked about Harmony. He'd been young when she'd visited, but it had been easy to see the strain between the two sisters.

"Still." Ruby went silent as she continued tracing the imaginary pattern. "Maybe they have it wrong."

He fought an urge to cover her hand with his. He cleared his throat. "Who's 'they' and what do 'they' have wrong?"

"Maybe it was her past that made her sad."

Austin's mother's feelings weren't relevant to the ranch's history. "Wouldn't you rather talk about cattle drives and wolves?"

She looked curious. "Are you encouraging me to quit this topic?"

"I'm suggesting something more exciting."

"I suppose that depends on how you look at it."

"Action, adventure, danger?" He had to think those could make a history book interesting.

"It must have been a hard decision for her to uproot and move here." Ruby paused. "And an even harder one for your grandmother and great-grandmother."

"I suppose." He'd never given it any thought.

"I'm curious," she said with a disarming grin.

"No kidding," he scoffed even as he fought his unwanted reaction to her smile.

She was beyond gorgeous when her expression lit up like that. Their gazes locked and held.

His heartbeat deepened and his palms itched with the need to touch her. He could smell her fragrant hair, almost taste her sweet lips.

Her eyes went opaque. Time stilled and the air hung heavy between them.

She slipped from the stool and he started to reach out, anticipating her warmth folding against him once more.

"You must be tired," she said and sidestepped him.

He dropped his arms in disappointment.

He wasn't tired. He was electrified.

She turned for the door. "Good night, Austin."

"Good night," he answered to her retreating back. But he knew it wouldn't be one. It was going to be a long, frustrating night of unfulfilled desires and exasperating dreams.

It had been a close call last night.

Ruby wasn't a fool. She had seen the desire flare deep in Austin's eyes. And she could feel her own answering response as it fanned out over her skin.

Whatever was between them was powerful. She'd have to stay on her guard and stay focused on her work.

Her manuscript had to be solid. A compelling story was the only way to get the attention of a publisher, readers, and the senior faculty at U Ainsworth. That meant it had to be unique, ideally based on a thesis not explored by other writers who'd studied the evolution of the West.

She knew the female angle was the edge she'd been looking for. What she needed now was to flesh it out.

She'd eaten a quick and early breakfast, hoping to get out the door before Austin came downstairs. He might understand the inner workings of the ranch. But she doubted he was the best source on the female lineage. Plus, a little time and space between them seemed like a very good idea.

She made a clean getaway and started along the cobblestone path that encircled the towering house, sprawling in two directions. After rounding the far end, she came across an open door with an older woman sitting on a bench outside.

The woman, who was smoking a cigarette, was dressed in a white smock over navy slacks with a blue-and-white-checkerboard cap on her salt-and-pepper hair. She was obviously a cook.

"Good morning," Ruby said, buoyed by the gray hair and wrinkled face, and wondering how long the woman might have worked here on the ranch.

"Mornin'." The woman's answer was crisp. It was hard to tell if she was smiling or frowning.

"I'm Ruby." Ruby offered her hand, hoping to break through her apparent aloofness.

"Mrs. Innish."

They shook.

"You're up early," Ruby ventured. Should she take the initiative and sit down on the bench or wait and hope for an invitation?

Mrs. Innish gave a chopped laugh. "This isn't early."

"It's early for me," Ruby said good-naturedly. "I'm guessing you make breakfast then?"

"Breakfast, lunch and dinner for all the household staff. Never mind the snacks."

"It sounds like you work hard." Ruby took a chance and sat down, perching on the edge.

Mrs. Innish stubbed out her cigarette in an ashtray and arched a brow Ruby's way. "You're a guest at the house?"

Ruby shook her head. "No. Not a guest. I'm here working."

Mrs. Innish looked her up and down. "I know you're not staying in the staff quarters."

"Staff quarters?"

Mrs. Innish canted her head toward the wall behind her. "For married cowboys and household staff. Anyone who doesn't live in the bunkhouse."

"I'm a writer," Ruby elaborated, taking another look at this section of the house. The roofline was lower, the windows were smaller, and it bordered on the parking area instead of the elaborate gardens and ponds.

Mrs. Innish got to her feet.

"I'm writing a book." Ruby spoke quickly, rising. "It's about the history of ranches in the Colorado mountains. Would you mind if I asked you a few questions?"

"I've got work to do in the kitchen," Mrs. Innish said gruffly, making to leave.

Ruby pressed. "I plan to focus on the women and their contribution to the industry's growth. I could come inside, if you're okay with that. That's what I'm doing with some other family members, tagging along while they work. That is, if you don't mind?"

Mrs. Innish's features pinched together.

"How long have you worked at Hawkes ranch?" Ruby asked.

The woman looked thoughtful. "Coming up on forty years."

"That's amazing," Ruby enthused. "Always as a cook?"

"I did laundry at first."

"Also hard work, I bet."

"Plenty of things were hard back then. Different."

"Different how?"

"Well, the roads were a rutted mess, electricity was hit and miss, and there was no such thing as the internet. Girls were never cowboys. Didn't even think about it."

"Would you have liked to be a cowboy...uh, cow person?"

"It's ranch hand now in the generic." Mrs. Innish started for the door.

Ruby quickly shifted into step with her. "Did you ever think about being a ranch hand?"

"The heat, the cold, the flies and the manure? I know what those boys went through by the look of their laundry. No thank you."

"But you like cooking." Ruby gazed around the bright, modern kitchen, sniffing appreciatively at something baking in the oven.

The room was industrial in scale, much plainer-looking than the family's kitchen with plenty of stainless steel, a giant two-door refrigerator built into the wall, miles of counter space, open shelves with cookware, and four deep sinks. Cornerwise to the fridges were three built-in ovens and a gas cooktop with eight burners. In the center of it all was an oversized island with its own small sink, two wooden knife blocks and a stack of cutting boards.

Two flats of eggs were out on the counter, sitting next to a huge bowl of fruit salad.

Mrs. Innish tied herself into a clean apron and went for the fridge.

"How many people do you feed here?" Ruby asked, peeping through the oven window to see trays of biscuits baking to a golden brown.

"Twenty to thirty, depends on the season, and the day, really." Mrs. Innish hefted large packages of sausage and three pounds of bacon.

"That's a whole lot of mouths to feed." Ruby took in the two long, rectangular wooden tables and spindle chairs at the far end of the room. They were utilitarian and worn, but sturdy-looking, and she counted thirty-two chairs. "You do this all by yourself?"

"I have help when I need it. The others take turns pitching in." She pulled a frown as she crossed to the stove and settled four big black griddles over the burners.

"Can I help?" Without waiting for an answer, Ruby shrugged out of her coat and hung it on a wall hook near the door.

"I don't see how you can—" Mrs. Innish stopped talking as Ruby wrapped herself in an apron.

"I'm good in the kitchen," Ruby said, knotting the ties around her waist.

"Know how to make pancakes?" Mrs. Innish asked doubtfully.

"You bet." Ruby's mother had been a pancake artist, with a great recipe and a talent for making them in all shapes and sizes. Ruby had learned young and could do it with her eyes closed.

"For thirty?"

"It's just multiples of four. Well, almost." The math wasn't perfect, but the point was the same.

Mrs. Innish gestured to two of the flat griddles. "Then let's see what you've got, young lady."

Ruby took a breath and glanced around, quickly spotting a large stainless-steel bowl. She was quietly delighted by the turn of events. There was nothing like working side by side to get a person talking.

"What brought you to the Hawkes ranch?" she asked while she located a sack of flour, some salt and a can of baking powder.

"I answered a job ad in the newspaper." The bacon strips sizzled and popped as Mrs. Innish laid them out on a griddle.

"Did you grow up in Colorado?"

"Wyoming."

"On a ranch?"

"In Slipper Pond. It's outside Rock Springs."

"So, you moved away from home for work."

"I wanted to make some money."

"Understandable." Ruby went to the fridge for milk and helped herself to half a dozen eggs.

Mrs. Innish pulled the trays of biscuits out of the oven. "It wasn't like now. Jobs weren't a dime a dozen."

"You were courageous to move all this way by yourself."

"Didn't have much of a choice."

"Really?" Ruby was intrigued. She mixed up the dry ingredients, hoping Mrs. Innish would continue.

"I was the oldest of seven kids. Couldn't exactly hang around and sponge off the family anymore."

The door at the far end of the kitchen whooshed open.

"Mornin', Bea," a male voice called out. "I hope you don't mind one more.'

"Dr. Bentz." Mrs. Innish's face instantly lit up, her face breaking into a smile. "I didn't know you were on the ranch."

"Complicated delivery last night," the doctor said. "But we've got a pair of healthy twin foals this morning."

This was a different vet than the one who'd worked on the

bull. Ruby put him at about forty-five. He looked lean, fit, and cheerful, with a shock of dark hair, ruddy cheeks and pale blue eyes.

"The biscuits are fresh," Mrs. Innish said. "And I'll make you some eggs. Over easy?"

"You know just what I like," Dr. Bentz said. Then he looked to Ruby.

"I'm Ruby Monaco," she offered.

"I've heard of you," he said knowingly as he took a seat at one of the tables.

"Oh?" she asked, guessing maybe that the veterinary community was small in Jagged Creek.

"Hardy said you were writing a book."

"That, I am." Ruby cracked the eggs into the bowl, not wanting to get behind on the pancakes. But she wondered what the cowboy might have said about her. "Did he say anything else?" She glanced at Dr. Bentz to gauge his expression.

He looked amused. "He'd like a starring role."

Ruby didn't know whether to be flattered or amused. "In my book?"

The doctor nodded.

"It's not a novel."

Dr. Bentz grinned. "I don't think he cares. He fancies himself a cowboy hero."

"I'll be sure to talk to him." She'd only met Hardy a couple of times. But if he was a willing interview subject, she'd track him down again.

"Pancakes are falling behind," Mrs. Innish said tartly as she carried a breakfast plate to Dr. Bentz.

"Sorry," Ruby offered, suddenly realizing she might have irritated Mrs. Innish by monopolizing Dr. Bentz's attention. She'd disappointed the woman on the pancake front to boot. Neither of those was a good thing.

She quickly whisked up the batter and ladled a dozen cakes onto the griddles.

While she worked, another staff member entered the kitchen and called out good morning—then another and another.

As she grilled the pancakes to a golden brown, Ruby listened in on the lively conversations around the two tables, realizing she'd stumbled across a terrific source of information. She was willing to bet these people knew exactly what was what here on the ranch.

Five

In the corral outside the main barn, Austin stared incredulously at Hardy while the ranch hand slid the saddle from his sweaty Appaloosa gelding. "What do you mean you talked to Ruby? Why did you talk to Ruby? *When* did you talk to Ruby?"

Austin had been on the lookout for the elusive woman all day and hadn't come across her.

"At lunch in the cookhouse."

"What was she doing at the cookhouse?" Austin didn't much like the sound of that.

"I don't know." Hardy headed across the corral toward the barn and the tack room.

Austin quickly hoisted his own saddle and followed, taking long strides over the loosely packed dirt. He'd met with his father over lunch, giving Garrett a progress report on repairing the signal booster tower and the ear-tag system. It hadn't exactly been well received.

"What did she say?" he persisted now. "What did you tell her?"

Hardy turned his head and gave Austin a perplexed look. "She was talking about her book. What else?" Then he chuckled as he took in Austin's expression. "Man, I'm forty-four. That young gal's not interested in me."

That hadn't been at all what Austin had meant. "I didn't think she was."

"Well, you sound jealous."

"I'm not jealous." Austin wasn't thinking about Ruby's affections. At least, he hadn't been thinking about them up to this moment.

They passed through the open door of the main barn, their boot heels clacking on the concrete of the wide center aisle.

It occurred to Austin that Hardy wasn't the only single cowboy on the Hawkes ranch. There were plenty of good-looking cowboys much younger than him. And Austin was sure that any of them would chat Ruby up given half the chance.

"I've got stories, you know," Hardy said.

"What stories?"

"Like the drive along Golden Ridge with the mudslide. Without my keen eyes, it might have hit us dead-on. Then I dug all night to get us out. I was hero there."

The perilous drive had happened when Austin was just a kid. He'd heard the tale, but Hardy wasn't the only one who'd worked hard that night.

"You were the hero?" Austin asked skeptically.

"It was me who thought to split the herd. Then I took the rear half around the peak. We were three extra days getting home."

"What about Lucky Luke Scranton?"

"Forget Lucky. All he did was rake in the glory."

"Not like you," Austin said with an ironic shake of his head.

"It's about time someone told the real story."

"So that's all she wanted?" Austin was relieved to hear it. Adventure stories, they could share. There were no scandalous family secrets to be found in the Golden Ridge mudslide.

"Yes."

They turned into the tack room, taking the rear door to the rows of saddle racks on the wooden walls.

"Hey, Rudy," Hardy called out to the tack room manager who was at the other end of the rectangular space.

"Howdy, boys," Rudy called back then returned to whatever he was doing.

"Plus, the house," Hardy said to Austin as he deposited his saddle pad and hung his saddle.

Austin emptied his arms. "What about the house?"

"When it was built. How long it took. All that furniture your great-grandma had hauled in here. I think she liked that part." Hardy nodded. "She liked hearing about the furniture and especially the parties. I told her old Nettie Harbottle would re-member the parties. She was apparently popular back in the day. Hey, did you know Ruby's been down to the Topaz House? Wouldn't have thought it. She doesn't strike me as the type to chitchat with the old folks. But what do I know?" He finally paused for a breath.

"Is she going to talk to Nettie?" It felt like this thing was slipping from Austin's control. He'd brought Ruby here so she *wouldn't* talk to random people about his family. Clearly, that wasn't working.

Hardy shrugged. "I would if I was her. Shorty said when his dad was a kid, he'd sneak up to the main house and watch the parties through the back window. Moonshine and everything, it sounds like. Wild times back then."

"Great," Austin muttered. That was exactly what he needed Ruby to hear about.

"Ever sorry you missed all that excitement?" Hardy asked.

"No." Austin wouldn't trade modern ranching to go back in time.

It was true the family hadn't thrown any kind of a party since Austin's mother's death. But he remembered his parents and his grandmother hosting them when he was a child. Thought they weren't nearly as lively as the ones from decades past.

His grandmother Peggy-Lyn was far more reserved than her mother-in-law, Kathleen. Austin's great-grandmother had grown up in Chicago during Prohibition. Family lore had it that her father had made his money as a bootlegger back then.

Austin's great-grandfather, TJ, had met Kathleen in the city and fallen instantly in love. Then, after her father had been shot under suspicious circumstances, Kathleen's inheritance had been a driving force in building their grand house.

"She also asked about your mom," Hardy added almost as an afterthought.

Austin stilled. "What about her?"

"Weird things, like did she have hobbies or like to travel. Like I'd know something about that."

"Anything else?"

Hardy gave him an odd look. "She already knows about the accident. Everybody knows about that."

"I know they know." It wasn't the accident that worried Austin.

Hardy had finished putting his tack away, but he seemed to be waiting hesitantly for Austin's next question.

"Thanks for telling me," Austin said, forcing a casual tone into his voice. "Maybe don't talk about the family with her anymore."

"You got it, boss. Sorry if I stepped out of line."

"Nothing to be sorry for," Austin assured him. "But pass the word. If she's asking questions, everyone should send her to me."

"Will do."

"Have a good night."

"You, too." Hardy took his leave.

It was coming up on seven, so Austin headed straight for the house, hoping Ruby was already there. He entered through a side door near the laundry room to strip off his muddy boots and wash the outer layer of dust from his face and hands.

Then he tracked her down at the far end of the great room.

She was gazing at the family photo gallery; a picture of his mother, he saw as he grew closer. He didn't like that she was focusing on Jessica.

"I looked for you today." His words came out as an accusation.

"I was around," she said easily, either not hearing or ignoring the edge in his tone as he stopped beside her.

"Around where?"

"Wandering. Here and there." She turned to look his way. "You obviously know the place is huge."

He got to the point. "I didn't bring you out here to grill the staff."

"Grill?"

"I just had a chat with Hardy. I know what you're up to."

She moved to the next photo. It was his great-great-grandfather Winston at the poker table in the Cactus Spur Saloon.

"Because I told you what I was doing?" Her tone was still easy and even.

If Austin wanted her to defend herself, it was clear he'd have to be a lot more direct in his accusations.

"Is this where he won that introduction to Lillian?" she asked.

"He did. He won first right to ask her on a date."

"And then he won her heart," Ruby sing-songed with a sappy little smile.

The smile was disarming, and Austin had to struggle to stay annoyed with her. "Don't change the subject."

"What's the subject?" She blinked, her eyes looking far too innocent to be innocent.

He hardened himself and blurted out the obvious. "You, looking for dirt on my family by insinuating yourself into the ranch staff circles."

She stopped smiling but her tone was still breezy. "I'm not writing a tabloid exposé, Austin." She moved on to the next photo.

He took a step to follow. "You can get all your information from me."

"That's ridiculous."

"No, it's not."

"I can't write a book based on one person."

"Sure you can."

"It's not a biography. Is that Kathleen?" She pointed to the black-and-white photo of his great-grandmother in a dark, sparkling, low-cut dress, with a cigarette holder, standing in front of the old grand piano.

"That's her."

"I hear she liked to party."

"Entertain." He didn't know why he was making that distinction.

Kathleen had been a rebel. She might have had tongues wagging way back then, but he'd always thought he would have liked her. He admired his great-grandpa TJ for marrying such an interesting woman.

"*Entertain*, then." There was a trace of amusement in Ruby's voice. "She was very beautiful."

"I agree."

"Tell me something about her." Ruby turned her attention from the photo to Austin.

"I never met her."

"Well, who knew her? Any of the retired cowboys or staff members? Someone must have been around in her heyday, even if they were only children."

"I don't know who she knew." The last thing he'd do was point Ruby to a new source of information.

"Tell me about the mob money."

"There was no mob money."

"That's not what I heard. Bootlegging, criminal gangs, murder." She looked intrigued and excited.

He girded himself once more against her sex appeal. "Gossip."

Ruby made a show of looking around the house. "*Somebody* paid for all this."

"Is that what you're going to write?" he demanded.

"I don't know what I'm going to write."

"Yeah. You do. The most salacious things you can find."

She looked affronted at that. "Not necessarily. And Kathleen's father's murder isn't a state secret. It's a matter of public record."

"Buried in old court cases, not splashed across the pages of a book and drenched in speculation and sensationalism."

"Why, thank you, Austin." Her voice had gone tart. "I so appreciated the vote of confidence toward my deeply-rooted sense of professionalism."

"You can't blame me for wondering."

They locked gazes and stared at each other in silence.

"Here's the deal." He was making himself crystal-clear. "From here on out, you're with *me*." He stabbed a finger against his chest.

Ruby's brow quirked in an amused misinterpretation of his words.

"Tomorrow," he quickly clarified. Although he'd have given pretty much anything to spend tonight with her.

Before a mental image of that could form, he ruthlessly shoved it aside.

She'd made her feelings abundantly clear last time they'd kissed. And now they were even further at odds. Nothing was going to happen between them.

* * *

Ruby was getting nowhere fast.

She wanted to poke around, talk to more people, hear stories and see things.

But that wasn't happening. When Austin insisted she stick with him all day long, he hadn't meant he'd be a tour guide.

He meant he'd be her jailer.

So here she was, sitting on the hard tailgate of a pickup truck, in a meadow halfway up a mountain, watching Austin and two other ranch hands build a fence around the new signal booster tower.

They'd informed her it was to keep out the bears. She couldn't help glancing over her shoulder every now and then to the distant woods, wondering what might be lurking beyond their edge.

When she couldn't see a single thing moving around in the tree line, she told herself any wildlife would stay away from the sound of the generator and the air-powered fence-post driver. The machines were uncomfortably loud from where she was sitting, and she could only imagine the noise traveled for a mile or more.

She turned back to where the men were working under the warm autumn sun.

She tried to keep her attention on her book outline, to further frame up her approach to those intrepid women from the past who'd coped with a whole lot more than the danger of bears. But Austin had grown sweaty, his gray T-shirt clinging to his shoulders as he muscled a fence post into position. The man was sexy anywhere, but he was sexier than ever out here in his element.

She thought again about his words last night. *You're with me.*

It had been on the tip of her tongue to shout, *Yes!* Yes, she'd be with him, all night long, if she had her way. Sex with Austin might be reckless, but it would be fun. They were both single adults, and the physical attraction between them was undeniable.

A rush of desire started to stir and she shifted on the tailgate.

She thought she was beginning to understand the motivation of those early Hawkes wives in leaving the comfort of the city for a tough life in the wild mountains. If Austin was an example of the Hawkes male gene pool, she could see giving up electricity and plumbing. And who needed shopping, entertainment or culture when they had a guy who looked like that?

Seeming satisfied with the position of the latest fence post, he set down the bulky driver and lifted his hat to wipe the sweat from his brow, pausing for only a moment before hefting the big driver to the next post laid out on the ground.

Aside from the zap and clunk of the power tools, and the low throb of the generator, the scene could have taken place a hundred years ago. All three cowboys were dressed in jeans and boots, their muscles corded as they toiled in the dust that rose around the worksite, their battered Stetsons shading their eyes.

She forced herself to focus on the details, to make the best of the situation by taking notes on the sights and sounds, scents and feel of the open range. Capturing that in words would add a timeless flavor to her book, ground the reader in exactly what it was like to live in the raw wilderness. Closing her eyes, she inhaled deeply, noting dried grass, musky leaves, a hint of rain in the distant clouds.

The compressor motor chugged to a stop. Hardy called out and Austin answered, the words indistinct across the distance. Beyond their voices, the wind swelled over bare branches and birds sang and swooped. She listened more closely and heard the tall grass rustle, the flies buzz around, and the deeper hum of a bumblebee as it flew above her head. Then a mosquito bit her forearm and she smacked her hand down hard.

Good detail that. There were biting bugs of all sizes on the ranch, especially around the livestock. She'd been warned about the horseflies. They were big enough to take an actual bite.

A mosquito was plenty annoying for her. She wiped the blood spatter off with a tissue. The little welt was already swelling on the inside of her arm.

The wind paused and the buzz of the insects grew louder. She hopped off the tailgate to walk around, hoping to keep them at bay. Clouds were rolling down the valley now, clinging to the mountaintops, spectacular as they piled high into the stratosphere.

Ruby spotted two riders coming their way. Their horses all but glided through the tall grass, and the cowboys both looked relaxed and comfortable in their saddles.

She felt a shot of envy. She'd only ridden once here with Austin, and she'd loved it. Moving silently through the picturesque forest and open fields was completely different than going in circles at the riding stable where she'd taken lessons as a child.

She took the opportunity to jot down some notes on the flowing manes and tails, and on the shimmer of their coats under the slanted rays of the sun. The horses looked—she'd have to call it happy. Something about their body posture made her think they loved their lives out here.

And why not? What horse wouldn't like high-end barns and corrals on the Hawkes ranch, not to mention the thousands of acres of trails and meadows. It was surely horsey heaven.

As they drew steadily closer, she realized one of the cowboys was McKinney. Ruby's envy redoubled as she watched the woman's skill in handling her horse.

Austin spotted the riders and stopped what he was doing. He walked to the generator and shut it down then waited on McKinney and the other rider.

Hardy and Anders left the waiting fence posts to join Austin. Curious, Ruby moved within hearing distance.

"What's up?" Austin asked as the pair reined their horses to a stop. He patted the neck of McKinney's horse as she dismounted. The man with her dismounted, too.

He was tall beside McKinney, with square shoulders, a shock of dark hair, and an easy gait in boots, faded jeans and denim shirt. His gloves were worn and his Stetson battered. It was easy to see he'd been a working cowboy for a long time.

"We're heading for the home corral," McKinney said to Austin. "The new Denver bull's on its way up the road. Thought you might be interested."

"I am," Austin said.

McKinney caught sight of Ruby. "What's she doing here?"

"Watching," Austin said as he stripped off his gloves.

"Why?"

He tucked them in his back pocket. "Why not?"

"How is watching you lot helping her write a book?"

Ruby closed the distance, since it seemed silly to pretend she couldn't hear them.

"I told her she could follow me around," Austin said, glancing her way.

McKinney rolled her eyes. "Well, that's weird."

"No, it's not."

"You're hardly the most interesting person in the family."

"Says who?"

The other rider smirked and tipped his hat up while McKinney gestured to the fence posts.

"You're *building a fence*," she said.

"That's what we do on a ranch," Austin countered.

McKinney turned her attention to Ruby. "It's boring."

Ruby agreed, but she didn't want to offend Austin. "I'm jotting down some atmospherics."

McKinney narrowed her eyes at Austin. "I don't know why she's got your back."

"She doesn't have my back," Austin said. "It's what she wanted to do."

McKinney waved a dismissive hand and turned back to Ruby. "Have you done anything fun since you got here? Gone riding?"

"Just once," Ruby said. "A short ride my first day here."

McKinney said, gesturing to the other cowboy's horse, "Hop up. Hand over the reins, Caden."

Austin frowned.

"Oh, no," Ruby quickly put in, taking a step back. Never mind what Austin would think. She wasn't taking away a cowboy's horse. "That's not necessary."

"Sure it is," McKinney said.

Caden walked his horse her way.

"I'm inexperienced," she said.

"Help her with the stirrups," McKinney said to Caden.

He looked surprisingly unconcerned about letting Ruby ride his horse.

Ruby looked to Austin again. While she'd love a chance to ride with McKinney, she didn't want to alienate him.

"Whatever," Austin said through what looked like a clenched jaw.

"You sure?" she asked him.

He nodded to the chestnut horse. "Go head. Take a ride."

"Need a leg up?" Caden asked.

"I don't think so." Making up her mind, and happy about the opportunity, Ruby moved to the side of the horse.

She grasped the saddle horn, slid her low-heeled boot into the stirrup, and swung herself into the saddle. It was smooth and roomy against her jeans. The horse shifted beneath her and twitched its ears against a circling fly.

"That's better," McKinney said with satisfaction.

Caden handed Ruby the reins and adjusted the stirrups to her feet. "Matilda is even tempered," he said as he worked. "She doesn't spook easily, but she does like to run if you let her."

"We'll go slow," McKinney told her.

"This is very kind of you," Ruby told him with appreciation.

"If you're going to write about us, it might as well be authentic," McKinney said as she mounted up and urged her horse into a walk. Unlike Austin, she appeared to take the idea of a book in stride.

Ruby pressed her heels into Matilda's flanks. The horse seemed more than happy to fall in next to McKinney. The leather creaked and the horse's hooves made a soft whooshing sound through the grass.

"I can't believe he dragged you out here and made you watch that," McKinney said as they started down the rise.

"He didn't drag me." It might not have been Ruby's first choice, but she'd made the best of it.

"Well, he must like you."

The suggestion startled Ruby. "What makes you say that?" She hoped they hadn't somehow given away their attraction. She inwardly braced herself, wondering how she could frame their relationship without lying.

"He's a loner. No offense, but having you around slows him down."

"I'm trying to stay out of the way."

McKinney looked over at her. "That wasn't a criticism."

"I didn't take it badly."

"I'm just surprised, is all. You, the book— It's exactly the kind of thing Austin hates."

Ruby couldn't suppress an amused grin at the contradiction. "He hates me, but he likes me?"

McKinney grinned right back. "I'm saying he hates the situation, so he must like you."

"I don't think he likes me much."

There was no denying Austin was attracted to her. But liking her was a whole other thing. He clearly wished she'd leave the ranch and get completely out of his life.

"How's the book coming?" McKinney asked.

"Good. Fine. It's coming together."

McKinney pulled a face. "That was a real question. I wasn't looking for platitudes."

Ruby couldn't help but appreciate McKinney's forthrightness.

"I have a bunch of notes, but I'm struggling with the outline. Right now I'm working on the theme and approach."

"Is that a bad sign?" McKinney looked genuinely concerned. "Or is it just too early in the process?"

"Some of both," Ruby said.

"What could we do that would help you?"

Ruby was warmed by the sincerity of the question. She decided there was no harm in being open with McKinney. "I've been thinking about the women on the ranch, the wives specifically, the resiliency of the ranching women."

McKinney gave a slow, considered nod. "I like that. But it doesn't seem like *way out here* to me. My frame of reference starts and ends on the ranch."

Ruby hadn't considered including McKinney as one of the principles in the book. But now that she thought about it, she liked the idea. She liked it a lot. The other women had all been newcomers, while McKinney was born and raised.

From what Ruby could see, McKinney had held her own with her three brothers in what was still widely considered a man's world. She was yet another example of the resiliency of the ranching women. She might, in fact, be the pinnacle of that resiliency.

A shiver ran down Ruby's spine as her book outline bloomed to life in her mind. She could see it clearly. And now she had a thousand questions for McKinney.

"Do you like being a ranch hand?" she asked, trying to control the sudden surge of excitement.

"I do. I like the animals," McKinney answered, looking serene. "I like the outdoors, the physical work—at least for now. I'm not naïve. I know I'm a Hawkes and what that means. I'll eventually transition from ranch hand to some kind of management position. We all will. Including my brother Tyler."

"You expect Tyler to leave the navy?"

"Yes. Soon, I hope. That'll take the pressure off me." McKinney gave a little laugh. "On the other hand, who wants to sweat their way through the heat, the storms and the bugs forever."

"The bugs." Ruby clucked with sympathy, looking to build empathy and intimacy between them. "I'm astounded by the bugs." She waved one away from her face.

"You get used to them. Well, sort of. So, you're focusing on the women, huh?"

"I am. What do you think?"

"I think it's about time. Have you had a look through the stuff in the old house?"

"'The old house'?" Ruby's chest hitched again. There was an *old house*? And it had *stuff*?

"Down the creek road from the main barn. It's pretty overgrown. You'd have to take a horse, or you could use an ATV. But the attic is—" McKinney shooed away several flies. "I don't even know what all's still stored up there."

Six

Hearing nothing but silence in the old house, Austin mounted the staircase to the second floor. He couldn't believe McKinney had sent Ruby here unsupervised. What had his sister been *thinking*?

He stopped and listened to the silence at the top of the stairs, holding out a faint hope he'd arrived before Ruby. But then he heard footsteps above him, and faint music began to play from the attic.

The access was from a back bedroom, up a steep staircase and through a hatch door.

The hatch was open. As he climbed the stairs, his attention went to a turntable in a mottled blue-plastic case spinning a black record. The scratchy, upbeat band music featured a trumpet player and seemed to pull the attic back in time.

Ruby was in a corner, kneeling in front of a battered trunk, bobbing her head back and forth to the beat. She wore a vintage felt hat—speckled gray with a gold ribbon and a big, shiny, gold flower on the side. She was looking intently at the patchwork quilt held in her arms.

Hearing or sensing his presence, she turned. She looked startled for a second, but then she smiled. Her cheeks flushed, and her eyes were alight. "This is absolutely *amazing*."

"The music?" He didn't find anything thrilling about early swing.

"Well, that, too." She gestured expansively around the room. "But I mean all of it, everything."

He looked around and wondered what she'd unearthed before he'd arrived. "You shouldn't be up here all alone."

"This is *handstitched*." She held up the patchwork quilt of cream, blue and yellow. "You have to wonder who made it."

"Haven't a clue." He stepped further into the cloyingly warm sloped-ceiling room.

The air was stale, the small windows at each end of the attic both closed tight. Light came from them and from a single light-bulb with a chain for a switch dangling from the ceiling.

"Can you imagine how long this took?" she asked.

"You shouldn't have come up here." He went to the closest window, released the latch, broke the stuck seal free, and pushed it open.

"McKinney gave me permission to look around."

"She had no right to do that." He walked past Ruby and opened the other window, appreciating the gust of fresh air.

"It's her ranch, too."

"She doesn't speak for the family." He paused to peer into the trunk, inhaling a strong scent of cedar. He doubted the thing had been opened in decades.

Ruby tipped her head to look up at him. "But *you* do? Come on, Austin. How is that fair? This is terrific stuff."

He was sure it was terrific stuff for her. Problem was, he was flying completely blind. Anything could be stored up here.

She rose to show him the quilt. "The stitches are impressively even. Somebody spent hours and hours and hours sewing this. Maybe it was Lillian, or maybe Gunner's wife Wanda. I bet it was Wanda. She seems more like the type. But if I look around some more, maybe I'll find out for sure."

"How do you know about Wanda?"

With a static crackle through the small, aging speaker, one song ended and another began.

"I found an album." She pointed to a battered brown-leather book sitting on a small, cluttered table. Its flaking gold-embossed letters spelled *photographs*. "Wanda was Winston's mother."

"I know who she was."

"She looks… I don't know, down-to-earth, like a practical,

sensible person who might have sewed things. I really can't see Lillian having the patience."

It irked Austin to hear Ruby chatting so familiarly about his ancestors, like she somehow knew them after just a few days.

"You know almost nothing about Lillian."

Ruby's expression faltered. "True. But she seems so fashionable in the pictures, like someone who bought things at a boutique or had a seamstress do the work for her."

"Boutique? In Jagged Creek? Back then?" That didn't even make sense.

"Maybe she traveled. Or maybe she ordered from a catalog."

"You're speculating."

"While looking for *facts*." Ruby gestured around the big room again. "You can't have it both ways, Austin. Either I can suss out the truth, or I can fill in the blanks. But you can't stop me from one and then criticize me for the other."

He drew a deep sigh of frustration. "Do you always push this much?"

"That's your counter? That I push too much? You really need to work on your rhetorical style."

"You're *such* a comedian."

"I'm not trying to be funny. I'm trying to do some research." She set aside the quilt and peered back into the trunk. "It's like a treasure hunt."

It felt more like clearing a minefield to him.

She gently lifted a brown plush bunny. It was threadbare with floppy ears, had one slightly yellowed eye and a tattered plaid bowtie around its neck.

"This belonged to someone," she said reverently, smoothing back its ears.

Austin was trying to be annoyed with her, but her easy tenderness wormed its way past his defenses.

"This has been very well loved." She turned it around to look at the back then hugged it to her chest.

Austin wished he was a little bunny.

"I bet you—" She hopped to her feet and turned around. "I bet you I can find a photo of this little guy." She sat the bunny down on the table, leaning it against an old lamp, facing her as if it could watch while she opened the leather photo album. "Can you picture it?" she asked as she flipped the pages. "A little boy or girl dragging their beloved bunny all over the house and yard. That bunny has a name. I bet it's a cute name."

Austin didn't see any chance of them figuring out the toy's name. And he didn't really see the point in that. Plenty of kids played with stuffed toys. It might be interesting to find this particular toy in a picture, but he didn't see the name making any difference.

"Aha!" she called out triumphantly. She pointed to a photo on the page. "It was Franny's. That's so amazing."

Austin peered down. He saw the bunny in the arms of a young girl in the black-and-white photo. Her hair was braided and she was wearing a dark dress with a white frilly collar with some kind of oval pin at the throat. "That could be anyone."

"She's sitting next to Gunner."

"How do you know that's Gunner?"

Ruby shot Austin a puzzled expression. "Look at his scowl, the furrow of his brow. That's young Gunner all right. So, the parents must be Clem and Alice." She gave a little laugh. "Hello, Alice. I see you survived the chicken coop none the worse for wear. She's very pretty."

Austin agreed. His four-times-great-granny was very pretty, with dark wavy hair twisted up in a bun. Alice wasn't smiling. None of them was. But her eyes looked happy. If he had to guess, he'd say they were very light brown or maybe blue.

"Thank you, Mr. Bunny," Ruby sang out happily, giving the toy a squeeze on its belly. She looked silly but beautiful joking around in that old hat.

"What makes you call it 'mister'?"

"The bowtie, obviously. And he looks like a boy. Don't you think?"

Austin didn't have an opinion on the bunny's gender. But he was impressed by Ruby's power of deduction. He studied the photo a moment longer, checking out his tall, clean-shaven, many-times-great grandfather.

Ruby's conclusion seemed right. The family of four was standing on the porch of this house when it was fresh and new. It made sense that it was Clem, Alice, Gunner and Franny.

His heart tripped a little as he looked at them. It was the first time he'd seen a photo of Franny. He found himself wondering if there were more pictures of her in the album, and of his other relatives at various ages. Maybe there were even more albums in the attic.

He glanced around with renewed interest while Ruby jotted a few things down in her notebook. The song changed again, a slower tune this time.

"Do you do this a lot?" he asked her.

"Write books?" She shook her head. "No. Mostly, I'm an instructor. I also work with graduate students, advising on their areas of research. Some of them have written books."

"I meant what you're doing now."

"What am I doing now?"

"The bear, the photo, the quilt and who made it—pulling threads from here and there to pull together a picture of a person."

She blinked with what looked like confusion, and it took her a moment to respond. "It's all a jumble right now. I don't have the first idea of where any of this is leading." Then she brightened. "But I do love immersing myself in the experience. It makes it..." She paused. "Three-dimensional. Does that make sense?"

"I guess." He supposed it did in a certain way.

She returned to the trunk and leaned inside, choosing a flat white box nestled in the bottom. She wiped off a thin layer of dust that scattered into a sunbeam. She balanced the box on the corner of the open trunk and worked off its lid, revealing faded blue tissue paper.

Despite himself, Austin was curious. He took the lid from her hands and set it aside while she peeled back the fragile paper. Underneath, they found silky blue fabric covered in gold beading.

"What is it?" he asked.

She lifted it from the box, rattling the tissue.

It was unmistakably a flapper dress. The bright royal-blue fabric was interspersed with patterned gold at the shoulders and hem. Lines of stylized gold beading came together at the center in a diamond shape, with a long tassel fringe dangling saucily from the midthigh hemline.

"Go, Lillian," Ruby whispered in awe, holding the dress up in front of herself. "I can see why they played poker for the chance to ask her out first," she added with a grin. "The girl had courage."

"Looks like she was about your size." He couldn't stop himself from picturing the dress on Ruby.

She looked down and swayed her hips back and forth, letting the tassels swing. "Dancing in this must have been so much fun."

"Try it on." The words were out before Austin could think it through.

"You sure?" Ruby loved the idea of trying on the heirloom dress, but the offer took her completely by surprise.

"Go ahead. Immerse yourself in the experience." Austin looked completely serious and also slightly entertained.

She held the dress out in front of her for a better view. It did look like it would fit.

"Turn around," she said.

"I can't watch?" he teased.

"No. You can't watch." She ignored the shimmer of arousal that skittered over her skin.

He turned his back.

She removed the hat then peeled her teal blue sweater over her head and stepped out of her boots and black slacks. Gingerly, and with care, she pulled the dress over her head. The fabric was cool against her skin, silky smooth and shimmery thin, but with an unexpected weight from the beading.

The long black fringe swung against her thighs. Her brown ankle boots weren't the right look, but she didn't have a choice but to step back into them since the floor was dusty planked wood. She reached around to pull up the zipper then combed her fingers through her loose hair to fluff it back up after the hat.

"About done?" Austin asked.

"It's safe to turn around."

He turned, stilling and staring until the silence stretched to uncomfortable.

"Well?" she prompted.

He visibly swallowed. "Nice. Very nice."

Her chest squeezed dangerously at the compliment. "It fits," she managed, telling herself to get a grip.

The point here wasn't to look good for Austin, it was to get a feel for how the Hawkes ancestor—she was still guessing Lillian—had felt dancing in the dress.

Ruby swayed to the beat of the music. "I think living in the roaring twenties would have been fascinating."

"I wouldn't complain about the fashions," Austin said, moving her way and surprising her by holding out his hand. "Dance?"

"You know how?"

He looked affronted. "What kind of a question is that?"

She nodded to the record player. "This is swing."

"Have a little faith." He took her lightly into his arms, moving to the beat.

She was just getting her feet sorted out beneath her when he gracefully swung her around at arm's length before turning her into a spin.

She laughed out loud. "You're good at this."

"I had lessons." His hand settled at the small of her back, his feet moving heel and toe to the beat.

"Cowboys take dancing lessons?"

"That's just my day job." He spun her again.

She grinned as she came back into his arms. "I got the impression it was more a lifestyle than a job."

"Sure. But we dance. At least, many of us dance. It's a great way to impress women."

"I'm impressed," she admitted, falling easily into the beat with him.

"You know what you're doing," he said.

"The fine arts faculty runs a recreational dance club. I'm not much for jogging or the gym, so I go there for exercise."

He swung her around once more, improvising a few steps.

"I feel very immersed," she said on a laugh as he drew her back in.

He grinned, stepping close enough their bodies brushed together as the song hit its finale.

She drew in a few deep breaths, grinning up at him with exhilaration. *That* had been fun.

The beat of the next song was slower.

He raised his brow in a question.

Anticipation built inside her. She knew she shouldn't. But she wanted to. She very, very much wanted to slow dance in Austin's arms.

She nodded.

He smiled and wrapped his arm around her waist, taking her hand.

As they swayed to the beat, she let herself mold against him, turning her cheek to rest against his chest.

The fabric of his shirt was thick, stiff against her face. But the warmth of his body soon made its way through. His hand was big and callused. His arm was sturdy, and his shoulders were broad, defined, hardened with muscle and sinew.

He touched his cheek to her hair and she heard him sigh.

The fringe of her dress brushed his jeans. Their thighs were tight together, slow steps matching on the creaky wood floor. The faint breeze wafting in from the pine forest offered little relief for the heat building between them.

He stroked his hand lightly across her back.

She felt a deep shiver in response, and he gave her a gentle questioning kiss on the temple.

She knew her answer should be no. But she didn't pull away.

This wasn't what she'd planned. It was nothing like she'd planned. But she could never have planned for a man like Austin, never mind anticipate how she'd feel about him.

They might be at odds. Yet she was intrigued by him. What's more, she respected him, and she couldn't seem to stop herself from liking him.

"You're beautiful," he whispered.

She felt beautiful. Who wouldn't feel beautiful in a dress like this, light on her feet, swaying in the arms of a buff, sexy cowboy?

He pulled his head back and she met his gaze. His brown eyes were deep, dark, filled with intent and purpose.

She wanted to kiss him. And the reasons not to were falling away in her mind.

Their steps slowed to a stop.

He brought their joined hands to her cheek, brushing his thumb along her skin. His lips curved into the faintest of smiles as he canted his head and leaned down.

She met him halfway, wrapping her arm around his neck, anchoring herself as his lips brushed hers. The kiss was soft at first, then firm, then harder, then deeper, as she pressed herself against him.

Arousal flared in her breasts, her belly and below. He wrapped her fully in an embrace, lifting her from the floor. The kiss went on, and his hands moved lower, cupping her rear and pulling the dress up her thighs.

As it bunched at her waist, she wrapped her legs around him.

He smoothed his way across her silky panties, exploring as her body tightened with need and her breath came more quickly.

She popped open the snaps of his shirt, kissing his smooth chest, exploring the contours, loving the heat and the taste of his skin.

He groaned, taking a couple of steps to perch her on the edge of the table. There he unzipped her dress, pulling it down over her shoulders, kissing her exposed skin along the way.

He cupped the lacy fabric of her bra. Then he whisked it off, stepping back to gaze at her breasts in the dappled sunlight.

They ached for his touch and she didn't have to wait long.

He flicked his thumb across her nipple and she bit down on her bottom lip.

His kisses began again, and his caresses became bolder, until she was squirming and reaching for the button of his pants.

He drew down her panties, and she kicked them off. His fingertips slid up the center of her bare thighs, meeting at the top.

She tugged at his jeans, shoving them out of the way.

In moments, they met, heated and slick. She kissed him deeply, gripping his shoulders, flexing her hips in answer to his thrusts.

He slipped a hand beneath her, holding her closer still, his free hand sliding up to cradle her head, fingertips burying themselves in her hairline.

Time stood still, and the world fell away, as breathless sensations rocketed from the core of her body to the top of her head and out the tips of her toes. Her breasts were hot and heavy, sending pulses of passion into her chest.

Tension spiraled tighter and tighter within her. Her skin tingled, and she squeezed her eyes shut, dragging in gasping breaths and crying out as light, heat and sound imploded inside her.

Austin's voice was hoarse as he called out her name.

And then she was floating, light as a feather, high in the cool air, the summer breeze soft around her, cushioning her landing.

Austin held Ruby—hot and slick in his arms—breathing deeply, trying to wrap his head around what had just happened between them.

He didn't know what to say.

Should he apologize? Should he tell her she was wonderful? Should he tell her it was the most fantastic sex of his life? Because it was—hands down.

He drew back to look at her, hoping to get a clue from her expression.

She looked slightly surprised and a little befuddled, her swollen lips parted, copper-toned skin dewy with moisture, brown eyes still clouded from passion.

"Should I apologize?" he asked.

Her gaze flicked to where their bodies joined then came back up again. "Are you sorry?"

"Not in the least." He was astonished, amazed and completely satisfied—physically, anyway. "Are you?"

She shook her head. "I sure didn't plan that." She slipped her arms back into the dress to cover up.

He took that as a cue to ease back and give her space. "I sure didn't either." Not that he hadn't fantasized about it. But even in his fantasies, it hadn't been that good.

He wished he could ask if it had been as good for her. He fervently hoped it had been as good for her. He wanted to know every feeling she was experiencing.

"You okay?" he asked, daring himself to be more specific.

"Don't I look okay?" She rubbed her cheeks and smoothed her hair.

"You look incredible," he said.

She smiled and his chest expanded in reaction.

"You look pretty good yourself," she said.

"So, what are we going to do with this?" he asked, acknowledging they'd just crossed a line and they couldn't take it back.

"Hope we've finally gotten it out of our systems?"

"And if we haven't?"

"Then I suppose we'll do it again."

Her bold admission took him by surprise. "You're open to doing it again?"

She gave him an admonishing shake of her head. "I didn't say that."

"You implied it."

"I don't think so."

He leaned in, keeping his tone light and teasing. "I *do* think so."

Her grin widened. "Nice try."

He gave an unrepentant shrug while she glanced around the floor beneath them.

He leaned down to retrieve her blue panties, guessing that's what she wanted.

"Thanks." She took them.

He stepped back and put his own clothing back into place.

The music had stopped while they'd made love.

Bra in hand, Ruby slipped down from the table and walked to where her clothes were stacked neatly on an old rocking chair.

She looked incredibly beautiful as she changed in a stream of sunlight. But she put herself back together way too soon, and he was beyond sorry their interlude was over.

"What now?" he asked.

"I look for more treasure." She gazed around the room.

"What are you hoping to find?" His reasons for worrying about her unfettered access to his family's belongings all remained. But he didn't have it in him to voice his mistrust.

"That's the beauty of this. I won't know until I see it. Look what we learned from the stuffed bunny. The music set the tone for sure." She started forward and passed him on the way to the record player.

He fought an urge to reach out, to pull her back into his arms, maybe dance again, certainly make love again. He'd settle for simply holding her close, feeling her heartbeat and inhaling her subtle sexy scent.

She blew the dust off a new record and set it on the turntable. Rosemary Clooney's voice filled the room.

"We've changed eras," he said.

"New atmosphere."

He didn't want the atmosphere to change, but there didn't seem to be anything he could do about it.

She cocked her head and stared at an antique secretary desk with an upper cabinet, a dropdown writing table and four drawers. A moment later, she was heading for it.

"Know anything about this?" she asked as she walked.

"Not a thing."

"Haven't you ever been curious?" She cautiously opened the doors of the upper cabinet.

"About this old stuff? Not really." He'd heard the adventurous and sometimes comical stories of his family's history, and he treasured some of them. But he'd never been interested in dusty furniture and clothing.

"You're weird," she said as she withdrew a stack of letters from one of the small shelves.

"Just what a guy wants to hear." He wasn't past thinking about their lovemaking yet.

Her back was to him, so he couldn't see her face, but he felt sure she was smiling.

"Need me to give you an ego boost, cowboy?" she asked.

"I'd take one," he answered, walking her way.

She flipped through the envelopes. "You're the best I ever had."

Despite her slightly mocking tone, the words bolstered his self-esteem. He placed his hands lightly on her shoulders. "Now *that's* what a man wants to hear."

"That was sarcasm."

"Didn't sound like sarcasm," he said, his voice rumbling next to her ear.

She gave him a light elbow. "Quit acting insecure. You know you're good."

He didn't know that. He hadn't given it a whole lot of thought before. Sure, women had seemed happy with his lovemaking. But until Ruby, he'd never done a postgame analysis like the one that was going through his head right now.

Were his kisses too hard, too soft? Had he paid enough attention to caressing her? Was he too fast, too slow?

She held up an envelope. "Mind if I read this?"

He focused. The letter was addressed to his great-grandmother Kathleen from someone named Bertie Briner.

"Briner was her maiden name," he said, half to himself, dredging the nugget of knowledge up from somewhere deep in his mind.

"Her father?" Ruby asked, canting her head back to look up at him.

"Her father was Willie. I was never told she had a brother. But maybe. Or it could be an uncle."

"Only one way to find out." Ruby tugged on the letter, but he kept hold.

"I want to read it first."

She turned, bringing them face to face. "Why?"

"Because I don't know what's in it."

"It's from her brother or her uncle. What do you expect to be in it?"

"It could be anything."

Ruby tilted her head, a sparkle in her eyes. "Like plans for a bank heist."

"My great-grandmother wasn't a criminal."

"Her dad was a bootlegger."

"Only during Prohibition. And that was a stupid law anyway."

"Is that how it works? You can break the stupid laws?"

"Better than breaking the smart ones."

She tried again to tug the letter from his hands.

He resisted.

"Don't be a chicken," she said.

"Seriously?" Did she actually think taunting him would work?

She made chicken noises in her throat.

"You're ridiculous."

She leaned into him and batted her long eyelashes. "Can I please read the letter?"

He inhaled sharply as his desire revved back to life. "Flirting is beneath you, Ruby."

"Don't be too sure about that." Her eyes dancing with amusement, she tugged suddenly and this time the letter broke free. "Why thank you, kind sir."

He reached for the letter, but she held it away from him.

It was a ridiculous contest since he could take it from her in about two seconds.

"Was that a bribe?" he asked, matching her lighthearted tone.

"Why? Would it work?"

"No."

"Then it wasn't."

"What was it?" He'd stopped caring about the letter. He was far more interested in how Ruby was feeling about him.

She sobered, and their gazes held. "I don't know. Do I have to know?"

He slowly shook his head.

She quirked a little half smile. "Raw animal passion?"

"Are you ever serious?"

"That was serious." She paused. "I don't know what happened there. But you, me. It kind of seemed inevitable."

He liked the sound of that.

He really liked the sound of that.

"Open the letter," he said.

She separated the edges of the envelope with her slim fingers and extracted a crisp sheet of paper. "You sure?"

"What's the worst it could say?"

Seven

In the end, Ruby found three letters to Kathleen from her uncle Bertie Briner. They were mostly inconsequential chitchat, so it was a mystery why anyone had kept them all these years. But Ruby was happy they had.

After Kathleen's father, Willie, had been shot and killed in an alleyway, his brother and partner in the bootlegging enterprise seemed to settle into a life of quiet obscurity. Bertie wrote to her of trips to the library and the park, and of a woman named Ophelia who owned a tea shop under the apartment he rented. It was hard to tell if Ophelia was a love interest or just a friend. Either way, Bertie clearly found her beautiful and enchanting.

Intrigued by the relationship, Ruby had to caution herself against going on a tangent. Her book wasn't about Kathleen's family, it was about the Hawkes.

One of Bertie's letters mentioned Cloris Reed. It sounded like Cloris was a teenager at the time the letter had been written. It also seemed like Kathleen may have taken the girl under her wing.

While talking with Cloris earlier at the Topaz House, Ruby had already learned Cloris had grown up on the Hawkes ranch. And now it seemed likely she'd been close to Kathleen.

Although Ruby would drop the Ophelia thread for the purpose of her book, she was absolutely picking up on Cloris and Kathleen's relationship. So, before Austin could show up at the breakfast table and take her into custody for the day, she'd grabbed a cup of coffee and one of Victor's hot, flaky biscuits, slathered it in butter and homemade strawberry jam, and headed for her car.

It was over an hour into Jagged Creek, and cell service was almost nonexistent along the gravel road. There was no chance of Austin calling to ask her to come back or to wait for him.

It was clear that her research made him uneasy. After the seismic shift of their lovemaking yesterday, he'd seemed more comfortable with her poking around the old attic. But she didn't expect his new attitude to last.

The sex between them had been nothing short of cataclysmic. But it had also been temporary and she knew the euphoria would wear off for both of them. Nothing had truly changed. Their physical attraction had been there since minute one. They'd simply chosen to bring it to its conclusion.

He'd still try to control what she learned about his family.

Savoring bites of the large biscuit, she let her mind roll back to their lovemaking. She didn't regret it. In fact, she was thankful she'd given in to her instincts and let the moment flow. Austin was an amazing lover and she'd treasure that memory for as long as she lived.

She started a playlist on her phone, pairing it to the car's radio, singing and tapping the beat on her steering wheel as she sped along the gravel road. Each time she drove it, the trip down the ranch road seemed to get a bit shorter. Soon, she rolled up to the Topaz House and swung her car into a visitor parking spot.

It was another bright fall day with the lush lawn forming a vivid emerald blanket around the stonework. The red leaves of vine maples lining the driveway stood out against the blue sky. She climbed out and soaked in the freshness and tranquility for a moment before heading inside.

Cloris was knitting in a sunny corner of the lounge, nestled up to the big fireplace. She looked comfortable and cozy in a pink fleece track suit with tiny rhinestones scattered across the shoulders. Her white hair was curled neatly around her face.

Her needles clacked through a loose knit square of rainbow wool and she looked up as Ruby approached.

"You're back." Cloris smiled in recognition.

"How are you doing today?" Ruby asked.

Cloris leaned forward, lowing her voice so that it sounded

conspiratorial. "It's a bread pudding day. Bread pudding days are good days."

"That sounds delicious."

"Whisky sauce." Cloris gave a wink. "You should stick around and have some."

"I might do that." Ruby pointed to a chair. "Do you mind if I sit down."

"Suit yourself." Cloris went back to her knitting, her needles clacking again. "Though I don't know why a pretty young gal like you wants to hang around with us old fogies."

"I like talking to you. I'm a history buff."

"You should be out looking for a man your own age. Won't be finding one here."

"You think I need a man?" Ruby knew marriage had been viewed differently in Cloris's day. She felt compelled to defend the concept of single womanhood even as her thoughts flicked back to Austin.

"Not need. But want? Sure." A twinkle came into the old woman's eyes. "I remember being young."

Ruby split a grin.

"Hard to picture now." Cloris gazed at her winkled hand. "But I was a looker."

"I bet you were. I heard you might have been close to Kathleen Hawkes back then."

Cloris nodded. "She was a pip, not like the rest of those stuffy fuddy-duddies."

"I heard she held parties?"

Cloris nodded again. "She put Pimm's and champagne in the punch. It was her secret recipe. And the dancing. We'd dance 'till dawn to the Cowboy Drifters."

"They were a band?" Ruby asked.

"They were good."

"Local?"

"Up from Denver. I kissed the banjo player once. He was twenty-three."

"How old were you?"

"Seventeen. Daddy saw and wouldn't speak to me for a week. And that was the end of the Cowboy Drifters."

Ruby could only imagine. Seeing what she had so far about the cowboy code on the Hawkes ranch, kissing a cowboy's teenage daughter would not have gone over well.

"Mrs. Hawkes understood I had a teenage crush on him," Cloris said, her gaze going a little bit dreamy in the sunlight. "She set me straight on men, told me a few things about life. I never forgot them. They served me well when my Mr. Reed came along. I made the man wait. I think that's what kept him interested." Then she gave a self-deprecating grin. "Well, at least until the engagement."

Ruby respected Cloris's choice and silently cheered Kathleen.

"Were you married a long time."

"Fifty-three years."

"Wow." Ruby was very impressed.

"Most of them good."

"Most of them?"

"There were a few rough patches with him out on the range. Cowboys don't always make the best husbands."

Ruby's thoughts flicked to Austin before she quickly shut down the line of thinking. "Because they're gone a lot?" she guessed.

"That, and they're hanging around with other cowboys, whooping it up, getting into mischief." Cloris shook her head.

Ruby wondered if it would be rude to probe. Before she could make up her mind, they were interrupted.

"Mrs. Reed," one of the Topaz House workers cheerfully called out as she hustled her way into the sitting room. "The puppet show's about to start."

Cloris lit up. "That's today?"

"It's right now," the woman answered. "Sorry to interrupt," she said to Ruby.

"Not at all." Ruby quickly rose. "I wouldn't want her to miss out."

Kiera appeared as Cloris rose and took the worker's arm to walk away.

"It's the final rehearsal for a local amateur theater group," Kiera told Ruby. "The company will do matinee shows on Saturday and Sunday for the local kids. The actors and puppeteers get to do a final polish in front of a live audience, and the seniors get to enjoy a lighthearted show. It's a win-win."

"It's really nice that they do that." Ruby was impressed with activities and entertainment provided by Topaz House.

"Good conversation?" Kiera asked.

"It was. She told me about Kathleen's parties. It sounds like the two were close."

"Kathleen never had a daughter, only the one son." Then Kiera laughed lightly. "But I guess you know that already."

"I've put together a pretty good genealogy chart. I just learned Kathleen had an uncle back in Chicago."

"Was he in the family business?"

"It sounded like he retired after his brother died."

Kiera gestured to the lounge chairs. "I'm on a break, if you can stay."

"Love to." Ruby enjoyed Kiera's company and she'd love a little girl talk.

"Tea okay for you?" Kiera asked as she headed for a small counter in the corner.

"Thanks." Ruby followed to see if she could help.

"Are you getting anywhere with the family?" Kiera dropped a teabag into a Brown Betty teapot and added boiling water from a spigot in the sink.

"It's going better. McKinney put me on to the attic in their old house."

"And what did Austin have to say about that?"

"He was hesitant at first. But he came around."

Kiera glanced Ruby's way, looking far too perceptive. "He did, did he?"

Ruby struggled to keep her expression neutral. "He just had to get used to the idea."

"And you helped him?" Kiera guessed, lifting the lid from the teapot and dunking the teabag up and down.

Seeing a line of white porcelain mugs on an open shelf, Ruby busied herself by pulling two of them down and setting them right side up on the counter. "We came to an understanding."

Kiera flashed a grin. "Oh, I want to pry. I mean I don't want to pry. But your expression really makes me want to pry."

Ruby wasn't sure what to say. She barely knew Kiera, but there seemed little harm in admitting she and Austin were attracted to each other—not all the details, of course.

"There may have been some...flirtation involved."

"You go, girl." Kiera poured the tea.

Ruby realized she'd given the wrong impression. "I didn't do it to manipulate him." She felt a little flustered now. "It just... sort of...you know...happened."

"Uh-oh." Holding one of the mugs Ruby's way, Kiera frowned with concern.

"What uh-oh?" Ruby wrapped her hands around the mug of warm tea.

"It would have been better if you had."

"Manipulated him?" Ruby thought she must have misunderstood.

"Are you attracted to him?" Kiera asked.

"He's a good-looking guy."

Kiera nodded vigorously. "They all are."

"And?" Ruby wasn't getting the point.

Kiera started for the lounge chairs. "Those Hawkes boys are heartbreakers."

"It's not exactly my heart that's involved," Ruby admitted.

Austin was sexy. He was exciting and captivating. And she could appreciate a fling with a cowboy as much as the next woman. But she didn't know him anywhere near well enough to be risking her emotions.

"Good," Kiera said as she sat down. "I'm glad to hear that. I like you, Ruby."

"I like you, too." Ruby took a chair cornerwise to Kiera.

"I'd hate to see you get hurt."

"No chance of that." Ruby was touched by Kiera's concern, but she was only here for as long as it took to do her research. "My life is in Boston."

Kiera settled back and sipped her tea. "I take it there's no significant other back in Boston?"

Ruby vigorously shook her head. "I sure wouldn't flirt if there was." And she'd done way more than flirting.

"I'm not surprised by that. But people have all kinds of relationships these days, some more open than others."

Ruby grimaced over the lip of her cup. "I can't even imagine."

"Me neither. Not that I'm judgy about it."

Ruby hadn't given it any thought. She didn't have any friends in open relationships—at least, none that she knew about. In any event, the topic hadn't come up.

"Have you been to the museum?" Kiera asked, saving Ruby from forming an answer.

"There's a museum?" How had Ruby missed something so relevant?

"They don't advertise. It's very informal. It was set up in Madeline Compton's back parlor—more of an archive, really. The Comptons donated some of their land, plus a whole lot of money, for the college. The college is basically next door to their home—so, next door to the archives. Some of the students operate the archive."

"You have a town *archive*?" Ruby was even more excited by that.

"Sure. I know Madeline really well. I can show you—later today or next time you're in town."

Ruby sat eagerly forward. "What time are you finished?"

Austin wasn't proud of himself for what he was about to do—snoop in Ruby's bedroom. But when she'd missed dinner, then eight o'clock had rolled around, he had to wonder if she'd moved from the ranch back into town.

Making love with her had been fantastic for him. And it had seemed the same for her yesterday. But when he hadn't seen her this morning, and as the hours had ticked past, he'd wondered if she'd masked her feelings. Maybe she regretted giving in to their physical attraction—regretted it enough to leave.

Glancing both ways down the second-floor hall, he slowly

and silently opened her door. He breathed a sigh of relief to see her belongings on the dresser and the bed, her small suitcase upright in the corner.

He hadn't chased her away.

He didn't even care that she'd been gone all day without an explanation again. All he cared about was that she was still around.

Voices sounded downstairs and he quickly pulled back into the hall, shutting the door behind him.

"Well, that's good news." McKinney's voice carried up the stairway.

"It's another treasure trove." Ruby's voice this time.

Austin couldn't help smiling at the sound.

"Kiera Brooks called it the Compton's back parlor," she continued. "So I was expecting... I don't know...a sitting room with a patterned rug, French Provincial chairs, a Tiffany lamp and a china cabinet. But it's a whole building. Madeline said it used to be a garage."

"I think it started out as the 'rug, chairs and lamp' thing a long time ago," McKinney said as Austin headed for the stairs. "As I understand it, Mrs. Compton eventually moved to the second floor above the garage then expanded the whole thing."

"She has high ceilings, stacks of shelving," Ruby said. "Everything is cataloged, cross-referenced."

Austin could see them now, standing together in the dining room.

McKinney braced herself on the back of a chair. "There are a lot of students cycling through to do the work."

"I read that you had a college," Ruby said. "But it sounded like everything was remote."

"Most of the classes are. They have agreements with institutions in Denver and Phoenix. Do you want some pie? Did you have dinner?"

"Pie sounds wonderful."

Austin came to the bottom of the stairs, but they didn't hear him, their backs turned as they left for the kitchen.

He hesitated, unsettlingly tense as he considered Ruby's possible reactions to seeing him today. He'd hate it if she seemed regretful or embarrassed. He wanted her to be happy. He wanted to see a smile on her pretty face, even better if there was an intimate twinkle in her eyes just for him, for the secret they shared.

The front door shut with a bang, startling him as his brother appeared in the foyer.

"You're back," Austin said, moving to greet Dallas.

"Sierra didn't want to miss the rodeo."

Austin had a moment's pause. "Tell me you're not riding in it."

The annual Jagged Creek Rodeo was coming up in just a few days. Dallas had competed in it as a teenager before he'd turned pro and had usually won half the events. But he'd only just recovered from his shoulder injury.

He shook his head. "Not competing. But the mayor asked me to be grand marshal in the parade."

"Well, that sounds safe enough."

"That's what my wife said." A sappy grin crossed Dallas's face as he referred to Sierra as his wife.

Austin chuckled. "So, how did the trip go?"

"Some was good, some disappointing." Dallas hung up his Stetson. "Bought a nice stallion in Omaha. Eight-year-old quarter horse, kicks high, got a heck of a spin on him."

"Young," Austin noted.

Dallas grinned as he walked forward. "Good long future for that boy."

"And what's next?"

"Done enough rough stock shopping, for now, I think. We need to finish the barn, put up a round pen, expand the paddock. Sierra has the house construction under control. Four bedrooms and one very big kitchen."

"You did say you wanted kids."

"And we've got room for them. Drink?" Dallas nodded to the wet bar.

"Feel like pie?" Austin asked instead. He was anxious to go see Ruby.

"Apple?"

"Blueberry."

"Even better."

The kitchen door opened, and McKinney and Ruby came back through, each carrying a generous slice of blueberry pie topped with vanilla ice cream.

Ruby's gaze caught Austin's.

He paused, bracing himself.

But then she smiled and glanced guiltily at her dessert. "You caught us."

"Hey, Dallas," McKinney said. "I didn't know you were back."

"Got in this afternoon."

Relieved, Austin returned Ruby's smile. "We were after some pie ourselves."

"Good trip?" McKinney asked Dallas.

"Came back with some new stock."

"Where's Sierra?"

"She didn't know there was pie."

McKinney pretended to guard her slice. "Get your own."

Dallas chuckled and headed for the kitchen while McKinney moved to the dining room table.

Austin shifted closer to Ruby. "How was your day?"

A wariness darkened her eyes, and he guessed she was recalling his reaction last time she'd disappeared.

"I went to town," she said then seemed to wait for his criticism.

"See anything interesting?" He kept his tone neutral, disappointed by the tension but knowing it was his fault not hers.

"Yes."

"Good."

She cocked her head, looking skeptical.

"What?" he asked.

"Why are you suddenly okay with it?"

He arched a brow.

Was she really asking what had changed between them?

McKinney called out, "Let her past, Austin. Her ice cream is melting."

He glanced reflexively at her plate and saw the ice cream was melting. "You should eat that."

"It wasn't a bribe," she told him in an undertone.

"I never thought it was."

"Then don't treat it like one." She sidestepped and waltzed past him, leaving him wondering what he'd done wrong.

Luckily, McKinney and Dallas kept the conversation flowing while they all ate their way through the slices of pie.

Austin barely paid attention.

Ruby's lips had darkened from the purple berries and all he could think of was kissing them.

Hand on her bedroom doorknob, Ruby heard footsteps behind her.

"Hey," Austin said softly.

She wasn't surprised he'd followed her upstairs. Although she hoped he'd been discrete about it. McKinney and Dallas were still chatting in the great room.

She turned. "Do we have to do this right now?" She was too tired to defend spending another whole day in town, and she was way too tired to dissect what had happened between them yesterday.

"Yes," he said gently but resolutely.

"I'm tired," she said.

"Turning into a pumpkin?"

"That was a coach, not Cinderella."

His gaze intensified. "We made love, Ruby."

She reflexively glanced up and down the hall to confirm they were completely alone.

He continued. "There's something for us to talk about."

She turned the knob and pushed open the door. It would be a whole lot worse to stand around talking about it in the hall. "Make it quick."

He followed her inside, shut the door and leaned back against it, pausing, his gaze scanning her. "You doing okay?"

"I'm perfectly fine."

He nodded thoughtfully. "I missed you today."

"Is that your way of asking where I was?"

"I know where you were."

She lifted her brow questioningly.

"With Kiera Brooks at the Comptons'."

"Are you spying on me?"

He smiled as he shook his head. "I overheard you talking to McKinney."

The smile got to her. She fought her burgeoning feelings, but this was one very sexy man standing in front of her. She struggled to focus. "How is that not spying?"

"It wasn't on purpose." He seemed to sense her change of mood and straightened away from the door, taking a step forward.

She held her palm up to stop him.

"What's that?" he asked, clearly amused.

"Stay right where you are, cowboy."

"I missed you today."

"No. You worried about what I was up to today."

"That, too. But I missed you."

She flattened her lips, steeling herself against the desire he roused in her.

"You're not going to say it back?"

"I'm not going to say it back."

He cocked his head. "Doesn't mean it's not true."

"You are *so* full of yourself."

But he was also right. She had thought about him and missed him today, especially during the long drive into town and back again when her mind wasn't occupied. She'd imagined his arms around her, their passionate kisses, their naked bodies rocking together.

"Your cheeks are flushed," he teased, easing forward a little more.

She reflexively reached up. "I'm hot."

"I'll say you are."

She wanted to tell him to stop, even opened her mouth to say so. But the words didn't come out.

"I'm not here to push you into anything," he said.

She knew that and nodded.

He gently took her hand, searching her expression as he spoke. "You're okay? Really?"

"No regrets, Austin."

He drew in a deep breath, his chest rising then falling. "I like it when you say my name."

"Austin, Austin, Austin," she teased.

"Was that you flirting?"

"Oh, I hope not." But she knew it was.

He took her other hand. His hold was loose, belying the strength in his broad palms and long fingers. "Because I'm open to it."

"We can't keep doing this." Much as she wanted to throw herself into his arms all over again, they'd already taken things too far.

"Because…?"

Her lips softened and her breasts tingled. She couldn't come up with a reason.

"You can just say no." He turned his hands and interlaced their fingers.

"I know."

"Or…" He slanted his head, bringing his lips a few inches closer to hers.

"I thought we were going to talk."

"Sure." Humor threaded through his voice.

"You're incorrigible," she whispered.

"What do you want to talk about?"

She couldn't think of a single thing. "You started this."

"Guilty as charged." His breath puffed with the words.

It drew her reflexively his way and their lips brushed ever so slightly together. "You said we needed to talk."

"We're talking."

"Not really."

They weren't saying anything of any consequence. Then again, their body language was unmistakable.

"Oh, man." She closed her eyes and kissed him.

He returned the kiss, shifting his hands to the small of her back, taking hers with them and pressing her breasts into the rock wall of his chest.

Passion zipped along her spine, warming her limbs and raising goose bumps on her skin.

She wanted to touch him, but her hands were trapped. She wanted to tear off his clothes and hers, and fall onto the bed in a tangle of arms and legs, wrapping around each other to make love again.

But he broke the kiss and drew back, his breathing deep and heavy. "I don't want you to regret this."

She didn't want to regret it either. But she didn't want to stop. The last thing she wanted to do was shut this thing down. Then again—

She struggled to control her breathing, to slow her heart-rate, to force some reason back into her mind that was awash in hormones.

"Are we the two most indecisive people in the world?" she breathed.

"It sure seems like it."

"I don't want to stop."

He eased back further, letting her hands go. "But part of you does."

"Maybe." She wasn't going to lie, either to herself or to him. "I know better than this."

He heaved a sigh and pulled away. "I sure wish you didn't. But I get it."

"I'm sorry."

He shook his head. "Nothing to be sorry about. I was the one who pushed it. Honestly, Ruby. I only wanted to make sure you were okay with what happened yesterday."

His compassion touched something deep inside her and she felt herself weakening all over again.

"You need to go," she said, shooing him away with her hands. "Quick."

He grinned in what looked like triumph. "Well, at least there's that."

"Don't gloat."

"Who's gloating?" He stepped backward for the door. "I'm crushed."

"You'll get over it." Her logic and reason were returning. That had been a very close call.

He paused. "I'll show you something interesting tomorrow."

Her curiosity instantly rose. "What?"

"It's a surprise."

She took in his mischievous expression. "Is making me wait some kind of payback?"

Nothing he'd done so far said he was vengeful. But she had blown hot and cold on him since she'd gotten here. Even she was confused about how she was feeling.

"It's restitution. But it'll be fun." His smile said he was enthusiastic, not bitter.

"Okay. Then I'll wait."

His eyes twinkled in amusement. "Generous of you."

They stared at each other for a silent moment, electricity still crackling between them, each of their chests rising and falling with steady breaths.

"You should go," she forced herself to say.

He pulled the door open behind him. "I'm gone."

Eight

Austin missed Ruby overnight and he looked forward to spending the day with her. After breakfast, they climbed into one of the ranch's pickups. Their destination was an easy ride from Dallas and Sierra's new house, so they'd saddle up a couple of horses and leave from there.

His overarching plan was to encourage her interest in the distant past. So a visit to the line shack originally built by Gunner and his son Winston seemed like a good move.

Austin's two-and three-times-great-grandfathers had put up the small structure before the family even had title to the land, and it was still in use today. Over the years, they'd fattened thousands of cattle up on the plateau in midsummer while they preserved the valley grasses for later in the season.

The place wasn't full of artifacts like the attic had been, but he hoped Ruby would find it interesting. He had a tale or two he could tell about the cowboys' adventures in it over the years.

"How long are you going to keep me in suspense?" She broke the silence as they sped westward on the gravel road toward an access point.

"You don't like surprises?" He'd found he liked teasing her, keeping her in suspense.

"No." Her tone was even, not amused but not annoyed either.

He glanced her way, keeping the light note in his voice. "You strike me as a person who likes surprises."

"I don't know what you base that on." She crossed an ankle over the opposite knee and propped her elbow on the back of the bench seat. "I'm a planner, focused and methodical."

She'd worn her Western leather boots, a pair of boxy, low-waist jeans that looked incredibly sexy topped with a purple-and-blue-stippled sweater under her puffy black jacket. Tiny gold earrings sparkled on her lobes in the sunshine, and her dark hair was pulled into a ponytail that anchored a royal-blue, Hawkes-ranch-branded baseball cap on her head. He'd like her wearing his family name—liked it far more than was logical or smart. But he liked it all the same.

"If you say so," he responded.

"You're seriously telling me you don't see that in my personality?"

"You've had a few impulsive moments since we met."

"Those were anomalies." The humor that came up in her eyes belied the admonishment in her tone.

"Understood," he deadpanned in return. "Can I say I like your anomalies?"

"You may—"

He expected her to add the word *not*, but she didn't.

He slowed for the turn onto the rougher, private dirt road that led to Dallas and Sierra's building site. "I like your anomalies."

"We're flirting again," she noted.

"I can't seem to help myself."

"You should concentrate on driving."

He swung into the first curve alongside a small creek. "I can drive this road blindfolded."

"Let's not do that."

He split a grin.

"Is there something historical about your brother's place?"

"No. We've had the land for decades, but nobody's ever lived up here before."

"I don't understand."

"That's the point of a surprise."

"Than what are we doing here?" she persisted as the road funneled them between towering pines and the dense, leafy undergrowth.

"I told you I'd show you something interesting, and I will."

"Well, at least it's a pretty drive." She gazed out the window at the sparkling sunlight as the narrow creek came into view once more.

It snaked its way under fallen logs and over smooth boulders, glassy in some places, burbling white in others. He knew it was thick with rainbow trout. His youngest brother Tyler still fly-fished here when he was home on leave from the military.

"Ever been fishing?" he asked her.

"I'm from Boston."

"You have a harbor."

"No. I've never been fishing. My parents are academics."

"So, that's how you ended up as a professor?"

"No." Her brow furrowed. "Well, not exactly. They encouraged me to further my education, sure. But I liked college. And I loved history. I didn't feel any particular pressure from them to finish my PhD."

"Are you sure about that? I felt a lot of pressure to become a rancher."

She turned his way, looking curious. "How so?"

"Can you keep a secret?"

She looked surprised by the question. "Sure." She held up her palms. "Who am I going to tell?"

"It can't go in the book."

"Not everything has to go in the book."

"Your word?"

She hesitated for a moment. "Yes."

He didn't exactly know why, but he felt confident she'd keep her word.

"My grandfather left me tens of thousands of acres in his will," he said. "I didn't know about it until the clause kicked in when I turned thirty. The land was put in my name. What else could I do?"

"Sell it?"

He shook his head. "It's part of the family holdings. I couldn't break it up."

"I can understand that. In fact, I admire it." She gripped the side handle above the door as they bounced through a series of potholes. "Originally, the thesis for my book was the demise of the big family ranches in Colorado. I picked the Hawkes ranch because you were one of the few that remained intact and thriving."

"'Originally'?" He picked up on the word.

"That was before I thought about the women. Focusing on their contributions and resiliency is a much stronger idea—more original and innovative."

"I don't know about that." His mother came into his thoughts. The distant past was one thing, but he hated the idea of someone delving into his parents' personal lives. "I don't see anything wrong with your first idea."

"It was okay. I could have done something with it. But the women's contribution is way more interesting. *Wow*." Her tone turned to amazement as they came out on the plateau meadow next to White Foam Falls.

Straight ahead of them, the forty-foot waterfall gushed between moss-covered rocks and into a deep green pool. The half-built house was to the west, near the northern tree line. Further along, the barn was taking shape next to the barbwire-fenced pasture and a row of corrals.

"It is absolutely gorgeous up here," Ruby enthused. She unrolled her window and leaned her head through the opening. "I can hear the falls."

"It's a nice spot." Austin had always thought of it as remote, so he'd been puzzled when Dallas had chosen the section as his part of their grandfather's inheritance.

As had happened for Austin a year earlier, and would happen for Tyler next year, Dallas had been told of the inheritance from his grandfather's will on his thirtieth birthday. At first, Dallas had threatened to sell the land and move away from his troubling teenage memories. But then he'd come up with the plan to raise rodeo stock. Now, he and Sierra were hard at work getting the operation set up before the snow fell.

Austin brought the pickup to a stop at the edge of the construction site. An air compressor kicked in, nail guns banging as the construction crew put up the wood sheathing.

Ruby climbed out of the vehicle, adjusting her cap to block the sunshine as she took in the half-built house.

Dallas spotted their arrival and started their way, removing his leather gloves and tucking them into his belt as he approached.

"It's coming along," Austin called out admiringly to his brother.

"Everything's on schedule," Dallas answered. "The electricians arrived today. How are you doing, Ruby?"

She gazed into the distance. "I didn't expect it to be so beautiful."

Dallas grinned. "Personally, I was sold on the thigh-high meadow grass. But Sierra's partial to the view of the falls."

Ruby's expression sobered. "Is Sierra here? I really want to apologize for showing up at her wedding like that."

Dallas waved away Ruby's concern. "Don't even worry about it. She didn't mind. It gave us something to tease Austin about."

"How was it my mistake?" Austin redirected the conversation. After what had happened between him and Ruby, the last thing he wanted was for Dallas to start joking about them dating again.

"You didn't bother asking who she was or what she wanted," Dallas said with incredulity.

"He's got you there," Ruby said with a smirk, clearly ready to throw in her lot with Dallas.

"Here comes Sierra now," Austin said then immediately regretted it when Ruby's smile faded. "It's fine," he quickly told her, shifting a step closer to lend support. He knew Sierra well enough to know she wouldn't hold anything against Ruby.

"Hey, Austin," Sierra said cheerfully as she approached.

Dressed in worn jeans, practical boots and a warm sweater, she gave him a quick hug.

"Nice to see you again, Ruby," she added as she drew back.

"I'm so sorry about your wedding day," Ruby blurted out.

Like Dallas had, Sierra waved away the apology. "It was a minor blip. It was kind of funny." She cast her amused gaze Austin's way.

"It wasn't *that* big of a mistake," he protested.

"We all thought you'd be perfect for Austin," Sierra said to Ruby.

It was clear Ruby didn't know how to react to the statement.

It was just as clear that her deer-in-the-headlights expression piqued Sierra's curiosity.

"I should be so lucky," Austin said heartily.

"Yes, you should," Dallas agreed. "We might as well go saddle up."

"Want to see inside?" Sierra asked Ruby.

"You don't mind?"

"I like showing it off…and getting advice." Sierra took in Ruby's outfit. "You seem like you'd have a sense of style."

"I'm no decorator," Ruby protested.

"I bet you have a better eye than Dallas."

"Hey," Dallas protested.

"Don't worry, darling." Sierra said, her tone placating. "You have other skills, I'm sure. We'll meet you at the RV. Ruby needs a better hat."

"Is there something wrong with my hat?" Ruby asked as the two women wound their way through the construction materials toward the front door of the building. She'd grown fond of the comfortable cap. It kept the sun off her head and shaded her eyes.

"You need a proper brim for trail riding. You're up high, and horses don't pay attention to the branches over their head. But don't worry, I've got plenty you can borrow. I barely even ride, but every place we visit, Dallas takes me shopping to the leather goods' store. I have more gloves, hats and chaps than a woman can wear in a lifetime."

"Chaps are a thing?" Ruby had always thought they were decorative.

"For a working cowboy, yes. For an occasional recreational rider like me, not so much. You want to borrow a pair?"

"Not if I don't need them." Ruby would already feel like she was playing dress-up by wearing a Stetson.

They crossed a partially built wraparound porch to walk through the wide-open front doors. In the relative quiet, she inhaled the fresh scent of newly sawed wood, taking in the bare studs that delineated the layout of the rooms. The floor was concrete. The ceilings soared high above the main room, showing off a bank of feature windows that rose to a peak.

"You can go straight through here to the back porch," Sierra said then pointed to their right. "And it'll stay open through to the kitchen on this side. I didn't want to be super fancy about a dining room or anything. I mean, there's space for a big table in the front bay window. But when you're cooking, you should be part of the action."

"I like it," Ruby said, moving into the kitchen. It was roomy without being overwhelmingly huge. She tried to picture it finished. "Will you put in an island?"

"In the middle here." Sierra stood and extended her arms. "The sink will be below the window. Around the end of the counter, it goes pantry, mudroom, and down the hall to the bedrooms. We changed the plans to have the master on the same wing as the kids' bedrooms. I can't see having them all the way on the other side of the house. Especially when they're little."

"So, kids are in the plan?" Ruby was a little surprised, given Dallas and Sierra had only been married a couple of weeks.

"We both want kids." Sierra led the way down the hall. "We've decided when they come, they come. The Hawkes ranch is very family friendly."

"Do you have siblings?" Ruby had no experience at all with a big family.

"Half siblings. They're quite a bit younger, and I barely know them. It was just me and my mom growing up." Sierra paused. "Maybe that's why a busy, chaotic household appeals to me so much. What about you?"

"Only child." Ruby looked around the big house. "My dad headed up International Studies at Boston U. I grew up in faculty housing. We entertained a lot, visiting professors and professionals mostly, so definitely not a chaotic household."

"Did you like it?"

"Sure." The staid, steady pace of her life had seemed perfectly normal at the time. She hadn't given it a lot of thought since.

"No husband and family in the plans for you?"

Ruby faltered at the question.

"Sorry." Sierra was quick to apologize. "None of my business."

"It's not that. I almost never think about it." Ruby realized her hopes and dreams had been wrapped up in her education and now in her career.

When she had pictured a long-term relationship, it was with an urbane, like-minded man. She'd imagined they'd buy a nice condo and find time for plays, art exhibits, high-class restaurants and maybe a little travel in between their professional achievements.

"That's because you're so successful," Sierra said.

"Not really."

Sierra looked incredulous. "You're a professor."

"My job's not even permanent."

"You'll get there. You're a hard worker. It's easy to see that."

Ruby appreciated the vote of confidence, even if Sierra didn't know anything about her work ethic. "I envy your conviction in knowing what you want."

"It's new to me," Sierra said and started back toward the main room. "Less than six months ago, I was out of a job, homeless, and had been dumped by my fiancé."

"You're exaggerating."

Sierra shook her head. "McKinney took pity on me and invited me to visit. Then I met Dallas."

"And that's all she wrote?" Ruby guessed.

Sierra laughed. "Not even close. We drove each other crazy at first."

Ruby couldn't help thinking about Austin. He didn't exactly drive her crazy. But she suspected he might say that very thing about her.

An unabashed smile came up on Sierra's face. "But there was something, something sizzling just below the surface."

Ruby thought about the sizzle between her and Austin.

"What?" Sierra prompted, taking in Ruby's expression. "Is there a guy like that back in Boston?"

"No." Ruby quickly shook her head.

"Well, you're obviously thinking about someone." Sierra snapped her mouth shut. "And I'm being unbelievably rude."

"You're not. I mean I don't mind." Oddly, Ruby didn't mind the curiosity.

Sierra was easy to warm up to. The woman all but oozed empathy, and Ruby found herself wishing they were girlfriends so she could just lay it all out on the table.

Sierra searched Ruby's expression. "I'm happy to talk or to listen. I mean it. Anytime." She unexpectedly reached out and squeezed Ruby's hand.

Ruby's chest filled with emotion. "Thanks."

Boot heels sounded on the porch and Austin called through the doorway. "You two about done in there?"

In her heightened emotional state, Ruby felt the timbre of his voice right down to her core.

Sierra gave her a quick shoulder rub and started for the porch. "Come on back for dinner," she said to Austin as she went outside. "We'll throw something on the grill."

"Uh, sure," Dallas added a split second later.

Ruby heard his hesitation. "We don't want to intrude."

"No intrusion," Dallas said with a friendly welcoming smile.

Ruby looked to Austin, leaving the choice up to him. He knew his brother. Hopefully, he could tell if Dallas was being sincere or merely being polite.

"Can do," Austin said easily. "If this one doesn't slow me down too much."

"Hey," Ruby protested, even though he had a point.

"You can take an ATV," Dallas offered, giving Ruby a look of concern.

"I'm not *that* bad," she told him. "I took some lessons at a stable near Canton."

"You didn't tell me you'd had lessons," Austin said accusingly.

"Sure, I did."

"You said you'd ridden *a few times*."

"I have. At a stable south of Boston. Why is that so weird?" She held his gaze.

"Well, you two kids have fun." Dallas jokingly mocked them.

Sierra frowned her husband's way and jabbed him lightly with her elbow.

Catching the gesture, Ruby's face flushed with heat. It was easy to guess Sierra had suspicions about Ruby's feelings for Austin.

The shack wasn't much to look at, but Austin hoped Ruby would appreciate its storied past. Before she'd showed up, he hadn't given much thought to the continuity of the seven generations who'd used it. But he was now. In contrast to the modernization, life at the line shack had remained pretty much unchanged in all that time.

Oh, they had better food now, better tack, and it was much easier to get here, especially now that Dallas and Sierra were settling in near the falls. But the chores of tending a herd were virtually the same.

"When was it built?" Sierra asked. Her saddle leather creaked as she dismounted onto the meadow.

"In the early 1900s. Most of what became the ranch wasn't ours then. And this was open grazing."

The shack was unassuming; a rectangular building with a low-peaked roof covered in tarpaper, a narrow stovepipe sticking out at the back. The lumber had grayed with age, and the two windows on either side of the door were old enough for the glass to have thickened at the bottom of the panes.

She removed her borrowed cowboy hat. "Have you ever stayed here?"

"Plenty of times." He dismounted and followed her to the hitching rail, looping the chestnut gelding's reins around it. Blunder was a fifth-generation Hawkes working horse, and he'd seen every corner of the spread.

Dallas had put Ruby on a dappled gray quarter horse named Sal. Austin hadn't met the gelding before today, but he seemed gentle enough. And it was clear the younger horse adored Blunder.

"So, it's been a working building for over a hundred years."

"Yes, ma'am. We upgrade the bunk mattresses every once in a while. And we dug a new outhouse around 2010."

She gave a pained grin. "Good to know."

"It's not fancy," he said, leading the way to the small porch that held two Adirondack chairs and a water barrel. "But I thought you'd appreciate authentic."

"I do appreciate authentic."

"Just not when you have to use the facilities?" He opened the door and it groaned on the hinges. A whiff of stale air came from the inside, and he propped the door open with a little wooden wedge.

"Authentic," she said and wrinkled her nose.

The floor flexed as they walked inside. Two bunks took up the far end of the room on either side of the small wood stove. Saddle racks sat at the foot of each bed. There was a counter with a basin and dishrack in the front corner, with shelves for food and dishes above it, and a picnic table in the middle of it all.

"What's it like staying here?" Ruby asked as she looked around, squinting in the dim, dusty light.

"You want to try it out? We can sleep over." He walked to a bunk and pretended to test the mattress with his palm. "Comfy."

She followed along, taking in the plaid wool blankets. "Dallas and Sierra are expecting us for dinner."

"Wuss," he said on a chuckle, turning her way.

"Judgmental much?" she countered with a grin.

The small, shadowy cabin suddenly seemed intimate. "I supposed learning about history doesn't mean you want to live it."

"I happen to have a fondness for plumbing." Her gaze settled on his.

"Can't exactly blame you for that." He couldn't resist, so he touched his hand to her shoulder, watching her expression.

Her gaze darkened from caramel to chocolate. She bit down on her lip. "I think Sierra suspects."

The abrupt statement confused him. "Suspects what?"

"That there's something going on between us."

"Why? Did she say something?" He tried to gauge Ruby's level of concern.

She shook her head. "It was more the way she looked at us."

Austin considered the possibility, trying to decide how he felt about it himself. His new sister-in-law seemed very discrete.

But she might say something to Dallas, who would absolutely confront Austin and ask for details.

"How do you feel about saying something?" he asked.

She looked worried. "I wouldn't even know how to describe… us. I mean we're unencumbered adults. We can do whatever we want."

"We don't have to admit anything to anyone." Whatever Ruby wanted was fine with him. He just needed to know what it was.

"You think we should lie?" She made it sound like he was the one who'd be embarrassed.

He wouldn't. "That's not what I said."

"But is it what you meant?"

He narrowed his gaze. "Why are you doing this?"

"Doing what?"

"Picking a fight."

"I don't want to fight. I'm just curious. What would you tell people? I mean if you were going to tell them anything. Or if they were to ask."

"Oh, Dallas will ask all right." Austin was sure about that.

"And what will you say?" There was a challenge in Sierra's tone now.

"Whatever you want me to say. I don't care who knows I slept with you. We can make it a headline in the *Jagged Creek Crier*."

"So, it's the sex?"

He drew his head back, knowing he'd said something wrong. He waited a beat, but she didn't give him any hints. "It seems like that would be the secret part."

"Sure. Yeah. That makes sense."

"You don't think it makes sense?" He was more confused than ever.

"I never said that."

He tried to talk through the logic. "Everyone knows we're working together. It's obvious we're getting along now. What's left that they don't know about besides sex?"

"Nothing." Her expression was neutral now.

He didn't know whether to trust it, so he spoke slowly. "So, we agree?"

"We agree." She gave a smile that wasn't quite convincing and turned away to explore the cabin.

Austin hesitated for a moment.

"How long do people live out here?" she asked, a bright edge to her tone.

"A few days, maybe a week."

She touched the enamel basin and the dish towel hanging off to one side. "Without a shower?"

"There's a creek down the bank." He knew from experience it was ice-cold, but it did the trick.

She moved her gaze upward, seeming to catalog the items on the shelves. "What about in the winter?"

"We don't run cattle up here in the winter. Something's wrong."

"No, it's not." She still didn't turn his way.

"Quit acting like… I don't know…like you're someone else."

She turned then. "What do you mean by that?"

"I can tell I did something wrong."

"You didn't."

He didn't believe her denial for a second. "I won't know what it is unless you tell me."

She flattened her lips.

"Ruby, I'm a guy. I'm a cowboy. You have to hit me over the head with whatever it is I did."

"You didn't do a thing."

"Right." He stepped closer to her. "I'm not buying that. And if Sierra is suspicious, she's going to tell Dallas. If you don't tell me what to say, then how can I—"

"Say whatever you want."

"Stop," he said softly.

She hit him with a frustrated glare.

He didn't know why this was turning into an argument. "Tell me what I did wrong."

"It's not for me to tell you—"

"If you don't, nobody else will."

"—how to feel," she finished.

He blinked in surprise. "How I feel? How I feel is *fantastic*. I like being with you. The closer, the better. The more naked, the better. We keep saying it's a bad idea. And we're right. But I don't care." He leaned closer, slowly enunciating each word. "I. Don't. Care."

He kissed her then—because he desperately wanted to do it, and because it was the only reasonable course of action.

She kissed him back.

Better still, she gave a low moan in her throat and pressed herself against him, wrapping her arms around his neck.

He wanted to strip off their clothes and tumble naked onto a bunk, to make long, slow, love with her until they were so satisfied that neither of them could move a muscle. He wanted it bad, so bad.

But this wasn't the place. They'd already made love in an attic. Here on the sagging springs and worn wool blankets with months of range dust clouding the air would be even worse. She deserved satin sheets, a pillow-top mattress, flowers, and champagne.

He broke the kiss, cradled her head against his shoulder, dragging in oxygen while ordering his hormones to stand down.

"What's wrong?" she asked, her voice muffled against his shirt.

"Wrong place," he said. "Wrong time."

She tipped her face his way. "You have somewhere you have to be?"

"In my bed or maybe yours, or in a five-star hotel suite, but not in a tacky old line shack."

"I'm a historian."

"You're also a woman." He allowed himself to look into her eyes. "A beautiful, kind, successful woman who deserves the finest things in life."

Her lips curved into a smile. "You're getting a little romantic on me there, cowboy."

He knew she was right, and it didn't bother him at all. "Maybe that's what we tell them."

"Who?"

"Dallas and Sierra." Austin cradled Ruby's face, stroking his thumb across her smooth cheek. "When they ask, we can say things between us got romantic."

Nine

Dallas and Sierra hadn't asked any questions, but the word *romantic* followed Ruby through the night and into the next afternoon.

What had Austin meant by it? A braver woman would have asked him. Then again, the answer might have disappointed her. For now, she was savoring the early bloom of an emotional fantasy, and she wanted to ride the high just a little bit longer.

She put a new record on the turntable, filling the attic with the crooning of Nat King Cole as she poked her way through boxes and trunks, eventually ending up back at the secretary desk. Inside it, she found a tattered dictionary and three well-thumbed novels: *Marjorie Morningstar*, *The Man in the Gray Flannel Suit* and *On the Road*. She checked the opening pages, hoping for an inscription, a clue to the reading tastes of Austin's ancestors. But nobody had written anything in the books.

In the top drawer, she found pens and pencils, erasers and a bottle of long-dried-out glue. When she came across a yellowed pad of paper, curled at the edges, she ran her fingers over the top page, feeling indentations from writers long past. She used the edge of a pencil to shade it, hoping to bring to light what had been written.

She sighed when she realized it was indecipherable.

When she discovered one of the drawers was locked, her excitement mounted. Most people put the good stuff under lock and key.

She got down on her knees and peered into the lock. Not that it did her any good. She wasn't a locksmith or a criminal.

But she did know the mechanisms on older furniture were usually simple.

She hunted through the reaches of the dusty top drawer and was rewarded with a paperclip. She bent it straight and inserted it into the lock, wiggling it around.

It didn't work, so she jiggled the drawer. That didn't work either. As the first side of the Nat King Cole LP ended, she was ready to admit defeat. But then she spied a thin metal ruler. Giving one last try, she slipped it into the crack at the top of the drawer and gently pressed the edge against the latch's resistance.

The record player's needle lifted, clacked and latched into place as she shimmied the ruler with one hand and lifted the drawer with the other—up and down, up and down.

When the lock actually gave, she sucked in a surprised breath. She held the breath, afraid of accidentally reengaging the drawer. She gingerly slid it open, her smile widening as it came free. She pulled it fully open to let in some light.

The first thing she saw was a box of sketching pencils. Stacked beneath them was a yellow-covered, spiral-bound sketchbook. She sat back on the floor as she lifted the unexpected treasure. Somebody had been an artist.

The paper crackled as she peeled back the cover, her curiosity burning, and hoping against hope the artist had signed their drawings.

The first page was a portrait. It was a pretty, young girl, very lovingly drawn, and she looked oddly familiar. Since Lillian's daughters had died as babies, and Austin's grandfather, Carl, was an only child, Ruby couldn't imagine who the girl might be. There was no signature, no initial, no clue beyond the sketch itself.

She turned the page.

The next portrait was a beautiful woman. The artist had expertly captured her fine features, but there was something more. There was depth to her expression, especially her eyes, a melancholy longing, like some who'd sent her beloved off to sea.

Ruby snickered at herself for the fanciful thought. Colorado was a long way from any ocean.

But again, the woman looked familiar. It definitely wasn't Lillian or Kathleen. It wasn't Peggy-Lyn either.

Ruby squinted. Then she blinked and her jaw went lax. The woman was Austin's mother, Jessica. It was an amazing portrait. Whoever had drawn it had real talent. But…

Ruby closed the sketchbook, turning it over. It had a twenty-four-dollar price tag from a popular chain store, but there were no other clues on the ownership. It wasn't from generations past. So, what was it doing locked up in an old desk in the attic?

She sat back, propping herself against an armchair to rest the book against her bent knees. She opened to the first page again and realized the little girl was McKinney.

She scanned through a few sketches, searching for initials or a signature. She came across a forest, a mountain stream and then she paused on a drawing of White Foam Falls. Whoever had made the sketches had obviously known the ranch very well.

She turned another page and blinked as she focused. The subject was Jessica again—Jessica in a lacy, diaphanous negligee. She was lounging back in a classic evocative pose, her knees bent to the side with one arm stretched over her head. She was lying on a quilt in a meadow of wildflowers. Her lips were pursed, her eye sultry, her hair mussed, as if she'd just made love.

The artist had to be Garrett.

Ruby tried to imagine Austin's gruff, grizzled father with a sketch pencil in his fingers. It was tough to make the image work, but he clearly had secret talent. She gazed down at the sketch again and smiled. Garrett had a true talent and deep, deep love for his wife.

She felt a surge of pity for him. He must have been devastated by her death.

In fact… Ruby skimmed her way through the remaining portraits and landscapes. The later drawings might have been sketched just before she'd died.

There were a dozen blank pages at the end of the book. She almost gave up on learning more, but suddenly there it was, an inscription on the inside back cover. The pencil lines were faint against the buff background. But it was legible.

Jess. I'll wait forever my love. JJ.

Ruby gave her head a small shake. JJ? Who the heck was JJ?

The downstairs door rattled and footsteps sounded in the hall.

She jumped to her feet, heart leaping with adrenaline. She didn't know what she'd found here, but she knew she couldn't let Austin see it.

She stuffed the sketchbook inside the drawer and pushed it closed. The edge caught on the lock mechanism and it stuck there, gaped open nearly an inch. He'd see it for sure.

Her gaze darted around for the ruler but couldn't see where she'd set it down. The footfalls crossed the hallway, heading for the stairs.

She yanked open the drawer, pulled the book from the desk and rushed across the room, stuffing it into her shoulder bag then fighting to get the zipper closed.

"Ruby?" It was Sierra's voice.

Ruby whirled even as she breathed a chopped sigh of relief— not that she wanted Sierra to see the sketchbook either. Nobody should see it, not until Ruby figured out what it meant.

"McKinney said I'd probably find you here." Sierra was dressed in soft gray slacks, a pastel blouse with some cute, dusty-blue ankle boots.

She grinned and pulled a bottle out of her canvas tote bag. "I raided the wine cellar."

"Hi." Ruby's voice came out breathless. She hoped Sierra wouldn't notice and ask questions.

"It's a bordeaux, Grand Cru." Sierra peered at the label. "I think it's good, but I'm only guessing."

Ruby steadied herself, forcing a lighthearted tone into her voice. "Are there bad wines in Garrett's cellar?"

Sierra chuckled. "You have a point. Are you okay with red?"

"I like either."

"Good." Sierra set her tote down on the table and withdrew two stemless wineglasses. Next, she pulled out a corkscrew.

"You came prepared," Ruby noted.

"I could have been a Girl Scout." Sierra peeled the heavy foil from the bottle top and twisted in the corkscrew. Then she grimaced as she tugged hard on the cork, grinning when it finally popped free.

"Music?" Ruby asked, taking a moment to reestablish her equilibrium by turning to the record player. She removed the Nat King Cole album and slid it back into the paper sleeve.

"What've you got?" Sierra asked.

"The latest seem to be from the '60s."

"Anything by the Beatles?"

Ruby thumbed her way further through the stack. "*Please Please Me.*"

"Sold." Sierra finished pouring the wine.

Ruby started the record spinning and turned down the volume.

They each sat in a wooden kitchen chair, and Sierra slid one of the glasses of wine to Ruby.

"Now," Sierra said with satisfaction, fingertips resting lightly on her glass.

"Now?" Ruby echoed, curious.

"We didn't want to pry last night." Sierra gave a light laugh. "Well, Dallas didn't want to pry. I was all for it."

It was clear Sierra was talking about Ruby and Austin's relationship. Ironic how that seemed like a tame topic of conversation now.

"Pry?" Ruby asked, feigning confusion.

Sierra leaned eagerly forward. "What's going on between you two? He looks at you. You look at him. The electricity crackles away." She lifted her wineglass to her lips.

"A fling." Ruby didn't see any point in lying or beating around the bush.

Sierra sputtered. "Seriously?"

Ruby gave an unapologetic shrug. "He's a good-looking guy."

"That's for sure."

"And we're both single." Ruby took a sip herself, appreciating the smooth rich flavor of the wine. She didn't consider herself a discerning wine drinker, but this was delicious.

Sierra raised her own glass in a mock toast. "I like your attitude."

"We're not planning on broadcasting it."

"Of course not."

"But it doesn't have to be a state secret."

"Austin's a really great guy."

"It's not that kind of a relationship." As she said the words, Ruby thought once more about Austin describing it as romantic.

"So…" Sierra made little air circles with her raised glass. "You're saying nothing will come of it?"

Ruby took another sip. "I won't be here very much longer."

"I'm really sorry to hear that." Sierra paused. "Austin deserves someone like you."

"You don't even know me," Ruby pointed out.

"I know you a little bit. You're smart and funny, and you're obviously hardworking."

"I might also be a serial killer."

Sierra squinted at her for a moment. "Seems unlikely."

"Why not?"

"You come across as too open and honest, and I'm a good judge of character. That used to be part of my job as a life coach—judging character. Besides, what serial killer would target Austin?"

"Vulnerable, he is not." Ruby hadn't known Sierra was a life coach. But it seemed to fit, given the way she listened so intently—like she was using every one of her senses in every conversation. "Life coach?"

Sierra gave her brow a conspiratorial waggle. "If you ever need any advice."

Ruby didn't plan to. "I'll keep that in mind."

Sierra considered her a moment longer. "I think you're good for him."

Ruby chuckled at that. "I frustrate him."

"That's good. He needs a little of that."

Ruby had to agree. It didn't seem like many people challenged Austin. She couldn't help thinking back to some of the critical things Kiera'd had to say about the Hawkes family's position in the region.

"It annoyed him a lot when we first met," she continued. "But I think he might be getting used to it now."

"I'd say so, if you're sleeping together." Sierra topped up their glasses as she spoke.

"Thanks." Ruby was happy to drink more of the delicious wine. But she found Sierra's statement oddly entertaining. "Has that been your experience? Professionally speaking, I mean. That men need an emotional or intellectual reason for sex?"

Sierra sat back and gave an eye roll. "Fair enough." Then she became watchful again. "But women are different. You must feel something."

"Lust."

"Sure, sure." Sierra waited, clearly looking for Ruby to fill in the silence.

"I don't know exactly what I feel. I mean I wouldn't have sex with someone I didn't like." Ruby pictured Austin's intimate smile and smoldering eyes, heard his deep voice, and relived the shimmer of awareness it sent up her spine. "But our friendship is brand-new, and I am leaving soon. And it really is a professional more than a personal relationship." She stopped herself there, wondering what had prompted her to open up so easily.

"All that is very logical," Sierra said gently.

"Are you in life coach mode?"

Sierra split a grin. "I can't help myself."

"I can see why you're good at it."

"You're trying to override emotion with logic. That never works."

Ruby disagreed. "I think it always works."

"Why?"

Ruby's book and career had to be her priority. "Because I'm categorically focused on research. Austin is…" She paused. She didn't want to lie about her feelings for Austin, but she was afraid to be honest. She tried another tactic. "I won't let anything—" she searched for the right word "—extracurricular get in the way of me doing my job. She stopped talking and waited for Sierra to rebut her weak explanation.

"So, the book's going well?" Sierra surprised her with the change in direction.

"Yes," Ruby answered even as she tried to figure out Sierra's strategy.

"I'm glad. Can you tell me anything about it?"

Ruby pushed down the twinge of disappointment as the conversation moved past Austin. She was more interested in talking about her work than about a man—obviously. "Do you want the thirty-second explanation or the three-minute one?"

"I'll take the full three minutes." Sierra grinned as she put her glass to her lips.

"Okay. I was looking to beef up my publishing credits, and I decided to document the historic family cattle ranches in the high country before they disappear. The Hawkes family interested me because their legacy has lasted so long. I was imagining cowboy stories, the action and excitement of an open range back in the day, how the ranch had grown and thrived over the years. But then I noticed the women."

Sierra stilled, her interest clearly perking up.

Ruby took that as a sign she was on the right track with her theme. "Never mind that the ranchers couldn't have succeeded without them, or that they were strong and brave, each hardworking in their own way, but they were also incredibly colorful characters. Austin's grandmother ruled with an iron fist, his great-grandmother was part of a Depression-era crime family, and a chance to ask his great-great-grandmother for a date was the prize in a poker game."

"No way."

Ruby took a drink. "And I feel like I've only scratched the surface." She couldn't help thinking about the sketchbook and the secrets Austin's mother, Jessica, might have hidden.

"Dallas didn't tell me any of those stories."

"I think they're embarrassed about the bootlegging money. As I understand it, that's what built the big house."

Sierra chuckled. "Well, I'm definitely buying a copy when your book comes out. Tell me more about the poker game."

Ruby relaxed into the conversation, coming to like Sierra more and more as they sipped their way through the bottle of wine.

Winetasting was a big draw for the Hawkes' tent at the annual Jagged Creek Rodeo. Open on three sides, covering eighteen hundred square feet of grassy field on the coveted upwind side of the rodeo ring, Austin's family had hosted the mix-and-mingle event for more than three decades.

Hawkes ranch cowboys rodeoed with the best of them, winning money and prestige, competing with the neighboring outfits for the most points over the weekend. Austin usually helped out as a pickup man, managing the stock in the ring while leaving the events for cowboys who could use the prize money.

He was on a break now, circulating through the tent on behalf of the family, moving between bales of hay and rough-hewn tables while keeping tabs on Ruby, who was cheering on the team-roping event from the bleachers. While the rodeo continued in the ring, the announcer's voice blaring in the background, dozens of spectators ponied up a charitable donation to taste five wines selected by Austin's father from the family cellar.

As Mayor Simons and his wife moved on, Sierra wandered up beside Austin, a glass of white wine in her hand.

"She's pretty," Sierra observed.

"Mrs. Simons?" Austin's gaze flicked to the back of the older woman's aqua-and-cream patterned blouse.

Sierra nudged him with her shoulder. "Ruby."

He looked to the bleachers again, seeing Ruby in profile, the blue Hawkes ranch cap on her head.

She jumped up, raising her arms, roaring along with the crowd at the roping team's time. She wore a red-checked, buttoned shirt he'd never seen before, half tucked into a pair of blue jeans.

"Austin?" Sierra prompted.

"Hmm?"

"I said Ruby's pretty."

"Well, that's obvious." He didn't get Sierra's point. Who

would debate the fact that Ruby was an incredibly stunning woman?

"You know I'm an empathetic listener." She paused and waited.

Austin narrowed his gaze as he looked her way. "I know you're fishing for information."

"I don't have to fish. I talked to Ruby."

Austin felt a lurch of surprise. "About what?"

"You know what. So, what do you think of her?" It was obvious Sierra either knew or guessed they'd had sex.

He wasn't going to confirm or deny. "I just agreed she was gorgeous."

"And smart, and kind, and funny."

Austin agreed with all those things. "Don't bother playing matchmaker."

Sierra widened her eyes in mock innocence. "Me?"

"Yes, you, Little Miss Newlywed. She's going back to Boston soon."

"So she says." Sierra shifted her gaze to the crowd in the bleachers. "I was going back to California."

Austin knew it wasn't anywhere near the same circumstance. "She has a life and a job to go back to."

Sierra sobered.

Austin felt like a cad for sounding so insulting. "I didn't mean—"

"You honestly think anything would have dragged me back to California once I'd fallen in love with Dallas."

"I'm sorry."

"It wouldn't."

"I know."

"I could have had the greatest home, the best job offer in the world. My ex could have begged me to forgive him and come back."

"I didn't mean—"

"I'm saying none of that would have mattered." Her gaze softened. "Dallas mattered. Nothing but Dallas mattered."

"Because the two of you were in love."

"Exactly."

Austin's gaze returned to Ruby, who was sitting forward on the wooden bench, watching pensively while another team pounded down the ring. Dust rose up from the deep-piled dirt, and the announcer called excitedly through the loudspeaker.

"Sierra, Ruby's not in love with me," he said. "And I'm not in love with her." Austin liked her. He liked her a whole lot. And he was crazy attracted to her. And he'd love nothing more than to spend endless hours in her arms, making love and talking and laughing.

A cheer rose up from the crowd.

But it wasn't love. It was way too soon to even hope for love.

Not that he was hoping for it.

What he was hoping for was to finally get her alone for a while. She was stunningly beautiful as she grinned and cheered out there in the sunshine. She was even more beautiful naked in his arms.

"You should give it a chance," Sierra said.

It hit him for the first time that it was dangerous to let wild fantasies roam free. Ruby was the most grounded person he'd ever met. She knew what she wanted and how to go about getting it—with a zeal that was sometimes frustrating.

"She's here to work," he said. "We haven't even been out on a proper date."

"What's stopping you?" Sierra asked. "The Oberfeld Hotel has a great restaurant. They also have nice rooms."

His chest tightened at the thought of sharing a hotel room with Ruby. "Logic and reason."

Sierra flashed an amused grin. "Not the best weapons where it comes to matters of emotion."

"They are *always* the best weapons." He was reminded of Ruby's words in the line shack.

"I'll remind you I'm a professional."

He scoffed out a laugh. "I don't need life coaching."

"You sure?"

"I'm positive."

She placed her hand lightly on his shoulder. "I'm around if you need me."

"Here we are." Madeline Compton joined them, glass of wine

in her hand. She was dressed for the occasion in jeans, boots, and a black barrel-racing shirt covered in gold and bright purple appliqué. "Some of the Hawkes. Just the people I was looking for."

Sierra was quick to switch gears. "Good afternoon, Madeline. I hope you're enjoying the tasting."

Madeline smiled, her face creasing while her pale blue eyes lit up. "It is up to its usual high standards."

"I'm glad to hear that," Austin said. "I'll pass that along to my father."

"Please do. Thank you. Now—" She glanced around the crowd in the tent. "Where's that lovely young woman I met last week? The one who's writing the book."

"You mean Ruby." Sierra gave Austin a meaningful sidelong glance, and he wondered if she was meant to say more. Like anybody had to sell him on Ruby.

"Yes. Ruby. Is she around? I'd like to talk to her."

Austin felt a hint of uneasiness. "What do you want with—"

"She's watching over there in the stands." Sierra helpfully pointed. "At this end, close to the top row. You see? She's wearing a red shirt and a blue Hawkes baseball cap."

"I see her. Thank you, Sierra."

Austin muttered sarcastically under his breath. "Thank you, Sierra."

Sierra's sidelong look told him she'd heard.

"Is it something we can help you with?" Austin asked Madeline, fishing for information.

"No, no. Not at all."

"If it's about the ranch…" he probed.

Madeline waved her weathered hand dismissively. "What would she know about the ranch?"

"She's writing about it."

"And more people should do that. Jagged Creek is an important town." Madeline finished the last of her wine and set the empty glass down on a barrel as she walked away.

"What's she on about?" Austin asked half to himself as he watched her head for Ruby.

"I guess she liked Ruby."

"Of course she liked Ruby. Who wouldn't like Ruby? I mean what, specifically, is Madeline planning to tell her?"

Sierra dipped her head to the side. "I don't think she'll dis you."

"What?" Austin was confused.

"Madeline likes you. She won't say anything bad to Ruby."

"I'm not worried about Ruby liking me."

She liked him enough to make love with him, and he'd take that any day of the week.

A waiter came by with an offer of drinks.

Sierra accepted a glass of white. "Then what's the deal?"

Austin opted for a cold bottle of beer. "What deal?"

"Why are you so worried about Madeline talking to Ruby?"

Austin considered his answer. "I don't like gossip. This book idea." He took a drink to give himself a beat. "I mean who knows what all she'll write about."

"Like?" Sierra asked.

He shrugged.

She waited.

It took him a minute to realize she'd gone into life coach mode. He took another drink to stall for time.

"Nothing."

Sierra looked amused now. "If you say so."

"I say so."

"Your words, maybe."

"Quit psychoanalyzing me."

She laughed at that. "I'm not a psychologist."

"You're nosy."

"Hey, you're the one who's fretting about Madeline."

"I don't fret." He didn't. He worried just enough about a problem to come up with a solution. It was a completely different thing.

Sierra's gaze shifted to the bleachers. "She really is very pretty."

"Madeline?" Austin joked.

"Right. Madeline."

Ruby recognized Madeline when the older woman stopped at the foot of the bleachers in front of her. She smiled and waved, and Madeline motioned for her to come down.

There was a break in action, the announcer walking the spectators through the rules of the saddle bronc event. Ruby had learned a whole lot today. Beyond the rules and the spectacle of the events, she'd watched the action behind the chutes, making notes on the rhythm and the jobs everyone undertook to get a competitor and the livestock out in the ring.

She apologized as she shuffled past people in the crowded stands, coming to a staircase that took her down to the packed dirt.

"Hello." She greeted Madeline as her boot hit the ground, taking in the woman's flashy appliqué. "Nice shirt."

Madeline gave a happy smile. "I love an excuse to wear it. It brings back so many memories. I used to be a barrel racer."

"No kidding." Ruby was impressed. She'd watched in awe of the speed and riding talent of the barrel racers.

"It was a very long time ago. Are you hungry? I was just on my way to the burger barn."

"You bet." Ruby was delighted with the opportunity to talk with Madeline about her memories of living in Jagged Creek.

They made their way, single file, between the bleachers and the rodeo ring. It was crowded, dusty and loud as music blared through the overhead speakers. But the energy was lively and positive. Spectators chatted and laughed, and the aromas of brats, burgers and cotton candy wafted on the air.

Ruby realized she was quite hungry.

"Barney's makes the best," Madeline said as they cleared the spectator area and came to a horseshoe of food trucks and stands. "We can sit down inside."

Barney's Burger Barn had a blue-and-white sign over the wide door that led into what looked like an actual barn. The smell of grilled beef and French fries intensified as they stepped over the threshold.

It was slightly quieter inside the building. The floor was creaky wood sheeting under Ruby's feet, and a rope barrier steered them to the long service counter. The lineup was short, and a young man dressed in white quickly offered to build their burgers. The array of toppings and add-ons was immense.

Ruby chose cheese, extra tomatoes, avocado and chipotle

mayo. The young man piled it high on a sourdough bun and added yam fries on the side.

"We probably should have split one," she said to Madeline as they approached the cashier.

Madeline had skipped the avocado but added bacon, regular mayo and relish for a more traditional burger with regular fries. "Have a little faith. All that cheering works up an appetite. I'll take a cola," she said to the cashier."

"Ginger ale," Ruby added, reaching for her purse.

"I've got this," Madeline said.

"I didn't expect you to buy me lunch."

"I'm the one who invited you." Madeline swiped her credit card over the reader.

"Still," Ruby said. But there wasn't much more she could do about it. "Thank you. That was very kind."

Madeline lifted her tray and Ruby did the same.

"Over there." Madeline marched deftly through the jumble of folding chairs and tables, grabbing an empty table near the wall.

They'd no sooner sat down than a fresh-faced young woman stepped up to wipe the table. "Need anything?" she asked cheerfully.

"Ketchup on the side counter?" Madeline asked.

"Right over there. Help yourself," the young woman answered.

"I'll grab some extra napkins," Madeline said to Ruby then bustled away.

Ruby pulled the paper off her straw, poked it into the ice and ginger ale, and took a long drink. Then she breathed in and looked around, settling into the surprisingly comfortable chair. The table had a wobble that she guessed was from the uneven floor.

Madeline returned. "Here we go." She set a handful of ketchup packets and a couple of napkins in the middle of the table.

"This was a good idea," Ruby said. "I didn't realize I was getting so hungry and thirsty."

"Hard work all the cheering." Madeline squeezed a stream of ketchup on top of her fries.

Ruby chose a long, crispy, yam fry and took a bite. It was wonderful. She swallowed. "These are terrific."

"Wait until you try the burger." Madeline used both hands to grasp the monstrosity, leaning over her plate to let the juices drip neatly down.

Ruby tried to copy her technique, slightly intimidated by the thickness of the burger.

"Don't be shy," Madeline said.

"I'm going in," Ruby joked before opening wide to take a bite through all the layers.

"Mmm," she said appreciatively as she chewed.

"Right?" Madeline asked with a nod.

"This is amazing." The bun was firm but tender, the burger grilled to perfection, and the chipotle mayo had just the right amount of spice to set off the texture of the avocado. "Is Burger Barn a restaurant in town?" Ruby hadn't come across it yet.

Madeline shook her head. "Barney's travels from event to event."

"Too bad."

"I'll say." Madeline took another hearty bite.

Ruby made it about halfway through the burger and through only a few of the yam fries before she had to take a break and slow down.

"I'm feeling so much better." Madeline dabbed her lips with a paper napkin. Then she took a sip of her cola. "I have a question for you."

"Sure." Ruby was almost through her ginger ale and wished she'd ordered a large. She was still thirsty.

"We have a few summer courses running at the college. Nothing like the full fall and winter semesters, of course. But one of them is American History. It's entry level, a 100 course. But it counts for credit at most of the colleges in the region. So, it's quite popular."

"I didn't know the college was open for the summer," Ruby said. She couldn't help be excited for the residents of Jagged Creek to have access to higher education year-round right here in their hometown. She couldn't imagine many towns of their size had an institution like Compton College.

"If you have the time. And, honestly, no pressure. But if you have the time, would you consider coming in as a guest lecturer?"

Ruby was honored to be asked. She didn't have a whole lot of spare time, but she wanted to step up and contribute, to pay Madeline back in some small way for all her work in the archives. Plus, she'd love to meet the local college students spending their summer learning history.

"It could be a single lecture." Madeline rushed on. "Or two or three. We'll take whatever you can give us. I know the kids would love to hear from a professor from U Ainsworth."

"Don't oversell me," Ruby said. "I was just passed over for a permanent position."

Madeline leaned forward, looking interested. "Why?"

"They didn't say."

"Who did you lose out to?"

"Doctor Bert Bartholomew," Too late, Ruby realized she hadn't kept the mock British accent from her voice or the sneer from her face. "Sorry." She reflexively put her fingertips over her lips. It was unprofessional to dis another member of the faculty.

Madeline laughed.

"So, what are you going to do about it?" Madeline popped another French fry into her mouth.

"Beef up my research and publishing credits for the next job opening. Write a compelling and significant book on women's contributions to the rise of historic cattle ranches in the Colorado high country." She took a breath. "Impact *that*, Doctor Bartholomew."

"You go, girl."

"I'm going." Ruby gathered her burger from the plate, ready now for more.

"So?" Madeline asked as Ruby took a big bite.

Ruby raised her brow in a silent question.

"The lecture or, hopefully, lectures?"

Ruby gave an enthusiastic nod. It was going to feel good to participate in the Jagged Creek community.

Ten

That evening, Ruby was a popular dance partner. So was Austin's sister McKinney.

Austin was jealous of newlywed Dallas who had a perfect excuse to dance every dance with Sierra. He wished he could do the same with Ruby, but it would raise more than a few uncomfortable questions.

He gritted his teeth as she laughed and chatted her way through a lively number from the local band on stage. The sun had set and the canopy of white lights shone bright above the raised wooden dance floor, obliterating the stars in the clear black sky.

As the song wound down, he marched her way.

She looked surprised to see him—not much of an ego boost. Her partner, a hand from the Jamison Cattle Company looked annoyed.

He ignored the cowboy. "Dance?" he asked Ruby.

"Sure," she answered. "Thanks," she said breathlessly to the Jamison guy.

Austin took her in his arms, grateful when the band segued into a slower number. "Having fun?"

She nodded, and her grin nearly split her face.

Again, not much of an ego boost for him since she'd danced with four other guys so far.

"What a wonderful day!" she said on a laugh. "I loved the events. Oh, the bronc and bull riding were scary. How did Dallas *do* that? I can't even imagine. If I was Sierra, I'd sure be keeping him away from competing." She gave a little shudder.

"It's not as dangerous as it looks. I mean it's dangerous.

That's why Dallas got hurt. Don't get me wrong, I'm glad he quit the circuit."

"I'll bet. Did you worry about him?"

"He's a grown man."

"I know. But he's your brother."

"And a hothead. At least, he was for most of his life. It wouldn't have mattered if I worried or not. He was going to do what he was going to do."

She held his gaze. "And you?"

"I'm not a rodeo rider." A split second later he realized he should have asked if she'd worry about him if he was—missed opportunity there.

"I meant are you a hothead."

"No. I'm—" He considered his answer. "I'm disciplined and decisive."

"Uh."

"Well, that sounded skeptical." He angled them toward a quiet corner of the floor.

"I'll give you the decisive part."

"Why only that?"

She gave a secretive smile and her gaze darkened a shade. "You're not so disciplined with me."

His low hum of desire gave a sudden surge. "Are you getting tired?"

"It's eight fifteen."

"Hungry?" He wanted to get her out of there, somewhere they could be alone, where every cowboy in a forty-foot radius wasn't waiting to pounce.

"If you saw the hamburger I had for lunch, you wouldn't ask that."

"Ruby," he intoned in growing frustration.

"What?"

"I'm trying to get you alone."

"Oh. Why didn't you say so?"

"I was being… I don't know, gentlemanly."

"I think you mean oblique."

He ignored the criticism. "The Oberfeld Hotel has a nice lobby lounge."

"I think you mean the Oberfeld Hotel has hotel rooms."

He gathered her closer. "I'm being gentlemanly again."

"By not flat-out asking me for torrid sex?"

"Yes."

"But you are asking." There was humor in her tone.

"If you're interested, I'm definitely asking."

The song was winding down and he knew he had to make his move before someone else asked her to dance.

"Come on." He hopped off the back of the stage then reached for her waist to lift her down.

"We're escaping out the back?" she asked as he took her hand.

"Saves answering questions."

"Won't people wonder where we went?"

"Sierra won't." It was on the tip of his tongue to bluntly ask Ruby if she'd shared their secret with his sister-in-law. But it didn't matter either way, and the last thing he wanted to do was disturb the mood.

They were sneaking away from the rodeo grounds for a romantic liaison at the Oberfeld Hotel. Nothing else mattered right now.

"You talked to Sierra?" Ruby asked as they skirted the back of the food stands, cutting across the field to the parking lot.

"She thinks you're pretty."

"She's not exactly my type. Plus, she's married."

"Very funny. She was fishing to see what I thought of you."

They came to a rail fence at the edge of the parking area and ducked through.

"And?" Ruby prompted.

"And what?"

She sent him a scowl. "This is me fishing."

He wrapped an arm around her shoulders and tugged her close. "You're asking if I think you're pretty?"

"Fess up, cowboy."

He stopped, turned her into his arms and lifted her off the ground, kissing her firmly on the lips. "Yes, Ruby. I think you're pretty. I think you're gorgeous, spectacular, breathtaking."

"You don't have to get carried away."

He sobered, lowering he slowly back to the ground, keeping his arms around her. "I always get carried away around you."

She smiled, looking even more beautiful in the faint starlight.

He took her hand and they walked along a row of pickup trucks parked on the grass. A warm wave of contentment swept through him. He wished the walk would take hours and hours.

Suddenly, Ruby stopped dead in her tracks.

He stopped, worried. "What happened?"

She was staring at the parked vehicles, a stricken expression on her face.

He looked around but didn't see anything. "Ruby, what is it?"

She swallowed. "Who's that?"

He looked in the direction of her gaze. "I don't see anyone." He took a step to one side for a different angle. "Do you still see them?" He wondered if she was embarrassed to be holding his hand.

"There," she said. "On the side of the truck. John Jamison Cattle Company."

"Is this about the cowboy you danced with?"

Ruby shook her head, looking mystified. "No. No, not exactly."

"He's with the outfit."

"That wasn't what I meant."

"What did you mean?" Austin was baffled by the conversation.

"Nothing."

"*Nothing*? You look like you saw a ghost."

"It's just that I've come across that name before."

He didn't buy it, but he didn't understand what was going on. "They've had a spread in the valley for a few generations."

"Oh."

"Are they going to be in the book?" he asked. It was deflating to know she was thinking about her research while he was totally fixated on her.

"No." She paused. "Maybe. I don't know."

"Okay—" He waited for her to explain.

She took in his expression. "Sorry about that."

"I don't know what *that* was."

"I was surprised is all."

"By the name on the side of a pickup truck."

"I was trying to remember where it was that I saw it." She started walking.

He fell into step. "Did you remember?"

"In the archives, maybe."

They walked in silence a little longer, getting closer and closer to his truck.

He didn't want to ask. But he couldn't not ask. "You still want to go to the Oberfeld?"

She twisted her head his way. "Sure. Why wouldn't I?"

"You seem distracted."

She smiled reassuringly. "I'm not that distracted."

He wanted to press for more but told himself not to be foolish. A sexy, wonderful woman wanted to get a room with him. His only question should be how fast he could safely drive to the hotel.

Cushioned on the fresh sheets of a huge, plush bed, Ruby had lost herself in Austin's arms, making love twice over, neither of them wanting the closeness to end. Afterward, they'd lounged in the oversized tub then wrapped themselves in robes and sipped champagne while sharing a giant slice of chocolate cake.

But now the interlude was over.

Though it was tempting to spend the night, they'd driven back late to avoid uncomfortable questions from the family in the morning.

She felt like she'd barely closed her eyes when her alarm was ringing.

At breakfast, Austin looked surprised to see her arrive, but nobody else paid any attention to her. The conversation revolved around completing the fall roundup and preparing for winter. Ruby knew she should listen closely so she could jot down some notes later, but now that she was no longer wrapped in Austin's arms, no longer satiated by their lovemaking, her mind began considering the John Jamison angle. If there was a John Jamison alive today, and it wasn't just the name of the ranch's founding ancestor, he could be the JJ who'd sketched Jessica and McKinney.

If he'd done the sketches, then he'd had a relationship with Austin's mother—very likely a romantic one.

Did Garrett know or suspect? Did McKinney remember any of it?

"You can't avoid sunk costs." The sound of Austin's voice caught Ruby's attention.

"I don't know what the rush is all about," Garrett responded.

"Look at how fast Dallas is moving," Austin said.

"Dallas is building a house. You want Sierra to live in a tent?"

"He's also buying horses. He'll have a loss this year, but it's the only way to make a profit in the coming years."

"Livestock has a payback."

"Technology does, too. It'll save us money," Austin countered.

"That hasn't been my experience so far," Garrett responded dryly.

"Medical records, for one thing. Nobody needs to fight with paper and a clipboard in the rain anymore. You just—" Austin gestured with his hand. "Scan. Boom. It's done."

McKinney spoke up. "I feel like I've heard this argument before."

Garrett shot her a quelling look. "This is not an argument."

It sounded like an argument to Ruby. Neither Austin nor Garrett seemed truly angry, but she couldn't help contrasting their raised voices to what happened in her family home. Her parents did point, counterpoint in a calm, methodical fashion. Sometimes they even had charts and graphs.

"It's a debate," Austin said.

McKinney swirled her butter knife in a circle in the air. "Can we wrap up the debate? There are cattle out there who couldn't care less if we use a clipboard or an ear tag."

"That, my dear," Garrett said emphatically, "is my point."

"Cattle don't read balance sheets either," Austin put in.

"You have to give him that one," McKinney said with amusement.

"I read balance sheets," Garrett said.

"And they'll look better than ever next year."

"I'll hold you to that." Garrett set his coffee mug down with finality.

Ruby finished the last bite of her buttery waffle and swallowed a mouthful of coffee as everyone rose from the table.

Garrett and McKinney headed for the hallway that led to a side exit while Austin lowered his voice. "You didn't have to come down for breakfast."

"You came down," Ruby pointed out.

"I have to go to work."

"So do I."

"You know what I mean."

She lifted her brow. "That my job's less important than yours."

"Are you picking another fight?"

"I'm making a point."

"My point is that your book doesn't need to be fed and watered."

"It only needs to be written."

He touched her hand and leaned in closer. "I don't want to argue."

"I think this is a debate."

Humor came into his tone. "I'll end it. You're right and I'm wrong. Your work is every bit as important as mine."

Since Ruby didn't have anywhere to go with that, she changed the subject. "Madeline Compton asked me to give a lecture at the college."

Austin pulled back, looking surprised. "On what?"

"History." She was amused now. "It's kind of my thing."

"Hawkes family history?"

"American history, generally. I very much doubt you'll come up."

"Very funny."

"I told her yes. But... I'm feeling funny about doing it while I'm staying here."

"Funny how?"

"I don't want to take advantage of your hospitality." Ruby

had been thinking about the best way to approach this. "I could maybe—"

"'Take advantage'?" He sounded baffled.

"I could finish up here then move back to town before I do the lecture. Or lectures, if there's time."

"Is there someplace you have to be?"

"No."

"Then why leave?" His expression turned intimate, sensual. "I want you to stay."

She wanted that, too. But what she wanted and what she ought to do were different things. She didn't mean to, but her voice came out as a plaintive whisper. "You know I can't."

"I don't mean forever."

Their gazes held and she felt a mixture of longing and regret. Last night had been spectacular. It had also been foolish on her part. It was obvious now she was setting herself up for heartache.

After a moment, Austin breathed a sigh and smoothed a wisp of hair from her temple. "Last night was great."

She nodded.

"I wish it had lasted longer."

She managed a smile. "If it had, we'd both be out of commission right now."

He smiled back. "True enough."

"Austin?" McKinney called out.

Ruby took a quick step back, suddenly realizing how close she and Austin had drawn to each other. "I thought I'd go talk to Madeline today," she said before he had a chance to walk away. She rushed on. "Check out the college and, you know…" She trailed off with a shrug then, hating that she was telling him only half the truth.

She would talk to Madeline about the college, but her most important goal was to find out more about the Jamison family. And she sure couldn't do that while following Austin around the ranch.

"On my way," he called over to McKinney. More quietly, he said to Ruby, "Just don't leave. Stay. Give a lecture. Whatever. But stay here."

She nodded because she wanted to stay. It obviously couldn't be for much longer, but she didn't want to think about leaving Austin just yet.

Ruby wrote *Jessica affair?* and *McKinney's father?* in the outline of her book. Then she crossed it out. But then she wrote it down again. Her preferences on how the Hawkes family story went couldn't change the facts.

She'd at first been massively relieved to discover John Jamison, the original founder of the ranch, had died decades earlier. But then she'd learned his great-great-grandson had been named after him. The current John Jamison was fifty-seven and at the head of the Jamison Cattle Company.

Ruby had found a picture. He was a very handsome man.

She'd made the two-hour drive to the Jamison ranch and tracked him down in the yard. She'd introduced herself, told him who she was and what she was doing, and he'd been quite willing to talk. After some preliminary questions, she asked him if he'd been friends with Jessica.

The expression on his face answered her question. She quickly changed topics, but the damage had been done. He became vague and guarded in his responses, and she knew he'd been Jessica's lover.

She couldn't help searching his features then, watching his mannerisms, listening to the cadence of his voice, looking for traces of McKinney.

Because the more she thought about it, the more suspicious she'd become. The sketches of McKinney so lovingly drawn— perhaps by her father. His eyes were blue, like McKinney's. The rest of the Hawkes had brown eyes. Their chins and noses were quite different. But there was something about his mouth, the curve of his upper lip, the way it pursed when he was listening.

She'd looked for other clues, studying his hand gestures. Then she had an idea.

She turned a fresh page in her notebook and asked him to write down his email address.

He did. And he was left-handed.

McKinney was left-handed.

Ruby thanked John for his time and told him she had everything she needed. She turned away, knowing he was likely to let his guard down when he knew the interview was over. At the last second, she turned back and asked him how well he knew McKinney.

Her stomach sank and guilt assailed her when she saw she'd hit the nail on the head. She quickly added Austin, Dallas and Tyler to the question to cover her interest.

When John said not very well, she smiled easily and said she hoped he had a nice day.

He wished her the same and she walked away.

But now…now she had an explosive secret to either use or bury.

On her outline, Ruby drew an arrow from Alice to Wanda to Lillian to Kathleen then Peggy-Lyn to Jessica and finally McKinney. Then she drew a double cross over the line that led to McKinney. Ruby had planned to use McKinney as the culmination of the changing roles and impact of the Hawkes women the growth of the ranch.

She couldn't do that now—not knowing what she knew. McKinney might legitimately be a daughter of the valley, but she wasn't a Hawkes. Ignoring the truth and pretending she was, would discredit Ruby's book and her research if it ever came out—and it would, things like this always eventually did. The ensuing scandal would guarantee she'd never get a permanent job at any credible university.

She tossed down her pen and ran her fingers through her hair, giving in to a low moan of frustration.

It was late. But she was keyed up and edgy.

Earlier, Austin had caught her gaze from across the dinner table. He'd smiled softly, his eyes shining with a secretive glow. He'd seemed relaxed, in a cheerful mood, even joking with his father, which she'd never seen before.

When they all rose to retire to their rooms, he'd given her hand a surreptitious squeeze and told her to sleep well.

Ruby wondered how she possibly could.

She retrieved the sketchbook from where she'd stashed it in a drawer and sat cross-legged on the bed to page her way through it once more.

She compared the inscription on the back page to John's handwritten email address. They were a match.

A DNA test would tell her definitively if he was McKinney's father. But she didn't see that happening.

The residents of Topaz House might know something about Jessica and John's relationship. But Ruby didn't dare ask. She wouldn't ask Madeline either. That meant she might never be positive one way or the other.

She set down the sketchbook.

If she stopped looking right now. If she never found out if John was McKinney's father, maybe she was fine. She could write her book as she'd planned and, if it ever came out…well… she'd argue what? That her research had been shoddy?

She clamped her jaw, wishing she had a glass of wine or maybe a shot of bourbon in her room. She decided on a bath instead. The room had an oversized tub with a jar of bath salts on the counter. Soaking wouldn't solve her problem, but it might help her get to sleep.

The thought of Ruby lying in bed just a couple of doors down was keeping Austin wide awake.

When the house settled to dead silence, he gave up trying to sleep and slipped from his bedroom to softly knock on her door.

When she didn't answer, he slowly pushed it open, expecting to find her asleep in bed. He hadn't yet decided if he'd wake her.

Before he fully digested the sight of the empty bed, he heard splashing in the bathroom and smiled. Surprising her in the bath was even better.

The comforter was wrinkled on the bed and a book was sitting at the foot.

He removed the book, transferred it to the dresser top then pulled back the comforter. He supposed he ought to dry her off first, but he was planning to scoop her naked from the tub and into his arms.

He smiled with anticipation as he padded to the en suite door.

"Ruby?" he called out softly, not wanting to frighten her.

"Austin?" She sounded surprised.

"It's me." As he eased into the bathroom, her naked body came into soft focus through the haze of steam and water. "I couldn't stay away."

"I—" she braced her hands on the sides of the tub and sat up "—wasn't expecting you."

Her skin was pink, water dripping from her shoulders and breasts. Her damp hair accentuated her delicate face that was scrubbed free of makeup.

"You couldn't sleep either?" he asked.

"No. I guess I was keyed up." She rose and reached for a towel.

He was disappointed when she stepped from the tub and wrapped it around herself.

"'Keyed up,'" he echoed softly. "Yeah. That's how I'm feeling, too." He moved closer.

She swallowed. "Should you be here?"

"Everyone's asleep."

"I know." She glanced furtively at the open bathroom door. "Still."

"Relax," he said soothingly. Then he joked, because he was feeling confident in her feelings for him. "Unless you're not happy to see me."

She gave him a smile. "I am happy to see you."

He used another towel to dry her hair.

Then he kissed her.

She was warm and fresh, and he wrapped his arms around her, letting the kiss take on a life of its own and the passion build between them.

Her towel dropped to the floor and he lifted her naked into his arms.

She pulled his T-shirt over his head, dropped it to the floor and peppered his chest with damp kisses as he carried her into the bedroom.

When he stopped at the edge of the bed, she stiffened.

"Did you...?" She glanced worriedly around the room.

"I locked the door." He guessed her concern.

Her eyes widened in what looked like trepidation and guilt, and her voice dropped to a harsh whisper. "Did you see?"

Baffled, he glanced appreciatively at her naked body. "Oh, I can see."

She looked to the bed. "But—"

"What?" he asked, lowering her so her feet touched the floor, worried that something was wrong.

Her gaze caught on something in the distance and she froze, her pink-flushed cheeks going pale.

He looked to see where she was looking. It was at the dresser. Specifically, the book he'd moved off the bed.

Both baffled and curious, he stepped toward it.

"Austin *don't*." She grasped his arm.

"Don't what?" He searched her stricken expression. Then he glanced to the dresser top and saw a sketch. It took a moment for him to realize it was the mountain vista from the line shack. And it was very good.

He pulled free of her grasp to take a better look.

"Did you draw this?" He lifted the book, marveling at what looked like her hidden talent.

"No," she said quickly, shaking her head.

He flipped a page and she put her arms into a long, pale cotton shirt, doing up a couple of buttons.

He recognized White Foam Falls.

Ruby moved to his side. "Please don't look any further."

"Who drew these?" He couldn't for the life of him imagine who on the ranch had this kind of talent.

"I don't know for sure."

"Well, where did you get them?"

She gave a sad shake. "Please don't, Austin."

"Ruby, what is going on?" He turned another page. He froze. He stared. His jaw sagged in astonishment.

It was a sketch of his mother.

She was in a negligee, in a meadow, looking like she'd just—

"*Where* did you get this?" he rasped.

Ruby squeezed her eyes shut for a second then gripped the lip of the dresser. "The attic. I found it in the attic. In a locked drawer."

"The attic? You *stole* it?"

"I wasn't going to keep it."

Anger bubbled up inside him. "What were you going to do with it? Publish these?"

"*No.*"

He tossed the open sketchbook back on the dresser. "Put them in a book for all the world to see?"

"I wasn't going to do that. I swear."

"I trusted you," he ground out, his anger growing along with regret.

"I know. I—"

He scrambled to gauge the damage he might have done by trusting her. "I *told* you about my grandfather's will." He was furious with himself now. "Is that going to be in your book? Are you going to tell everyone our private family business before Tyler and McKinney even know they're going to inherit? I *trusted* you."

"No," she repeated, shaking her head. "It's nothing like that. I was only—"

He waited.

"Researching," she said. "I found the book, and I didn't know what it meant. I wanted to find out more."

Despite himself, he glanced at the sketch again. Who could have drawn it? Why would his mother have posed that way? He was missing something. He had to be missing something.

Then his gaze caught something else. His mother's name, Jessica, handwritten in an open notebook on the dresser.

He focused on the word *affair* then on *McKinney's father* followed by a question mark. He lifted the notebook, reading more, trying to make sense of it.

"Austin, don't," Ruby said weakly.

He saw arrows from Alice down to Kathleen through Peggy-

Lyn and ending with McKinney. The McKinney arrow was stroked out.

He lifted his gaze to Ruby. "You're not saying—"

"I don't know anything for sure." She took the notebook from his hands. "It's wild speculation right now. I was thinking and doodling at the same time."

The slight tremor in her voice told him she was lying.

He flipped a page in the sketchbook then another and another.

He came to a drawing of McKinney. McKinney as a little girl, maybe three, squatting by a stream and gazing at a butterfly that had landed on a wildflower.

"You *know* who drew these," he stated, convinced that she did.

Ruby pressed her lips mulishly together.

He gave her a look that said he'd wait an eternity for an answer.

There was a trace of a tremble in her hand as she reached for the sketchbook. He gave it to her and she turned to the last page, revealing an inscription.

He read it and his last hope this could be a mistake evaporated. "Who is JJ?"

Ruby's voice was dry, barely above a whisper. "John Jamison."

Austin's blood pressure spiked. Anger roiled through his chest at the thought of John Jamison sneaking around with his mother.

"You're sure." It wasn't a question. He knew deep down Ruby wouldn't have told him a name if she wasn't sure.

"Not 100 percent. I don't have DNA or anything."

He steadied his breathing, forcing himself to stand still instead of storming out the door and heading straight for the Jamison ranch to demand satisfaction. He couldn't do that. It would bring everything in to the open and destroy his sister's world.

And it wasn't all on Jamison. His mother had been a participant in this. Though it was harder to be angry with her. He loved her deeply.

A thousand questions rolled through his mind. Who else had known? Could his father have known?

Austin dismissed the thought. His father couldn't possibly have perpetuated such a huge lie.

"Austin?" Ruby's tone was low and tentative.

His thoughts moved to McKinney and stayed there. It would kill her if she ever found out she wasn't a Hawkes by blood.

"You aren't going to use this," he said emphatically to Ruby. "You can't use this."

"I'm thinking it through," she answered.

"*What's* to think through?"

"It's complicated. I can't flat-out ignore a fact. I'm trying to figure out how to—"

"You said it yourself. Not everything has to be part of the story."

"It's not that easy with this."

"It's exactly that easy. Just don't write about it. And you don't use the sketches. He scooped up the sketchbook. No way was she getting her hands on it ever again.

She looked stricken. "I *wouldn't* use the sketches. I don't have—"

"Why not? They're facts, aren't they?" His exasperation was growing. He had to get out of there.

He couldn't stand that this was happening to his family, and he couldn't stand the idea that Ruby would betray them.

"You better leave," he said.

It might be midnight, and she might be half naked, but he had to get her out, send her away from his family, stop her from doing any more damage than she'd already done.

He could have kicked himself for his own stupidity. He'd been dead wrong to let her stay on the ranch. This was all his fault.

"Now?"

"Right now," he said through a clenched jaw. "And don't come back. Don't ever come back."

He stalked from the room and firmly shut the door while regret and anguish pulsed through his brain and his heart.

Eleven

Ruby's heart was hollow as she checked back into the Oberfeld. The comfort and beauty of her generously sized room meant nothing this time. Even the big bathtub held zero appeal. All she could think about was lying in Austin's arms in a room like this, content from lovemaking, cocooned in warm, citrus-and-sandalwood-scented water.

She barely slept, instead tossing and turning with frustration at the vivid memories.

Rather than showering in the morning, she dressed haphazardly and marched out the door. She headed down the hall and through the lobby, out onto the street where she hoped she could leave the painful memories behind.

With no particular destination in mind, she soon found herself crossing the front porch at Topaz House. She hoped Kiera was working. She could sure use a friendly face right now.

As she walked in the doorway, Kiera looked up from the reception desk and broke into a smile that warmed Ruby's heart.

"Hey, you!" Kiera came to her feet. She skipped forward and gave Ruby a hug. "How are you doing? It's been too long."

"I looked for you at the rodeo." Ruby hugged her back, grateful for the enthusiastic greeting.

"Didn't get there this year," Kiera said.

"Oh?" Ruby knew it was one of the most popular events in Jagged Creek.

"Busy with stuff at home. Did you have fun? Had you ever been to one before?"

"It was my first time." Ruby tried to keep up her smile. "I liked it. I had a burger with Madeline."

"Burger Barn?"

Ruby nodded.

"Those are to die for. Did you make it through the whole thing?"

"Not even near."

"Come on in. What's up? Are you here to talk to the residents again?"

Ruby hesitated. Unexpectedly, her eyes heated up and she had to blink against tears.

Kiera immediately looked concerned. "Whoa. What's wrong? What happened?"

Ruby shook her head. She couldn't explain without betraying the Hawkes family.

"Come and sit down." Kiera led her to a quiet corner of the lobby and they both sat in plush chairs. "What has you so upset?"

Ruby took a breath. "Austin and I had a falling out."

Kiera sat back, looking resigned. "I'm sorry it happened. Those Hawkes guys… I tell you."

Ruby wanted to defend Austin. This hadn't been his fault. But she couldn't explain. It was easier to let Kiera think Austin had simply broken it off between them.

"I'm no longer staying at the ranch."

Kiera shook her head. "Did you get what you needed?"

Ruby had, and then some. Right now, she had too much information. "I have enough."

"Good. Well, at least there's that." Kiera paused. "How far did it go with you two? I mean it was obvious you were attracted to him, and it sounded like he was attracted back."

"We slept together," Ruby admitted. There was no harm in Kiera knowing that much, and Ruby really needed someone to talk to.

Kiera took her hand. "Dang." Then her expression changed. "I mean dang if you regret it. If you don't, then you go, girl."

Ruby couldn't help but crack a smile. "I really don't know yet." She realized it was true. She was hurting badly right now, but how could she regret all those incredibly magical moments in Austin's arms?

"That's perfectly normal," Kiera said briskly. It takes time for the haze of passion to fade. I wish you'd been the one to walk away—show those Hawkes dudes they can't have every little thing they want out of life."

"It wasn't all Austin's fault." Ruby couldn't bring herself to let him take the blame.

"Oh, no you don't," Kiera said with an adamant shake of her head. "He doesn't get a pass on this."

"I did something," Ruby admitted.

"What? Killed a heifer? Set the house on fire?"

"No. Nothing like that."

"Then he had no call to do whatever he's done. Now, how can I help? Do you want to talk to the seniors? Or I can go on break. We can head for Madeline's and sleuth through records there if you like."

"Uh-oh." Ruby's promise to Madeline slipped her mind.

"What's 'uh-oh'?"

"I told Madeline I'd give a lecture to a class at the college."

"That sounds exciting."

"I was looking forward to it. But—" Ruby didn't plan on sticking around Jagged Creek any longer than necessary.

"Right now, all you want to do is hightail it out of town," Kiera speculated.

Ruby nodded miserably.

"You shouldn't do that," Kiera stated with conviction. "Don't let that Hawkes family chase you away. You came here for a reason. Finish your research. Do the lecture, if you feel like it. They can all lump it out there on their ranch with the cattle and the horseflies."

Ruby had to admit Kiera's advice seemed sound. She couldn't abandon her work and start a new book project at this late date.

For better or worse, she was stuck with writing about the Hawkes ranch. She was also stuck with focusing on the women. It was by far the most compelling approach to the material.

Where it came to Jessica and McKinney, she'd have to somehow strike a balance. There had to be a way forward.

"Can you really take a break?" Ruby asked, appreciating Kiera's practical advice.

"The archives?" Kiera asked, looking eager.

"If you don't mind?"

"Love to help."

In the end, Kiera took the whole day off, and the two women plunged into the research. Madeline stopped by and agreed to schedule Ruby for a lecture as soon as possible.

Ruby forcibly pushed Austin from her mind, filling it with everything she could find about the Hawkes women, the town's women, and the women who'd lived on the neighboring ranches.

When they finally finished, Ruby offered to buy Kiera dinner. But as they crossed into the lobby of the Oberfeld, those raw memories of Austin slammed into her, making her breath stagger.

"You, okay?" Kiera asked, concern on her face.

"Fine." Ruby struggled to shake off the feelings but they wouldn't go away.

"You sure?"

"No. I need a drink."

"Coming up," Kiera said and gently steered Ruby toward the lounge.

"Two vodka martinis," Kiera called out as they passed the bartender. "Olives okay with you, or do you want a twist?"

"Olives are good." Ruby would be happy with anything that had a kick.

They took a cozy table for two near the window, overlooking the garden lights that were just coming on.

Kiera leaned silently on the table and waited, looking compassionate and safe, an excellent listener.

"We spent the night here," Ruby told her. "Well, half of the night. It was after the rodeo, and it was fantastic, and I can't get it out of my head."

"Of course you can't," Kiera said as the bartender set their drinks out in front of them.

"Would you like me to open a tab?" he asked.

"Yes," Kiera immediately answered. "We'll do dinner in a little while."

The man nodded and left.

Kiera dabbed the skewer of three olives in the frosty glass. "What happened to split you two up? I mean don't tell me what you don't want to tell me. But it must have been something big."

Ruby didn't know how to answer. She took a healthy swallow of her drink, grateful for the warmth of the liquor going down her throat and spreading its way into her system.

"Did he do the usual Hawkes dude thing?" There was a frown on Kiera's face. "Go cold as soon as he got bored?"

"What? No!" Ruby realized she'd reacted too forcefully.

Kiera stopped dabbing. "Really?"

"It wasn't anything like that. Austin didn't—" Ruby took another drink. "It wasn't anything like that."

"Sorry." Kiera looked contrite now. "I didn't mean to insult either of you."

"It's okay." Ruby wasn't insulted. She was so raw and sore and heartbroken that there wasn't room in her body for any other emotion. She squeezed her eyes shut for a moment, trying to get herself under control. "Thing is, I found something I shouldn't have found."

She opened her eyes to see Kiera's brow rise.

"And now." Ruby drew a shuddering breath, remembering Austin's reaction to the news. "It'll compromise my book if I don't use the information."

Kiera gave a chopped laugh. "This will sound nasty. But good for you. For once, the world doesn't revolve around the almighty Hawkes family."

"You really don't like them." Ruby couldn't help wondering what had happened between Kiera and the Hawkes to make her so cynical.

"I really don't."

"Care to share?"

Kiera shook her head. "It's old news. We're talking about your book here. Listen, nobody wants to be on the bad end of scandal, but people should also own up to the truth."

Ruby hadn't thought of it that way. But Kiera had a point. There was an argument to be made that McKinney deserved to know who her father was.

"No matter what?" Ruby asked, not completely convinced.

"Usually. I mean who does a lie protect? The liar? It's not usually the victim."

"In this case, it's hard to say."

Hiding the truth protected John Jamison and Jessica. But it also protected McKinney. Her life would be shaken to the core if she found out. Then again, her father lived only two hours away from her and she didn't know it.

"So there's an argument to be made both ways," Kiera said reasonably.

"I suppose." Ruby toyed with her glass.

"My opinion," Kiera said. "You should do what's best for your book and your career. You're not responsible for the Hawkes family's indiscretions and lies."

Theoretically, Ruby knew Kiera was right.

Ruby was a historian. She prided herself on her professionalism, which meant she couldn't make value judgments. That past had happened the way it had happened. Hiding or shading the truth didn't change it.

And her career was back in Boston. Her life was back in Boston. She had enough material for a fascinating story, and she owed it to herself to get it written and published to set herself up for advancement. That was the entire reason she'd come to Jagged Creek in the first place.

But then a vision of Austin's anguish came up in her mind, messing with her conviction. She thought about his love of his family and their ranch, and his hard work to improve it. She couldn't help remembering his wry sense of humor, his vehement opinions and his passionate lovemaking.

Deep down, she knew what was right professionally. She also knew she'd be sacrificing his family's future for hers.

Austin regretted kicking Ruby out in the middle of the night. He'd lain awake afterward wondering where she was and what she was doing. Had she made it to Jagged Creek? Would she stick around awhile or head straight home to Boston?

He had to fight an urge to drive into town and find her. He desperately wanted to be with her. He absolutely couldn't wrap his head around the thought of never seeing her again.

He made his way down the stairs and heard the voices of his family around the breakfast table. They sounded happy, laughing, talking overtop of each other. Dallas and Sierra had stopped by, early as it was.

"How long can you stay?" McKinney asked.

Austin was surprised to hear his youngest brother Tyler's voice.

"I'm on shore leave for three weeks, and then I have to decide—" Tyler spotted Austin and broke into a grin. "There he is."

Tyler shot up from his chair and strode to meet Austin, pulling him into a tight hug. He looked fit, neat. He was in civilian clothes, but he carried himself like a soldier.

"Where'd you come from?" Austin hadn't seen Tyler in several months.

"Shore leave for now," Tyler said happily. "What's with you sleeping in?"

"It's barely seven." Austin wasn't about to own up to his restless night.

"Are you getting old and tired?" Tyler returned to the table, where he'd piled his plate high with pancakes, eggs and sausages.

"As if," Austin retorted taking his own seat next to his father and across from Dallas.

He wasn't hungry, so he poured himself a cup of coffee. Caffeine was what he needed to get his mind straight again. He'd let Ruby into their lives and made a mess of everything. She was gone now, and he had to accept it.

"How was the Mediterranean?" Dallas asked Tyler.

"Work on your tan?" McKinney put in.

"I was on a destroyer not a cruise ship." Tyler smiled fondly at his sister's teasing.

Looking at his three siblings now, Austin couldn't help assessing their features. Tyler looked like Dallas, who looked like Austin, who favored their father. The men all had brown eyes, nondescript noses, square chins and skin that tended to a deep tan.

They were all tall, within an inch or so of each other. Tyler's face was slightly more angular. Austin's a little heavier across the brow. But anybody meeting them would know they were brothers.

McKinney's skin was light in tone, her eyes blue, more round and wider set. Her hair was light brown with a copper sheen. He'd always discounted those things, along with her slight build, because she was a woman. She wasn't supposed to look like them.

"Did you shoot at anything?" she asked Tyler, humor still threaded through her tone.

"Only at the bad guys," he joked back.

"You shouldn't joke about what you're doing out there," their father said.

"We observe a whole lot more than we ever shoot," Tyler amended.

Austin shifted his gaze to his father, wondering if he'd known or suspected anything about his wife's infidelity. Was it possible the marriage had been that rocky without his father even noticing?

His dad caught his gaze. "What?"

"Nothing." Austin shook his head, looked away and took a swallow of his coffee. There was no way to ask the question that was on his mind. "Here to help with the roundup?" he asked Tyler instead.

"I can't see him sitting around the house," Dallas answered.

"We're already down one." Garrett sent a critical look Dallas's way.

"Hey, I'm here if you really need me," Dallas responded.

"He's mostly in the way now that I'm decorating anyway," Sierra said with a smile to Dallas.

He put an arm around her shoulders and gave her a squeeze.

"I'm coming up to see," McKinney said to Sierra.

"Happy to get on horseback," Tyler put in, taking another bite of his breakfast.

Austin had always enjoyed the big lively breakfasts with the whole family. But right now he wished Ruby were here. He knew she was an only child and wondered what she'd think of the chaos. He found himself smiling then cut off his unruly thoughts and helped himself to a couple of pancakes, dousing them with maple syrup. She was never going to have breakfast here again.

"We're going after stragglers in the Wind Valley," McKinney told Tyler as she used the tip of her spoon to start peeling an orange.

"All's well with Rambler?" Tyler asked about his golden palomino quarter horse.

"He's always here ready for you," their father said.

The four siblings exchanged looks and smirks.

Sierra looked confused but didn't ask any questions.

Their father made no secret of wanting Tyler on the ranch instead of in the navy. Now that Dallas was back in the fold, Austin suspected Tyler would be next on the list.

Austin would be happy to see Tyler come home, too. But his brother had to make that decision for himself.

"Where's Ruby?" McKinney seemed to suddenly realize Ruby was gone. She looked to Austin as she popped a section of orange into her mouth.

"Back in town," he answered, trying to sound offhand.

"Who's Ruby?" Tyler asked.

"So suddenly?" Sierra looked around as if she expected Ruby to appear.

Austin wished Ruby would appear. He wished she'd walk back through the door and— His thoughts stopped there, because he couldn't imagine what came next. He couldn't talk, joke, laugh and make love with her while she was busy destroying his family.

"This morning?" McKinney added, clearly confused.

"She left early," Austin answered.

"Why?" Sierra asked, peering at Austin. She knew more about his relationship with Ruby than anyone else.

Austin gave a shrug that was for everyone, adding what he hoped was a surreptitious warning look for Sierra.

Dallas raised his brow in a question, but Austin didn't answer.

"Who's Ruby?" Tyler asked again.

"She's writing a book," Dallas answered.

Austin took a big bite of his pancakes to avoid answering any more questions.

"Is she coming back soon?" Sierra asked.

"She's great," McKinney told Tyler. "She's a history professor from Boston."

"She almost crashed our wedding," Sierra added.

"Then she moved in to write a book on us," Dallas added.

"She likes Austin," McKinney said.

Austin swallowed. "No, she doesn't."

Everybody stilled and five sets of eyes swung his way. He realized how harsh his tone had sounded.

"What happened?" Sierra asked, looking concerned.

Austin put his attention on his breakfast. "Nothing happened. She…finished and left. It's good she's gone. She was intrusive." He took another bite.

McKinney looked perplexed. "I thought she was finding all kinds of great stuff."

"She was," Sierra said, watching Austin closely.

"She had this idea to focus on the women of the family." McKinney gave a playful little toss of her hair. "In other words, *me*. It's about time, I say."

"Do you expect to be famous?" Tyler asked McKinney.

"Honestly, my money's on Great-Grandma Kathleen. But I'm hoping for a strong supporting role."

Austin spoke abruptly before he could stop himself. "The book's not about you."

There was a split second of silence while McKinney's expression fell.

"What is up with you?" Dallas asked.

Sierra put a gentle hand on Dallas's arm and Dallas looked

down in confusion. It was obvious she knew Austin had had
something to do with Ruby's sudden departure.

Austin quickly came to his feet, moving past the moment.
"Nothing. I'm good. Tyler, you ready? Rambler's stabled in the
main barn. Let's get going."

Ruby enjoyed giving the lecture. The fresh, curious enthusiasm of a classroom of students was exhilarating. The class had
run long as she'd answered question after thoughtful question
about people and lifestyles. She much preferred a version of history that went beyond dates, names and prominent inventions.

But now it was over, and her own thoughts crowded in again.

She hated to go back to her hotel room. Everything about
it spurred memories of Austin, from the color scheme in the
room to the fresh scent of the sheets, even the feel of the shower
cascading over her in the shower. She didn't dare have a bath
in the oversized tub, even though it was one of her favorite in-
dulgences.

Austin was everywhere, and no matter how hard she fought
the memories, she couldn't seem to shut them down.

Instead, she let herself into the quiet, cavernous space of the
archives and took a small table in the corner of the sitting area.
Surrounded by shelves and file cabinets, books, boxes and a
few display cases, she shrugged out of her jacket, opened her
laptop and raked her hair into a ponytail.

She pulled up her book outline and focused on the page. She
was going to force herself past this writer's block. She needed
to flesh out the chapters, link them to the theme and thesis, en-
sure she had a strong through-thread. Now was the time to figure out if there were more elements to research in person. Once
she was back in Boston, it would be too late.

She was a linear thinker, so she pulled up the notes page for
one. *Courage* was the working title. It had been her first instinct
to use as a starting point.

But she questioned herself now. Maybe she should use *fear*.
After all, it was fear that led to courage.

Or maybe it was courage that led to fear.

Despite her best efforts, Austin popped into her mind again.

It was courage that had led her to Austin—courage that first day when she'd showed up at the ranch, heart racing, palms sweating with each step she took. Then courage again when she'd gone back to confront him a second time and ask for his help.

But she wasn't afraid of him. She was in awe of him. He was a modern-day hero, taking on physical challenges and risks every single day while pushing against his father, trying to apply technology to an age-old industry, all to hold his family and ranch together as the world changed around them.

Ruby had to admire that. And he did it all with intelligence, energy and integrity. He'd treated her the same way, even though she was a thorn in his side, even when she'd caused him grief, which she had done and would keep doing.

She'd made him angry. But his anger wasn't frightening. His anger hurt her deeply because it was justified and because of the wedge it drove between them.

She wasn't afraid of Austin. She was afraid of losing him.

The sound of footsteps intruded on her thoughts.

"I didn't know you'd stayed," Madeline said, sounding pleased as she approached the table.

Ruby looked up. "I'm working on the outline."

"Surrounded by inspiration?" Madeline asked as she slid into one of the plastic chairs. Then her expression sobered. "What's wrong?"

"Nothing," Ruby lied. Then she forced a smile on her face.

"You look pensive."

"Just lost in thought." Ruby gestured to her screen. "I'm working on the book outline."

"How's it coming along?"

Ruby felt a sudden wave of emotion and a well of heat behind her eyes. She didn't want to explain. She couldn't explain. "It's not coming—" Her voice cracked. She swallowed and tried again. "I thought I had something I could use." She covered her mouth with her fingertips.

Madeline reached out a hand wrinkled with experience and gave Ruby's a squeeze. "But you can't?"

Ruby admitted the truth to herself. Her heart sank even as a weight lifted off her shoulders. "I can't."

Madeline gave a sympathetic smile. "Then use something else."

Ruby shook her head. "It's not that easy." It would feel good to do the right thing by Austin, but she was also compromising her book and, thereby, her career.

"It's never easy. You've been here for...what? A few weeks now?"

"Yes."

"And you haven't noticed?"

Ruby didn't know what Madeline meant.

"It was never remotely easy. People built this town, these ranches, this community and, in the early days, they scratched it together with their bare hands. We've been hit with disasters, droughts, wars, the Depression, never mind the day-to-day challenges of isolation and deprivation. The highway still gets hit with avalanches. Phone service goes down for days at a time. An emergency surgeon can be two hours away. But always, every time, when one path is closed, we find another, or another."

Guilt grew within Ruby. "When the cabin burns down, you move into the chicken coop."

"Now you're getting it."

"I can't see the chicken coop. I've tried. I've really, really tried."

"That's because you're still mourning the loss of the cabin."

Ruby put her finger on it then—the flaw in the metaphor. "But the house is still standing, and other people will see it. And I'll be living in the chicken coop looking like a fool."

"Ahh," Madeline said. "And you can't hide the house."

"Someone would find it."

"Burn it yourself?"

Ruby compressed her lips. "It's not flammable."

"Too bad you can't time travel," Madeline said on a lighter note. "Back to before the house existed."

Ruby stilled. Her mind sped up with a new idea. She'd have to lose McKinney altogether, plus Jessica's later years. But she'd still have Kathleen, Lillian and all the rest to play with. The story might not be as strong, but it wouldn't be disingenuous, and it would get rid of the horrible feeling that she'd betrayed Austin.

"You have something?" Madeline asked with a growing smile. "You *do* have something."

"Maybe," Ruby said and put her hands to the keyboard. "Maybe I do."

Twelve

Austin was working harder than ever, but it wasn't helping. His body might be dead tired when he lay down in bed, but he couldn't fall asleep. He lay there night after night, sweet memories of Ruby dancing through his mind, leaving his arms feeling empty and his heart full of regret.

He knew he'd done the right thing, knew it down to the marrow of his bones. But he missed her so much, it physically hurt. Over and over again he tried to come up with some middle ground—a way that he could be with Ruby despite the harm to his family.

He thought about leaving Jagged Creek, about following her to Boston. He could transfer the title to his land to Dallas or Tyler or even McKinney. But Dallas didn't want to ranch cattle, Tyler was still on active duty, and McKinney was too young. He couldn't put that kind of a burden on her shoulders.

Especially since she'd be recovering from the shock of learning the truth about her mother. His father would also be recovering from the shock. Austin couldn't walk away from them right when they needed him the most.

He smacked a bottle of bourbon down a little too hard on top of the bar, the bang echoing in the empty great room. It was getting late, and he was dreading another long night.

He tipped back his second drink and swallowed it down.

"That's not a good sign." It was Sierra's voice.

Austin turned to see she was alone, silently heading his way on soft sneakers and wearing khaki slacks and a pastel pullover sweater.

"Where's Dallas?" he asked, not happy about being disturbed.

He didn't want to chat politely. He wanted to wallow in his own misery for a while longer.

He poured himself another drink.

"Sure, I'll take one," Sierra said as she drew closer.

He felt like a heel. "Sorry."

"Don't be sorry. Just pour me a drink." Her tone was teasing and there was a smile on her face.

"Bourbon?"

"Sounds good."

He flipped over another heavy crystal glass. "Neat okay?"

"Neat's fine."

He poured for her and handed over the glass.

She sat down in one of the big leather armchairs and peeled off her shoes, curling her feet under her as if she was settling in.

The big stone fireplace beside them was dark and cold, keeping with his mood. He felt bad now that he hadn't lit it when he arrived.

"Sit," she said.

He didn't see he had much choice. He took the chair opposite.

"How's it going?" she asked, her gaze soft and sympathetic.

"Fine." He took a more controlled sip of the liquor this time. "You?"

"All good." She paused. "They delivered the appliances yesterday. And the kitchen cabinets are up."

"Good," he said absently, nodding his head.

"But you don't care about that at all."

He looked her way. "What?"

"Austin, why did Ruby leave?"

His stomach contracted at the mention of her name. "She was never going to stay."

"Not forever," Sierra agreed.

He gave a sharp nod. He didn't trust his voice right now.

"But why then? Why that exact moment?" Her compassionate gaze was steady. It invited his confidence.

"What are you trying to do?" he asked with suspicion. He knew very well what she'd done for a living.

"I'm worried about you."

"Don't worry."

"Sure. Okay. No problem," she joked sarcastically.

"There's nothing for you to worry about."

"I know."

The silence stretched to uncomfortable between them, and Austin shifted in his seat.

"But there's something for you to worry about," she said softly.

He opened his mouth.

"Don't bother lying," she told him. "I do this for a living."

"You think I need life-coaching?"

"Yes."

He gazed through the crystal into the bright amber of his drink. "I can't tell you."

She shifted and set her drink on the table beside her, leaning forward. "You can. Whatever it is. I can keep a confidence."

"It's not that I slept with her."

"I already know you slept with her."

Austin wanted to talk. He desperately wanted to talk. But it wouldn't be fair.

"I can't," he said on an embarrassingly plaintive note.

"Austin."

He came to his feet. "No. No. I'm not going to tell you something you can't share with Dallas. It's not right. It's not fair. I'm not coming between the two of you."

"Okay, now you're scaring me."

"Please, Sierra." He needed her to leave. He didn't want to be tempted to unburden himself at her expense.

She rose to her feet then reached down and polished off her drink.

He was glad.

He wanted to be glad.

He desperately wanted to be glad that she'd walk out and leave him to his misery. But a small, panicked part of him wanted to stop her from going.

He gritted his teeth to keep quiet.

"Austin." She took a step his way and put her hand on his arm.

The tenderness of the gesture pierced his soul.

She seemed to sense it and just stood there, her light touch telling him she wanted to help.

"I never thought I'd say this," he rasped. "I need life-coaching."

"Everyone does at some point."

Uncertainty tightened his chest. He knew if he stepped over this line, he could never go back. What he was about to do would alter the people he loved forever. But he also knew he couldn't keep going on like this.

"Ruby and I had a fight."

"Okay."

He returned to his chair and Sierra did the same.

"She knows something, something terrible, and she's going to put it in her book for the world to see."

"About you?"

"Worse." His stomach churned and he had to open and close his mouth twice before getting the words to form. "Garrett is not McKinney's father."

Sierra blinked, but other than that, her expression remained impressively neutral as a silent moment slipped by.

"You didn't know," she guessed.

"I had no idea."

"How do you feel about that?"

"How do I *feel* about it?" He struggled to sort through a rush of conflicting emotions. "I feel betrayed."

"By Ruby?"

"*Yes*. Why did she have to do that? Why did she have to dig into our family that way? We had a good thing going."

"You and Ruby."

"Yes, me and Ruby." They'd had a great thing going. So great, he couldn't get her out of his mind, not for a minute, certainly not for a night so he could get some sleep.

"You miss her," Sierra said.

It was his curse. "I don't want anything to do with her."

"This works better if you're honest."

"Do you have any idea what she's doing to our family? What's she's doing to McKinney?"

"No." Sierra shook her head. "I don't."

"My baby sister is going to find out she's not a Hawkes, that her entire life was a lie. That her brothers are only her half-brothers and that the father she adores isn't even related to her."

"I can't begin to imagine how that would feel. But Austin—"

"What?"

"Ruby didn't do it."

"Not yet, but she will."

She'd been clear about that. Scandals would make her book interesting and exciting. It would sell copies, make a name for her, get her the promotion she wanted so badly.

"Your mother did it."

Austin's jaw sagged.

"She was the one who had an affair. She was the one who hid the truth."

He wasn't understanding Sierra's point. "We can't change that now."

"No, we can't."

"We don't have to broadcast it to the world. We don't have to destroy lives after all this time."

Sierra seemed to consider his words. After a moment, she leaned forward again. "Are you in love with Ruby?"

Austin reared back. "No!"

He wasn't about to love a woman with no ethics, a woman who'd betray his family for the notoriety and professional advancement. What kind of a man would do that?

"You're sure?"

"Just because I like having sex with her doesn't mean I'm in love with her." But even as he said the words, he knew it was more than sex. He loved tumbling naked with her, but he also loved talking with her, laughing with her, even debating with her.

"Let's think this through," Sierra said.

"I don't want to think this through."

"I'm not surprised."

"Stop."

"I don't believe I will. Ruby's gone, and you miss her desperately, and you hate yourself for missing her because, in your mind, she's a threat to your family. I mean, how could you love her? How could you possibly love her?"

Austin's stomach was churning again. He hated how close Sierra was getting to the truth.

"It's okay to love her," Sierra said softly.

"It's not."

"Your mother and McKinney have nothing to do with your feelings for Ruby."

He completely disagreed there. "They have everything—"

"If Ruby wasn't in the picture, and you knew about McKinney."

"I wouldn't know about McKinney if Ruby wasn't in the picture."

"*If* she wasn't," Sierra said more emphatically, "what would you do—with the information?"

Austin hadn't thought about it from that angle. What would he have done if he'd found out himself? Bury the secret and hope it never came out? Tell someone, his father or McKinney?

"Let the lie fester?" Sierra challenged.

He scowled at her this time.

"Whatever Ruby does or doesn't do, you have to make a choice."

The realization spiked painfully into his brain. The knowledge was his responsibility. He had to do right by his sister.

"So," Sierra said with breezy finality, "it's okay to love Ruby."

It took a moment for Sierra's words to penetrate.

She was grinning at him. "Good news, huh?"

He suddenly felt lighter, and he broke into a wide smile.

It was okay for him to love Ruby.

It was *okay* for him to love Ruby.

Ruby tucked the printed copy of her outline into a manila envelope, sealing it for the mailbox in the hotel lobby. Her book was going to be good. It would be a solid representation of the Hawkes women's lives, their contribution, and their resilience as they'd helped build the cattle industry in Colorado.

She pictured Austin's expression when he read the outline, the relief he'd feel that his family was no longer at risk and, hopefully, the forgiveness he'd feel toward her for not using the information about Jessica's affair. She wanted to be happy about all that, but her heart faltered at the thought of leaving him forever.

Her bag was packed. She'd said her goodbyes. And she'd checked out of the hotel on her phone. All that was left was to drive the rental car back to Granby and catch her flight home. Soon, Jagged Creek would be nothing but a memory.

The closer the moment came, the more her chest ached with hollowness.

She forced herself to march across the hotel room and extend the handle on her roller bag. She left the key card on the desk and did one final look around the room to make sure she had all her stuff—that no shirts were still hanging in the closet, no power cords plugged into the wall.

It was empty.

She had every single thing she'd come with.

Well, everything except one.

Her hand tightened on the handle, squeezing firmly as her eyes welled up and her throat went raw with pain.

She was leaving her heart behind.

She'd denied it as long as she could, but there was no getting away from how she felt. She'd fallen in love with Austin more quickly and more thoroughly than she'd ever imagined possible. But there it was. And there was nothing she could do to fix it.

A knock sounded on the door.

It was past checkout time and housekeeping was obviously about to kick her out.

It felt fitting somehow, being ushered from the hotel, forced out of town because she didn't belong there. Madeline had told her to come back anytime and lecture at the college. But Ruby knew she wouldn't be back.

The knock sounded again.

She gathered her frayed emotions and lifted her chin, tugging her suitcase behind her as she pulled open the door.

Austin stood there, tall and broad-shouldered, in all his handsome, cowboy glory, the man she now knew she loved beyond reason.

Her heart took a lurch, her chest filling with joy and then pain as she stared at him, stupefied, unable to comprehend his presence.

He glanced at her suitcase. "You're leaving."

"What—" She couldn't manage any more.

He seemed calm, not angry, but maybe that was a cover. "Can I come in?"

"It's past checkout time."

"I don't think they'll mind."

She knew she should tell him she'd changed the book. She didn't want him to launch into a lecture about his family's privacy. And she didn't think she could stand it if he were any more disappointed in her. It would break her heart to have their last moments together be another argument.

He eased forward and she backed up a few steps.

"I have something to tell you," she said, opening her bag to retrieve the envelope.

"Don't." He took a quick step forward as the door swung shut behind him.

He put his one finger gently across her lips, shocking her to silence.

"Let me be the one to talk," he said.

"But, you don't—" she started to speak around his fingertip.

"I'm sorry, Ruby," he told her in a gentle voice and his hand fell away.

Her lips parted in surprise.

A gleam came into the depths of his eyes. "Don't do that."

She couldn't exactly stop herself from being surprised.

"Don't look at me like that," he repeated. "I'll lose my train of thought."

She blinked.

"I acted like it was your problem," he said and drew back a little. "I thought it was your problem. I blamed you, and that was wrong."

She was confused. "Austin—"

"No." He shook his head. "Let me get this out. It's my problem. It's the family's problem. But I think I've found a way—"

"*What* problem?" she blurted out.

He stopped.

"I don't know what you're talking about."

His brow furrowed. "McKinney. My mother. The secret and the lie."

Now Ruby was more surprised than ever. She was the one who'd dug it up. She was the one who threatened to make it public.

She couldn't figure out what was going on here. "How do you mean?"

He shifted closer again. This time he took her hand from the suitcase and slipped her bag from her shoulder, setting it on the carpet. He took both hands in his, sending a surge of warmth up her arms to her shoulders to the center of her chest.

"You never lied," he said. "You never betrayed anyone."

She'd betrayed him. She loved him, and she'd never forgive herself for putting her career ahead of his happiness.

It was a book. A single, insignificant book. There would be other research projects, other papers, other books. But there was only one Austin.

How could she have been such a colossal fool?

"You found the truth," he said.

Her voice caught in her throat. "I'm sorry."

But he shook his head and smiled. "Don't be sorry. The truth is the truth. Keeping it hidden doesn't change it. We have to deal with it. *I* have to deal with it. Like I said, it's not your problem."

"But I made it yours," she pointed out, regret filling her all over again.

He gave a teasing smile. "Thing is, I think I've found a way to make it yours."

She frowned at the odd turn of the conversation.

He let go of one hand and cradled her face with his palm. "Don't go, Ruby."

"Don't go where?"

"Stay. Don't leave me."

She was truly speechless now.

He leaned in and his voice dropped to a whisper. "Help me figure this out. This is a family problem." He gave her a gentle kiss.

The brush of his lips was light, but joy and desire instantly filled her. She stepped in and kissed him back. The passion quickly deepened between them.

He broke the kiss, just barely drawing back. "Oh, man, I missed that. I missed you so much." He hugged her to him. "I love you, Ruby. We'll figure out what comes next together."

He loved her.

He *loved* her?

"You love me?" she asked, breathless because all the oxygen had been sucked out of her lungs.

"More than anything in my life."

"But—I messed everything up."

"You didn't. It was messed up before you even got here. I just didn't know it yet."

She was scrambling to make sense of everything. "You're not angry?"

His smile grew wide. "I'm not angry. I'm a little nervous." He smoothed back her hair. "I just told you I loved you, and you haven't said anything back."

Relief poured through her, followed by joy, followed by the strongest surge of love. "I love you back, Austin." She wrapped her arms around his neck, coming up on her toes for another kiss. "I love you so much."

It was long minutes before their kiss ended.

Ruby was more breathless than before.

If not for the very real possibility of a housekeeper entering the room at any moment, she'd have hauled Austin onto the bed.

"Here's the thing," he said, sounding breathless himself.

"There's a thing?" She didn't want there to be a catch. Her world was too perfect at the moment. She didn't want it to get messed up.

"Yeah," he said with a sultry smile.

She hoped he was about to proposition her. Forget about

housekeeping. They probably wouldn't show up for a while anyway.

"I know how much you like artifacts."

"I do."

"I brought you something great."

"You did?" Just when she'd thought the moment couldn't get any better.

He reached into his pocket and extracted a ring—a gorgeous diamond solitaire bracketed by tiny rubies.

"It was Kathleen's. I can only imagine the exhilarating provenance."

Ruby's heart thudded so hard she could barely speak. "Austin, are you—"

"Absolutely." Love radiated from his expression. "Please marry me, Ruby. I think this ring was created just for you."

"Yes," she breathed, hugging him tight. "Yes."

He kissed her soundly then slipped the ring on her finger.

It sparkled and shone against her skin.

"It's perfect," he whispered. "Kathleen might have worn it, but its true home is with you." He kissed her finger then wrapped his arms around her, cradling her tightly against his strength.

Since Ruby had already been packed, Austin drove them straight back to the ranch, dispatching a couple of hands to return her rental car and announcing the good news. McKinney and Sierra were in the great room, now admiring the ring, exchanging hugs with Ruby and welcoming her enthusiastically into the family.

"You pulled it off," Dallas said.

"She seems too good for you," Tyler added.

"I won't argue with that," Austin said, his gaze firmly fixed on Ruby while his brothers talked.

"I guess Sierra was right," Dallas added.

Austin looked to his brother, puzzled as to what Sierra might have predicted.

"I used to tease her about staying because she was between homes and jobs," Dallas said.

"You did not," Tyler put in with horror.

Dallas shrugged unrepentantly. "My wife has an excellent sense of humor. She always insisted she'd have walked away from anything for me."

"Man, you *really* don't deserve her," Tyler said.

"Ruby proved the theory," Dallas said. "She gave it all up for you."

"I'm one lucky man," Austin agreed. "But she's renting her apartment, and I think she already has a job in Jagged Creek."

"How did that happen?" Dallas asked.

"Madeline has big plans for the college. Ruby's a get for her." Austin paused, his gaze going back to his fiancée. "She's a get for me, too."

"No kidding," Tyler said, nudging Austin with an elbow.

"What's all this?" Their father made his way down the stairs.

"Austin found a finger for great-grandma's ring," Dallas told him.

Garrett gazed at the three women in silence for a moment. "Didn't see that one coming."

"Sierra did," Dallas said. "Took Austin a while to clue in though."

"I'm going to introduce myself," Tyler said, breaking away.

The statement took Austin by surprise.

"I guess he hasn't even met her," Dallas noted.

"I hadn't thought about that." Austin watched Tyler give Ruby a hug and join the conversation.

"You're sure about this?" his father asked him.

"I wouldn't have asked her if I wasn't sure."

His father gave a brooding nod. "Is she still doing the book?"

"Yes. She showed me her outline."

Dallas hit Austin with a penetrating and quizzical look. It was clear Sierra had shared the information about McKinney— as Austin had expected she would.

"I liked the outline," Austin said, levelly returning his brother's gaze. "She improved it. Very much."

Their father watched the exchange with intent. His voice was terse when he finally spoke. "I want to see it."

"I'll ask her," Austin said.

"Make it happen."

Austin caught Dallas's eye once more. It was clear both men were thinking the same thing.

Their father knew.

He knew about the affair, and he knew about McKinney. It seemed likely he'd known all along.

Austin's amazement was tempered with admiration.

His father had loved her as if she were his own. He hadn't treated McKinney any differently than his three sons. In fact, in many ways, she'd been his favorite. The strength of character that showed was beyond impressive.

His father had protected McKinney all these years. They'd eventually have to tell her the truth. But not today. When the time was right, Austin knew instinctively he'd have his father's support.

"Somebody open the champagne, already!" McKinney called out, moving the two groups toward each other.

"On it," Dallas offered and headed for the wine cellar.

Austin went to Ruby and wrapped an arm around her. He gave her a quick kiss then whispered in her ear, "Overwhelmed, my love?"

She leaned into him and held her hand out in front, admiring the ring as she whispered, "Only with joy."

* * * * *

BAD BOY
GONE GOOD

KATIE FREY

A little over a year ago I confided to a friend I met online via a Mills & Boon Facebook group that I wanted to write for Mills & Boon.

Suzie poured over every sentence in my first novel and encouraged me from first draft to submission.

She is a huge fan of Mills & Boon and always wanted to see her name in a Mills & Boon book. So today, I help with that.

Her daughter's name is Evie.

Suzie Bethell-Thompson. This book is dedicated to you.

To the fans and friends out there, reaching out with kind words to new writers can make a huge difference.

Thank you.

One

Two Truths

"This was nice," Evie Hartmann said, all the while thinking to herself that her date with Ben had done more to confirm her previous friend-zone designation rather than lighting a spark for eternal passion. *Or any passion really.*

But it had been nice, the Michelin dinner, catered by a chef Ben had flown in for the occasion. Reminiscing about the "good old days," then doubling down on the fact they were both far too young to yet have amassed many "good old days," much less reminisce about them. Throughout the evening, neither had commented on the odd moment of stilted awkwardness, both aware of what the other wanted, and similarly aware that they were miles away from common ground.

Evie bit the inside of her cheek. *It was one thing to know what was good for you, and it was another thing entirely to want it. But, damn, did she wish she wanted it...or him...*

Ben Kingsley, who was the nicest guy on the planet and

more handsome than half the leading men in Hollywood, nodded in her direction, lifting a hand to tilt the rim of his hat up. It was a reflexive gesture for a cowboy, and one she'd missed during her stint in LA. Although she'd missed the presence of cowboys, the lack of suitable roles had brought her home. Or, more pointedly, her consistent pattern of being a runner-up but never the leading lady. She might be coming home a failed actress but was determined not to feel that way forever. Thus the date with the golden-boy neighbor.

He swallowed, Adam's apple bobbing. "Absolutely. I'm so glad you're home."

Evie zoned out again. There was a sincerity in his tone, a gruff warmth that had her second-guessing her decision to friend-zone him. She *wanted* to be wrong about it. More than anything, she'd *wanted* to be wrong about how she felt. Hell, she'd been wrong about so much else lately. Fate owed her a do-over. She was, after all, a red-blooded female, and she still found it hard to imagine that any female might look at the delectable treat of a neighbor and not want more.

So what was wrong with her?

It had been a week since she'd come home. A week since she'd decided she'd had her last failure in Hollywood. It was time to stop running and face the life she'd been born into. Time to be an adult.

Since her homecoming, she'd been busier than a queen bee, attending society luncheons, a ribbon-cutting ceremony at the Bozeman hospital, and two family dinners, both complete with her siblings and their picture-perfect significant others. Once again, the family table was filling up, the seat next to hers the only empty spot at the table.

Evie was the only one still alone, and she was *tired.*

Ben cleared his throat, the noise riding on the evening

air, reverberating in the wet heat of late summer. "Real glad you're home, Evie," he added, smiling and taking a step closer to her. He was undeniably handsome, but more than that, he was perfect. Just perfect in all the ways that should matter to her.

Why couldn't her hormones buzz? Was she broken? Evie squeezed her eyes shut a moment, willing herself to focus on the moment. *Real glad you're home,* he'd said.

Home. Hartmann Homestead. Two hundred and fifty thousand acres of rolling ranchland, grazing fields and sparkling waterfront that bordered on Yellowstone National Park. It was nice to be back. Good for her. *Just like Ben would be.*

"Right. Me, too." Evie nodded, shifting from foot to foot. It was hot, but despite the summer heat, she pulled her elbows against her body, hugging herself, endeavoring to send the message to Ben that he shouldn't come any closer—not yet anyway. A kiss between them would complicate everything, changing the course of friendship between her and the boy next door. The boy she'd been friends with longer than anyone. *Or almost anyone.*

Her eyes searched for the bunkhouse in the foreground, but as Ben took another step toward her on her porch, she abandoned her search and backed up toward the door, trying to shake the feeling that he was the *wrong* boy next door.

"Uh, good night, er, buddy. I'll call you tomorrow. Thanks for tonight. Er, dinner was just lovely, and I had a great time."

It was embarrassing—how fast she turned on her heels. She was inside before Ben had a chance to answer, let alone make a move, but it was just as well. She wasn't at all sure she was ready for either response just yet.

Evie pressed her shoulders against the oak of the front

door, second-guessing, for a moment, her decision to whip inside like an insane person. At least no one—

"That good, eh?"

The person interrupting her was none other than Amelia, or Mia, her newly euphoric and recently engaged sister.

"We might be twins, but if you're reading this as euphoria, your own feelings have gone to your head."

Mia took a few steps toward the entrance door, offering a mug in Evie's direction. She raised it to her lips. Hot coffee, black. "I'm gonna be awake all night if I drink this." Evie shoved the mug back at her sister, frowning. But instead of taking the mug back, Mia pulled a flask from her back pocket, unscrewing the lid of the slim, flat-backed silver bottle and lifting it to her nose.

Mia poured the contents of the flask unceremoniously into the mug. "If you're pressed against the door like that, I reckon there's only a handful of reasons that could warrant your reaction. All of those circumstances remedied, in part, by a stiff drink. Besides, staying awake all night isn't always a bad thing." Mia winked.

"It's not what you think." *Not exciting. Not titillating. Just...boring.* Evie eyed the drink, then accepted it. The mug was warm in her grasp. Ever since making things official with her new beau, Antone Williams, Mia had been incorrigible. Incorrigible and deliriously happy.

Some people had all the luck.

"You're not trying to force things to the next level with 'Besotted Ben'?" Her sister hooked an eyebrow in her direction, then turned and padded toward the main sitting room, feet soft against the polished plank flooring.

"Hey," Evie called after her. "Don't call him that," she offered weakly. *Besotted Ben* was the moniker the Hartmann siblings had coined for him from the moment he'd made his affections known when Evie was seventeen, over a decade prior. Evie had found ways to avoid encouraging his feelings, and they'd stayed friends. Ben had always offered a muscled shoulder to cry on, and a supportive ear whenever she'd needed it. Of course, she'd never told Ben about *him*. That would have changed everything between them. Maybe it had been self-preservation. Maybe it had been the worst part of herself. The part that hadn't wanted to admit to what she'd done, because keeping the memory of *him* to herself made it easier to wallow in it.

Mia didn't answer, just walked away. Evie hesitated, pausing a moment before she threw back the oak door. Stepping outside, mug in hand, she took a deep drag of her sister's Irish coffee.

Evie hadn't told any of her siblings, as close as they were, about the voice mail her agent had left on her phone. No sense in reminding everyone that the worst thing she thought about herself was true: she was a failure. At twenty-eight years young, she might be too old for Hollywood, but she wasn't too old to assume her position at the ranch and become a part of the legacy she'd been born into. Hell of a consolation prize, if she could get her perspective corrected. Still, falling back on the family fortune didn't exactly feel good. But after eight years in Hollywood and not a major screen credit to her name...well, it didn't take a career counselor to analyze her next move. Right now, there was only one thing—well, one responsible thing—that could improve her mood.

Her feet led the way to the only path she could take. The decadent ranch house was behind her in five minutes, and she felt lighter with each step that put distance between her and the wealth of expectation there. There was only one surefire way to keep her mood light: a midnight ride on Lady.

Lady, a great dame of a horse, was a third-generation Pryor mustang, and her best friend, after Amelia. Against advice, she'd brought Lady to LA, riding her at every opportunity, but they had been few and far between. Now her proximity and access to the horse was one of the best parts about being home, as was riding for hours, uninterrupted, across the rugged landscape. Tonight the sky was clear, and she could think of no better way to unburden her cluttered mind.

When she arrived at the stable, she tugged at the door, playing with an unfamiliar padlock. *Since when had Nick started locking the barn? Of all the infernal ideas, this one took the cake, as they had never suffered any outright felonies at the ranch.*

It was nearly midnight, and she hadn't brought her phone. Connecting with Lady, and leaving her problems behind, was a little easier to do without the shackles of technology, but now she deeply regretted the oversight. She needed light to find the spare key.

Perhaps it was a reflex, grounded in the flashbacks of her adolescence, but she stared at the bunkhouse. If ever there was a reason to go and knock, this locked barn was it. She was dressed nicely, date-ready, in a patterned sundress that flowed around her knees. A bare section of legs slipped into heeled cowboy boots. She was glad to have her denim jacket but decided to remove it nonetheless, folding it over her arm. She pushed back her shoulders and made her way toward the bunkhouse. She would bet money that her brother Jackson, more at home with the ranch hands than in the main house, especially when his serious live-in girlfriend, Hannah Bean, was working, was drinking with the boys on a Friday night. So, if she wanted her midnight minute of solitude with Lady, she just needed to charm a few cowpokes and demand they let her in, big brother notwithstanding. Easy enough.

"The last girl I dated was an extra on *The Bachelor.* I'm allergic to oranges. I prefer cats over dogs." Brady ticked the statements off on his hand as he recited them, grinning with his challenge.

In the two months since his return to Montana, August Quaid had spent a lot of time living rough with the cowboys. He frowned, pretty sure he could spot Brady's lie. Each statement was more ridiculous than the last, but they all sounded like bullcrap to him.

The walls of the bunkhouse felt tighter than ever, rough-hewn logs sweating in the summer heat, but the general chatter of the men was muted, with everyone focusing on their guess. Instead of answering, August studied his fellow ranch hands. Jackson, the youngest Hartmann son, and his stand-in best friend since the death of the eldest Hartmann heir, Austin, scratched his chin and smiled across the room. August returned the grin. There were worse places to be than with these men, a found family of sorts, spending this Friday in precisely the same fashion as the last, the only difference being the drinking game.

"This feels like a drinking game for sorority girls," August said finally, exhaling before he took a deep drag of pale ale.

"You're just cranky because it's Friday night, and you're here with us, again." Alex, the youngest of the hands, nodded at him, smiling wide across his fresh, clean-shaven face. Alex was new to Hartmann Homestead but had been on the back of a bull since before he'd been old enough to ride. His interview, which involved corralling an unbroken stallion, had landed him a job offer before Jackson had even requested the background check. A hand like that would be useful this season, especially if this drought didn't break soon. He was exactly the type of ranch hand August needed to recruit and hire now for his own operation. He'd been away from Bozeman too long, and he was grateful Jackson had taken him back into the fold, no questions asked, so he could get his sea legs under him before he implemented the transition at Quaid Corp from fracking Goliath to a leader in organic ranching in Montana.

Across the bunkhouse, Brady aimed a crushed-up beer can in his direction, and it sailed in a clean arc across the room, missing him by a wide margin, to the delight of the other ranch hands. Brady had ridden in Jackson's crew for four years and was the closest cowboy to him in age.

"Just guess already. Two truths and a lie. If you guess right, I drink. If you guess wrong, you drink." Brady leveled his eyes in challenge. He didn't like August much; it was clear from the narrowed eyes and frowning mouth that tightened each time he glanced in August's direction. They had the same look: tattoos, beard, and white shirt tucked into worn jeans. Difference was, Brady hadn't flipped a modest trust into one of the largest land-lease corporations in the USA, leveraging every personal asset he had to self-make millions. Brady just had a nice beard.

Well, so did August. Whether he liked it or not, he was the bad boy of Bozeman, a title he'd kept despite his absence of nearly a decade.

But the distaste between the Hartmann foreman and the Hartmann neighbor ran deeper than that. Heck, everyone knew it. Brady lacked the two things August had cultivated and treasured his whole life: the trust of Nick Hartmann, managing partner of the estate, and the friendship of Jackson, the younger Hartmann brother, horse whisperer and PCRA runner-up rodeo champion. And no one, even the new hires, could feign ignorance as to the respect August had garnered from Austin, the eldest Hartmann sibling. The same brother August had made a blood oath to, ten years prior. Now, two years after Austin and his wife died in a helicopter accident, August had no chance to renegotiate the promise he'd made him a decade earlier.

"Look after the family if anything ever happens to me."

Especially *Evie, Austin's favorite and the younger twin sister of the Hartmann bunch.* August couldn't think of her. *Not again.*

Self-made fortune aside, August was a neighbor, and the Hartmann boys had grown up friends, even if the Quaids hadn't been as rich—far from it, in fact. Their income inequality had never bothered the families much. Anyway, the Quaids had been comfortable. However, the implication of August's father in a Montana meth ring via the DEA ten years ago had robbed August of what little respect his family had had, and at twenty-three, he'd packed up and made his own fortune betting on land leases for fracking.

Turned out his ability to read people, negotiate and spot shale was a valuable combination indeed. The oil and gas industry had made him rich enough to buy his own seat at any table, meth-dealing father be damned, and so back home he'd come. No evil eye from a ranch hand could ruffle him. He wasn't here to rebuild his dad's legacy. He was here to start his own, and he didn't have to apologize to anyone.

Jackson hadn't batted an eye when August had knocked on his door a few months prior. They'd picked up where they'd left off, fast friends and found family.

August picked up the crunched can, walking it the two

paces to the garbage can. The can hit the recycling bin with a clash and he straightened his posture. It was tough being back in Bozeman.

If the road to hell was paved with good intentions, the road home to Bozeman was paved in shame. Sure, he'd made a fortune, but at what cost? Setting up pristine land for oil and gas to frack? Against his mother's wishes, he'd sold his fracking interest and was intent on making a fresh start. Bad-boy persona or not. He reached for a new can of beer. Perhaps a few games of Two Truths might make the next three months here a little easier to bear. He needed to spend some time staking his land, and figuring out how to roll out his plan, courting state money for Montana's largest solar farm. He'd never been a very good cowboy, but maybe, just maybe, his legacy would prove otherwise.

So here he was, drinking with the boys. A bearded, tattooed, rich-ass cowboy that had earned the spot at this table.

"I don't think you're allergic to oranges, but I also know the last thing you dated was your left hand, so I'm thinking the most honest thing you've admitted to is your preference for felines. Drink up, buddy." August's deductions were met with a begrudged shot from Brady, much to the delight of the other six men in their bunker.

"You know me, I always did have a soft spot for puss—"

Thankfully, another cowboy aimed his crunched beer can in the direction of the outspoken Brady, the can connecting square on his shoulder with a resounding smack before falling to the floor. The two cowboys to his left applauded and the older, German ranch hand raised the beer. *"Nett,"* he said in his native tongue.

"Winner plays." Another cowpoke raised his glass in cheers, and August resigned himself to another long night of drinking with the boys. Might as well enjoy it while he could. Before he knew it, his own cattle would arrive and his barn would be staffed with a different set of cowboys. He wondered briefly if a new challenge would be enough to help him forget the angelic face of Evie Hartman. *Promises made to her dead brother notwithstanding.*

"I'm not playing." August frowned, waving his hands in refusal.

The men whistled and howled, with Brady adding an in-flammatory "that's the thing about you, Texas, we would see right through ya anyway. You're too big-city for us now."

"We could spot your lie ten feet away. You're about as square as they come. Bad Boy of Bozeman—ha!" Alex, another ranch hand, teased.

"Bald reif hält nicht steif," Sven offered up in a support-ive tone. The men stared blankly, the ruckus pausing just long enough for August to hear a tentative wrap at the door.

"Sven, for the last time, none of us understand you if you talk in German," Alex protested, bouncing a soft tap off his buddy's shoulder.

"Early ripe, early rotten," August muttered under his breath. He'd been studying German, more for the distrac-tion than anything else. Having Sven around to bounce dialogue off offered the perfect opportunity to polish the rudimentary vocabulary he'd learned through the apps he'd installed to listen to while riding. Sven was one of August's men and had maintained the Quaid grounds during his ab-sence. As for learning German, August was determined to better himself, understanding all too well the difference an education offered. Yes, he had an Ivy League degree—the meth money had enabled the finest Yale education money could buy, and it was not an asset the bank could seize—but he also had a thirst for knowledge. And he looked for-ward to telling Brady to screw himself in *haute Deutsch.*

"Show off," Brady frowned. "Typical August Quaid. Too good to play with the likes of us—remind me why you're here again?" Beside him, another cowpoke smirked.

Alex picked up a guitar, strumming a country classic and humming while two other hands, John and Jack, tapped feet in synchronized rhythms.

To learn the ropes, you had to fit in. It was how he'd gotten a grip on land leases, and how he intended to use his skills for good with respect to zero-carbon-footprint ranching. *Fit in, learn what he could, and replicate using green technology.* August frowned. Then picked up his beer can. If he wanted to charm Montana politicians and change the face of power in Montana, understanding the culture was an important part of the role.

"I've always wanted to go paragliding," The first truth was easy. Boring, perhaps, but easy.

"I've never broken a bone." The lie was out before he could hide it, thinking back to the summer he'd chased after Evie, regretting the worst decision of his life, only to be thrown from his horse. Damn rattlesnake had scared his horse, and he'd never caught up to her, wasting precious minutes to suck the venom and tourniquet the bite he'd suffered after being thrown.

He tamped down the memory. She'd packed her bags before he got back from having the damn arm set.

The cowpokes were mumbling between themselves, trying to determine what the lie was. There was one last truth circling in his mind. A truth so relevant that it choked him and escaped before he could come up with a better lie. "I'm moving to get out of the oil industry."

"The hell you are." The voice chilled him. He turned, recognizing the woman before he saw her, the four little words reverberating in his chest with a stunning familiarity.

John howled. "Liar, liar, pants on fire—she's got you. You gotta drink, buddy." The older ranch hands scrambled, recognizing not only the woman in their bunkhouse but respecting her lineage. Of course they agreed. Of course they thought his truth was a lie, because it was inconceivable that he'd ever leave Quaid Ranch. *Which was precisely why he had to go.*

Evie smiled at him. "You aren't very good at this."

Damn, she was even hotter than he'd remembered. Dark hair the color of coffee was twisted into a low chignon at the base of her neck, and her skin was a luminescent ivory in the low lighting of the barn. Her lips were parted and delectable. He wondered for a moment if she tasted the same. Teenage Evie had tasted like cherry lip gloss. Forbidden fruit had always been his favorite.

"Schönes Mädchen." Sven smiled, offering up the term of endearment for Evie, who'd long had a soft spot for him.

"Sven," she said, returning the smile. Evie was looking everywhere but at August, and he wondered if she was purposely avoiding eye contact with him. She looked the same as before. The same in all the ways that mattered. Her eyes, squinting at the corners, flashed with self-satisfaction. Her dress moved with her, the scalloped edges fluttering as she made herself at home. She pointed at a cooler, lifting an eyebrow in the direction of the drinks. "Who do I have to be related to in order to get a drink around here?"

Jackson leaped forward with a speed that risked a faceplant, tipping a slim-necked bottle in her direction. Evie accepted it and shifted from foot to foot until another cowpoke stood, waving at his seat.

"Winner plays," he said, blushing.

"She's not playing here," August started, unable to control the rush of blood to his own cheeks at the thought of Evie

Hartmann playing a drinking game with the crew. They were nice men, but this game had the tendency to spiral after a few shots, and they were already forty-five minutes in. Frankly, he was surprised he'd said that before Jackson had thought of forbidding her.

"You're not the boss of me," Evie leveled at him, lining her beer cap up with the steep back of her chair. The heel of her hand came down onto the bottle, and with practiced efficacy, she uncapped her drink and proceeded to take a deep gulp from the bottle. Gone was the girl who didn't know her way around a bar; Little Evie was all grown up.

Her insistence to play was met with howls and whistles from the men. "This isn't a game for Goody Two-shoes." Brady raised an eyebrow at her. For once, August agreed with the man, perhaps not for the same reason, but he was undeniably in support of the result. The last thing he wanted was for Evie to play Two Truths and a Lie here, with these men.

"Three statements, two of them true, one of them a lie. We guess right and we win, you drink. If you win, the guesser drinks," Jackson explained, blushing furiously in the process. "And don't tell Nick I let you play."

"Nick isn't the boss of me, either. Two truths and a lie. Seems easy enough." Evie sat back in the chair and crossed her legs. The track of skin on her thigh, between her dress and the top of her cowboy boots, was pearlescent in the low-lit bunker. A lesser man would wonder *only* at how soft her skin would be to the touch, and August, in a concerted effort not to be a lesser man, forced his eyes up to her face, watching as her nose scrunched in concentration.

"I speak fluent French," she said, mimicking Brady as she ticked the statements off slim fingers.

The thought of her fingers pressed against his chest, tentative but confident...

Her first statement didn't impress the men and was met with a groan. Brady rolled his eyes, muttering under his breath. Evie shook her head, guessing at the insinuated murmur, a faint color rising to her cheeks.

"I, er, never had an operation. No stitches, nothing." She clung to the last word of her statement, speaking it like a defense. The lie couldn't be easy to spot.

Brady crushed up another beer can, the crackle of aluminum offering a brief distraction from Evie's pause. Under his breath, he muttered, "Could she be more boring?" *Just loud enough for her to hear.*

"You're supposed to make ze statements a little...salacious." Sven offered an apology for the men's whispers.

"Using word-of-the-day toilet paper again?" Jackson teased, clearly ready to say anything to change the topic.

August was glad of it. The last thing he wanted was more "salacious" trauma from the youngest Hartmann on the premises. "I'd be happy to walk you back," he offered. "This game isn't for everyone." *Especially not her.*

He hated to see his worlds collide, or worse, be reminded of the world he'd never be a part of. The Bad Boy of Bozeman could never be with a good girl. And especially not the little sister of his dead best friend. The one he'd promised to protect.

"I'm a virgin," she said instead of accepting his offer, meeting his eyes directly for the first time that evening, her face stone-cold and calm.

Her final statement was met with a howl, the men stomping their feet and whooping. "This game's not for everyone, my ass," Jackson huffed.

"Girl came to play, boss." Brady whistled.

"Mamma Mia," said Sven, miming the sign of the cross. "Burning loins, indeed."

At twenty-eight? Still a virgin? August was the *only* cowboy not to howl, the *only* cowboy not to join in the ruckus. There was ruckus enough inside his own mind.

"That's a lie," he said quietly, thinking it to be impossible. How could she spend so much time in LA, goddess that she was, and not... The men were ignoring him, but Evie met his gaze, her regard unreadable.

"Je me suis jamais fait opéré," or, in layman's terms, *I've never had an operation.* He'd never been gladder to have learned French than in this moment. Gladder, and, as he considered the weight of her statement, more disappointed. So, her virginity was a lie. She was twenty-eight. He wasn't sure why he was surprised other men had had her.

Probably, better men.

She remained calm, confirming to all in the bunkhouse that Evie Hartmann was all kinds of grown-up.

Instead of taking his shot, August Quaid got up and walked out of the bunkhouse.

Two

The Longest Goodbye

"August," Evie called after him.

Her disclosure *was* inappropriate, but she had been goaded into making it. Everyone jeering at her, *Miss Goody Two-shoes,* and the worst part of it was that it was all true. She *was* a virgin despite how hard she'd tried not to be eight years earlier. She didn't feel a speck of guilt for lying to the cowboys. After all, it wasn't as if she'd *overtly* lied. Lots of people exaggerated their medical realities. Plus, wasn't there a whole doctor-patient confidentiality or some such nonsense protecting her biological, er, situation? And wasn't her virginity a medical reality, depressing though it may be?

She saw him, walking in a quick clip away from the barn. Hurrying, she doubled her pace. *How dare he be indignant?*

"August," she called again, this time layering a little more insistence into her tone. She watched as he slowed and eventually stopped. He ran a hand through his hair and put both hands on his hips in resignation.

"Where's the fire, August?" she asked, pulling up beside him, her chest heaving.

"Fire? Aren't you the one with *burning loins*?"

She cringed as he repeated the teasing phrase from the bunkhouse.

"What do you mean by all this? Coming into the boys' bunkhouse, roiling up the men with your indecent disclosures?" He paced in front of her as he shook his head.

"My indecent disclosures?" She bit back a laugh. He was upset about the drinking game?

"Telling everyone, telling them you're not—"

"—not a virgin? I didn't *tell* anyone that. I played a drinking game, and honestly, you're overreacting." *Like usual*.

"Overreacting?" He scoffed. "A drinking game with the ranch hands, and what would your mother have to say about that? Or your brothers, for that matter?" August turned, squaring his shoulder toward her, and studied her directly for the first time that evening. His eyes, with a blue that matched the inky, velvet cobalt blue of the night sky, pierced hers. A shock of dirty-blond hair fell in front of his face, and he pushed it behind his ear. He looked the same, but different. More grown. More *man*.

If the Hollywood execs were halfway smart, they'd make a show called *August Walks*. August Quaid was so attractive that women from all over the nation—heck, all over the world—would tune in just to watch him walk around in those jeans. She could see the promos now—heck, Netflix and Amazon would fight to license the rights. *This week, August walks around a supermarket. This week, August walks around a hardware store.*

It was a million-dollar idea.

Sure, August had been a very attractive adolescent, moving in next door when she was eleven, and he, fifteen. In a lot of ways, they'd come of age together. *In a lot of ways, apart from one.*

"And what's wrong with drinking with the ranch hands? Don't seem to remember you having a problem with us hanging like that before?"

"Before?" His eyes flashed and he raised his shoulders, pulling against the broad chest with the motion. "You mean when we were all kids drinking together in the barn?"

It had been eight years since they'd spoken. *Eight years.* How could it feel like yesterday?

She felt her face soften as she smiled at him. "Right. I mean, how many nights did I slink away with Jackson, meeting you on the side of the creek with the whiskey and a few stolen cigarettes? Didn't worry very much for my virtue then?"

"Not with your big brother around to protect it," August confirmed wryly.

Ah yes, Jackson. And Austin. If only they had been a little less diligent.

Evie shrugged, walking a few steps toward a white picket fence. She stepped up on the bottom rung, letting the top of the fence press into her belly, and leaned, arms outstretched.

"You used to do that," she heard him say behind her.

"I used to do a lot of things." She spoke the words across the field, not caring if he heard them. Out here, it was impossible not to think about all the things she used to do, including the inappropriate ones. The stolen kisses. The lingering cuddles on a picnic blanket next to the river. The time she begged for him to be more. More than her best friend. More than the guy she kissed the taste of her dad's brandy off. More than a bad-boy fantasy incarnate.

She turned to look at him, still reveling in the memory of his masculinity on her tongue. Masculinity and brandy.

Then she felt him move closer to her and looked down to see his hand beside hers on the top of the fence rail. Then his other hand circled around her to grab the rail, his body hot against the back of her legs, the curve of her butt. Her heart thudded against her chest. She felt his stiff jeans through the thin cotton voile of her dress, then she felt him lean into her, holding her against the fence as he once had.

She felt young and alive and not one bit bored.

It was the opposite of her date with Ben.

Opposite because *August wasn't good for her.*

"What are you doing?" she wondered aloud.

His hands left the fence railing and found her hips, and, with his guidance, she stepped down from the fence, spinning to face him.

"Don't come into the bunkhouse and talk about the other men who have had you." August said gruffly. She pressed her eyes shut and inhaled. He smelled like pine and persimmon. Spice, and rugged male.

He tightened his grip on her hips, and she reveled in the feeling of possession.

"Had me?" She said the words tentatively, feigning ignorance as to what he'd meant. She hadn't known August would be back when she'd decided to come home. Well, hadn't known for sure. He was a complication for her good-girl agenda, but a delicious one.

"Evie, please, don't make this—make you, back at the ranch—harder than it has to be." His thumb brushed over her hand, which remained braced on the top rail of the fence.

It was maddening that he would dare insinuate that she had anything to do with this being any harder than it had to be.

She could have been—had wanted to be—easy, had he not been so precious about her virtue. It was maddening.

The one time she'd been ready to give it up, and the only man she'd ever really wanted hadn't wanted her back.

She bit her lip, forcing herself to think more appropriate thoughts. More productive thoughts. *Ben Kingsley. The good guy, her counterpart in Western royalty. The responsible step in her adulting future.*

"Look, August, I get it. You don't have to pretend anything. I came back here because I don't want to be 'Little Evie' anymore, flitting around Hollywood, chasing a dream that's never gonna happen. I'm grown, and I know the difference between getting what I want and getting what I can actually have."

"What's that?" he asked, his voice quiet.

She didn't, *couldn't*, clarify what that meant.

Evie pressed her eyes shut. It was intoxicating being this close to him.

I want to kiss you. The thought was undeniable, but Evie swallowed the sentiment. "It's a new era for the Hartmanns. Nick has got Rose, and he's redefining our approach to cattle. Jackson and Hannah are working on the mustang sanctuary, and Mia is full-on into politics and whiskey these days. I just want to matter again, and I'm going to figure out how to do that. I'm going to be realistic."

"Realistic? Little Evie wants to grow up, but instead, she decides to come and play Two Truths and a Lie with the ranch hands? I don't buy it, Evie."

"Good. I'm not for sale anyway," she gasped, angry at how easily he'd seen through her. She twisted from him, but his hands tightened on her hips.

"Not so fast," he warned. "I'm not through with you."

"I decided to come tonight so I could see my horse. The barn was padlocked and I heard the voices—your voice—and I decided I could do with a drink, which, frankly, felt necessary after the day I've had." She was speaking fast, each sentence running onto the next. She was nervous to be alone with him after all this time. Nervous because he *could* see through her, and it was terrifying to think about what he might find.

"They keep the barn locked now. There are a lot of drug runners in Montana these days. Things aren't the same as before." August's voice was low and warm, and his thumb brushed her hip in a soft and steady stroke, as if, perhaps, he wasn't all that mad she'd crashed his party. The way his voice had scratched as he'd said *drug runner* stuck with her.

At least, this time, it wasn't his family. This was all getting real, and quick. *Things aren't the same as before.*

"I didn't know you spoke French so well," he added, interrupting her thoughts, the shadow of a smirk on his face.

Damn that drinking game. "Mais oui," she answered, leaning forward. At least that part was all true.

"I guess you are full of surprises." His thumb brushed against the pad of her thumb.

"Nothing here surprises me anymore." Except the feel of his hand against hers.

He laughed. A deep chuckle that started in his belly and shook his body. "Oh, Evie, you are a breath of fresh air, I'll give you that."

A laughingstock. The last thing she wanted to be was a laughingstock, and August issuing the chuckle stung all the more. She squirmed, pivoting out of his grasp, and once again pressed herself against the fence to stare out along the horizon.

She felt his hand warm on her back and sniffed as his chuckling ended. "I woulda thought you get enough fresh air out here, hardly need me for that."

"I guess Big Sky beats LA," he said. "But even I can

admit, I missed the life you breathed into this place. It's hard to see you, but I'm glad you're back."

Against her own will, she turned yet again to face her childhood crush. "Is that so?" She breathed deeply to slow her traitorous heartbeat, taking another step toward him. *Hard to see her?* He was the one who rejected *her* eight years ago. He was the one who had made her run to LA, any excuse to start over. To grow up.

"Yep." He nodded. "Real glad."

Then he dipped his head, letting his lips meet hers with an urgency that caught her entirely by surprise. She wanted to focus on the kiss and lose herself in the feeling of his scruff brushing against the satin of her cheek. Focus on the hot pressure of his lips against hers. On the roving hands claiming her body, exploring the curve of her hip with the brazen confidence of a past lover, although, as her virginity would attest, he had been no such thing.

It felt good. Right, and thus, frightening. August Quaid was her own personal brand of kryptonite and she could not allow herself to indulge in any more of her childish whimsies. He had been right about one thing: it was time for her to grow up. That was probably why he'd rejected her. She'd thought about it often enough. He'd said "no thanks" a little too easily. She could remember the facility with which he had left her crying in the field alone with her horse. She twisted away, breaking free of a kiss she could drown in.

Did only the weak have traitorous lips? Well, she'd be weak no longer. He wasn't part of her plan, nor could he be. She was going to take her place at the Hartmann table and stop letting everyone around her down. Starting now.

Still, she savored the challenge, unasked but answered all the same. "I'm not through with you, either, August, but don't worry. You don't have to pity-kiss your friend's kid sister. We're cool. I mean, with how things ended. That's ancient history, and no, before you ask, I never told the boys, so it can just stay between us. I'm dating Ben. Well, I mean, I went on one date with him. But I'm gonna go on more."

Ben Kingsley. The nicest golden boy in Montana. Maybe the world. As far from August as one could get. Not that she was comparing the two cowboys.

"Ben?" He froze, confusion branded across his face. "I'm sorry. I had no idea." His hands were gone, leaving in place the memory of his grip. She felt both cold and hot all at once at the loss of his touch.

His phone served a blessed interruption. He pulled it from the back pocket, offered a quick glance at the screen and nodded. "I gotta take this."

She nodded, chin out. "I'll see ya, August."

"Yep," he promised, walking away.

No lingering glance. No offered apology for the fevered kiss. Typical August, he always left her wanting more.

"Gordon," August said, voice terse on the phone, using all his self-control not to look over his shoulder to see if she was watching him walk away. He didn't need to watch. It was a scene he'd seen before. A scene he dreamed of more often than not, one that had him waking in sweat-soaked sheets, leg burning where the snake had bitten him. The snake had made it impossible for him to move fast enough to get to her. To fix things. To try and take back the worst moment he'd ever lived. Eight years, and it still woke him up. Still haunted him. Even though he should know better than to lust after a girl so far out of his league. He could make millions, but it wouldn't be enough. Not then. Not now. Not ever.

"I thought you were playing tonight," Gordon started,

calling him into reality, his voice clipped and dry. He was Danish and spoke with the affectation of a person who was always bored, regardless of the topic of conversation.

Shoot. The game. It was too late to make it into town now, but if he hurried he could go online.

"I am. Count me in for the second quarter." Quickening his pace, he made a beeline for the bunkhouse, forcing himself not to think about the kiss he'd just shared with the one who got away.

"I'll send you the login," Gordon promised. "Minimum buy-in is ten K tonight, but the good news is there's a whale in the group. He lost twenty K in the first round and is betting aggressively to make it up."

The whale was a novice player with a lot of money, the hobbyist poker player who bet on emotions with no regard for math. It was the kind of player August needed to parlay average winnings into major paydays. It felt good to earn money that had nothing to do with fracking. Or climate crimes. But mostly, he liked the fact that his involvement in the underground poker community fed his bad-boy persona, neutering any chance for him to get his hopes up with regard to women he couldn't have. Poker was a "low-brow" hobby in the mind of the Montana elite, so his involvement therein kept him from receiving most invitations he would otherwise be refusing anyway.

Tonight's game being an online one, mathematics would play a larger role in the bets. It didn't matter; August had always had a head for numbers. And it really didn't matter if he won or lost, only that he played. The splashier the bets, the more it would feed his reputation. So, he rarely missed a game.

By the time he arrived at his ranch, forty-five minutes later, his own crew was wrapping up a recreational skeetshooting session behind the barn. He went into the house and poured himself a mint tea. Her favorite. Maybe it was lame, but he always downed a glass before a game. He had a process, and maybe it was superstitious of him, but he wasn't about to risk it with a whale on the table. Ten minutes before the first deal.

Glancing about his room, he grabbed the leather messenger bag housing his slim notebook, the moleskin under his pillow and denim jacket. A glance at his wristwatch had him biting the inside of his cheek. Four minutes was barely enough time to log in, let alone get his spot. Evie, the kiss on the fence…it was precisely the kind of risk that could get him banned from the game. A losing bet, any way you looked at it.

He carried the key to the barn on a chain around his neck, and two minutes later, he was in the loft staring down at his horse as she stomped beneath him. He preferred to play in silence, and the barn allowed him to do just that. His efficient fingers activated his phone hot spot, and with his laptop powered up, he logged in to the private URL, careful to keep his webcam off. He didn't want to give anything away. Information was power, and the less his opponents knew about him, the better.

The other players were logged in. Seven hands were dealt, and the pot was already at $35,000. The whale, according to his right hand, Gord, was also in politics. In Montana. More specifically, the energy sector. The game had a lot more than one bet riding on it.

Gordon opened the game with a video stream.

"We have a few new players joining us this round," Gordon started, droning on with the boilerplate rules for the club games. "No-limit poker. By taking a seat in my game, you agree to abide by our house rules, as well as the rules for the specific conventions."

A dialogue box on the corner of August's screen popped up, blinking for him to click "I agree" before allowing the game to begin. As players clicked in, he saw the names.

Viktor Ivey. A seasoned player he'd won a few grand off the week prior, but he was seated left of the dealer, not ideal. Next to him, "Sailor," a new handle, followed by "Reese Chip" and "BigDaddy." August always played the same handle, Finovia, and was between Chip and BigDaddy, pleased at his proximity to the whale. Because anyone named BigDaddy was begging to lose money.

Poker jacks in the first deal, and forty minutes into the game, he was two hundred thousand ahead.

Nicely done, Gordon texted him after he won a white-knuckled bluff.

The barn was quiet. It was a darkness August found warm and welcoming. No one came here. Sure, the lock helped with that, but still, the Hartmanns' main barn had the comfort of a safe place. He sat on a three-legged stool in the loft, the only light the glow of his laptop as he hunched over a simple table. His fingers traced the initials carved on the scarred tabletop: *AQ + EH*.

He'd found the carving only a year ago and since then had moved his bets to the barn loft, touching the heart for luck, smiling at the adolescent EH who'd no doubt never thought her carvings would ever make it to the eyes of AQ. August Quaid and Evie Hartmann.

Forcing his attention back to the screen, he saw the cue he'd awaited all evening. The whale, excited. There was nothing incredible, only a king of spades laid by the dealer. Must have a pocket card to make a high double. August looked at his own hand, pocket aces, with one on the table. Rubbing the table with his hand, he clicked the "all in" bet, and four minutes later, cashed out with $240,000. Two hundred and forty thousand in clean money.

August shut the lid of his laptop, and with it, the last vestiges of light vanished. In the dark of the barn, he didn't have to pretend she didn't matter. He didn't have to pretend he didn't wish things were different, wish he could in fact be, as Jackson had put it, the kind of man Evie deserved.

He'd almost missed the game. Almost stayed a moment too long outside, risking his chance to hook the whale for another stolen kiss from *her*. He should be grateful she'd come clean about dating Ben Kingsley… She saw things clearly, understood better than he ever had, how important it was for people to stick to their own kind. The good girl didn't end up with the son of a meth dealer. Even if he'd made a fortune betting on himself. First, traditionally in the commodities market, and now, playing poker under an alias. This was exactly why he needed to stay focused, and, more importantly, stay far away from Evie Hartmann. He couldn't be with her, and the sting of that truth was enough to throw him.

Maybe one day, if he had his way with regard to the future of Quaid Corp, he'd earn the respect his family never had. Maybe then, things might be different.

Three

Don't Pretend to Want My History,
I Know You Like the Mystery

"What do you say, will you do it?" Jackson asked the following morning, the youngest Hartmann son riding abreast August on a silver mare as they made their way to the north paddock to check the conditions of the grazing meadow. The two months since August had returned to Montana had passed in a flash, and he still vacillated between wanting to spruce up his family's farm and sell it, or actually try to make a go of his insane solar project. To hedge bets, he spent his spare time shadowing Jackson, to learn what he could from the most successful ranching operation in Montana. In the past two months, they'd fallen right back into the friendship they'd earned in their youth, just like the good old days. Maybe it helped that Jackson had also been away from the family ranch, riding rodeo under an alias while August was away. But maybe, just maybe, August had changed enough to get accepted by the Hartmanns.

He swallowed the thought. Being accepted by Jackson, the black sheep of the Hartmanns, was hardly akin to being accepted by Josephine, the matriarch. In any case, he didn't *want* the acceptance. It would mean he'd have to actually choose. Actually try. Stop pretending his heart beat solely for Miss Goody Two-shoes herself. *Evie.*

August stared at the horizon ahead of him, flustered by Jackson's request. *Be Jackson's best man? At a Hartmann wedding? It would be the social event of the season, for the people to whom that sort of thing mattered. Not his people. The kind from the other side of the tracks. The wrong side of the paddock.* The truth of it stung.

"Didn't reckon you for the marrying type?" he said, offering a question instead of his agreement.

Jackson laughed, shaking his head. His hat tipped as he bent forward to stroke the neck of his horse. "Me, neither, but Hannah, I mean, she's something else."

Hannah had met Jackson when he'd ridden rodeo, operating under an alias in order to avoid the attention his name garnered. She, too, had secrets but hadn't kept them from Jackson. At least not for long. Together they'd overcome Jackson's aversion to all things family. More than August had thought possible, as evidenced by this most recent request. *Best man indeed.*

He smirked. "I guess you're not getting any younger." Warmth spread in his chest, and he swallowed, emotion thick in his throat. *What do you say, I know you've got my back, but will you stand up with me? On the big day?* Jackson's words were deafening, and on repeat in the quiet of August's mind.

"You don't have to give me an answer now. Just say you'll think about it."

August nodded. Think about it, he would. Standing up

with a Hartmann on the biggest day of his life wasn't an ask he took lightly.

Would it legitimize him further in Evie's eyes? He pushed the thought away. Kiss or no kiss, he didn't need Evie's approval. Wanted it, maybe. But he didn't need it.

They rode in silence, with the comfort that had developed over many years of friendship. August shook his head, remembering that Sven, his German ranch hand, had asked him if it bothered him that Jacks had disappeared for a few years, not even telling August about his pseudonym. Everyone had secrets, and Jackson had deserved to sow a few wild oats, if that was what he'd needed. And it wasn't exactly as though August had been up-front about his own feelings concerning Jackson's little sister. Besides, he'd been closer to Austin. Sadly, just not close enough to fill the void the bitter fight between the brothers had created.

With Austin dead, August had never been more grateful for the chance to get closer to Jackson. He'd lived too much of his life as an orphan. Jacks wasn't judgmental, and August never felt like the loser son of a drug dealer when he was around him. Just like that, Jackson was happy enough to find another black sheep. And so August had gained back a dear friend. The only dear friend who could see through his charade of pretending Evie didn't rattle him to the core. But it didn't help that he was also Evie's brother. The one person he had to hide his feelings from the most.

"Gotta say, man, I'm happy to have you back," Jackson admitted casually.

"Sure. Well, you know, I gotta make up a viability report. Profit and loss statements so I can do a proper job evaluating next steps for the ranch."

Jackson nodded, fully familiar with August's conundrum.

"Guess it's not like your old man is gonna talk you out

of anything. This decision is all yours, buddy." Jackson was chewing on a long piece of grass, his words clipped as he squeezed them out of the side of his mouth.

"I know. But still, I gotta do right by my ma. I'm going to see what the costs would be to make our ranch operational, and compare it to my solar farm initiative. Let the numbers decide." *Even if all he could think of was the damn solar farm. Well, that, and Evie.*

Jackson laughed. "Always a gambler, I see. Can't wait for you to find something, or someone, else to obsess over. I'm telling you, Hannah keeps me busier than I've ever been, but it's worth it," Jackson said, his voice layered in sarcasm. It was true. August didn't usually gamble, not when he wasn't sure he'd win. There was one thing about betting on yourself, and another thing entirely to take an uncalculated risk. He was here for all the risks, but he just needed to weigh them appropriately first.

"I guess I'm just gambling on the fact that you still might have something useful to teach me about horseflesh." August grinned, kicking his heel into the flank of his stallion, causing the horse to pull ahead.

"Got you bested there," Jackson shouted after him, making up the space between their horses in seconds.

"That why you asked me? To be your best man?" August pondered aloud, wondering if Jacks could be persuaded to talk of anything other than his happy relationship. The current drought was threatening to be a bad one, and keeping the cattle moving through the shaded valleys of the pasture adjacent to Yellowstone was a good plan. And August wanted to know if his idea was right. He needed to know if his instincts could translate to ranching, or if he should just stick to poker and whatever land leases he could find in Texas. The place where no one knew his history. But if the allure of anonymity was so strong, why was he reveling in this moment now?

Was it okay for him to want this life? To feel like he might deserve it when he knew for a fact he didn't? It was easy, being friends with Jackson. But maybe that had more to do with Jackson than him.

"I asked you because I figure you're the least likely to force me into the insane groom obligations… You know, Nick would turn a suit fitting into a seven-hour engagement."

"Suit fitting? I gotta deal with that?" August frowned.

"Come on, man, you're the only unstuffy friend I got." Jackson clucked at his horse and slowed the pace. August watched as the muscle in his jaw twitched and felt a stirring of pity. A seven-hour suit fitting *did* sound pretty miserable.

"Okay, I'll do it. But the bachelor party happens under the stars, not in a club. It's not my scene, man." August smiled. It was an easy compromise, if there was one person who hated clubs more than he did, it was the same guy who loved sleeping rough, out in the elements. Jackson Hartmann.

True to form, Jackson flashed a wide smile. "All right, can't exactly deny my best man, now, can I? But let's see what the crew says. And of course, I would need to see what my current wedding plans entail."

Jackson clicked at his horse, closing the distance between them, then slowing at the edge of the river.

"You mentioned something about a few beers? If we're gonna talk weddings, then I'm gonna need a drink." *Or six.* August smiled.

Evie listened to the voice mail again, wondering if the fiftieth listen might somehow change the message.

"Evie, look, I had hoped not to do this over voice mail, but I can't seem to get a hold of you."

Evie bit her lip. After scrolling her call log, she hadn't noticed so much as one missed call from her agent, and somehow her agent's effort to invent excuses made the message sting a little harder.

"You know, darling, I think the world of you, but for some reason, Hollywood doesn't seem to feel the same way. Even more, feedback that you're coming across a little too *provincial* on-screen, and you know as well as I do, it's hard to lose a bad stink in these circles." The message was interrupted by a lively soundscape in the background—boisterous voices, clanging dishes and laughter—and Evie took the opportunity to blink away a hot tear. "Of course, it goes without saying," the voice mail continued, "I'll keep an ear out, and you'll be the first person I call if I see any roles that might fit your innocent Annie Oakley vibe." More laughter flared in the background. "It's been a real treat working with you—please do stay in touch."

And just like that, her agent of five years disconnected.

"Press four to repeat the message. Press seven to delete it. Press nine to save."

I'm not listening to this again. With superhuman determination, she managed not to press four, but even drawing on every ounce of strength she had, she couldn't delete it. *Nine.*

Although she never wanted to hear the message again, she knew should replay it over and over and over again until the crushing rejection was ingrained. Little Evie, a movie star? It was absurd.

Making things work at Hartmann Homestead had never been so important. She had nowhere else to go. Nowhere else to hide.

As she stared out the window, a sharp knock at her door broke her reverie. Mia pushed in, hair in a messy bun, wearing one of her signature graphic tees with a pun on it. Ever since she'd moved into Antone's luxury ranch, she'd become a different iteration of herself. A new Mia. *Or maybe she was finally being the Mia she'd always imagined herself to be?*

"Another long day at the office, I see," Evie grinned at her twin.

"Right," Mia said, the dig not lost on her. "Whatever. I'm comfortable." She smiled.

Comfortable and happy, if her wide smile was any indication.

"I just got off the phone with Mom, and we're having one of her 'Hartmann dinners' next week. Themed, because, well, it's Mom, and she's bored. I think she said understated costume, so, heavy on the accessories. The whole gang is coming." Mia issued an eye roll, flopping onto the bed next to her sister.

Evie stared out the window again, the happy reflection she saw in her sister a harsh reminder of all the things missing in her own life. "That sounds painful." She grimaced. She was certain that this dinner wasn't just happening out of the blue. Their mother always had an agenda; she was famous for them.

"I'm pretty sure I'm busy," Evie started, only to be interrupted by a swift jab to the ribs.

"If Antone and I are going, you're going," her sister threatened.

"I'm up for it if you are." Evie smiled, an idea forming.

"Up for the soiree you mean."

"Up for trading places," Evie corrected.

"Who's bored now?" Mia smiled.

The whole gang would no doubt include Ben, the apple of her mother's eye, and no one entertained boring people better than Mia, who pretty much made a career of getting sheikhs and royals in the mood to spend month-long stays at the luxury branch of the estate: Hartmann Homestead & Spa.

"Are you seriously proposing a bait and switch?" Mia's eyes were gleaming, as she no doubt wondered if they'd be able to pull it off. Her question, rather than immediate refusal, was a good sign.

Evie had been home eight days. Just long enough to rub shoulders with most people on the ranch, but with enough makeup and the right costume, not even her own mother could tell them apart. Plus, the thought of having to flirt with Ben for an evening, again, was unappetizing at best. And in the twenty-four hours since August had kissed her, she'd been able to think of little else. A switch was the perfect way to bring a little adventure to the party, not to mention a much-needed distraction.

"I'm game if you are," she grinned. Mia studied her sister. "You'll keep Antone company, no funny stuff! I'm telling him about the swap—" Mia wagged a finger at her. "But if this is what you need to get Ben on the right track, I'm for it. Why not?" She smiled.

"Wait." Evie's head spun. "What do you mean, 'get Ben on the right track'—you can't do anything I wouldn't do." She sweated at the thought of it. Although she couldn't help but wonder, *would August be able to spot the switch? Of course he would.* Then, as an afterthought, she wondered, *would Ben?*

"It's a little late for that." Mia smiled, making a dash for the door before Evie could reconsider, or follow up with a fresh threat.

Evie's phone buzzed a welcome distraction. Maybe it was her agent? Having second thoughts, or perhaps with an "innocent Annie Oakley" role, whatever that was? She answered, sweating fingers sliding off the screen.

"Evie here," she blurted.

"Hey, answering on the first ring, it's my lucky day."

Not her agent. Ben.

"And why is that?" She pressed her eyes shut, imagining she was a coquette in a French film. She was a phenomenal actress, even capable of feigning interest where there was none. *It hadn't been enough for Hollywood, but this was the role of a lifetime.* For the right guy, anything was possible.

"Just wondering if you might want to go out again. You've been a little…quiet?" he offered.

Quiet? She'd issued radio silence and was incapable of answering texts with flirty banter. *To Ben.* In the past twenty-four hours, the only texts she'd wanted to send were to August, and that wouldn't do.

"No, not quite, just busy. I had a little admin to wrap up from LA. You know, the same old story, call the moving company, check in and coordinate with the transporters, take a pulse on where my things were, but I'm through with it now." Or she would be when she eventually did make the calls to check in on her worldly possessions.

"I guess you haven't heard?" Ben asked dryly.

"Heard?" She pressed the phone closer to her face, as though the added proximity might make his message a little clearer, or a little faster. It was a bit annoying, the way he danced around his news. Finally guardian to some new information, and he was holding it hostage.

"About your brother? Jackson's getting married."

Evie sank into the down duvet of her Queen Anne four-poster bed. Jackson, married? She wanted to be happy for him. No, she *was* happy for him. One could be happy for someone and intensely jealous at the same time, right?

"I guess it's just the first of a few marriages in our future," she muttered absently, thinking of Mia and her picture-perfect Antone, already in on a gag together.

"In our future? Yeah, I'd like that." Ben laughed.

"Are you misinterpreting me on purpose?" she pressed. It was the opposite of cute. It was maddening.

"Not at all, I didn't mean—I was just joking," Ben backtracked, the perfect gentleman. *Kinda boring, really.*

"No, I'm sorry, it's just been a hard day. Look, I have to go. I need the details on this wedding." Her mind was already running, and not in the direction she needed it to go. "I guess you're coming to Mom's party next week?

She had to clear her head. Go for a ride or something. On the back of a horse, she might feel a little more herself. Lady had that effect on her. And maybe August would see her, see how totally fine she was, how that kiss meant nothing to her, and how she was moving on, *no problem.*

"Yeah, I'm going. Save me the spot next to you. Really looking forward to it, Evie."

Evie stared at the phone for a few minutes after he disconnected. What was wrong with her? Ben was perfect. She was the broken one here, and she absolutely refused to stay that way. She squared her shoulders. But first, a harmless switcheroo with Mia. *What harm could it do?*

Four

Eat, Pray, Lust

"August."

He heard the voice carry over the wind, and wondered only for a moment if it had been his imagination.

"August, I know you can hear me. Wait up," said the voice, this time a little more insistent.

Evie. He stopped in his tracks.

Without turning, he put a hand on his hip, studying the horizon. He had a meeting with the Montana energy commissioner and figured he'd take a few snaps of the roofs of the Hartmann property. Jackson had mentioned offering up the barn roof for solar panels, and the Hartmanns' support could only help his application. Not that he needed it. But more solar panels meant more green energy. So, here he was, taking pictures. He turned and raised his camera to his eye, finding Evie in the center of his viewfinder, brunette hair blowing behind her. He snapped a quick shot. Purely to test the light.

"And just what do you think you're doing here?" she demanded as soon as she was within spitting distance.

"Picking up Jackson for lunch. Best man duty."

"With a camera?" She nodded toward the camera he carried.

He nodded. Her cheeks were pink, but he could still make out the freckles that dusted the bridge of her nose. Her eyebrows, dark against her pale skin, knitted together. "Well, I'm sure he's waiting, then."

August nodded. "Sure he is."

She took a step past him, then froze. "You coming to dinner tomorrow?"

Six days. It had been six days since her admission under the moonlight.

Don't talk about the other men who have had you, he'd said. But even without her talking about them, it was all he could think about. Even though he knew better.

"Is that an invitation?" he asked, studying the back of her head. She was tall, but still small enough to fit in the crux of his arm.

"It most certainly is not." She spun around, eyes blazing.

"What's got you so mad?" he asked, calm despite his burning curiosity.

She stared at him, her hazel eyes reading into his with an intensity he remembered from their moonlight encounter. "I don't owe you any explanations, August. Remember that."

"Easy, girl. I don't need your invite. Jackson already told me, dinner with your whole fam. And fan club."

Jackson had given him the heads-up. Ben was invited. So, tomorrow he'd get a front seat to their flirtation. Perfect.

"I guess I'll see you tomorrow, then," she answered, through gritted teeth.

"With Ben." *He couldn't help it.*

He could see the tension creep into her shoulders. Her posture, generally impeccable, straightened even further. "Right. Ben will be there. I didn't realize *you were his date.*"

Not the answer he was expecting. "I didn't mean I was going with Ben. Just that Ben was also gonna be there." Despite himself, he issued the statement like a challenge. Daring her to bring a man better suited to fire her up than himself. Of course, the fire had never been the issue. He still burned for her.

Her lips drew into a thin line and she nodded, then shifted her weight from foot to foot.

"Er, before you leave. I wanted to apologize. For last week."

That got her attention. It was the right thing to do: apologize and move forward. It was one thing to lust after Evie, and quite another to act on it. Even if she had kissed him back…

"You don't need to apologize." Her eyes widened, and she bit her lip. "Just—don't let it happen again."

Don't let it happen again.

"I won't," he promised, as much to himself as to her.

"Right. Fine, then. Let's just never talk about this again. I have a boyfriend." She bit her lip again. The sweetest lip he'd ever tasted.

Boyfriend, was it now?

"Doesn't matter much. It didn't mean anything." He turned to leave. "See you tomorrow, Little Evie." He walked away before she could have the last word. The last word to a chapter he was never gonna read didn't matter anyway.

"I might have something for you."

Evie felt a rush of nerves twist in her stomach. The adrenaline had been cranking since she'd seen her agent's name flash up on her caller ID. *Amber Atley.* No sooner had she deleted the message than her agent had called her back. So much for Hollywood whiplash—she had quite the case of it now.

"I thought you didn't think we were a good fit anymore?" A part of her knew she needed to be nice. That was show business. But her agent's words had stung. What had changed in the two weeks since she'd left Hollywood? Not her. She hadn't slimmed down or gotten any "sexier." She wondered for a moment if it was obvious to everyone that she was a virgin… *Maybe that was her problem?*

To be honest, not being a good fit agent-wise was a nice way of putting Amber's previous rejection. Evie could recall being fired by her agent as clearly as though it had happened yesterday. Maybe because the last time she'd listened to it… had been yesterday. She'd accepted it. *She wasn't going to be an actress.* It was a childish dream. It was unbelievable that she was twenty-eight. How much time had she wasted? Just to find herself back where she started.

Maybe acting was more about escape than art. Maybe she was doing the right thing by facing the music and the expectations her family imposed. Or maybe…she should cling to this last chance to escape. She picked up a pink gel pen and wrote her name in loopy writing, shading in the curve of her E with pink sparkly ink. Then, underneath, she added *Pro* and *Con*.

"Don't turn into one of those oversensitive actresses," her agent admonished, her voice sounding far away through the phone. "Throwing every piece of constructive criticism back in my face. It's just, I got a call about a part that might be perfect for you."

Con: people trivialize your concerns.

Evie hated herself for being interested in going back, but she was. She doodled a little more. "Go on, then." She was in her bedroom and crossed the room to study herself in the large mirror that hung over the fireplace. *No, she didn't have a label that said "virgin" written anywhere. That wasn't it.*

"A wannabe burlesque dancer gets stranded in the wilderness, then escapes with a lumberjack after surviving on her own for two weeks. Very Eat, Pray, Lust, if you will."

Eat, Pray, Lust? Wannabe burlesque dancer? Still sounded like a made-for-TV movie and not an Oscar-worthy drama, but it could be interesting.

"I don't know the first thing about burlesque." *Or living wild in the woods.* But somehow, the lure of a new project was enticing. Especially if Amber was calling about a lead role...

Maybe she'd rather face her failure in LA than face her failure here at home. Two weeks, and she wasn't any closer to finding love. If anything, it felt farther away than ever before.

Whatever she was doing with Ben was not going to work out. Especially not when every fiber of her body craved August. Seven days since his kiss, and she hadn't spoken to him apart from their weird two-minute chat this morning.

Doesn't matter much. It didn't mean anything.

And yet every time she closed her eyes, she felt his lips against hers. Taking his pleasure as though it were only hers to give. If it didn't mean anything, why couldn't she just forget it?

Yeah, come to think of it, getting far from August to an audition and a potential B movie seemed like a great idea. *Except that it didn't. She felt sick just at the thought of her determination to be a grown-up vanishing after one illicit kiss.*

He might look like a grown-up version of the man who broke her heart, but she couldn't forget the reason they weren't together. *He hadn't wanted her.* If insanity was doing the same thing and expecting a different outcome, she sure as hell wasn't going to repeat her naive seduction routine, not with the one boy who would pretty much guarantee a total ostracism from her family.

Her guts twisted again, this time with an unfamiliar longing.

"What do you say, Evie? You in? Ready to come back and roll the dice again?" Her agent was back to making nice, encouraging promises.

"I only just got back here. Remember? To rediscover my roots? Recenter?"

The girl in the mirror stared back at her, frowning. *The girl in the mirror was thinking about it. One last try for the dream. To grow up on her own. To find success in LA— leading man not required.*

If distance made the heart grow fonder, maybe a little trip to Hollywood was just what she needed to get her head on straight with regards to Ben and August. Not that August was an option. *Ugh. Yeah. Distance was imperative.*

"One audition. I swear you're perfect for this part. The brief says they are looking for ingenue sex appeal, and your Montana roots are perfect for the whole stranded-in-the-wilderness trope. I mean, I imagine a high school in rural Montana is basically like camping." Amber laughed, the shrill sound culminating in a snort. "I may have told the casting director you could start a fire from rocks, or whatever it is that gets those wilderness gurus riled up."

"Amber," Evie warned.

She didn't know the first thing about starting a fire, but she knew just the man who could show her…

"Look, one audition. I wouldn't ask apart from the fact that I really do think you're perfect for the job. Literally perfect."

"Timeline?" Evie reached for her moleskin agenda and flipped it open, pen in hand. It was nice to have *someone,* even a sniveling agent, tell her she was perfect for something.

"Audition's in two weeks. Filming in three months, in Canada. Project should wrap up quickly. I guess it just depends how long it takes to cast the lumberjack."

"All right. I'll do it. But if this doesn't work out, forget my number." *Just as Amber had threatened.*

She didn't have to think about the lumberjack. The chances of her getting this part were slim. She knew that better than anyone. So, why was she excited to escape again?

"Right. I'll text you the details."

It was unseasonably warm once again. Despite dusk falling fast, the air was still sticky and hot.

"Are you looking forward to seeing Ben this evening?" Her mom's question had resulted in a last-minute overture to the golden boy. Ben had been delighted that Evie had been the one to reach out, and he'd been available. Irrespective of his wildly successful ranching operation, he made time for her whenever she called. It was nice but it also made her uncomfortable because she wasn't ready to do the same for him. But here she was, having a picnic with Ben, and only hours after she'd extended the invitation. Her mom must be thrilled.

And so Evie had been talking for the better part of an hour. Because whenever she stopped talking, it was just awkward. They were on horseback. It seemed easier, inviting him to go riding, than sitting through another dragging date in a café. Somehow, on the back of a horse, she could just squeeze her thighs together and let Lady take her away. It was as though this date came with its own four-legged getaway plan, and she found the realization wildly comforting. Horses were a perfect distraction. Horses and streams of incomprehensible chatter. At the moment, she was partaking in both.

"Eat, pray, lust?" Ben asked, eyebrow hooked.

"That's not the title," she said, suppressing an eye roll. "Remind me again why I told you about this?"

"You like to confide in me?" he drawled, smiling at her.

There he was. The Ben she remembered from her childhood. "I knew you were in there somewhere." She smiled back. *This was Ben, the one that teased her, offering up good-natured winks and an open ear. This was the version of Ben she found the most charming. She could do worse than end up with a guy like him. She could do worse, but maybe he could do much better.* The thought was followed by an image that haunted her. The brooding face of August Quaid. *She needed to want what was good for her. Now more than ever.*

"In there? What do you mean by that?" He was riding beside her, his black stallion enormous next to her brown mare. Somehow, he seemed sexier today. Maybe it was the horse?

She stretched, her cotton shirt pulling tight against her chest in protest of the motion. It was nice just hanging out. Maybe that was what she needed to do. Envision these dates as friend dates, and give Ben some time to grow on her.

"I just mean it's nice hanging out." She smiled and kicked the corner of her dislodged picnic blanket back into place. "Your call yesterday was followed by Mom's. The wedding is officially all she can talk about, and now I'm fending off wedding plan obligations as fast as they are hurled at me." She smiled. It was easy to smile and talk about Jacks, her favorite brother.

"I bet," Ben smiled encouragingly.

She smiled back. It was safe talking about family. Heck, family was the reason she wanted this to work so badly. She cleared her throat, then continued. "I mean, I like Hannah loads, but it's like they're having a shotgun wedding without the gun. Like, where's the fire?" She grinned. It was true, in the two weeks since she'd been home, she'd become quite close to Hannah. The Bostonian doctor was always quick to laugh and even quicker to negotiate seconds on dessert. It was definitely an endearing quality, and Evie couldn't help but like her.

"You don't think…" Ben blushed, then pressed his heels into the sides of his mount. The stallion hurried his pace.

"Are you embarrassed to say it?" She smiled, squeezing her legs around Lady to follow suit.

"'Course not. I just meant you don't think this is *actually* a shotgun wedding type of situation, do you?"

"Like, because she's pregnant?" Evie spelled it out, wondering if it was possible for Ben to flush a deeper shade of vermilion. She'd never known a man to blush so much. She liked that she made him nervous. But she didn't like that all that thought did was trigger more questions. Like, *could she make August blush? What would that entail?* These thoughts did nothing but provoke a blush of her own. She'd likely have to do a lot more than suggest a hidden pregnancy to make the bad boy of Bozeman blush.

"No. Yes. I mean, I don't know," Ben said, his voice quiet over the click of hooves on dry dirt. He shrugged. "I don't suppose it really matters anyway. Jackson is more in love than I reckon a man has a right to be. In situations like these, why wait?"

More in love than a man has a right to be. What was that supposed to even mean?

Now it was her turn to blush. What must it feel like, to have someone love her that much? It was why she was here. Why she'd come home. *Family.* The one role she couldn't fail at. The role she'd been born to play.

"Do you think it's stupid? Me flying out for the audition, I mean." She asked the question tentatively, quietly. Unsure what she wanted him to answer. Then he clicked his tongue and nodded toward a scatter of birch trees a few hundred yards ahead, to the left.

"I packed some food. What do you say we stop for a few minutes? I'm getting hungry."

She nodded. She was hungry, too. And she didn't want to seem too eager to hear his answer. Because she was.

Once they stopped, Ben offered a hand to help her dismount, but instead of accepting it, she just swung her leg over the edge of the saddle and neatly hopped off alone. Girl power.

Ben was rifling through his saddlebags and pulled out two bottles of artisanal lemonade, still chilly. Circling to the other side of his horse, he fished out a small cloth bag housing what looked to be a few chunky cookies. "I asked our chef to pack us a little something on the off chance you got hungry. I know better than to let you starve."

She and Mia had always been the type of girls who didn't support diets very well. Perhaps that was why the Hollywood expectations had made her crazy. She accepted a cookie, eyeing the second package.

"Goat cheese sandwiches with toasted walnuts and drizzled honey and fig compote. I thought you'd like these."

She took a cookie and bit into it. *Damn perfection.*

"If you think feeding me will get you off the hook for an answer to my questions, you're wrong." She picked up an acorn and threw it at him.

Ben tied the horses to a thin birch tree and sat nearby, his back leaning against the trunk.

He picked a long piece of wheat grass and put the blunt stem into his mouth, chewing on it as he mulled over his thoughts.

That was the thing about Ben. He thought about what he said. He didn't act rashly.

Ben didn't kiss you in a fit of passion, pressed against a fence railing, then storm off. She swallowed the bite of cookie.

It was kind of annoying, actually. The long, pregnant pauses.

"It's not a hard question, just tell me. Do you think I'm making a mistake to go to this audition?" She was pushing. Not the ladylike behavior her mom liked. But still. Her mom wasn't here.

Ben pulled the grass stem from his mouth and smiled. "Sure is. A hard question I mean." He munched on the grass stem again for a few moments. "Way I see it, you're going to head to this audition. And probably, you're gonna get the part. So, am I really doing myself a favor if I tell you to go for it? Don't think I am. Yep. The way I see it, you need to just think about what you want, then go for it. But what I want? No. Guess I don't think it is a good idea to audition, push comes to shove."

A cold wave overtook her. It was an honest answer, she supposed. But why was she hoping for him to say something else? It could have been her mom. Or her big brother talking through Ben. It was logical. Sweet, even. But he didn't want her to escape. Only *she* wanted that. Because she was broken. Because something was wrong with her. *Because she only wanted things that were not good for her. She only wanted hurried kisses pressed against the fence. She only wanted men she couldn't have. Shouldn't have. Wouldn't have.*

"Right. No, that's a good point. I guess, I mean, I'll probably go for the audition. Very unlikely I'll get the part and it oughta get me out of some of this last-minute wedding planning."

"Guess you have a point there." He nodded. But there was something in his tone that put her on edge.

"Hey. Speaking of wedding planning, I reckon we better get back. Even if these sandwiches do look delicious, I'm just not hungry." *More to the point, she just didn't want to be there.*

"Yep. You have a point. Time's a wasting and I'd hate to lose the light for our ride back." He was unperturbed.

Always annoyingly practical and agreeable.

She took a sandwich to eat in the saddle. "Right. And you probably could do with some time on your own, I'm sure. Besides, I'll see you at the party later tonight, right?"

"That you will." He tipped his hat and smiled.

But she didn't smile back. She just nodded, still processing his comment that he didn't think it was a good idea for her to go to the audition.

As Lady settled into a steady saunter, she let her thoughts bounce around at the same rhythm.

Ben was annoying. The way he agreed with everything.

Apart from how important it was for her to follow her dreams.

She didn't say anything else until their goodbye. What could she say when her thoughts were entirely occupied by someone else despite her every effort to the contrary?

"Of all the infernal ideas. A costume party for dinner?" August had spoken aloud although he was alone. Jackson was the worst. He'd accepted the invitation on autopilot, glad of it the moment he crossed Evie on her way to the barn. But now? Forty-eight hours later, the dinner was looking like a bad idea.

He was going. He couldn't believe he was going.

"Damn it," he muttered. Of course he was going. A dinner party with the Hartmanns, Jackson, Mia, Nick and Evie? Throw in their spouses, and one neighbor intent on marrying the only woman who'd kept August interested for any real period of time... What could be less awkward? In all seriousness, though, it was important for his transition to respectable rancher and upstanding member of the renewable energy circuit. August wasn't stupid. The Hartmanns had a stronghold in Montana politics. It would be good to brush up on his relationship with the extended family before he submitted his grant proposal.

Costume party. What the heck did one wear to a costume party? August mused in front of the mirror. He reached for his phone, ready to reach out to the one person who could help.

The only person he wanted to talk to.

The one person he should avoid.

I need help.

He knew the minute he'd sent the text it was a bad idea. So, why did he send it? Why give in to his most baseline of urges?

He stared at his phone. Nothing.

Minutes later, she texted back.

Tell me about it. Wink emoji.

Emojis were flirty. Not that he had much text-flirting experience. He was used to high-rolling bars and after-work watering holes filled with glamorous women mostly interested in rich men. It didn't matter if you were a bad boy in those circles. Only that you were rich. Which he was. Self-made, and ridiculously rich. But still in a whole different league than Hartmann wealth. He'd have to prostitute canyons and rivers for the next ten years to even approach a fraction of the generational wealth their family had amassed. And he was better than that. He was done being the bad boy. At least, bad in the way that mattered.

He frowned in the mirror again. *What did costume party even mean?*

His phone pinged with Evie's message again.

People aren't going to *really* dress up. Just accessorize and you'll be fine.

He was typing an answer before he could wipe the smile off his face.

I think you're vastly overestimating my ability to accessorize.

I don't think I'm overestimating anything, she wrote back, adding a smiley-face emoji.

What did that even mean?

He definitely understood accessories better than her cryptic emojis.

What are you wearing? he responded.

Nothing.

His heart dropped.

Kidding. It's a surprise. I'm dressing up as my best self.

Whatever that meant...

Thanks for the help. See you tonight, he replied.

Then, for good measure, he added a purple devil emoji. Without being entirely sure what it meant.

* * *

In the end, he'd decided to accessorize with a leather jacket and grease-stained muscle shirt. Oil. It was what had made him rich, and there was the added benefit of leaning into the degenerate vibe everyone in Bozeman expected of him. He looked like a biker, with his full sleeves of tattoos and athletic build. And yeah, the long hair and beard kinda added to the look, so the costume worked on a lot of levels. He couldn't decide if he was mad or pleased that the matriarch of the Hartmann family found his heritage distasteful. Even better, he was still, more or less, dressed as himself. Simply *accessorizing* as he'd been advised. He added a pair of sunglasses, which he intended to wear indoors if needed.

Thirty-six minutes later, he was standing in front of the Hartmann residence, and, strangely, he was nervous.

Jackson opened the door wearing a gold-and-burgundy chunky-knit scarf and glasses, the two accessories passing his suit off as a Harry Potter costume.

"Right this way." He ushered August through the heavy oak door and down the hall.

As familiar as August was with the grounds, he was unfamiliar with the home, having spent most of his childhood sleeping rough with the boys, outside. Still, it was hard to forget the opulence of Hartmann Homestead. It looked the same but, eight years later, felt altogether different.

The home was as he'd remembered, polished wide-plank flooring, overstuffed leather couches draped in sheepskin throws and raw silk pashminas. Josephine, Jackson's mom, had a thing for candles, and there were easily one hundred cream pillars lit in the living room, the yellow light casting a warm glow in the space. Large oil paintings of Yellowstone National Park, framed in heavy, gilded frames, were suspended from the ceiling with gold cords. Their home reminded August of a chateau, and the family? Royalty.

The back of the modern ranch featured floor-to-ceiling windows bracketed by lush mustard velvet drapes. It would have been intimidating if August hadn't been wealthy himself. If August hadn't stayed in homes like this all up and down the Eastern Seaboard each time he negotiated a new deal with foreign capital. Heck, he was about to drop $170 million on his next energy project. This home shouldn't intimidate him. But. It did.

Jackson stopped, and August followed suit. "The place looks great." He offered the compliment easily.

"Thanks, but my mom gets all the credit," Jackson said, indicating the Hartmann matriarch. "This is where I leave you to find Hannah."

August grinned. "Thanks, man, um, Harry—I'm sure I'll see you around.

Josephine was seated in a white leather chair that backed a large grand piano. She was wearing a sheath dress embellished with long, beaded fringe, and her blond hair was pinned in tight 1920s-style wave-curls, held in place with a crystal fascinator. She smoked, indoors, from a large cigarette holder encrusted with rhinestones.

Then he shook his head. This was a Hartmann party. Those were probably diamonds. The matriarch looked his way briefly, then turned away. *Was she sneering?* For a moment, he second-guessed his oil-inspired costume, but then, he saw *her*.

She was dressed in a black dress that clung to her body with little room for imagination. Although why anyone might want to imagine anything other than the perfection she was offering up was beyond him. Her nose was dotted with a black heart, and she had rhinestone—maybe diamond?—cat ears to finish the look. Her hair was blown out in soft chocolate waves that fell over her shoulders. Nude lipstick did little to camouflage the perfect pink tint to her lips, and she looked very feline indeed. But something was different. As sexy as the woman was, she walked differently. A little too sexy, but in an obvious way that didn't remind him of his Evie. *Not that she was his.*

"August, so nice to see you." She took a few steps toward him, a wide smile across her face.

He swallowed, dry-mouthed at the sight of her, then straightened.

"Who wants a dark and stormy," a voice called from the hallway.

The second Hartmann twin arrived from behind him, looking stunning. She also had a black heart-shaped dot on her nose but, in addition to the makeup, had freckles penciled on her face and wore a flower-adorned antler headpiece.

"I'm Mia. It's been ages since I've seen you. Look at you, all grown up." Blushing, she thrust the drink tray forward.

Beside him, Jackson smiled. "And you remember Hannah." He was completely unruffled by the introduction of Evie as Mia.

August noticed. Noticed it was *her* right away. They'd done this before as teens. Swapping spots. He'd always figured it out before the family most of the time, as if spotting the difference between the twins was his own brand of skill. Tonight he saw through the charade at the first widening of her pupils. The first time she shifted her weight from foot to foot. But why the swap?

"I hear you've been suffering all my fiancé's useless factoids about ranching," Hannah said with a Boston accent, fiddling with a matching chunky-knit scarf.

"Nice to see you again, Hermione." He grinned.

The music was tasteful, a string quartet playing in the background. August scanned the room, looking for clues as to why the twins had tried to swap for an evening and to try and figure out if anyone else was in on it.

Ben was there. Dressed in a light blue blazer with gold buttons and a subtle gold crown. If you could classify any gold crown as subtle. Prince Charming—*that was cute*. He was talking to Nick and a redhead that August quickly deduced to be Rose. Nick nodded at him but didn't make a move to walk over. So, it was gonna be that kind of evening. Chilly indeed.

Antone Williams, recently retired NFL player and boyfriend to Mia, was chatting with "Evie," leaving a hand possessively on the small of her back, clearly in on the swap. So, the gang was all here, although Antone seemed to be the only one in on the swap.

"You're looking quite *dear* yourself." He smiled at twin he was sure was the real Evie.

Why the added facade?

"How are things? Now that you're back, I mean." It was the first twin. The cat. "Any more drinking games?" Her eyes glinted.

That was the problem with the girls—they told each other everything. Mia had never approved of Evie sneaking away, and had let him know just what she'd thought of him flirting with her sister back in the day. Of all the things he'd expected to do this evening, defending himself to Mia, while she pretended to be Evie, was not one of them.

"I just want to give your mom this. Excuse me a moment." He made a beeline for the hostess, and offered up the Château Lafite Rothschild he'd brought for the occasion.

"The 2009 vintage," he said as he handed over the bottle of red.

"August, thank you for coming to my party. Turns out we have a bit to celebrate this evening, and as a nod to the hilarious circumstances under which our future bride and groom met, I thought we'd all try on a new look for the night."

He'd known about Jackson's alias and nodded, but Josephine continued before he had a chance to answer.

"Although, it looks like you haven't branched out much from your brand."

She still had it. That way of talking to you like you were nothing. He rolled his eyes. Apparently, his self-made fortune of tens of millions of dollars wasn't enough to redeem him in her eyes.

"I'm just glad you didn't come as an inmate." She laughed.

"Mother," Mia, rather, Evie, warned.

"Just a laugh between friends, *dear.*" Her mom shook it off.

A suited member of the waitstaff passed by, balancing a tray of pimento cheese and bacon melts. He snagged one.

"Er, right. Well, I remembered you were a fan of the Lafite, so I do hope you enjoy this one."

He glanced at his watch. Only eight o'clock. This was gonna take forever.

"The bathrooms?" he asked.

"This way," "Mia" gestured.

He followed her, watching her walk away in the okra dress. How could she be an identical twin, yet so singularly attractive to him? How could he want her even now, as she leaned into a charade meant to hoodwink him, as though he wouldn't be able to spot the difference between the sisters? She was different than she'd been eight years ago. Grown. Womanly. And he wanted her with a hunger eight years in the making.

An enigma indeed.

Five

Dinner

August followed her down the hallway, each step taking him farther away from the bustle of the bizarre costume party and offering him more space to breathe.

She was nervous. It was another tell. Mia was better at faking that she wasn't nervous. For an actress, Evie still had a tough time acting in front of her family.

She was wearing spike heels, black, but he watched as the red soles flashed with each step. Click, click, click, she set a languid pace down the hall, her impressive balance giving her a sway. He wanted her to slow down. To talk to him. Explain what was going on. Ask her about Ben. All of this would be easier away from prying eyes, thus the trip to the bathroom. But she was nervous. Walking too far ahead. Brushing him off. He cleared his throat. "Weird being at a family soiree without Austin."

She stopped in her tracks. Bringing up her dead brother

was a risk, but, hell, he wasn't here to play. He wanted to see more emotion through her Hartmann mask.

"Yeah."

Her voice was soft. Quiet. He stopped walking, not wanting his own footsteps to drown out her ability to talk.

"Austin was the one who encouraged me to get out of here. Start my own thing."

August cleared his throat again, emotion thick at the mention of his deceased best friend. It was true. Austin had also offered him the push he'd needed to take a step toward his destiny.

"Quite the idea man. You had to give him credit for that," Evie said, albeit dryly. She didn't walk away, though. His gamble had paid off.

"I never got a chance to tell you how sorry I was. About his passing." His voice was still a little thicker than he wanted it to be. It was hard to talk about this stuff. Especially with her.

"To be honest, I would have thought you'd have come to the funeral. You were his best friend."

Ouch. He deserved that. "I was drunk. Drunk for days after I found out. And the last thing I wanted to do was be a drunken idiot at his funeral." He drew his mouth into a thin line, more out of anger at himself from the memory. He should have tried harder to make amends with Austin. They had just grown apart, mostly due to August's manic drive to make himself something better. And in doing so, he hadn't been a very good friend. He'd been the bad boy everyone had thought he'd be, just in a different way than they'd expected.

He was sure he was speaking to Evie. He wouldn't have made that admission to Mia. Damn, it was one of the things he was least proud of. Missing the opportunity to send his best friend off. To say goodbye. *To say thank you.*

"Sounds like exactly what everyone expected you to do. What everyone expected you to be." She said the words quietly, but somehow they became amplified in his head.

"Is that what *you* expected?" *He couldn't help it. Somehow, he felt like that lost boy around her.*

"I don't know what to expect from you, August."

She resumed her walk to the bathroom. It was miles away, but he was glad that she was taking him on a random detour around Hartmann Homestead. It meant more time with her.

"Yeah, well, I expect better of myself. Don't worry. It just caught me off guard."

"You don't owe me any explanations." She shrugged, her slender shoulders conveying even more disappointment.

"Don't I?" he asked, allowing a gruff undertone to layer itself into his question. He wanted her to drop the act, but she wasn't going to crack this fast. He needed to change tack.

"I know a good petroleum joke..." He spoke from behind her, so Evie turned to face him.

"Is that so?" She wanted to switch the subject: talking about Austin was hard. Her shock at him bringing up her deceased brother was very emotionally charged. But that was how it always was with August. He didn't sugarcoat things. Everything was raw and too much and not enough and incredible.

"Sure. But it's a bit crude."

Evie smiled, then, despite herself, let out a rolling belly laugh. "You're cute. Didn't know you were into dad jokes, they look good on you."

"Ouch. Dad jokes were not the look I was going for."

It couldn't have been further from his target, judging by his frown.

She smirked. "What's wrong with dad jokes?"

"I guess they just aren't for me. I never wanted kids. Not gonna have 'em. I figure the Quaid name can end with me."

Her smile faltered.

Never wanted kids. Not gonna have 'em. She didn't say anything, didn't answer. It didn't, or shouldn't, matter to her if he wanted a litter of Quaids or none. Per the gossip in the bunkhouse, she was dating Ben. Nonetheless, she was taking him the long way to the bathroom. There was a water closet just off the living room, but now she led the way down the hall, past the library, to the guest suite that looked onto the north meadow.

"Quite the place you have here," he noted as they walked down the hallway.

"Another dad joke?" She grinned.

The staff had lit candles all over the first floor, in typical Josephine opulence, but his chuckles bounced off the polished floors.

"Now it feels like I live here pretty much on my own. Er, I mean, Evie and I take the north wing when I'm not at Antone's, and Nick and Rose live in the east wing, which feels like a whole other house, it's so far from our quarters. Jacks has the grounds cottage, and Josephine lives on the original homestead—about an hour away. Still, the staff are terrified of her." It felt weird. Continuing the ruse when he clearly saw through it, but somehow it was easier being someone else around him. Then she didn't need to face the turmoil that filled her. That set her on fire.

"Me, too." He laughed.

Hard to believe someone so imposing could be afraid of anything. But she didn't say it aloud. Just nodded.

"Whenever she comes over, it's like the staff pull out a protocol binder. Candles and canapés—it's as predictable as clockwork."

He laughed. "Candles and canapés. I mean, there are worse protocols."

Did he sound sad?

"Is it weird to be here?" It was the kind of question Mia would ask, and she smiled, as she was truly curious.

Sometimes it was easier to ask the questions that were really on your mind if you had a little anonymity.

"Weird? Sure. I mean, it's not a secret, what people think of me, I mean."

She didn't say anything, just reached for his hand. He looked at her.

"When my dad was arrested, I know what people said about my family."

She remembered. Shit, her dad was one of the people who had started the witch hunt.

"You know, I never had anything to with the drugs. Never. I didn't cook it. Sell it. Hell, I didn't even know my family was involved."

"That sounds like a cop-out. I mean, you not knowing anything?" She dropped his hand. She didn't want this version of August. She wanted the August that was unrepentant. Hardworking. Honest.

"Easy for you to say." He didn't need to elaborate. She got the point.

"It's why I won't have children. I saw firsthand how badly someone who shouldn't be a father can mess up their kid."

"You turned out okay." The protest was feeble. She added a squeeze to the hand she still held.

"My brother didn't."

He never talked about Ryan. Never. If August was the bad boy of Bozeman, Ryan was the villain. He was in prison with their dad.

She dropped his hand. "So, no kids." She wasn't sure

why the statement hurt. It wasn't like it made him less appropriate for her. Less possible. Yeah, she wanted kids. But he didn't want her. And she couldn't want him. Not without fulfilling everyone's worst fear about her. That she was a lightweight. That she was never gonna deserve the legacy she'd inherit one day. That she couldn't make the kind of decisions she needed to make in order to be a responsible adult.

"No kids. I have enough to make amends for as it is."

"Here's the bathroom." She pushed open the door to the guest suite. It was her favorite room in the house. The library, modern, with teak finishes, had a bookcase that swung out as a hidden door. It was the type of room you'd expect to be dark, like a cave, but instead, the door gave way to a room with a glass veranda roof, sixteen feet high and bathed in natural light. Whenever she needed space from her twin, she came to sleep here. Well, not since Mia had found her happily-ever-after with Antone.

"Not bad." He let out a low whistle.

The bathroom or her? From the way he was looking at her, she had to wonder.

"You know I used to have a thing for your sister." He looked at her. Directly.

"Is that so?" she managed.

"It is. Still do. Just a bit." He licked his lips. *Good God.*

"Well, my sister is dating someone," she reminded him. Which, technically, was true. Amelia was serious with Antone. And, technically, *she* was dating Ben. Even if she wasn't sure she wanted to be. "And from what I remember, you were the one who didn't go after her. Eight years ago. The one who didn't want to, er, I mean, I guess you weren't that into her."

Evie pressed her eyes shut. *She could still remember what it felt like, standing on the banks of the creek. Pushing the straps of her one-piece off her shoulders and offering her-*

*self up to August. Wanting to be with him. All the way. Only
for him to say that he didn't think it was a good idea. That
he didn't want to be her first.*

The humiliation had stayed with her. She hadn't been a
flaky teenager. She hadn't made the offer lightly—in fact,
hadn't made the offer to anyone again since. No way in hell
was she going to relive her deepest humiliation. Or give
herself to someone else. Not like that. Yep. She had scars.
And he'd been the one to give them to her.

*She had jumped back on the back of her horse, naked,
seconds after his second-guessing. Clutching her wet bathing suit in one hand as she rode away.* She needed to remember that moment. Especially now, when he looked like
sex incarnate. Or, at least, what she imaged sex would look
like if it took on a male form.

*No. He hadn't wanted to be her first. Hell, he was prob-
ably only interested now because of her damn lie from the
Two Truths and a Lie game... That she wasn't a virgin anymore. Ugh.*

"Not sure why she'd think I wasn't into her." He was
staring at her. Eyes unreadable. Then she felt a weight on
her hand.

His hand.

Just a comforting touch. Just a brief pat, but it lingered,
his hand hot against her skin.

"Well, I mean, I heard you never followed her. Guess I
shouldn't forget the kind of man you are."

*Think of something else. Anything but how electric it feels
to be this close to him.*

He straightened. She could tell her words had hurt him,
but, shit, so did the memory of the most embarrassing moment of her life.

"Not like anyone is gonna let me forget." He looked

around the room. Anywhere but at her. His hand gone as quickly as it had come.

"Just through there." She pointed to the door to the bathroom, then feigned a deep interest in a stack of books on the nightstand. In fact, they were her books. But he didn't know that. She picked up *Wuthering Heights* and thumbed through it.

He nodded. "I'll just be a few minutes."

"Yeah. I'll wait," she said. Mia would have left, proving the second charade of the evening to be her feelings, growing stronger by the minute.

There were times when a few minutes could feel like hours. Now she was living one such unending moment. A moment of waiting. Of wanting to come clean about who she was and what she wanted. Wanting to know her own mind well enough to stand up to her family. To the little voice in her head. To Mr. I'll Never Have Kids Even Though I Have a Body for Sin.

And sin she wanted.

She was mad and sad and a million other emotions all at once.

She heard the water running; he was washing his hands. When she'd first seen him that evening, her heart had thumped so loudly she'd worried her siblings would hear. Or that Ben would hear. Her pulse wasn't hers to control. He owned her heartbeats, it seemed. *Damn.*

It ws impossible to be immune to the tight white shirt, perfectly groomed beard and blond hair tied back into a messy man bun. Grease stains on his hands, shirts and pants, he looked dirty, strong and so very bad. His muscle shirt offered up a view to some new tattoos, and she had a question about one of them. It was a fresh piece of line art, a tree of life.

"Did I tell you?" Anxious to change the subject, she bombarded him with the question as soon as he opened the door to the bathroom.

"Tell me what?" He tested a smile. She saw a dimple peek at her and she melted. Could you really judge someone for the worst things they'd done? Or was it better to remember them only for the best of who they were? Was she being ridiculous? Hanging on to her hurt? No. She was being smart.

He was standing close to her, but it was comfortable. They'd been silent for several minutes, but it was as far from boring as any silence had ever been. The silence was electric. Instead of talking to her, he was looking at her, and she knew, without a shadow of a doubt, that he saw through her silly game. Time to drop the charade.

"I got an audition."

He nodded. Still not saying anything.

Her mouth was dry. *Why had she told him? The only thing more embarrassing about clinging to her virginity like it was something precious was definitely swapping places with her twin at twenty-eight. Was she surprised he figured it out? Happy?*

"It's a good part. A lead role. It's not a big-budget picture, but Paramount is interested in distribution. And it's a small cast. I'd be, er, an aspiring burlesque dancer. Who gets stranded following a plane crash. Very *wild.* I was thinking of channeling my inner Reese Witherspoon and giving it a go."

"I think you'd be perfect for the role." There wasn't a trace of tone, just sincere encouragement.

"Filming isn't long, only three months. In Canada, of all places. But yeah, I mean, my agent pitched me as a pro-camping woman of the wild." She shrugged.

At this, he laughed, but then forced his mouth out of the playful smirk.

"It's stupid. I mean, I have a lot going on here. And I don't even know if I like acting, really."

He nodded. Still not offering his opinion, just leaving her space to state hers.

"I could just go for a few days. For the audition. It's in LA, no surprise there." She looked down. At her own feet. Too afraid of the potential judgment. Whatever reaction he had, she wasn't sure whether she wanted to see it.

"Thought you were done with acting?" He hadn't even raised an eyebrow at the fact that she'd tried to pass herself off as Mia. Honestly, the sad thing was that no one had even noticed. Ben hadn't so much as batted an eyelid when Mia had slipped an arm into the nook of his. She'd purposely given Mia a different perfume for the night, wondering if Ben might raise a besotted eyebrow at the sub. But no. He hadn't noticed, and, as such, the golden boy had received his first strike, failing at a test he hadn't realized was being held.

If Ben had said it, she was sure it would have sounded like a statement, but August had asked her. No tone. No judgment.

"So did I. It's kinda hard to make it in Hollywood, in case you haven't heard?"

"Yeah." He laughed. "They said the same thing about the oil industry."

He flashed a cheeky smile at her, and the defense sounded more like a challenge.

"You're infuriating. You know that, right?"

"Sure, *Mia*. And you're cute. Swapping places. Thinking I wouldn't notice. That your own family wouldn't notice."

"It's never too late to be what you might have been." She quoted George Eliot, the Victorian novelist, and wondered why someone else's words made her feel more naked than ever.

"That's an odd thing to say," he mused, reaching for the copy of *Wuthering Heights* she was holding.

"Whatever. To be fair, they didn't. Notice, that is." She defended her switch, although the fact that he was the only one to see through it made her feel somehow worse.

"Yeah, well, I noticed."

"And how was that?" She stuck her chin out as though the new posture might prove her point. They were identical twins, after all.

"Even after years of playing with y'all, I never ever spent a night wanting to kiss Mia."

Her heart stopped.

"Is that so?" She licked her lips. Couldn't stop the reflex, which felt as natural as breathing. As sweating in summer heat. In *August* heat.

He didn't answer. Once again, the silence spoke louder than anything he could say. She watched as he licked his lips. *Good God. Was he gonna kiss her? Good God. Let him kiss her.*

"And I've wanted to kiss you. Since I got here."

He didn't ask. Didn't pause another moment, just took her mouth with a surety that caused her heart to leap into her throat. He kissed her so expertly she forgot she was in her family's guest room. Forgot that everyone at the dinner party was sure the "deer" was Mia, and not her. Not that it was better for Evie to be caught kissing the resident bad boy, not with Prince Charming at the same party. She should push him away. Get him to stop. Except that she didn't want him to stop. She wanted him to keep going. All the way. Even here, in a random guest room. Because it wasn't about the where. It was about the man. And about the way that man made her feel. All grown up, in all the best ways.

Her hands explored the broad expanse of his chest, and he pulled away from her as suddenly as he had kissed her.

"You taste good," he said, shrugging his shoulders in an apology.

"You don't know the half of it," she answered without thinking. It seemed like something an aspiring burlesque dancer would say.

"I could teach you, you know."

About how to offer him a taste? A taste of what exactly? Her blood sizzled at the possibilities.

"About living in the rough. I mean, I could help. Make your audition a little more…authentic?"

"Help?" She couldn't focus on anything except for how much she deeply regretted whatever impulse had caused him to take his hands off her.

"Help you prep. We could go for a weekend. I need to stake out some land on the west line of my ranch. You could come."

She licked her lips again, in a dare.

"If you want to," he finished.

Oh, she wanted to.

"This weekend?" She looked at him. It was Thursday.

She licked her lips, liking the way he stared at her as she did.

"Yeah." His voice was gruff.

"I'll let you know," she said instead of *hell, yes. Always leave them wanting more.*

"You do that."

"I mean. Yeah. I think this weekend could work. My audition is in two weeks, so sooner is better."

"Friday, then. We leave Friday."

She nodded. "Tomorrow."

He dipped his head and walked out of the guest room. They had a party to get to, and she had a date waiting.

Six

It's a Dude Deal

For seven years, August had read about all things oil, from fracking to land rights. He could read a soil test faster than most geological engineers. However, somehow, the most "honest" job he'd had, making money hand over fist negotiating fracking rights, had made him feel slimy. It was as if excelling at that job had just made everyone right about him. That he was bad. Because what could be worse than prostituting the land around him for money?

"It's never too late to be what you might have been." There was something about Evie's quote that had hit home. She'd made it offhand, but it haunted him, perhaps for its optimism. Sure, he'd done some slightly shady—while fully socially acceptable—business activities to generate his wealth, but it wasn't too late to be what he might have been. The kind of man who could make social change. Who could make a difference.

First step, he needed to secure more capital. Which meant the divesting of some land. The easiest sales were the ones in which both parties won, which led him to Cody, the last of Jackson's groomsmen, and the owner of the land that lay west of Quaid Ranch.

Thus the invitation to today's ride. Little did his guest know that he was about to be on the receiving end of a proposal to end all proposals.

"You gotta change this here." Cody had his attention. A few years August's junior, Cody had moved to Bozeman a few years back. His family had bought the dude ranch that bordered on the north lot line of Hartmann Homestead, kitty-corner to his own land.

Cody was pointing at the irrigation system and frowning. Didn't need an engineering degree to sort out that it was decrepit, and it definitely needed replacement if August was going to move forward with the modern updates necessary for successful ranching operations. But what Cody—what everyone—didn't know was that organic ranching was just a small part of his plan.

"Yep, kinda saw the irrigation upgrade coming." He nodded, wondering if he should have brought a notepad to write down the list of practical ideas he needed to implement. Mostly, he needed a good number two. His thought was that maybe Cody might be interested in a joint venture.

The cowboy was rich in his own right, but the dude ranch was small. Since Cody had taken it over, they'd gotten a fair bit of press. Most recently, Antone Williams had launched a whiskey distillery nearby, and the ex-NFL player had hosted a ton of tours; players staying at Hartmann Homestead partook in some elements of the expedition trip Cody coordinated on his dude ranch. Klein Korner had been written up in *Esquire* as the "Masculine Retreat to Kick-start Any

Gentleman's Misadventure." He was booked solid and, per Jackson, looking to expand.

Cody nodded. "Actually, there's a lot you've got to do here, if I'm being honest."

"That's why I asked you over. Honesty. Truth is, I've been out of the ranching game longer than I've been in it."

Cody nodded and kicked at a bit of gravel. "Can I ask you? Why ranching? I mean, didn't you make a bucket in oil and gas? Why come back here? Not like you need to work, if *The Wall Street Journal* was right about the man placed third in their ranking of today's top forty under forty."

August leveled his gaze at Cody. "I reckon you know about my folks?" Sometimes it was best just to get right to the point.

"Sure. Your old man is doing time. I heard. But at least, well, from what I understand, they didn't cook in the house."

Meth houses were common enough in Montana. But his dad's operation had been bigger. He had run four cooks, all working from trailers parked on the reserves, which had made things complicated for local law enforcement. August had stayed far away from the "family business." There had been more than enough honest work available. If you counted professional poker as honest work, then later, fracking. As a result, August had spent most of his adolescence out of the house, either sleeping rough, camping, or with Austin. *Or Evie.*

August had made his seed money for the oil and gas gig playing underground poker, and then, as his notoriety grew, he was able to get invited to some high-stakes games. *Legitimate games.* It was a different side of Montana, but at least he hadn't broken any laws. Just a few jaws. But flipping his modest winnings into a fortune had taken a lot more work. He'd been gone a long time, but he was finally ready to earn back the respect of this community, tattoos be damned. The rebel persona stayed, though. Perhaps that was why he still gambled. Because he wanted Montana's upper crust to accept him for what he was: *a bad boy gone good.*

"I came back because home is where the heart is." It was the truth. *He came back for her.* Even if he could never be with her, he could look out for her. Protect her, or look after her in whatever capacity she might need. He'd promised Austin he'd look after his sister. And he was gonna. He groaned.

"You know—" Cody smiled "—I've seen you play before."

"Play?"

"Poker. We could totally host an event at the dude ranch." Poker with the boys? *Why not?*

"Why don't you show me the barn," Cody offered, and August nodded, leading the way.

August heaved open the door, the hinges complaining loudly about their lack of oil.

"I know. Oil the door." He'd add it to his impossibly long to-do list.

The barn was full. He'd ordered a wind turbine, and a series of batteries, and they lay in pieces on the floor. This was the part he felt good about. The part of his plan he was most confident in.

"Quite the operation you've got here." Cody whistled, taking in the batteries August had been playing with.

"I've applied for a government grant. I'm hoping to build on twenty thousand acres. Solar, mostly, but I've been reading up about some amazing batteries. That's, er, the other reason I came home. Spruce up part of the ranch for sale. And turn the rest into a solar farm."

Cody looked at him. Well and truly shocked.

"Gee, I had no idea you were into that. I mean, weren't you the oil guy?"

At least he hadn't said "meth guy."

"Yeah, well, had to make money doing something, and poker, even the hands I was playing, wasn't going to make me rich enough to make a huge dent in what I want to do."

"And what's that?"

"Change the face of power in Montana." He was nervous to say it aloud. He hadn't spoken about his plan much, not with anyone related to the Hartmanns. There was still too much that could go wrong.

But Cody was smart. He seemed to *get* what August was trying to do. "You're gonna need quite the capital investment to get this going," he pointed out.

No. August didn't need money. "I reckon I have enough. First-phase budget I'm guessing will finish at around two hundred million."

Cody whistled. "Not exactly chump change."

"Yeah, but there are some federal grants for eighty mil. And I think I should be able to cash-fund the rest."

"Can you?"

He nodded. "I can. If I sell half the ranch."

Which he could do. His dad had signed over the land and the family's assets before the trial. Everything was in his name.

"You're looking to sell?"

It was impossible to miss the interest in Cody's eyes.

"I might be," August confirmed.

Cody didn't miss a beat, saying, "How big is the holding?"

"Forty thousand acres. I'd be looking to sell half."

"I wouldn't need the house." Cody had jumped right to the point.

"I figured. And I don't need the water." Which meant that the more expensive half of the land was available.

Cody nodded. "You worried about what Jacks might say if I buy this land?"

The Hartmanns were always looking. Always buying, and the Quaid land was adjacent. But August wanted a clean sale. Wanted to get the money for this project without the Hartmann wealth. On his own. No handouts.

"No. Can't say I am. I'm tight with Jacks, and I need this deal to work for everyone."

"Well, I'm interested. I'll talk to our team. Do you have any details on the land?"

"Sure." August felt good about the decision. He wasn't a rancher, and for the first time since he'd come home, he realized he didn't need to be to make it in Montana. He could make the Quaid Corp a leader in renewable energy, and turn its land into the largest solar farm in the state. This bad boy had a good plan. And maybe, just maybe, she'd notice.

"You're going camping?" Amelia's laugh rang through the Max Mara fitting room, in downtown Bozeman.

"Not like I haven't been camping before. I don't see what's so funny about it," Evie said, feeling her cheeks flush. Mia was talking to her from behind the curtain of the changing room.

"You know how much I hate weddings." Mia was complaining. Again.

"I know that's a flat-out lie," Evie countered, smiling. Her twin was a total sap.

"Not as big a lie as you…being some sort of camping expert?" Mia pushed back the curtain and twirled. "What do you think?"

The dress was an inky-blue silk maxi dress, and it fit her like a glove.

"I'm not sure it says *wedding*." Shaking her head, Mia disappeared behind the curtain again.

"I mean, if my agent thinks this role is a possibility, I'd be crazy not to go. And she might have exaggerated my aptitude in the whole *starting-a-fire-from-rocks*—or however you do it—niche."

Mia laughed but didn't say anything.

"Really, I mean, it works out. I'm gonna just go for a little camping with August. He's gonna teach me a bit about, *umm*, fire…and I'm gonna be all set for my audition in two weeks. Easy as pie."

Her words tripped together as she hurried to defend her decisions.

"You know we're twins, right?" Mia asked through the curtain.

"Sure. Yeah. I mean, of course, I know. What kind of question is that anyway?"

"I just mean, we're twins and I would never judge you. Like, never."

Evie stared at the curtain. She didn't hear anything, so she assumed that Mia was standing still, just talking to her through the divide.

"I know that," Evie answered.

"Well, I just mean, if you were looking for an opportunity to spend time with August, you just need to be careful. That's all I'm saying."

Evie heard everything that Mia wasn't saying. That August had destroyed her eight years ago. Crushed her heart to the pulverized mess that had kept her celibate and single until now.

Evie heard the quiet purr of a zipper and then watched

as Mia pulled back the curtain a second time, this time revealing a blush-pink baby doll dress.

"That's perfection," Evie said, her voice thick with emotion.

"You heard me, right? About August? I don't want to be the one to pick up the pieces of another disappointment."

It was her twin's way of warning her not to get carried away with August. Not that she needed the warning. But still, it stung that Mia's fallback was a warning and not encouragement.

"Don't be ridiculous. Nothing is going to happen with August. We're just friends now. He doesn't think of me in that way, never really has. You should know that better than anyone—"

"—no, *you* should know that better than anyone." Mia wagged a finger in her direction.

Evie reached for the gleaming copper-pipe clothing rack beside her. With the help of the saleslady, she'd chosen three dresses, none as demure as Mia's selection.

"You know, I'd appreciate your support." She reached her hand behind her back and felt around for the zipper of her jumpsuit. Dang thing was impossible to take off. "You of all people should believe in second chances." Especially after Evie had supported, without so much as a raised eyebrow, Mia offering up her driver's license as her own only a few short months ago. A trick that had landed her a fiancé. And this was her thanks?

"I'm going to start with the red one," Evie mused, fingering the barely-there silk slip dress while she enjoyed her twin's speechlessness. She pushed her way into the change room as Mia exited, taking a chance to pose critically in front of the large three-way mirror.

Evie shimmied out of the jumpsuit she'd put on in a

scramble that morning and slipped the red dress over her head. She eyed her reflection as she pulled the dress down over her stomach. It was tight in all the right places, but perhaps a tad short.

She pulled back the curtain moments later.

"Damn. There's not a subtle thing about that dress." Her twin didn't address the earlier rebuke, but was now smiling.

"Yeah, well, subtle isn't really my style."

Evie took a step outside the fitting room and took a place beside Mia in front of the three-way mirror. Sure, they were identical, but right now each of their personal styles was radiating.

What would August think of this dress?

"I want you to try on the black one. The one with the slit."

The second dress, Evie's favorite, was a lined, asymmetrical-cut dress, the inside a cream crepe chiffon, and the outside a black crepe. It was matte, billowy, yet slit to the hipbone on one side.

Evie nodded and spun back toward the fitting room.

The red dress was off, and moments later, Evie was pulling the crepe dress over her head.

The straps were impossibly thin, a hidden sewn-in bra doing most of the work to keep the dress up. The silk and chiffon hung off her. It looked like too much fabric, yet, when she took a step, exposing a mile of creamy leg, not enough. This dress was sexy without being over-the-top. Dressy without being in your face. It was the one.

August would love it.

She pushed back the curtain and stepped out.

"You're buying that dress." It was all Mia said. As if her choice was a statement of fact, and there was simply no other acceptable outcome.

"Yep. I'm buying it."

Mia took a few steps around her.

"Everything going all right in there?" A discreet saleswoman rounded the corner, then offered a quick gasp.

"You ladies look fabulous. I mean, wow."

Mia smiled, and Evie followed suit.

"Yeah, I think we found our dresses." Evie winked at the saleslady, who was pleased. They had chosen from the runway collection, and both dresses were displayed without a price tag, not that the price tag mattered much to either sister.

"Shall I pull some accessories?"

Mia nodded, and the woman disappeared, humming.

"I guess I need to ask. What about Ben?"

"I'm ending things with him. I mean, I have to."

Mia audibly sucked in a breath.

"You don't have to do any such thing," Mia corrected. "You're dumping him because you want to."

Mia walked into the fitting room beside Evie's, and Evie heard her pull down her zipper.

"Pass me my stuff. I need to change."

So much for the accessories.

"Fine, then." She chucked Mia's jeans and top under the adjacent curtain. "I guess I'm ending things with Ben because I want to." *Wasn't that reason enough?*

"You know, Evie, it's not a secret people are getting tired of your antics." Mia was huffing, gearing up for a full-blown fight. "You really think Momma is going to welcome a meth dealer around the table?"

Evie felt her heart still, and not for a good reason.

"I mean, you call me, upset that your career is in the toilet and that you want to come home and find love, and 'adult'—I remind you, those are your words—then when a freaking Prince Charming comes onto the scene, instead of putting your all into that relationship, you jump feetfirst into a disastrous flirtation with the one guy who's ever really wrecked you. The man with the worst family history imaginable, and more tattoos than common sense? I mean, what are you even doing? And now? *Now* you're going back to Hollywood to get your hopes up for another audition? I mean, at what point do I host an intervention?" Mia's voice was shaking.

It was the longest rant she'd ever heard from her twin. Mia was not the type to judge, but instead of shopping, it seemed Evie had signed up for judgment day.

"'Disastrous flirtation?' Is that what I'm engaged in now?" Evie's voice shook right back. Sure, maybe the family didn't know just how much August had turned his life around. Not all the Hartmanns had a Google alert on the name August Quaid. But still, didn't she deserve the benefit of the doubt? And if she felt that she deserved another shot at Hollywood, was there really an expiration date on the support she could expect from her own family?

"A weekend of camping? Really? Just you and him? Are you so desperate to shrug your good-girl image?" Mia pushed back, not waiting for another answer.

"Just what do you think happens on a camping trip?" Evie said, her pitch rising.

"I think exactly what you expect. That's what's going to happen. You and him, cuddled by a fire, the woodsmoke—"

"This isn't a made-for-TV movie," Evie interjected.

"Precisely. It's not. So, stop acting like your life is. Make some responsible choices for once."

That stung. Mia was hitting where it hurt.

"Haven't I done that? Do you know how easy it would have been for me to sleep with a casting director? So many of the girls do that. But me? Never."

"Yeah, instead you act like sex is something so precious you need to hurl it at the resident bad boy—"

"I'll just leave the accessories here." The saleslady's voice cut into Mia's diatribe. Damn, that woman was really desperate to sell her accessories.

"You do that," the twins answered in unison.

"Evie," Mia continued.

Evie heard the curtains swish as her twin stepped out of her fitting room. Evie still hadn't unzipped her dress, classically underachieving in the shadow of her twin.

"What then?" Evie snapped.

"I'm just worried about you. I just want you to be happy. Ben, I mean, he's for real."

"August is real, too." Evie surprised herself with the vehemence of her defense.

"I just don't want to see you get hurt. And you're on a path of self-destruction, if you ask me. First and foremost, but running back to LA when you left only weeks ago, determined to never go back, then falling once again for August…"

"Well, I didn't ask you. So, thanks for your concern." Evie wiggled out of the dress and slipped her clothes back on. She looked at the two dresses on the floor of the fitting room, then picked them both up. She could be both: the sexpot and the elegant Hartmann. Just not at the same time.

Evie didn't wait for Mia, and instead went directly to the cash register. "I think just the dresses for now." She dismissed the accessories the saleswoman had replaced on the copper rack.

"Sure, of course," the saleswoman said. "So, did you decide? The red or the two-tone?"

"Both," Evie answered, smiling. "I'm going to be both."

The object of August's lust and Hollywood it girl.

* * *

"I know you're waiting for an apology," Mia started, after ten minutes of silent driving.

Evie shook her head. "You don't have to apologize for what and how you think." She stared out the window. *Shit.* The truth was, Mia was right. But Evie didn't care.

"Maybe my career has never been in a better place. And maybe by breaking things off with Ben, he'll get even more interested. Isn't that how it works with men?"

Mia snorted. "Are you seriously giving me lessons now? You be nice to Ben, or I'll just head over and do the job for you if I have to. Can't you see the whole family is ready to see you succeed at something? I love you, Evie, but damn, you have to stop hurting yourself."

Evie didn't answer, just stared at the road. Another fifteen minutes, and she could be on the back of her horse, riding on her own.

Then she got a different idea.

"You know what? I think I'll get out here, and Uber back." Evie nodded toward Chez Pierre, on the edge of town. She loved that restaurant.

Mia blanched. Then pulled over. "Fine, Evie." She sighed, resigned.

Evie got out and slammed the door, perhaps a little too hard. Mia didn't even look back, just pulled away from the curb and drove away.

Evie had her phone out in seconds. Twelve percent battery. It wasn't ideal, but should be enough to get her another ride. Yes, she'd hoped for her family's respect, but for the first time in ages, she'd realized that in order to have that, she needed to respect herself first. And that started by getting her affairs in order.

So she texted *him*.

Her own resident bad boy.

* * *

His phone pinged with Evie's text. Are you headed to town?

Yeah, actually, gotta pick up some batteries.

Batteries? Not true. He had been in town to meet with his lawyer, but he was home again. He couldn't have thought of anything better than batteries?
For the camping lanterns, he added.
As if the clarification made it better.

I'm just getting a coffee. Chez Pierre.

August smiled. Then he headed for his truck. From the driver's seat, he sent back a purple devil emoji.

He'd lied. He wasn't, in fact, going into town, but when she'd texted him, he had responded before his brain had succeeded in reminding him to play things cool.

Chez Pierre was a decent restaurant. French food served with a thick side of French pretension. He spotted Evie right away. She was sitting at the window reading a book. It made him smile. Most women would be on their phones, or primping or applying lipstick, but Evie was reading.

He walked over to the table, waving away the offer of help from the front of house.

"Evie." He nodded to her. "Thanks for the invite. This place serves a mean cup of coffee."

She just smiled.

"Bought my dress for the wedding. I was in town with Mia."

"Sure." He nodded again, though her words didn't explain why she'd called him to meet her, or where Mia was now.

The waiter came by and brought with him two cappuccinos.

"I ordered for you." She smiled.

"Thanks." He smiled back, meaning it.

It was 2 p.m., and while her text had caught him by surprise, he hadn't hesitated to get into his truck. If Evie was asking him for coffee, he was not stopping to ask questions. Not even the questions he *should* ask. Such as, what if someone saw them out together? What would people say? What would Austin have said? Or Jackson? Or worse, Josephine...

"So, you ready?" he asked.

"For the camping trip? Yeah. Sure. I was born ready." She smiled. "You?"

Ready to spend a night with her, under the stars? He swallowed. "Sure."

She leaned forward, reaching for her coffee. Under the table, her knee brushed against his. He had never felt so aware of his limbs. *Or hers.*

"Looks like weather is gonna bless us. Should be a clear night, so we can work on all sorts of tricks for your audition."

She took another sip of her latte, and a bit of foam stuck to her lip. He stared at it, until she brushed her mouth with the back of her hand.

His mouth went dry.

"What were you doing in town—besides getting batteries?" she asked, pinning him with those hazel eyes.

He was glad of the question. Wanted to tell her himself before she heard from Cody, or worse, her brother. Evie had always hated getting news from her brothers.

"I was with my lawyer."

"Oh, is it about your dad?" She took a sip of coffee, eyes wide.

Of course her head went to that. The worst part about him. For a moment, he considered letting her think his family was getting out on parole. But no. He didn't want to play games. Maybe he couldn't have the kind of relationship he wanted with Evie, but, damn it, he'd take an honest one.

"No. I am selling the ranch."

He watched her face. Trying to gauge the reaction.

"C'est tout bon?" an intrusive waiter passed for the fourth time to ask.

"Oui," Evie managed to answer, face pale.

"Not the whole thing," he started. "I'm selling twenty thousand acres. Turning the other half into a solar farm. I know it's a big change—"

"I think it's amazing." She smiled at him, and for the first time that week, he felt sure of himself in all the right ways.

"I'll let you know how it turns out. How about you? Getting ready for your big audition?"

"It's been tough with my wedding duties, but I've been trying." She bit her lower lip and it was all he good do not to lean forward and kiss her. *Prying eyes*, he reminded himself. "Would you mind? If we run a few lines together? I mean, on our trip." She was running her words together. She was looking at him, then away, a classic flirtation, but as appealing as it was obvious. Then she broke the pattern and reached into a bag, pulling out a leather folio.

"Here is the scene I'm reading."

He reached for the papers. The scene was titled "Up in Flames." *How appropriate.* He knew they would be playing with fire tonight, on their camping trip.

August scanned the first page, fighting off a blush.

"Er, the audition also involves a screen test with the male lead. So, they sent me some of the spicy scenes."

He could feel the blood rush to his cheeks. And other

places. "Sure, that makes sense," he managed to answer. "But maybe we should rehearse these on our trip. I wouldn't want to give people the wrong idea."

She pushed a strand of hair away from her face, tucking it behind an ear. "You'll really read these lines with me?" she asked, voice a little breathy.

August nodded, then looked around the café. The other diners seemed oblivious to their interaction. So they should be, there was nothing untoward happening. Certainly, the electricity he felt was invisible to others, but that was how electricity worked. You couldn't see it, only feel it.

"Whatever I can do to help you get this part," he answered earnestly.

Evie reached across the table and took his hand, offering a quick squeeze. "Thanks, August, you have no idea how much this means to me."

He nodded. Thing was, he did.

Seven

All the Wine

"You look nice tonight."

There it was again. Nice. You look nice. The weather is nice. *Nice nice nice.* Just like her date.

He was perfectly *nice.*

Where were the fireworks? Where was the electricity? Where was the burning that kept her up at night, obsessing about the line of a tattoo, or the bulge she'd tried not to feel or stare at when pressed against a fence post... Or the lines she couldn't wait to recite, the chemistry she was dying to rehearse...

But instead of frowning, she pasted on a smile. Ben was the nice guy. This was the match her mother had dreamed of. The first son of the second wealthiest family in Montana. A Hartmann-Kingsley marriage would be the beginning of a new empire. A *nice* new empire. But an empire she didn't want. There was no getting past that.

"Thanks. You look nice, too."

God, was this her life now? *You look nice, too. Let's get canapés and feed ducks and never make a politically incorrect statement. As was appropriate for the Hartmann and Kingsley clans respectively.*

"I haven't eaten here before," he mused, staring at the menu of Chez Pierre. His hands reached to his already-straight tie, repositioning it for the fourth time.

"Let's get the snails. Very authentically French," she said, winking conspiratorially. Snails and a lot of wine. All the wine actually. That would be a good start. Then she could stop thinking about the coffee she'd had here earlier that day. With a man in a white T-shirt and jeans. And eyes that *saw* her. And instead of the constant second-guessing of her ability to decide what was right for her future, he'd offered to help her rehearse...

She'd show Mia. Give Ben her honest best shot. But at the end of the day, she wanted to be authentic. It was just tough to be confident about a decision, such as pursing August, when the people she loved most didn't support it.

Evie smiled at the waiter, a nice chap she'd met through Pierre—afterall she was here for the second time today—when Ben cut in.

"We'll have the snails to start. And what kind of beer do you have on tap?"

"Maybe we could order a bottle of chardonnay?" Evie suggested. "Est-ce que je pourrias voir la carte?"

The waiter smiled. *"Oui, mademoiselle."*

"Really, I just want a beer. Make it two," Ben said, dismissing the waiter, lips pursed.

"Of course." The waiter nodded.

Evie pulled at the neckline of her dress. She felt hot, or maybe it was just her nerves. She'd asked Ben to dinner to end this. They'd been out at least four times in less than three weeks, and it felt more like a dance than a courtship, with her dodging any attempts at a midnight kiss or hand-holding at the end of the night.

It had gotten to a point where dessert was causing her anxiety. *Dessert.* She had gotten into the habit of ordering coffee, then aperitifs, then a final call of limoncello, anything to delay the awkward moment on her doorstep where she would thank Ben for dinner, then rush inside without kissing him.

But now? It was she who'd initiated the dinner, and not because she'd wanted to, but because of Mia. Or, rather, what Mia had said.

Her twin had been right. Yes, part of her wanted a clean break before her camping weekend with August. Because maybe something would happen. Because maybe she *wanted* something to happen. *With August.* But a bigger part of her was still questioning everything. The part of her she hated. The part of her that was a reflection of her sister. The Hartmann part.

But this was a dance she couldn't keep up with. Still, as much as she didn't want to lead Ben on, she didn't want to let down her family. And yet, she couldn't bear to let herself down one moment longer.

"You're really gonna go, then? To the audition?" He was still smiling, but it irked her.

"Yep. In two weeks. But first, a quick camping trip this weekend to reconnect to the wilderness for a few days."

"As you come back now, right?" He smiled. He didn't ask for details about her camping trip. Thankfully.

The waiter arrived with two beers. Annoying. She'd asked for wine but perhaps not clearly enough. She should really brush up on her French.

"I've, er, got to pee. Please excuse me." Try as she might,

all she could think about was escaping to the bathroom. Because she knew she shouldn't be there.

Ben just nodded and picked up the menu again.

The bathroom at Chez Pierre had only a few stalls. In the stall next to hers, she heard another woman on the phone.

"I think he's gonna propose."

The woman was squealing. Happy. How you should be when on a date with the man you might marry.

"When a freaking Prince Charming comes onto the scene, instead of putting your all into that relationship, you jump feetfirst into a disastrous flirtation with the one guy who's ever really wrecked you." Mia's words echoed in her brain.

"I wish you were here. So you could film it. I gotta focus on not crying. This is freaking amazing."

The woman was hyperventilating. And had a kinda annoying, high-pitched voice.

Evie heard her leave the stall and then turn on the taps. She'd passed that awkward moment. The moment where she'd been in the stall far too long. She needed to get out. Flush maybe, despite the fact that she hadn't used the toilet. She didn't want Miss Newly Engaged to think she was the kind of person who didn't resolve her own business.

She didn't want anyone to think that about her.

She flushed a napkin down the toilet, then made her way to the sink. The girl was blonde, her hair curled in tight ringlets. She was younger than Evie and was intent on re-applying her lipstick.

"Er, congrats, it sounds like," Evie managed, activating the automatic tap with the wave of her hand.

The girl spun and smiled. "Thanks. Pretty sure it's gonna happen tonight."

After soaping up, Evie gave her hands a rinse. Then she

dried off with a towel from a basket on the counter. "That's great." She forced a smile.

"I know, right? I've wanted to marry this guy pretty much since the day we met."

"I'm happy for you," Evie said, feeling a bit empty. Not even her bathroom neighbor had subscribed to the whole love-comes-softly mentality. She was marrying the love of her life.

For a quick second, Evie wished she could trade places with *her*. The unnamed blonde who was about to be on the receiving end of a proposal she *dreamed* of accepting.

"Don't worry, it will happen for you, too. You're *real* pretty." The girl smiled and spun on her heels.

Evie stared for a long moment in the mirror before leaving the bathroom. *Real pretty.* She didn't want that to be the best thing about her. But what should she do if it was?

"Here's the thing, Ben. I'm not sure this is gonna work." Amazingly, she'd managed to get the statement out without backing down.

Sometimes, when you had a bad feeling, you just needed to lean into it. And just because she was calling things off with Ben didn't mean she was abandoning her plan to adult. It just meant abandoning the plan to adult with *Ben*.

She could be a good daughter and find other ways to fill her Hartmann shoes. She could get into horse breeding with Jackson. She loved horses.

Yes. A celibate horse lady. With a penchant for politics and bad boys. She was betting zero on actually getting the part in Hollywood. The audition was more an excuse just to get out of Dodge and maybe make this whole Ben thing less awkward. Besides, what was one more rejection?

It was fine, as long as it didn't come from August. Her butterflies about tonight's camping trip were there in full force.

Yep. Band-Aid was coming off now. Especially when her damn subconscious couldn't bite back the odd biting remark. Band-Aid *off.* Quick and painful, but then over.

"Not sure it's gonna work?" He repeated her statement as a question.

Seriously. How much clearer could she be? Perhaps she should have taken Mia up on her offer to do this for her.

"I just think we're better as friends," she tried again, nodding, hopefully with what looked like encouragement.

"It's not you, it's me," she added.

It's August, her subconscious tacked on for good measure.

"All right, Evie." Ben sighed. He pushed his plate in front of him and arranged his cutlery neatly at the nine o'clock position.

She felt a pang of guilt. He was taking this like a champ.

She took a sip of her beer. If she was going to make a dent in this bottle, she had to get drinking.

"All right," she parroted, nodding. The relief was already palatable.

Ben laughed. A light and easy laugh.

"No, I meant, all right, I know you. You always take a while to get used to change. And, I mean, this is a lot of change. Mia is now in a serious relationship. Jacks and Nick, both getting married. This is huge for your family. I can see how you might want to take things slow with me."

No no no.

She chose her next words carefully—so there would be no mistaking their meaning. "Actually, this isn't about taking things slow. I just don't think we have a connection."

Ben laughed again and shrugged. Apparently, she hadn't chosen her words carefully enough. "Evie, that's the thing. I know you. Love your family, fit in. You know my family, and there are no surprises."

Apart from the fact that there were. For example, the surprise that she was currently lusting after her unavailable bad-boy neighbor. "Sometimes surprises can be a good thing."

"Well, then why don't you surprise *yourself* and stop self-sabotaging."

He signaled for the check and smiled at her.

"I really don't think it's appropriate for you to say I'm self-sabotaging."

"Oh my God. Yes! I do!" It was the blonde, exclaiming from two tables over. As she'd predicted, her man was on one knee. From nowhere, a string quartet walked onto the restaurant floor, playing Max Richter. Evie pressed her eyes shut. She loved his songs.

"That could be us." It was Ben, his voice quiet.

She didn't know another way to say it. "We're not dating. I just want to make that clear."

"Whatever you say, Evie. Take all the time you need to get your head on straight. I'll be here."

Instead of addressing how patronizing it felt to be told by the nicest person on the planet that she was making a mistake of epic proportions, she just said, "As long as we're clear."

Problem was, she was fairly sure they weren't. And worse, she was sure that there were more of these painful conversations in her future.

"You're back early."

The voice greeted her, echoing through the lobby. It was her mom, of all people.

"Didn't know you were staying here tonight," Evie answered, not at all ready for another lecture. It had been an extremely long week and all she could think about was leaving. Sleeping under the stars. With August.

"Thought you were out with Ben this evening?"

Looked like the lecture was coming, one way or another. Evie kicked off her shoes and made her way into the library. Her mom was in the kitchen, and yes, she had every intention of going there. But not without a stiff drink.

Her Dark and Stormy poured, she pulled up her big-girl panties and made her way to the dining room. The Hartmann girls didn't spend their time in the kitchen; Josephine wasn't that kind of woman.

Her mom was dressed in a dove gray suit. The look was fitted, elegant. She wore a silk chemise in lieu of a dress shirt and looked glamorous.

"You look good, Mom," Evie started.

"And you look…" Her mom paused, assessing her. "Tired."

So, it was going to be one of those chats.

Evie pulled at one of the sleek chairs and took a seat at the marble-topped island. The dining room was her least favorite part of the home. Featuring walnut paneling, in stark contrast to the white marble, it was an aggressive marriage of contemporary modern style with farmhouse chic, and Evie wasn't sure she liked it.

Josephine poured her own drink. Vodka on the rocks. Calorie free, or so her stick-figure mother liked to remind her. Evie took a deep sip of her drink, regretting for a moment she hadn't taken a straw to slurp with. If she was going to disappoint her mom might as well go all the way.

"Early date, then?" Josephine asked with an eyebrow arched.

Not early enough.

"Actually, Ben and I are on a break."

Band-Aid off.

Josephine pursed her lips. A thin line Evie was all too

familiar with. Her lips had almost disappeared when Evie had announced her plans for Hollywood, so she was well versed in parental disappointment.

"I thought you were back. That you were charting a new course. Making smart decisions?"

"And I thought you were my mom, not my dating coach." *Or career adviser.*

Josephine clicked her tongue. To be fair, she couldn't have been used to this. No one talked back to Mom.

Josephine finished her drink, then pushed her stool back and stood. She made her way around the island, releasing the hidden door to a recessed bar fridge on the west side. Chilled vodka, always at the ready. Evie watched silently as her mom poured another drink.

"Want a vodka? Less cals than whatever it is you're drinking."

There it was. Frankly, it was amazing she hadn't grown up with a raging eating disorder. As she sipped her Dark and Stormy, she counted her appetite as her first independent revolt.

"Did I tell you? I leave for an audition in two weeks. The casting agent saw my reel already, thinks I'm perfect for the role." *It was kinda true.*

Josephine's lips retreated further, the line of her mouth tightening.

"No. You didn't mention."

"Yeah, well, it's quite the opportunity." Evie smiled, then finished her drink. After a moment's thought, she passed her glass to her mom, who added a shot of vodka to the waiting ice cubes.

"I didn't realize you were short on opportunity." Josephine replaced the vodka and closed the bar fridge with startling force.

"Well, that's adulthood, I guess. Picking the opportunities you're interested in."

"I thought adulthood was picking the opportunities that warranted further effort. The opportunities best in line with your status."

It didn't take a genius to deduce which opportunities her mom was referring to.

"Is that why you're waiting up? To hear about Ben?" Evie was tired. Tired of not feeling as if she was enough.

"I'm here because my son is getting married. I can't remember the last time I had this much to do. And the child I thought was making the best decisions of her life is now admitting to being a train wreck."

"Train wreck? Don't you think that's a bit harsh?"

"The fact that you think it's harsh concerns me. You won't get a thousand do-overs. Second chances are tough to come by."

Evie took a sip of her vodka, steeling herself for the lecture. That was just what this day needed.

"I suppose we don't all dream of marrying rich and being miserable." She eyed her mom. It was hard to forget that her father had left. She had been five when her dad had joined his other family for ten years. But she remembered the decade her mom had spent alone.

"Miserable? Look at my life. That just tells me you don't know the first thing about what I do. What I've built."

Evie looked at her mom. Really looked at her. Time had been kind. Well, either time, or a bloody good surgeon, Evie wasn't sure which.

"Do you think it was easy for me?" She made a sweeping gesture with her hand. "You think building this, maintaining everything, was easy?" Her mom's voice shook, and she stared at Evie, eyes full of challenge.

The picture window behind her mom set the stage, filling the room with a warm light.

"Easy? No, Josephine. I don't think anything about you is, or ever was, easy." Miraculously, Evie managed to avoid an eye roll.

"Well, I can tell you, raising a family isn't easy. And don't call me Josephine, I don't like it."

"Sure, my nanny told me all about it." Evie wasn't in the mood to let *Josephine* off the hook.

"You are throwing away a chance at a perfectly good union with a good man."

"I don't love him, Mom."

"You think I loved your father? I was beautiful but poor. And look what I built."

Evie felt sick. This was not the pep talk she had hoped for.

"Maybe 'built' is the wrong word. But still, I'm here."

"But are you happy, Mom? Is your life the one you want for me? Or for Ben, for that matter?"

Ben had always been the apple of her mom's eye.

"Hell, if you think Ben's so great, you marry him." Evie picked up her glass, leveled a look at her mom, and drained it.

"Me? Marry Ben? He's twenty years younger than me. Don't be ridiculous." Her mom blushed. Her mom actually blushed.

"Josephine. Er, Mom. I want to be in love. I want to want someone more than my own breath. I want to be nervous and excited, terrified and optimistic, and feel a thousand other feelings all at once. And yes. I know I come from a life of privilege. How could I not know that?"

"Indeed." Her mom looked at her intently. Evie felt, for once, that she had her mom's attention. It was unsettling.

"But maybe that privilege affords me the opportunity to

do what I want. Did you ever think of that? Sure, you were poor and beautiful. But I'm… I guess I'm, well, not as pretty as you. But I'm also not poor."

"You wouldn't know the first thing about being poor."

"Yeah, well, I don't think you know the first thing about being in love."

Josephine stood again. This time circling to the wet bar and serving herself a glass of water. "That's some way to talk to your mother."

"Maybe it's time we worked past that." Evie felt small. For the first time all evening, all year really, she felt like a child, asking her mom to be her friend.

"I just don't want to see you make a mistake." This time it was Josephine's voice that was small.

Evie stood and made her way over to her mom by the sink. She took her hand.

"I don't think you can find love if you worry too much about making mistakes. I'm not afraid to fail, Mom. I'm afraid not to try."

Her mom squeezed her hand.

"I'm proud of you, Evie. I just don't want to see you get hurt."

She squeezed her mom's hand back. "Me, neither. But I'm not afraid, Mom. Especially not if I know I have your support."

Her mom didn't say anything but squeezed her hand back.

Evie smiled and nodded. For a Hartmann, that was as close to permission as she'd get. Not that it mattered. Hartmanns didn't need permission.

For the first time in a long time, Evie felt as if she was making decisions worthy of her name. Present departure for camping with August included.

Eight

Into the Wild

"Basically, no one believes I'm doing this." Evie's voice carried on the wind as he rode behind her. They were off on their camping weekend.

He couldn't believe it either. But here they were, five o'clock, Friday night, and they were heading into the rough.

"I didn't tell anyone," he admitted as his horse pulled abreast hers. *The secret made it feel like eight years ago. Made it feel like she was his.* They settled into a comfortable saunter, and he didn't feel the need to say anything.

After twenty minutes of quiet riding, he pulled ahead of her. "I have an idea of where we can camp," he admitted. She just nodded, smiling.

"I'm following you, cowboy."

He road ahead, imagining, for a moment, what it might feel like to be the kind of guy Evie would follow anywhere.

An thirty minutes later, they rounded into very familiar territory. He knew she'd recognize this spot. They were on his land, more precisely, about forty minutes from an old hunting cabin he'd escaped to when he was a kid. He and Austin had spent countless nights here. He and Evie had spent just one. Well, not the whole night. Long enough for her to make him an offer he couldn't accept.

"I know where we are," she said. Her tone was difficult to decipher.

"Yeah, well, the terrain is perfect for impromptu camping, and if the weather turns on us, there's a lean-to not far from here." He pulled up and dismounted from his horse in one fluid motion, then turned to watch her as she did the same. He'd come ahead of time. Gathered rocks to line a firepit. Cut some pine boughs to set the tent on. Scouted a tree to hang the food in, and swung a pulley rope to secure it. It was Montana, after all. There were bears.

Here, in the wild, he didn't feel as if he was dating the good girl. Not that they were dating. It was more like hanging out with his old friend. And he wasn't stressed about Jacks or Nick catching them out here together.

"Should I go gather some firewood?" she asked.

"Sure. I'll stake the tents."

Tents. As in two tents. Because she was his dead best friend's little sister. And his current best friend Jackson's favorite sibling.

"Perfect," she said softly.

She wandered around, humming to herself. She was a hell of a singer, and he found himself massively distracted by her humming. It was a tune he didn't know, but one he liked. He wondered if she'd noticed that he'd brought a guitar.

It took about an hour to set up the two tents and unpack the gear from the horses. Once the mounts were watered and fed, he turned his attention to the neat pile of kindling he'd set out for a fire by the circle of rocks. Evie was squatting near the rocks, snapping twigs into uniform lengths. He'd taught her that as a teen.

"I know it probably doesn't matter, but I thought the twigs would stack better if they were all the same size."

Adorable. Pretending not to remember his tricks of the trade.

"I thought you needed *help* with this camping survival stuff." He grinned. Maybe she didn't need to be here. Maybe she just wanted to be.

"Nope. You promised to teach me how to light a fire, and sir, here I am. Ready to learn."

So you're here to play with fire? Is that it?

"All right." He circled next to her. "A promise is a promise." He picked up a few of the adorably trimmed twigs and leaned them together in a makeshift kindling teepee. "The trick is air circulation. You need to make sure the sparks have room to breathe. Give everything enough space."

He didn't want any space from her. Hell, the space he'd been allowing for had turned his own irksome spark of a feeling into a full-blown inferno.

"Right. Okay, so no need to trim them, then. I won't do that in the audition."

"Do it. I think it's cute. Probably exactly what an aspiring burlesque dancer would find important. It's a very sexy way to try and start a fire."

A faint hue of pink rose on her cheeks, and she nodded, a wisp of her bangs falling forward. He smelled her shampoo. Lavender. The rush of floral scent hit him in the gut. *Best friend's little sister. No-go zone. You're here to help her prepare for her audition.*

"So, first you set up the teepee. Then you need something soft. Imagine you're making a bed for the sparks."

A bed. Everything he said, or saw, felt layered with in-nuendo.

"They call it a tinder nest."

"Tinder? Like the app?'

Was she playing him? Enjoying this a little too much?

"Tinder like a fire starter. Focus, Evie." He grinned. "You'll want to find dry, fluffy materials for the tinder nest. Think dead grass, shredded birch bark, dry animal poop."

"If you think I'm going to bring dry animal poop to this audition, you've got another think coming. That's a little too authentic, although if I had some now, I'd throw it at you."

"All right. No dry animal poop. Bark, then. Focus on the bark."

"Sure. Then what?" She was leaning close to him. All he could think was of lavender. And touching her.

"Then you strike."

He could kiss her now. No one would know.

He knew it would be good. Good enough to outweigh the bad from their past. From their present.

He could strike.

"Flint and steel. Strike hard. This part I know." She produced a small piece of steel from her pocket, and a small dark rock. "Tons of flint along the riverbed." He watched as she created sparks. He blew on her efforts, his breath hitting strands of her hair.

He wanted to kiss her. More than he'd ever wanted to kiss anyone before.

"We did it!" She squealed as a hair of birch bark turned red.

The fire that followed was steady. They added twigs, starting small, then building up to the larger sticks. "You don't start with the heavy stuff. You need a structure, see? Need enough little twigs to build something that can take the heat."

She nodded, eyes wide, staring at the yellow fire. Then she got up.

"I'm gonna make you dinner." Evie grinned. "First the fire, then dinner."

"Next step, burlesque tutorial?" He laughed.

She laughed back. "You're lucky I'm not holding any dry animal poop."

Beside the fire was a metal pot. "I'll get the water if you want to start on the pasta sauce and then cook the noodles? There should be a cast-iron skillet in one of the saddle bags."

"It's a deal." She stuck out her hand, and after a quick pause, he took it.

"Then I'll get some wood. Bigger pieces. I saw a tree back a few minutes. That way, we can have us a nice fire later." *And he could spend a few more minutes reminding himself of the promise he'd made Austin. And the reasons he still wasn't quite enough for Evie.*

Cooking wasn't that hard. Evie didn't see what the big deal was. Wait till the water boils, then dump in the pasta. Chuck a bunch of stuff into the skillet and add butter. Seriously, everything was going way better than she'd expected. She could totally speak to her backcountry experience at her upcoming audition. It was easy to forget her sister's disbelief at her departure into the woods.

"You're doing this?" Mia had been shocked to walk in and find her packing earlier. "I thought you were joking."

"Yeah, well, it's the dawn of a new era. I'm taking control of my life. First step—prepare for this audition. Next step—get the part."

Mia had sat on her bed, watching as Evie sifted though piles of clothes, tapping her foot with the annoying tics of OCD that were ever present in moments of stress.

"What do you think a burlesque dancer would wear on a plane?" Evie had tried to keep it light. Had wanted her sister's foot to stop switching.

"So, you haven't changed your mind? You're not, per chance, solo camping?" Mia had pressed, putting clear emphasis on her irritating advice. As in, pick the right guy... Tap, tap, tap, tap, tap, tap, tap. Seven of them. Not good.

"No. I'm going with August."

Mia hadn't said anything, but her lips had drawn into the tight Josephine line.

"Very adult, Evie."

"Whatever, Mia," Evie had snapped back, feeling less adult than ever.

Well, it didn't matter what Mia thought. She'd already come clean with Mom, and next, she'd put her sister in her place. It was the dawn of a new era. An era in which Evie made choices for Evie. And yes, maybe August didn't want what she wanted long-term. And maybe this was only ever going to be a secret hookup or living-rough tutorial. That was gonna be her trick: don't expect more, and try to live in the moment.

Then she smelled smoke. Because she hadn't been living in the *recipe* moment.

Damn.

The pot with the water for the pasta now housed something entirely different. The noodles had melded into a co-agulation of gelatinous gunk. It didn't look savable. But she had to stay optimistic. *Nothing is lost, only changed.*

Evie pulled the pot from the fire. *"Owwwww!"* she screamed, dropping the pot.

August appeared in a flash and was at her side, pulling her into his chest.

"What happened? You okay?" His hands gripped her

shoulders, and for a moment, she forgot the searing pain in her hand. She felt his hands as though he'd branded her.

"I'm fine. I just grabbed the pot handle without a cloth."

He reached for a water bottle beside the fire, squirting the cold water onto her hand. It felt amazing.

"I am so sorry this happened." He was apologizing as if it was his fault. *Some bad boy.* She smiled and focused on enjoying this moment. Just the two of them, him doting on her, even if it was because she was an idiot. What would Ben have said in this situation? Then she frowned. Ben would never be in this situation. Still, if she'd learned anything over the past couple of weeks, it was that this August was hardly the same one she'd left behind eight years ago. He was grown up in all the right ways. Maybe it was time to let everyone start fresh. To take the best and leave the rest. Because, with August, the best looked freaking delicious.

"That's nice," she said, willing herself not to cry. *What kind of fool picks up a hot metal handle without a pot holder?*

"It's just first-degree—it was really smart of you to drop it right away."

"Yeah, but I'm afraid I ruined dinner." She pointed to the pot, now on its side in the dirt.

The pasta was still clumped together in a traitorous lump, but at least none of it had spilled onto the dirt.

"I can say without a doubt that that looks like the worst pasta I've ever been offered." August laughed.

She had known, of course. What kind of idiot overcooked pasta to the point that it became a congealed mush you had to slice through like a blob of hateful casserole?

"Not my forte, I'll admit it." Best just to brush the kitchen fail off. No one was perfect.

August speared a curious fork into the pot, then frowned

as he lifted the entire bulk of her disaster out in one pull. "I feel like your character isn't much of a cook, either," he said.

He was quick. Sharp-witted. He'd been quick as a kid, it was what she'd liked most about him.

Well, that, and the tattoos.

There were more now. New ink she didn't recognize. Now, *that* she didn't like. Didn't like that there was a permanent part of him she didn't understand.

He'd been splitting wood when she'd noticed some sort of Celtic pattern that wound up his chest—she'd seen the bottom of the ink every time he lifted the axe over his head. She'd been thinking about collecting a few more trunks, as heavy as they were, just to see him cut it. She was ready to trace every inch of those Celtic tats with her tongue. Or whatever sexy burlesque dancers did with stranded pilots.

"Do you know anything else about this character?" he asked her for the millionth time.

"Not really. I mean, the part is for a dancer, which works out for me. I mean, I studied ballet for years."

"Pretty sure ballet isn't quite the same wheelhouse as, well, burlesque?"

Evie frowned. "Keep that up and I'll force-feed you my pasta."

"Let's see it, then. Shake your moneymaker."

She laughed, then flicked the dish towel in his direction.

"If you dance for me, I'll make a second dinner."

"Second dinner?"

"Tip one for camping—always overpack on the food." He grinned.

"What's on the menu?" She was suddenly very interested. Even *joking* about her meal was unappetizing, but she was still hungry.

"You're gonna need to show me your culinary moves

first, before I so much as wiggle in your direction." She grinned.

Camping with August was getting really interesting really fast.

He almost hadn't packed it. Almost thought it would be ridiculous. The point of this campout was for her to get a feel for living in the rough.

But he'd wanted to impress her. That was why he had a bag full of all the fixings to make a lumberjack feast.

The marbled ribeye was streaked with fat. He'd bought it from the butcher Cody had recommended. The guy who supplied the meat at the dude ranch. He'd picked a cut off the bone, figuring it might be easier to prepare in the rough. The meat was already room temperature, thanks to the several hours it had taken to get to camp. It looked really good.

Evie came beside him and watched as he cut up the herbs he'd brought. In the iron skillet, he hacked off a thumb of butter, then scraped in onions and rosemary. Oregano and chives. Fennel and green onion. He didn't know how to cook much. You could say he was a one-trick pony. But he could grill one hell of a steak, on a fire, on a barbecue, heck, in a pan. If steak was the question, then he was the answer.

He chopped on autopilot, fishing a head of garlic.

She watched him, fascinated, as he pressed the flat of his knife over the head of garlic, pulling the sections out, free of their peel.

"Before I chuck this in, garlic, yay or nah?"

"Yay all day." She laughed. He smiled and added all the little sections into the buttery rue he was working on. *Couldn't have garlic breath alone.*

"Didn't figure you for a cook." She was watching intently, her injured hand apparently forgotten.

"Man of many talents, what can I say?" He smiled again. It was easy tonight, just being with her. Maybe it was easier because they weren't in town. Weren't in her house, or weren't hanging around with her brother. It was just her and him. Easy.

"I call this the lumberjack feast. Used to make it every time I was celebrating a win. My first contract. My first land lease. You get it." He smiled at her. He purposefully brought up the land leases, as though the poker wins were somehow less legit. As though earning money on his wit was somehow not good enough. *And right now? More than anything, he wanted to be good enough.*

"And what are you celebrating today?" she asked with a quiet curiosity.

Everything about today deserves to be celebrated.

"Actually, I did get some big news today." He was going to tell her. It *was* big news. A government grant of this scale legitimized him, and Cody's offer was the gravy on top. He'd only sell five thousand acres, and with $90 million in government funding, he had all the financing in place to get Quaid Green off the ground. But, at the same time, he didn't want to tell her. Didn't want tonight to be about him getting closer to someone that would be socially acceptable for her to date.

"Big news?" She smiled.

"Yeah. But you know what? I don't think tonight should be about that."

She shifted. He was aware of her beside him. Aware of her arm. Aware of her eyes, watching every movement.

"Something tells me your dinner is going to be a bit better than mine."

He liked it. Liked that she didn't press. Didn't want more than he was ready to offer. Maybe they could have a secret fling. *He could have his cake and eat her, too.*

Tonight he didn't want to think. Didn't want to remember. Just wanted to be.

"You know, out here, we can be anyone we want. I think that's what I like about being in the wild."

She leaned back, settling against the trunk of a birch tree. "I think, right now, I'm exactly who I want to be." She took an exaggerated inhale, the smell of the sizzling stake impossible to avoid.

"Me, too," he added.

Returning to his bag, he pulled out the potatoes he'd packed last minute.

"Smushed or roasted?" he wondered aloud.

"I don't think I've ever had smushed?" She laughed. "But will you teach me how to make them?"

"Teach you? Yeah. I'll teach you."

Out here, they could do what they wanted without answering to anyone. And more than anything, he wanted to teach her. Show her that maybe, even if he'd been late, even if he wasn't the first to have her, he'd be the best. *He needed to be.*

He chucked a potato her way, and to his surprise, she caught it and grinned.

"Then let's go, Professor." She winked.

He caught her wrist before she could chuck another potato his way, and brought it up to his mouth, licking a small speck of olive oil that had dribbled out of the aluminum foil. It was hot against her skin. He looked at her, stomach roiling. He was all kinds of hungry. But sometimes the best feast was a long time coming.

Nine

The Wrong Lie

"This is the best meal I've ever eaten." Her eyes rolled back in an exaggerated praise for his dinner.

He knew it was hyperbole. Overstatement for the sake of emphasis. But he appreciated it, and her enthusiasm was contagious.

It was dark, but in a perfect marriage of teamwork, they'd prepared the tents seamlessly, the sleeping rolls laid out, mosquito nets in place. Lanterns around the campsite were lit, and a few logs had been laid out for them to sit on.

When he'd sliced into the steak, cutting it into two, the meat revealed itself to be a perfect pink. His best work. The smushed potatoes were crispy on the outside, and pillowy soft on the inside. An orgasmic combination. He offered a spoon of reduced garlic butter over her plate.

"Yes, please. A thousand times yes, please."

"Now, that's the good girl I remember hearing about."

He smiled. It was surreal. Eating here. With her. Under the guise of teaching her how to live in the rough. They'd camped often enough as adolescents. If anyone knew how to sleep under the stars, it was a Hartmann. But she'd come anyway. On his impromptu invitation. Because it was more than an invitation. More than a tutorial on living in the rough. It was why he'd packed the steak.

And she knew it.

"Eight years. You've kept me away from this steak for eight years. What's your excuse?" She was joking but serious. It was classic Evie.

"Maybe I just wanted to perfect the recipe. Get it right before I shared it."

Was that why he'd walked away from her when she'd asked him to be her first? He'd wanted to get it right before her? Of all the stupid ideas... He hadn't been a virgin, but he also hadn't been...sure he was good enough. On every level.

"I know that's not always the right choice." He added the disclaimer and hoped she read between the lines.

"Well, I guess you could say this steak was worth waiting for." She took another bite and smiled.

He did, too.

It was really good steak.

Sometimes, the waiting was worth it.

"Last I heard you were playing poker. Is that what happened?"

"Yep. I still play. You'd be surprised the contacts you can make around a high-stakes table. But yeah, I played poker, long enough to turn my seed money into enough to leverage my first land lease. Then flipped my land lease to an investment portfolio run by Capital One, and parlayed that success into some venture capital for Quaid Corp."

"Yeah, Jackson told me a bit about it. He's very impressed."

What about you, Evie? Are you impressed?

"In poker, you read people. Negotiating property is pretty similar. I wasn't expecting to have the success I met, but I guess I felt like I didn't have a choice. I didn't want to come back here until my success was bigger than my family's failure."

She put her plate down. It was clean. But instead of getting up, she leaned toward him, resting her head on his shoulder.

"The people who knew you never cared about your family's failure, August."

"I cared." He put his own plate down, reveling in the weight of her head on his shoulder. And the weight that was lifting off him as he came clean.

"I know," she said quietly.

"I cared if you cared." It was getting chilly, and he stared at the embers of the fire as he carried on. "Or, if my family's failure meant you couldn't. Care. About me."

Shadows flickered around the hearth, the fire their only light source. It cast a yellow light on her face, and she looked fucking beautiful. Maybe it was how good she looked that inspired him to be honest. She had a face that provoked honesty.

"But... I only ever cared about you." She pressed her lips together in a tight smile and lifted her head off his shoulder. Direct. Undeniable. "None of that other stuff. I only cared about how it would affect you."

He'd known that. Or hoped it. But hell, hearing her say it, now, under the stars? It was an absolution.

"I feel like I owe you an explanation," he started.

"Don't you read people in poker?" She stood, backlit by the fire.

Quickly, he got to his feet. "Yeah."

"Well. Read me, then." She looked at him directly in the eye. And unbuttoned the top of her button-down, the plaid shirt falling open as each descending button was released.

"Can you read this?" She continued to undress.

He felt transported in time. Young and beside a stream. Watching his best friend's little sister, the girl he was madly in love with, slip off the straps of her bathing suit, offering herself to him.

But I'm a virgin.

He'd panicked.

And some other guy had had his pleasure.

But here she was again. As beautiful. Maybe even more so, because he'd stoked the fire he'd kept burning for her with another eight years of yearning.

"No woman has ever measured up to you, Evie." His voice was gruff, and he watched her, transfixed on her fingers.

"August." The single word stilled him. Then she winked.

"Just thought I'd dance a little better without this shirt." She smiled, then she slipped her arms out of the flannel top and it fell at her feet.

She stood before him in her jeans and thin tank top. White cotton, thin-strapped, modest, apart from the curves it hid.

He groaned.

"Follow me. I bet there will be fireflies by the lake."

He followed her without protest. Truth was, he'd follow her anywhere. And she knew it.

She pulled her phone out from her pocket, and, once

again, he heard her "summer tunes" playlist. The same hits from their summer, bringing him back in time.

"How's this for burlesque?" She laughed. "Deal is a deal. Us Hartmanns never welsh." She set her phone on a rock and motioned for him to sit. So, he did.

When the music started, he watched as Evie circled her hips. Ingenue meets sexpot. She fit the brief for this casting call. Damn, did she ever.

"I feel ridiculous." She got shy about twenty seconds in.

"I made dinner. Deal's a deal." He grinned. Never had he appreciated a deal as much as this one. Never had he negotiated as well, for a prize as heady.

She didn't say anything, just circled her hips. Then she reached for her ponytail and pulled off the elastic, letting her hair fall to her shoulders, waves falling in front of her breasts.

As if on cue, he spotted three fireflies, then two more, until they were joined by a chorus of twinkling insects. The universe was clearly calling in favors to set the scene.

She smiled wider, shaking her head.

The woman was sex incarnate. "Good God, Evie. If you want the part of a stranded burlesque dancer, and you pull even a fraction of this out for your audition, the part is yours." His mouth was dry as he watched her dance to the tinny sound from her iPhone.

"You're just saying that." But her eyes were shining.

He stood, unable to take it for even a moment more.

"Evie." He wondered for a moment if he should stop the music, but decided not to.

"Evie, I'm not just saying this. If you want the part of a sexy burlesque dancer, I can't think of anyone in Hollywood, or anywhere for that matter, that looks sexier than you, right now."

She stopped moving.

"If you're making fun of me, then stop."

Making fun of her? He hadn't been more serious about anything in his life.

"If I am able to promise one thing to anyone in any situation, it would be to you now, to promise that I'm utterly sincere. You're the sexiest woman I've ever seen. And I mean that."

She sank back, putting all her weight on her back foot. Then she took two steps forward, closing the space between them.

"I want you." She had been quiet in her admission, but sure. The words, succinct but sincere.

"I want you, August."

He didn't answer, frozen in place by her demand.

She wanted him.

"Touch me."

His head spun at the implications of her command. Was it due to the walk? The fireflies? The romance of the moment?

"For what?"

She stiffened at the question, his gruff denial of her request doing nothing but solidifying her resolve.

"Sex. With me. Now."

Damn. She was direct. He felt his own willingness strain against his jeans and swallowed. This was the Evie he remembered: Relaxed. Direct. Hair loose on her shoulders, and smile quick and easy. This was the Evie he'd run to Texas to avoid. The Evie he'd hoped to impress with his self-made fortune, and now, by his willingness to bet on himself, walking away from the company that had made him millions to invest in his own wit instead.

He reached for her face, his thumb brushing against skin so smooth that he wondered what she did to make it that way. It was like satin. Soft. Supple. His hand trailed down her cheek to trace the line of her jaw, then a finger danced on her collarbone.

He watched his finger, rough and calloused against her pearl-smooth complexion. He, inked and hard, she, pure and soft.

"I can't keep saying no to you." He paused, finger sweeping across her shoulder.

"Then don't." She tilted her chin up, the languid line of her neck offering a delectable plane to place a kiss on.

"I'm not Little Evie anymore." She looked at him, her hazel eyes dark and searching. *Damn right she wasn't.*

"I liked Little Evie," he reminded her.

"I'm not some Goody Two-shoes" She frowned, her lips pulling into a frown.

"Is that what this is about? Killing your good-girl image—"

"This is about me. Wanting you, more than I've ever wanted anyone in my entire existence. Can we stop asking questions now? Can you just take me already?"

Her words were more a challenge than an offer.

His hands moved to her face, but his tenderness was replaced with a feverish desire to claim her. Maybe she wasn't offering anything beyond tonight—he certainly had no illusions about a future place on her arm at a Hartmann wedding, for example. But what she *was offering?* Her…right now? Hell, he'd take it. He was done fighting. The part of him that was primal was stronger than his voice of caution. She was his best friend's sister, but here she was, offering herself up on a platter.

She raised her arms above her head, her shirt pulling up to reveal several inches of her stomach, white and soft and available.

His hands moved on autopilot, pulling the hem of her tank top up over her head. She wasn't wearing a bra.

Good God.

He fell to his knees before her, managing to avoid consuming the breasts on offer before him to press a kiss along the waistband of her jeans. She stood still as he undid the button of her jeans.

They had been here before. Eight years earlier. It had been her, unbuttoning her jeans, and him, insisting she could do better.

Now? Maybe he was better. Better than he had been. At least he was man enough to admit he wanted her with a hunger that was unparalleled in his life.

He pulled the jeans down her legs.

"August."

Her hands were in his hair, tugging him up, but he shook his head, pressing kiss after kiss on her skin as the slow descent of her jeans revealed more of her legs. Inch by inch, he discovered her. The hollow of her knee. The curve of her calf. The bump on her ankle. The freckles on her shin that reminded him of a star. Her skin smelled like baby oil. Like a woman who hadn't tried to be, but just was, innately sexy.

"I want to touch you, too."

She was talking, but her voice sounded far away. He began pressing kisses back up her legs, now free of the jeans. His hands roamed her legs, thighs and butt, until he met her at her apex, breathing her in. Evie was everywhere.

"You first," he said gruffly. Mostly because he knew there was no going back now. And he wanted her to scream for him. He tugged down the strip of elastic that held her underwear up and sucked in a breath. She shifted her weight from foot to foot, with the nervousness of a new colt.

His hands eager, he reached for her hips and urged her to the edge of the bank.

"Sit."

It wasn't a question, and she sank to the ground, sitting, then letting her back fall against the grass, wet with dew.

"This shouldn't happen here. You should be in a five-star hotel. Or a castle in France." He could afford those places now.

"I want to be here. And I don't want to wait."

Another kiss to the inside of her thigh, and she parted her legs.

She didn't say anything, but he could hear her thinking. As he licked her, explored her, touched her, her body started to tremble. Like a leaf in autumn, she clung to her control as he teased it away from her. He was good at this. He knew it, but this was different. It was Evie.

Good wasn't enough. He wanted to be magnificent.

He felt her pulse around his fingers, and her legs spasmed, but he didn't stop. As he pushed his tongue and fingers into deep corners of her, her cries were the anchor that kept his feet on the ground, his nose pressed against her.

"My God. August. August." She repeated his name and it had never sounded sweeter. Never sounded as right.

Reluctantly, he kissed her, then moved a kiss to her hip bone, then on the soft, perfect rise of her belly.

Her perfect belly.

Marred only by a lone scar.

Sometimes, in moments of acute pleasure, time suspended itself. And in these moments, the oddest memories could surface.

I speak fluent French.

I never had an operation.

I'm a virgin.

Je me suis jamais fait opéré. I've never had an operation.
Two truths and a lie.

But she'd said she'd never had an operation. And she'd made the disclaimer in French.

Which meant her lie was never having had an operation.

And her other truth? She was a virgin.

How was that even possible?

"That looks like an appendectomy scar." His head was clear. The weight of the possibility hit him like a ton of bricks.

Evie, naked and sated, blushed, her skin turning a uniform pink.

"What's your point?"

"You lied." He pulled himself off the bed of grass, forcing himself to stand, his want for her hard against the confinement of his jeans. *Not like this. He was going to be the good guy.*

"That's the point of the game," Evie shot back. "Two truths and a lie."

"Sure, but you lied about your lie." His eyes narrowed.

"Funny, all of a sudden admitting in front of a room full of cowboys that no one has ever wanted to sleep with me didn't seem like my best idea."

She stood. Naked. Before him. Her hair fell in front of her breasts in a lush curtain of soft brown waves. She was shaking again, but not in the good way he had been responsible for only moments earlier. *She was angry.*

"I think you know how much people have wanted to sleep with you before."

"Well, you look about ready to leave." Her voice had gotten quiet again, not mad. He had to tread lightly.

"Forgive me for not wanting to take your virginity—"

"Take it! It's not some precious thing."

But it was.

"Seriously." She took a step toward him, her hands at his waist, fumbling with his belt. "Take it. Take me."

"I'm not a saint," he whispered as she kissed his neck. "You have to stop this. Now."

"Yeah. I know. Not a saint. A bad boy. I know. The bad boy who is refusing to bed me." But she didn't stop kissing his neck. "August. I've wanted you to take me since that night in the field. Let's just live this now. Tonight. Unless—" she paused, fingers suspended "—unless…you don't want me."

He didn't answer her, just lifted his shirt over his head.

"I want you, Evie. I might not deserve you, but I want you just the same."

He reached for his wallet, then, condom in hand, he stepped out of his jeans. It didn't matter that she had lied. A small part of him had guessed it. Hoped it. Wished he hadn't been too late.

I want to be here. And I don't want to wait, her voice echoed.

"I want you now," she said, or at least he was pretty sure she had. Evie was ethereal under the stars. Touching her skin, reveling in its velvet softness, felt like a dream.

She bit her lip, and he felt it in his guts. Kissing her, he toppled onto her, his weight pressing her into the grass, wet with dew and hot with body heat. "I want you now," he parroted.

Evie wrapped her legs around him, and before he could second-guess why she would lower her standards enough to let him be her first, he sank into her.

Her hands were on his back. Fingers pulling him closer. Her touch, gasoline to his fire.

He kissed her. Tasted her skin, slick with sweat. She arched her body and spread her legs.

Her heat was slick and tight against him. She didn't flinch as he took her, and as he pulled out, she craned her neck forward and kissed him. Again and again, he buried himself in her, getting lost in the scent of them, sweating, together. He clenched his jaw as he focused on her, as, again and again, he took her.

He pulled back, still buried inside her, and paused.

"Am I hurting you?" For a moment, he second-guessed his passion.

"No." She raised her hips to prove her point, looked at him, and squeezed.

The muscle in his jaw tightened.

She reached up and sucked on his nipple just long enough to elicit a growl. He heard himself make the sound, an out-of-body experience. He wanted to move. Wanted to bury her in kisses. In love. But he was frozen.

"August." she wrapped her arms around her neck. "I've thought about this for so long. And it's so much better than I hoped."

She lay back on the grass, and he swallowed. It was uncomfortable. How much he wanted her. How much he felt.

"I'm a bit worried my heart is gonna explode," he said quietly.

"Don't worry." She kissed him. "We'll explode together."

She arched against him, and then he felt her whole body start the sweet shake he'd dream of for the rest of his life.

"August," she started.

But he didn't stop, just lost himself in her. Again and again.

Evie.

When he came, she cried with him.

Ten

Worth It

He wasn't going to ask if it was worth the wait. Or make a crass joke about making up for lost time, which to be fair, he'd done. Four times that first night, and once in the river. All transcendent. Then, day two. Rehearsing a kissing scene, and falling onto a bed of soft grass and wildflowers. It was shaping up to be the best weekend of his life, and he still had Sunday afternoon ahead of him.

Evie was addictive. Consuming. And she was his, even if it was just for now.

That was the problem with making love to her. It changed everything, especially his insane idea that he could quit her, cold turkey, when they got back to reality.

"What time is it?" Evie wondered, eyes still pressed shut.

He looked at his watch. *"Damn it."*

"That late?" She rolled off his sleeping bag and felt around the tent. Then she locked eyes with him, and he swung her panties around causally.

"Nope. I'm keeping them."

"August. I need my underwear."

"So do I."

She threw a sock at him, then pulled on her jeans, without the perfunctory underwear.

And just like that, he was hard again.

He looked at his watch. Two p.m. already, and it was a two-hour ride back to his ranch. Sunday was escaping him.

More than anything, he wanted to finalize the solar panel project *without* leaning on the Hartmanns. He wanted Josephine to look at him and see a guy worthy of her daughter. He wanted to stand at Austin's grave and feel like a man who had earned a spot next to Evie. Which made the appointments he'd lined up in the coming days more important than ever.

"I was thinking. I mean, I don't need to go home just yet." Evie took a step toward him.

"Err, not sure I'm following. We can't stay out in the woods all week, I didn't bring enough provisions ."

"I meant, I could go to your home. If you wanted."

He wanted.

"I mean, I could maybe help. With your applications and stuff…" She blushed. *Stuff.* She caught on quick for a virgin.

Ex virgin, he corrected.

"I mean, yeah. Sure. That sounds great."

"Which part?" She hooked an eyebrow at him and bit her lip. "The help with applications… or the other stuff?"

The vixen! "Let's get to mine and you can show me what you're thinking," he winked at her.

She was out of his tent in a flash to pack.

He had time for a quick dip in the lake.

He hoped it was cold enough.

They'd ordered delivery and binge-watched movies from the eighties. Eaten ice cream for dinner and each other for dessert. She served as a pretty good dessert, based on his penchant for seconds. And thirds.

But reality was a bitch. All the words they hadn't said left the air thick with tension. Tension, and a teeny bit of resentment.

"I'll drive you to the airport." It was August who broke the silence of their last dinner.

Evie pushed away an empty delivery pizza box, and frowned. "No. I need to stop by the house."

She waited for him to offer to take her.

He didn't.

"Right. Well, this time with you…" she felt a heat rise to her cheeks, and cursed the blush she knew colored her face.

"It's been great. Let me know how your audition goes. I want a play by play, every detail." He reached for her hand and drew it to his lips.

Those lips.

"Right. I know." She was repeating herself. Hard to keep her mind straight as he took one of her fingers into his mouth. Good God.

"I'll text you my flight details. Maybe when we land, we can talk about, whatever this is that we're doing." This is what Mia would have recommended. Getting the last word.

"Sure," he shrugged. Always the consummate cool guy.

She nodded, swallowing the feeling that everything was about to change.

Her hotel was about thirty minutes from LAX, but Evie had called ahead and a driver was waiting. She'd packed light, carry-on only, and was at her hotel before midnight.

After checking in with the front desk, she placed her call while pacing the lobby.

"Evie?"

Amber answered on the first ring. "Took you ages to call

me back. You ready for tomorrow? Did you get the pages I sent over? I'm at a party, I can barely hear you."

She pulled the dog-eared pages out and stared at them. "Yeah, I'm ready."

"Good. That's good. I called the casting agent again this morning. You're the fourth person reading for the role, and the last on their shortlist. The other women didn't light up the screen test, didn't meet the director's expectations. I think we have a real shot here." Evie heard every word as clear as a bell, despite the ambient chatter from the lobby. Amber's undertone just as clear: don't mess this up.

"Yep, well, you don't have to worry, I'm gonna get my beauty rest, then I'll be there, first thing."

The background noise was still muted. "Evie, it's hard to get rid of a bad stink here. This is a good shot, don't blow it. I'm not sure I'll get another chance with you."

She meant it as a kindness. For sure. Evie knew it. Amber wasn't mean, but pretty girls were a dime a dozen. Evie knew that.

"I know. You're betting on the right horse."

"That's what I like to hear." And, just like that, Amber clicked off.

Evie sat on the plush sofa in the hotel lobby, unsure about everything except for one fact: she wanted to call August.

Instead, she took out her journal and sketched her name. Evie Hartmann.

Pro: Optimistic.

Con: Optimistic.

Pro: Good Actress.

Con: Plays a lot of roles for a lot of people.

Who does she want to be? And who did she want to be with...

That was the only question that really mattered. She

needed to be the leading lady of her own life before all else. And leading ladies called the shots.

Something was wrong. He'd felt it the moment she'd left. He tugged at his beard. That wasn't true. He'd felt it earlier. The third time they'd ordered take out. When he'd realized her eagerness for pizza likely had more to do with a similar eagerness to hide what they were doing, what they'd done, from the people that mattered most to her. Like Mia.

But if this was all he could have. These few days, hidden from people who would judge them, from the ghost of his best friend and his surviving family, from the high brow, upper crust of Montana's elite, then he'd take it. Because a few days with her was better than nothing. Better than never. Better than before.

August stared at the stack of papers in front of him. It was hard not to think of her constantly. Of the way she withered beneath him, buckling every time he touched her. Like her body was an instrument only he knew how to play. And her sighs, the best music in the whole world.

Solar credits. He needed to focus on solar credits. He reached for his coffee, now cold. So why, in two weeks, hadn't she asked him out? Past his front door? Anywhere…

He reached for his phone. There was only one person who might have answers for him, and he was going to call her.

"Mia speaking." She answered on the first ring.

"Err, hey. This is August."

Silence. He could literally hear static on the phone line.

"I'm just calling, about…" He paused. How could he ask her? This call was ridiculous. He shuffled the papers in front of him, as though the solar grant paperwork might offer him some insight to the heiress he'd seduced.

"Evie. You're calling about Evie?" Mia finished for him.

At least her tone didn't sound accusatory. "I gather you know—"

"—she's been staying at yours? Yeah it doesn't take a brain surgeon to work that out."

Did the fact that they were less subtle than he'd imagined offer any relief? His stomach turned. No.

"She's in LA now."

"For her audition. I know. Look, I have a busy day, can I help you with something August?"

"Just, you know, wondering what you think about," he cleared his throat. "About Evie and I?"

The silence was thicker this time. Louder somehow. He pulled at his beard again, then drew a hand through his hair. He wasn't going to break this time. Wasn't offering her a way out of the question. Truth was, he wanted to know what Evie's twin thought of the idea. Of he and Evie. Dating. In public. Or whatever his open ended 'Evie and I' implied to her identical sister.

Her hesitation was as loud as her answer. "Do you guys want the same thing?"

"Really Mia? Answering a question with a question? I know you like politics but can't you just answer straight for once?" Maybe his outrage was a tad unfair, but this wasn't time for games.

"Aug, did you ever think I'm not the one you should be asking?"

August nodded, then, realizing they were on the phone and his nods would pass unnoticed, he added a quick "Right. I see your point."

"She's staying at the MacMaster Hotel. Venice Beach location. My advice? You really want to see if you have a chance at something real? Ask her yourself. I'll call ahead for you." Mia disconnected without waiting for an answer. That was her, straight to business, and upfront, when she wasn't pretending to be her twin. But it wasn't the directness that had him off guard, it was the suggestion. That August simply ask Evie herself.

He tightened his grip on the papers he held. It was decided then. He could read them on the plane.

It was easier than he'd expected. Booking the next available flight to LAX. It was good to surprise your girl, he reasoned, but he only pretended for a few moments that the surprise was for her. He had to see her. Had to kiss her. *Had to make sure they wanted the same thing.*

He was surprised at Mia's readiness to help. Maybe his reputation at Hartmann Homestead wasn't as bad as he feared. Maybe a small part of her was rooting for him.

He was on his second whiskey and coke when he heard the key card in the door. Somehow, being in her hotel room, had him questioning things. The only soundtrack to his evening was the thundering clouds outside, the storm that followed him from Montana, both figuratively and literally, darkening the room. It was pissing rain, but the storm mirrored his mood.

"August?" She dropped the key on the floor and flew toward him. "I didn't know you were coming!" she said, her face buried in his neck. She was every man's wet T-shirt fantasy, and his own personal kryptonite.

"I didn't know, either. I just decided I wanted to be here." He tried to shrug. Tried to pretend her enthusiasm at seeing him didn't affect him. Tried to pretend he couldn't see the outline of her bra through her damp shirt.

"You just flew here?" She let her purse fall to the floor, and kicked off her shoes with the familiarity of someone who was altogether too comfortable in a penthouse suite.

He shifted his weight from foot to foot. "What's a three-hour flight to see your girl?"

He tested the words, more to gage her reaction than his own. She blinked, then her face spread into a wide smile.

"Your girl now, am I?" She smiled, but there was a shadow across her face. He leaned forward, kissing her before the shadow spread.

"I'd like you to be."

There it was. The reason he'd flown at the drop of a hat to see her. Not only because he'd missed her, but because he wanted her to be his. *Officially.* Despite the promise he'd made to his dead best friend. Despite the fact that she was Jackson's little sister. Despite the fact that she was good and he was...*not good enough.*

"I'm so glad you're here, but I have to admit, I'm doubled booked tonight. Drinks with my agent, then later the casting director and male lead are joining. They want to make sure the chemistry is right."

He shifted, swallowing disappointment.

"Unless..."

Despite himself, he grinned.

"You don't want to come to drinks with my agent?"

He kissed her and she smiled. "Right then, we better go now."

"Isn't it a bit early for drinks?" he caught her wrist, pressing a kiss into it. He'd been right. She was including him, not hiding him away.

He cleared this throat. "Maybe for now, we focus on what we're good at." Before she could answer, he kissed her again, relieved when her lips parted in response. Sex. Yep. He'd remind her how good they could be together

She tasted like oranges and smelled like cinnamon. Somehow, now, even while facing the turmoil of possible rejection, it was easy to get lost in her.

He needed her the way most men needed oxygen. He

needed her to feel alive. To feel like the best version of himself, even if being with her meant he was giving in.

"God, I love when you kiss me." Her grin, and apparent forgiveness, was intoxicating. "I'll have you know I can offer up a pretty decent strip show, in the right circumstances."

"And what circumstances might those be?"

"For a guy like you?" She kept up the rhythmic trace of her hand across his abdomen. She was lifting his shirt, but he caught her wrist with his rapid reflex. This was his party. He wanted control, but first he needed to clarify a few things.

"You were wrong to think I'm better than I am. A better man would walk away. A better man would leave you alone. Go anywhere but here. I've tried to avoid you, but damn it, I don't care if we're in a hotel room or a forest, I want you Evie. Right now. Bad."

She kissed him. Again and again. She kissed him with an urgency that had him pressing hot kisses down the curve of her damp neck.

"We do have an hour…" She kicked her legs apart and unbuttoned the waist of her jeans.

Whoa. From virgin to sexpot. But he'd take it. This was one way he knew how to apologize. How to make a point.

She stepped out of her clothes, and he picked her up. Her legs were wrapped around his waist, and her hands were pulling his shirt up and over his head.

"Thirteen steps to the bed," he whispered into her neck. A singular advantage of hotel rooms, the bed was always close. He figured thirteen steps at most.

"No." She slid down his body and pulled at his belt. "I want you to take me right here, right now, fast and hard. On the floor." She wiggled her legs free, and pulled him to the ground, the slate tile of the penthouse lobby cool on his feet.

She tugged his pants down, then his briefs. He was harder than he'd been in his life, unsure whether it was due to her nakedness, or the insistence that he take her there, on the floor, rather than on the bed, a few feet to the left. He'd never wanted any woman enough to melt into a puddle on the floor. It was a first for him.

He kissed down the curve of her belly, then eyed the bed. He wanted her properly.

"August, don't make me beg." She pulled his hair, then shimmied out of her pants. His hand traced her thigh, finding her hot and wet.

He took her hand and put it on him. "I want you, too. More than I've ever wanted anyone."

She closed her eyes. "Show me," she whispered. *Or was it a challenge?*

A crack of thunder followed, and after a succession of flashes, the lights in the suite went out.

The blackout didn't matter. August reckoned there was enough electricity between them to heat the damn hotel for the season, let alone an evening.

He touched her again, rubbing her first with his hand, then with himself. Evie made the sexiest sounds when she was hot, and it was more than he could bear. Shifting his weight, he teased her again, still not entering her. His hands on her breasts, he moved from one nipple to the other. He covered her body with his, forearms pressed against the floor as he was prone atop her.

Then Evie surprised him. With a twitch of her leg, she flipped him onto his back and settled against him, slipping down the length of him, then rising up again, in a slow and tortuous rhythm. A glorious prison indeed. Her eyes were hooded and her lips red, bruised from the kisses and beard burn he'd inflicted.

As she inched down, each centimeter a velvet torture, it

occurred to him that she'd foregone the condom. So, he supposed they were exclusive. That was what the kids called it these days, right? He tried to recite the alphabet backward. Anything to delay the release he felt coming. She was exquisite. This was why he came. Maybe he didn't care if they were a secret. *If a tree falls in the forest, does it make a sound? If the neighbor gets the girl in secret, does it bring her down?*

He would never say another thing about slate tile again. Cold? Hardly—it was the flooring of the future.

This floor was his new favorite feature of the room. Of any room. Open his eyes? He'd rather die. Move from this spot? Not on his life. Even the memory of this moment would be enough for him.

"P. O. N. M. L." He whispered the letters with each rise and fall of Evie. *Was it his twentieth time through the damn alphabet? How could this moment feel timeless and urgent at once?*

"Kiss me," she said.

Or did she?

Her lips were on his, her silky skin brushing against him. *"G.F.E."*

She moved faster. Her cries echoed through the suite.

A groan. *Was it his?*

His legs felt weak.

When she spasmed around his length, he saw stars. Actual stars. He pulled her close, kissed her on her neck again, and let his hands tighten on her arms. Then he spilled into her and saw God.

"This is August Quaid, my neighbor from back home."

She'd introduced him as her neighbor. Without so much as a courtesy blush. Two weeks of near constant sweaty sex, forbidden kisses and Chinese takeaway and here she was, at the first opportunity, introducing him as her neighbor.

"Great to meet you, I'm Amber Atley," the woman, Evie's agent, introduced herself.

Amber, a short slim woman, pressed her elbows together as she leaned into the handshake, inclining her body just enough to offer a glimpse of décolté; but it was too obvious for August's taste. Especially in comparison to Evie, who was radient in a demure silk top and pencil skirt that hugged her in all the right places.

The night got steadily worse. First when Evie met her potentially-soon-to-be costar, Rob Case, followed by the appetizers and cocktails during which he suffered a front row seat to Evie flirting with the heartthrob of the day, proving an undeniable chemistry to the director and agent.

The cocktails culminated in a handshake from the director, and a wet kiss from the co-star, for the sake of the movie everyone assured each other.

One evening in her world and it was clear to him. She should stay here. She was about to get the career she'd always wanted. He was just gonna hold her back. The last thing he needed was for the media to confirm what he knew innately, that there was no measure in which he would ever be enough for Evie Hartmann. They could pretend all they wanted, frantic on a slate floored hotel room, but beyond that? To even think she'd want him was insanity.

At least he'd got what he'd come for. The answer.

He was too angry at himself to hear her muffled apology in their town car back to the hotel. She cleared her throat and repeated herself. "You could say something you know," Evie repeated, incredulous as to her silence.

But he didn't know what to say.

"I don't know what you were expecting." She crossed her arms across her chest.

"I don't know Evie. Maybe I was expecting better than this. Watching you fall all over yourself to impress a director. It's just…" He exhaled his distaste. It's just… she was going to make it. And he would just hold her back. And the truth of it disgusted him.

"I was hardly falling all over myself. I'm here to work."

"Not that you need to."

Maybe, just maybe, she'd choose him instead.

"I thought you wanted me to pursue my dream."

No. The dream wasn't to be with him, and he was a fool for thinking it might be. Things didn't work out like this for the Quaids, he wasn't signing up for a Hollywood happy ending.

"Well, maybe I'm not sure this is what I want." He stared out the window, cringing at the thought that their conversation was being witnessed by a driver.

"That's great August. Do me in the hotel room, and dump me in the cab. You're a class act."

But that was the thing. He wasn't.

She stiffened. "Is this why you came? To spy on me in LA? End things?"

Her ferocity caught him off guard.

"You know, this is exactly why everyone thought I should be with Ben. He'd never do… this. My family were right."

"I guess they were."

He stared out the window, wondering a moment if he could get a flight standby. When they pulled up at the hotel, she was out of the car in a flash. He lowered his window.

"I'm heading on to LAX. I'll see you around Evie."

He did up the window before he could read too much into her expression. This wasn't how he'd thought the night would end. Or maybe it was.

Eleven

Team Ben

Nick was riding beside Jackson. The call had not been one he'd been expecting, but Jackson welcomed the company of his big brother nonetheless. They didn't spend much time together these days. Kobe beef had really changed the face of their operation, and Nick was busy with a Japanese export deal.

"How are the mustangs?" Nick asked, riding abreast Jackson.

Jackson was riding his favorite stallion, unsure of what Nick was really there to talk about. "Fine. I can't complain." *And neither can you,* Jackson thought. They had sold four stallions since January, each fetching a startling price tag. Nick couldn't be here to reprimand him, revenue targets were on point.

"This is awkward," Nick started, clucking to his horse.

"Awkward?" Jackson echoed.

"Yeah, see, I wanted to talk to you about the wedding."

"Right—nothing awkward there. Planning is going super well." If Nick was just here to talk weddings, they should have invited the girls. Although, push come to shove, for this wedding, Jackson worried he was even more excited than Hannah. "Never thought I'd be so over the moon to get hitched, I'll tell ya that."

Nick tipped his hat, and Jackson was unsure if it was to reposition the rim against the sun or acknowledge the statement.

"Look, the last thing I wanted to do was insert myself in the wedding planning. But I do have a favor to ask. If it's too much—"

"Let's hear it, then."

"It's about your friendship with August."

Jackson felt his mouth draw into a tight line. This was exactly why he'd ridden rodeo under an alias. Being judged by the family for his every decision, having to live up to Hartmann rules. It was exhausting.

"He was Austin's best friend. And I'll be damned if he hasn't become one of mine." *Nick wasn't the enemy. Jackson knew it, but it was still hard not to anticipate the ask that was coming.*

"It's not for me." Nick raised one hand in defense.

"Did you know?" he continued. "Know that he flew to LA for her audition?"

Jackson stared, unable to form a coherent response. *They were friends. August had assured him his kid sister was off-limits.*

"You must be mistaken," he sputtered in answer.

Nick shook his head. "Mia called. She felt guilty about getting him a hotel room key card. Especially after Mom invited Ben over for dinner. A dinner to which Evie no-showed."

Mom.

"Yeah, well, you can tell Josephine he's coming to the wedding as my best man. Unless you're here to ask for the job."

They approached the main barn, their horses steering themselves.

"No, I'm not. I thought you could ask Ben? Feels like the least you could do after our sister stomped on his heart." Nick's voice was quiet. Almost tentative.

Ben? "I mean, he's a really nice guy, but my best man?" Jackson shook his head. "I know Mom has a great idea about a Hartmann legacy, Ben and Evie, I mean… come on." He rolled his eyes.

"I'm not asking for Josephine."

Jackson pulled up on the reins of his horse. *For Evie.*

"She put you up to this?"

Nick laughed. "You really think Evie would ask for something for herself? But she and Ben were out eight times in six weeks. They were constantly texting… And this thing with August? It could ruin everything. You know as well as I do, he's not the marrying type. He's pushing Evie back to Hollywood, which is anything but healthy…"

"Yep."

"Imagine how Evie would feel having it be Ben walk her down the aisle, you know, instead of the neighborhood degenerate."

"—August isn't a degenerate."

"Okay, I was quoting Mom. As others at the wedding will do. And you know they had a thing back—"

"You mean the puppy love when she was a teen? We can't all live with our adolescent actions hanging over our head. Just because August flew to LA doesn't mean they got together." Jackson shook his head, happy to defend his friend, and sister, for that matter. *But Nick had a point.* Heck, August probably despised weddings. He hadn't thought of that when he'd asked him to do the honor.

"Not saying they did. Just saying their *friendship* will cause tongues to wag."

"Yeah, right." Jacks exhaled.

"I'm just thinking of what will be the easiest. For Evie. Heck, for you. You really want to draw focus from your bride on your wedding day?"

"I'll think about it," Jackson promised.

The wedding was in forty-eight hours and Evie had been puking for the last five. Too much ice cream. Break-up bingeing if you could call it that, was not good.

So much for "adulting" Evie.

She'd been hurling for an hour. Like clockwork. Every morning, three mornings in a row. Morning. Sick. *Morning sickness.*

Shit. She pressed her back against the headboard. *Shit.*

This was not in any plan. Not his. Not hers. She couldn't tell anyone. Couldn't even say it aloud.

So she thought it.

I might be pregnant.

Shit. Shit. Shit.

Nope. They'd used protection. Religiously. Every time.

Every time except once. On the floor of their hotel room, in the middle of a storm. Urgent and fast and all her fault.

One time. *One time without protection and this is what happens.* How unfair. She'd waited her whole life to have sex, then, after the first month of having sex regularly, bam, she might be pregnant.

Turning on the bathroom tap, she swallowed a few gulps of cold water. She needed to get home. To Mia's bathroom. She'd seen pregnancy tests under the sink that time she'd blown a fuse straightening her hair and running the blow-dryer at the same time. In looking for a handheld curling iron to finish the job, she'd stumbled on a few boxes of pregnancy tests.

"Because you never know," Mia had said, winking.

And now? Evie had to know.

She was home in fifteen minutes, pedal to the metal. Her sister would be at work. She let herself into her twin's bathroom with the desperation of an addict looking for a fix. They were there. A hoard of pregnancy tests, underneath a hair mask.

She peed on the stick quickly, then waited, the back of the box offering little entertainment.

"Take the pregnancy test as early as one day after your missed period."

Honestly. Was it irresponsible that she didn't know exactly when her period was due?

Evie chewed on the inside of her cheek. Yeah, it had been awhile. She ticked days off on her finger, then abandoned the exercise. Whatever. She was late.

Not late enough to make her frivolous virgin self nervous, but definitely late enough to make her current morning-sick, sexpot self terrified.

"Wait two minutes before expecting results. Results may take ten minutes depending on HCG levels."

Evie was so unprepared for any pregnancy that she didn't even know what HCG levels were, let alone what they should be.

She didn't look. It had only been one minute and thirteen seconds.

"One line means not pregnant. Two lines mean pregnant."

She peeked at the test. One line. She flipped it back over.

She was just late. That was good news. Very good news. *Right?*

Her phone beeped. Two minutes. She turned the stick over.

Evie had crossed a lot of lines in her life. But never two. Not until now.

Pregnant.

She should have known better.

He should have known better.

She stared into the medicine cabinet mirror, trying not to judge her reflection.

Idiot, her reflection said to her.

Sometimes one fact, one truth, could change your life. And this was one of those choices. One of those facts.

The girl in the mirror didn't even think about options. There wasn't a circumstance in which she would consider not keeping this baby.

Evie didn't have anything against abortion, but for her, and the girl in the mirror, for this pregnancy, the only thing she could imagine less than having August's baby was… not having it.

She was pregnant. And yes. She couldn't say it aloud. But not saying it out loud didn't make it less true.

Shit shit shit.

She put both her hands on the bathroom vanity. Five minutes. She could cry for five minutes. Then her eyes would be dry. She stared at herself.

"I don't want to be a father." He'd said it.

Well, being a dad and being a father wasn't the same thing at all.

She hadn't had a dad. She'd had a father. The last name. Security. But no one to read her bedtime stories or clap at her ballet recitals. Her dad had walked out for ten years, gone to live with his other family. Came back when she was sixteen. Just in time to watch her heartbreak unfold.

She would do better for her kid. Whatever it took. Whatever, whomever, she needed to be, she'd do it.

The girl in the mirror looked strong. Sure. A bit sad, but strong as hell.

It was funny. She'd left Hollywood to find her purpose. To grow up. Then Hollywood came calling back. And right now, she knew beyond a shadow of a doubt that she was all grown up. Because she couldn't fail. Wouldn't fail. Not for August's baby.

She should start by telling Mia. But she couldn't. She didn't want anyone to second-guess her decisions. Didn't want someone she loved to *say something* she couldn't forgive. She'd tell Mia when she had a plan.

There was only one person she could talk to about this, and as much as she dreaded that conversation, she'd have it. There was one safe place. One person who would listen, and nod. And be nice.

It would be easier to accept the end of the affair now. It had to be.

She splashed water on her face.

"I'm sorry," she said to her reflection. "You know why I have to do this."

It was easier apologizing to her reflection than coming clean with August.

His phone buzzed with Evie's text. We need to talk.

At the same time, an incoming call, which he answered on the first ring.

"You wanna get lunch?" Jackson said over the phone. It would the perfect time to tell him about the sale of Quaid Ranch—or twenty thousand acres of Quaid Ranch. Cody had signed a few days earlier but, at August's request, the deal had been kept quiet. Could it be that things were lining up for August Quaid? Maybe he could reconsider things with Evie.

"Yeah, that's perfect. I'm hungry. Can we make it an early one?" He looked at his watch. "I can be at Santi's in thirty minutes. Does that work?"

Santi's was a run-down barbecue joint, but Jackson loved it. So did August. Heck, so did anyone who had taste buds that varied beyond Michelin cuisine. It wasn't fancy, but, damn, it was good.

"Perfect." Jackson clicked off, and August busied himself pulling together the paperwork for his project.

As for the talk with Evie, he would deal with her later.

Santi's was buzzing with people. A few CEO types sitting awkwardly at a picnic table outside, waiting for their ribs. More flannel-wearing cowboys, and a few musicians, strumming at guitars. The people flowed like water, in and out, from pristine backgrounds and muddy inlets, all because the food was second to none.

Jackson was waiting, sitting at a picnic table in the shade, texting. He looked up as August approached.

"I ordered. Two racks, wet, and sweet potato fries."

"Slaw?" August asked.

Jackson nodded. "'Course."

He slid onto his side of the picnic table, glad he'd brought his cowboy hat for this occasion. He wanted Jackson to see him as an equal. They were frinds; Jackson was the kind of Hartmann who *liked* Santi's. But he was still a Hartmann. And August was a Quaid. So, there was that.

"You brought a man bag?" Jackson frowned at August's tote.

Don't blush. It's not a man bag. It's a leather satchel.

"What else am I supposed to carry documents in?" he askied in lieu of prompt denial.

"Easy, darlin'. I'm just teasin'." Jackson smiled.

"Actually, I want to get into this before I lose your attention entirely." August pulled the bag onto the table and started fiddling with the zipper.

"Not like a bit of food is going to keep my head out of whatever has you carrying purses." Jackson laughed.

August smiled back. This wasn't hard. It was good news, a *fait accompli*. He had the commissioner on board. Had funding lined up. The sale of the land was signed, and the severance was approved. It was all coming together.

In one exhale, he let it out. "Thing is, I'm selling. Not the whole ranch, just some of it. Er, because I want to fund a project. It's a big deal. Solar energy. I mean, I'm going to launch a solar energy project. Twenty thousand acres and everything I've made down South keeps me in control—"

"You're selling twenty thousand acres? To start a solar farm? Why have you been riding around with me, then? Learning about about the land?"

August felt his stomach flip.

"Learning about the last, I mean, that's not why I was hanging with you. I *like* hanging with you Jacks, you're my friend."

Jackson's mouth tightened. "Not a good enough friend to talk to about this play. This is fucking huge."

His stomach flipped again.

"I know. It's big. But I'm all in for Montana. Everything I have. I laid it all on the line for this deal."

"Selling half your family's land?" Jackson shook his head.

"Yeah, I get that this is gutsy, but I locked up ninety million from the State. I've thought it all through. This is my chance to make a difference." *A chance to mean something. To be someone.* He didn't have to say it. Didn't have to spell it out. Jackson was smart.

"Twenty thousand acres?"

"Relax. I sold them to Cody. And he's besotted with Hannah's best friend, if you haven't noticed, so it's not like he's going anywhere…"

Jackson was interrupted from making further complaints by the arrival of two racks of ribs.

"Can we get two beers, too?" Jackson asked of the server. *He couldn't be that mad. Not if he was ordering them both a beer.*

Jackson scratched his chin. "Look. I wish you'd told me what you were up to sooner."

"Not sure why it matters."

Jackson picked up a rib, but instead of eating it, he waved it in August's direction. "It matters because friends tell each other stuff. And we are friends. Damn good friends."

August nodded. Jackson was right. "I've been on my own for so long, it's hard to trust people."

"I know. But I trust you, August. This is a hell of a project. I'm just sorry you didn't come to the Hartmanns before what I assume is venture capital."

August smiled. It was as close to an approval as he'd come. But Jackson didn't lower his rib. Instead, he continued. "Speaking of favors, I have some rearranging to do. For the wedding. Thing is, I need a stand-in for my best man, just for the ceremony. You totally have the bachelor party. And—" with his available hand, Jackson made the sign of the cross "—you'll always be the best man of my heart."

August nodded. Not a big deal. He'd been surprised that Jackson hadn't asked Nick from the onset. Optics were everything at society weddings, and Josephine was the mother of the groom.

But it was hard not feeling this was a precursor for the rest of his life. You can be my best man, but only at the bachelor party where no one can see. He could sleep with Evie, make love to her under the stars, in hotel rooms, at his house, but only if no one knew.

That was it. Why they could never be anything more.

"I get it, buddy, don't worry. If you are cool with the whole solar project surprise, I'm cool with a switcheroo for the wedding day." He exhaled.

"Thanks. Nick is gonna be delighted. He had this crazy idea that I should ask Ben. And the last thing I want to do is cause drama. I can't tell you how much I appreciate your chillness about this. I told him your trip to LA didn't mean anything."

Jackson tucked into his ribs. But August just stared, feeling sick.

"Ben?" he parroted. *If a tree falls in the forest, does it make a sound? Was his love for Evie as clichéd as that?*

Jackson didn't look up from his plate. "Yeah, you know he and Evie have been dating. Nick thought it would be a nice show of support from our family to have them walk down the aisle together. I mean, if there's a gesture I can make to have Evie feel more comfortable at the wedding, I'm gonna do it, right?"

"Sure." The word was stuck in his throat. The picture of Evie and Ben starting the wedding processional walking side by side. He was jealous. *They were meant to be over. She'd told him as much. But why did this request, and from his dear friend at that, feel like the nail to a coffin for a relationship he wasn't ready to admit was ill-fated?*

"Honestly, to hear Nick say it, Ben is ready to walk down the aisle for real. This oughta be a nice warm up."

August just nodded, wondering how liquid a 30,000-acre solar farm could be. He should have known this purgatory was too good to last. All of a sudden, her text made sense. *We need to talk.* He knew exactly what that meant. Her family had gotten to her. They were done. Well, two could play that game. He pulled out his phone and texted:

Evie, I think I know what you want to talk about. It's cool. We were never long-term, just do what you're gonna do.

With the swoosh of the send button, his stomach sank. But at least he was back in control of what mattered. His future. He'd been her first. Maybe that was enough. For her.

Twelve

Dress Rehearsal

"**Y**ou got the part." Amber had texted her the news.

Probably because she'd ignored her last four phone calls. She didn't need another rejection right now.

August had been, *well*, predictable. And in the worst way. He hadn't written her since she'd landed from her callback audition, forty-eight infernal hours ago.

She'd sent him four text messages.

What do you mean "it's cool"?

No answer. So, she'd tried again.

I really think we need to talk, August. Come on.

Punctuated with a tasteful monkey covering its eyes. Her emoticon game was strong.

When he hadn't answered with a purple devil or anything, she'd launched another missile.

I really think we need to talk, August. Come on.

Still dead air.

I bet you're busy. I'll let you work.

Emoticon choice: crossed fingers. That was just cryptic enough. As in, she hoped he got her message. Hoped he was too busy to let her know what was up. Hoped he'd get back to her.

With Herculean strength, she managed to stop herself from a pathetic fifth text. He'd given her the best nights of her life. Let her believe for a moment that he saw her, and loved her. And that moment was worth it. Was worth the soul-crushing silence and moment of self-doubt that accompanied his ghosting. *It was worth it,* she reminded herself. Still, it was hard not to feel like she was twenty. Naked and entirely rejected. She was naive and wrong. He hadn't wanted her, he'd used her. August Quaid wasn't one speck different from the man that everyone thought him to be. Or was he? Somehow the indecision felt worse than a diagnosis. If her thing with August—whatever it was —had been DOA, surely that would have been easier to live with than this *ghosting*...

And now? She was pregnant. Pregnant and yet somehow less adult than ever before.

When her phone had beeped with a text notification, her heart had literally skipped. Then, when she'd seen that it was Amber, telling her she'd gotten the part, it fell.

Which made no sense. She should be elated. Sure she'd

had her share of B list movies, but this one? It was slated for global distribution. With an actual movie star starring opposite her. This was a big chance to get what she'd always wanted, a foot in the door with the big studios. *Except that it wasn't what she'd always wanted.*

The whole time she'd been in LA for the callback, she'd wanted to be here. Montana. Near August.

"Tell me everything." It was Mia, entering her room without knocking. She was carrying two of Pierre's to-go lattes. At least she came bearing coffee.

Evie stuck her hand out for the coffee. Then she watched as Mia installed herself on the chair opposite her bed.

Evie opened her mouth to speak. She could talk about the movie part. Mia would then likely suggest making their coffees Irish, which, honestly, Evie could use right now. She felt dead inside. Totally numb. Because her messages to August were marked "read" and she'd had no reply.

But nothing came out. Instead, she started to cry.

"I'm sorry, Evie. I really thought you'd get this one. I mean I don't see why your no-good agent would have gotten you all riled up if you didn't have a decent chance."

This made Evie cry a little harder. Not sobs, but raw tears, now flowing freely. Because her twin sister thought she should be sad about not getting a part. Entirely trivial with respect to what she was feeling.

"Seriously. If you want to be an actress, just leave. August will support you. Or Ben— it doesn't matter."

"You think I'm crying about Ben? What about our twin connection? Come *on*, Mia. Can't you just be on my side for once?" Evie managed to hold back the rest of her emotion, forcing a long gulp of too-hot coffee down her throat.

"I am on your side." Mia was on the bed immediately.

"But Evie, you have a way of coloring your experience. I mean, you're such a romantic that you're literally the only twenty-eight-year-old virgin that even exists."

"I am not." Evie sniffed.

Mia hugged her. "I'm sorry. I didn't mean that. I'm sure there are loads of other virgins. And I honestly respect you for hanging in there until you're married."

Evie snapped her head up. "Is that why you think I was waiting? Because of the sanctity of marriage?"

Mia balked. "Er, isn't it?"

Evie let it all out. "No, Mia. I was waiting to be in love."

"*Was* waiting?" her sister asked softly.

"Was waiting," she confirmed. It felt good. Telling someone. As if the admission made it more real. No take backs.

"I didn't know it was so serious between you and Ben," Mia mused, smirking.

Evie threw a pillow at her.

"Very Cinderella story for you," Mia added. "I had always wondered about the tattoos…are they… everywhere?"

Evie blushed.

"Seriously? You're gonna be one of those girls? The kind who doesn't tell her best friend the details of her first time?"

Evie stared at her hands. Pressed her eyes shut. Then she opened them and reached for her phone. Still no reply.

"Is it okay if I am? One of those girls?"

Truth was, it didn't matter what Mia said. There was no amount of cajoling that could get Evie to dish on her time with August. It was enough just to share that it had happened. The memory was for her. Especially as she grappled with the reality that that might be all she got. And she had to somehow make it enough.

"I did get the part." She wasn't crying anymore. If she'd had any growing up to do, it was done.

Mia's smile widened, and her hand flew to her face, pushing her bangs away as though they were somehow keeping her from seeing reason. Then she offered Evie a hearty clap on the back. "That's freaking amazing. Honestly. Never had a doubt." She winked.

"I haven't told anyone yet, I just found out. Shooting starts fast. Just three weeks."

"Basically right after the wedding?"

"Yeah. If I take the part."

Mia smiled, then put her arm around her sister. "You know, I'm really proud of you, Evie. You always were the brave one."

"Brave?" Evie sniffled. "Don't you mean the scaredy-cat?"

"I think waiting for what you want, then taking it, no hesitation, is about the bravest thing you can do."

Evie just nodded. She had no regrets. The decision to be with August was one she'd make again, even if she'd known then how it would end. It was the easiest choice she'd ever made, but it didn't make her brave. Just stupid. And in love. And now? Alone.

He was late. Late because he had spent the better part of an hour staring at his phone. She hadn't written him in three days. Okay, to be fair, she'd written him three days ago, when she'd landed after her second audition, but nothing since. Yes, her text messages were begging for an answer, but somehow, waiting with his head in a guillotine was less enticing than one would think. He'd prefer if this, whatever it was, just fizzled out, without the heart-wrenching "conversation."

Technically, the ball was in his court. He wanted to write her back. Wanted to take another step, but he was paralyzed by the thought of what she'd say. Maybe to her, it had been a roll in the hay—okay, many rolls in the hay—a way to shake her virginity with someone who didn't matter, so that she could be ready for someone who did. He didn't want to be the chain that pulled her down. Evie could go anywhere. Be anything. Be with anyone. This space, the silence he offered up, was his kindness, even if it was a lot harder to maintain than he'd dreamed.

Montana royalty. The future she deserved. Jackson had been pretty clear. Sure. He hadn't exactly been open with Jacks about the torch he had been carrying for his little sister. But he knew what Jacks would say. No matter how much August had pulled himself up. No matter how much he'd earned, it would never be as much as Ben. Never come close to the Kingsley holdings.

Maybe it was better to let her have the happiness everyone knew she deserved.

So he didn't write. Didn't do much, apart from mope. Sven, his trusty ranch hand, had found him drunk two mornings in a row, sleeping in the Hartmann barn with his hand resting on the decade-old graffiti. *AQ + EH.*

Wasn't love putting the other person first? Wasn't him saying nothing and letting her have the future she deserved the biggest expression of love he could make?

He texted Cody. It was time to schedule some poker. A card game was a surefire way to clear his head. To think only of numbers and people to play. After all, everyone had a role in this Montana legacy, and his? The bad boy.

Thirteen

Anywhere But Here

"Is this how you thank me for getting you the keys to a penthouse suite?" Mia launched into a tirade before August had a chance to register who he was speaking to. "Blowing off my sister?"

"I thought the case of whiskey I sent Antone was thanks for your previous help?" he murmured, still a little drunk and *very* hungover.

"I know what you guys did in that penthouse. One case of whiskey won't be enough of a thank-you for that wham, bam, thank you, ma'am." Mia said.

How she could laugh at the situation was beyond him.

"Why are you calling anyway? If you need another case of booze, ask your fiancé. We're not friends, Mia. Don't call me." It was an aggressive reaction, sure, but the last person he wanted to see right now was a Hartmann. Unless...

""Relax. I'm calling to help. I know what you want, and I can help you get it."

The admission sobered him, and August ran a hand through his hair. Was it possible? Could one of the nuclear Hartmann family members actually be pulling for a Quaid?

"Seriously. I know how my sister feels about you. And about the hopeless match my mother is insisting on."

Despite himself, he smiled, nodding at the phone like an idiot who confused voice calls for Zooms...

"Let's start by making this wedding an opportunity for you to mark your territory, *mm'kay*?" Mia suggested. "I'm gonna text you a number, for a dance teacher. Call her, and practice enough not to embarrass us on the dance floor, okay? I'll text you later with part two of this plan."

Mia hung up without waiting for an answer, and for the first time since his solar grant went through, August began to wonder if his tides were truly turning.

"Don't act like I'm the first person to ignore a yellow engine light," she muttered into the phone. Mia had been laughing for three minutes straight. Traitor.

"Seriously. Can you come?" Evie flirted with the idea of lifting the hood, but as she stood in front of the hood of her car, she couldn't even remember *where* the weird lever thing was to open the hood. It wasn't as if she'd even know what to look for even if she did manage to open the damn thing.

Her twin stopped laughing long enough to remind her that today she was working in Billings. It was a hard no to a rescue mission.

"Want me to call Antone?" Mia offered.

"Nope, I'd prefer to keep this embarrassment as private as possible," Evie said.

It wasn't as if she didn't know where she was. She took this road home precisely because, in her youth, she'd often crossed paths with *him*. The Quaid Ranch was about twenty minutes away from here if landmarks served her right and she cut across the field.

"Or Ben?" Mia teased.

"No. Don't call anyone. Heck, I wish I hadn't even called you." She hung up on her howling twin and reached for her purse.

It was just after five, so she had more than enough time to make it in daylight. Maybe if she closed her eyes she could imagine she was a novice burlesque dancer, making her way through a wild forest to a hunky lumberjack... Imagining their weekend in the woods didn't make it any easier to forgive him. How dare he ghost her? Although she'd been pulling away too. A hand went to her stomach, patting the piece of him she carried with her. Was she so wrong about him? About how he felt about her? Was that what sex was like for everyone? Was their connection totally in her head?

She was about to find out.

Slipping in earbuds, Evie walked to the beat of Maroon Five and sang along.

Sing like no one is listening, indeed.

Perhaps if she'd been paying attention and not singing along, she would have noticed the grumbling clouds as they gathered. Or might've observed the smell of the damp air as it rolled in, when the cold front cut across the field, bringing with it the threat of heavy storms.

The rain pulled her from her reverie, starting as the odd freckle of warm wetness, but before she knew it, her clothes were slick against her skin. When she rounded the corner to the Quaid Ranch, she smiled with relief. His truck was there. August was home. And since he'd always been handy with cars, he'd have hers up and running faster than she could figure out how to open the damn hood. Not to mention that it was the perfect reason for her to stop by. Maybe his phone was broken. Maybe there was a reason he hadn't called. The more she thought about it, the more she started to think that it was more than likely she had had the whole thing wrong. There was *obviously* an explanation for his silence, and here she was, brought by the fates of car mechanics and rain to figure it out.

He didn't answer the door. To be fair, she hadn't knocked. Not when she'd taken in the second car, painted a sickening shade of pink. What kind of person paints their car hot pink?

She studied the car.

The same kind of person who bought vanity license plates.

"WCKDFUN." Because of course. That made perfect sense.

Instead of knocking, she rounded the corner of the ranch, the wraparound porch giving her access to a view of the living room though the main window.

It was raining hard, so at least her tears weren't as noticeable. She shouldn't be sad; he had the right to entertain any woman he wanted. He hadn't made her any promises. *Except it felt like he had.*

But maybe that had just been sex. She had no frame of reference. Maybe that was how August did it. Made every woman feel like they were the center of his world, just to promptly forget about them. Pop culture did seem to relativize that kind of behavior. He'd abandoned her before. What had made her think it would be any different this time?

She sank to the floor of the porch, crawling like an idiot as she took in the surroundings. Then her heart sank. August was dancing with WCKDFUN. She was as opposite to Evie as he could find. A Barbie, skinny in a way that was genetically impossible for curvy, tall women. Her platinum hair was white to the root, but it was the nails that made her cringe.

"You should get your nails done," her agent used to harp.

Well, Barbie evidently hadn't missed a salon day. Not ever, by the looks of the claws she had in August.

Her stomach sank. So, this was why he hadn't called her. Why he hadn't texted. He'd had his fun, and now he'd moved on.

Thunder cracked through the sky, and Evie frowned. There was no easy way out of this. She wasn't going to walk forty minutes back to her place. Not with lightning and thunder threatening her very life.

Nor was she going to interrupt what was clearly a date. Or a... Evie swallowed, her throat hot and eyes burning. Thanks to August, she had a pretty good idea what might be in store for Barbie, or whatever her name was. She pulled out her earbuds, not wanting to dull any sense that might prove useful right now.

Yep, she had a pretty good idea of what was happening. Or not.

Nope. Not happening.

She wasn't gonna let it happen. As much as she didn't want to interrupt the lovebirds looking like a drowned rat, she was mad. Mad and insanely jealous. This was supposed to be her goodbye to August. And now, Barbie was ruining it.

She crawled back to the front door, careful not to get noticed. She heard the lyrics to her favorite song through the window.

I wasted my nights. You turned out the lights... She struggled to think of the words. Something about happily ever after. And fairy tales being full of shit. Well, that was accurate enough.

She knocked.

In her mind's eye, she saw him cross to the door.

He opened it. The first thing she noticed was his smell. He smelled like pine and sap and woodsmoke. Like their weekend camping.

Do not cry. . This was supposed to be their goodbye.

"Evie? You okay?" August's eyebrows knit together in question.

"Babe? That's our hour." The blonde was reaching for her coat.

She charged by the hour? Evie felt sickness mounting in her throat. Maybe it wasn't the kind of date she'd worried about. Maybe it was worse.

"Are you okay?" August asked again.

"No." She managed to force the answer out.

"We on for next week?" The blonde pushed past her. "Babe, I'm going to let you deal with—" she gave Evie an exaggerated once-over "—whatever this is. I've got another booking, so I've gotta run."

"Another booking?" Evie felt her mouth tighten with the question.

Before Evie could register anything else about the woman, or her eventual bookings, she was back in her pink car.

"You wanna come in?" he offered, pulling his door open.

She frowned but walked in. What choice did she have?

It didn't look good. He was smart enough to realize it. He wasn't sure what he was doing, trying to be the kind of man Evie would choose, heck, answering her text messages would probably work better than dance lessons, but to be fair, the last person he was expecting to see at his door at the onset of a flash storm, soaked to the bone, was Evie Hartmann. First, was their fight, which had felt more like a breakup. Then the best man demotion. Some might say he didn't know when to quit. But looking at her, he could only grin.

You know you liked a girl when you signed up for private dance lessons just to impress her and her family at a damned wedding you didn't even want to go to in the first place.

August Quaid was fairly certain of a few things. He was a good dancer. Well, at least, he was good at the kind of dancing that was like sex. Slow, grinding, heat and hips and hands everywhere. He was hard just thinking about what it would be like to dance like that with Evie, the good girl incarnate, and show her just how good at *dancing* he could be. But something told him Jackson's wedding wasn't going to be *that kind of wedding.* And fortunately, Mia had hooked him up with this dance teacher. To teach him to waltz. Because being with Evie Hartmann meant knowing how to waltz. Knowing how to be the kind of man that liked waltzing. If the past six days of no contact with Evie had taught him anything, apart from how to cure a hangover, it was that he couldn't let her go without a fight. Especially if her twin sister thought there was even a shadow of a chance he'd win.

The tight line of her lips was not lost on him. Her mood was another thing of which August was certain. She was pissed, and, just maybe, hurt.

Her purse fell to the floor with a loud thud.

"You look good," he said reflexively. The words tripped off his tongue before he had the presence of mind to stop them. *She was mad,* he reminded himself. Because he'd been ghosting her. Because he was an idiot.

"Save it, August. I don't charge by the hour, but I am mad enough to want to get out of here as soon as possible."

"Mad? About Beth?" He ran his hand through his hair, gathering it into a ponytail and then twisting it into a bun. She liked his man bun, and he was ready to use every weapon in his arsenal.

He tried to grin at her.

Nothing.

Her eyes narrowed. "Are you going to explain yourself?"

He shook his head and then walked down the hall.

"August," she called after him. He heard the patter of sodden feet follow him.

"Just getting you a towel." Not that his floors were precious, it was more the prospect of wrapping the towel around her.

"That woman… Your, er, date," Evie raised her voice, words crashing together.

"Date?" Now he'd lost the plot. "Woman, what are you talking about?

He spun quickly, stopping dead in his tracks, and he felt her crash against him.

"Are you going to deny it? I mean, I was *here,* August. I might be naive, but I'm not stupid."

"No one is calling you naive. I'm pretty sure I'm the stupid one because I really don't see the problem."

"The problem? With you sleeping with someone else just a week after…" Her voice caught.

Her eyes widened, then her brows crested together. She inhaled quickly, a succession of breaths that were a poorly disguised effort to avoid a sob.

She was dripping on his floor. Soaking wet, her hair plastered to her head. Her white shirt offering a clear view of the purple bra underneath.

"You know," he said gruffly, "you're beautiful even when you're being ridiculous."

A tear escaped her.

He pulled her into his arms, and for a moment, she fought him.

"August, it's not okay for me just to be one of your women. A woman who charges by the hour, I just… I can't believe I was so wrong about you."

"You *were* wrong about me, and I'm sorry for that." What was the point of getting torturous secret dance lessons to impress a girl if they just ended up blowing up in your face and hurting the girl?

He pressed a kiss onto her mouth and she bit him. Hard.

"Screw you, then." She resumed her struggle, but he pulled her closer.

"Evie," he said her name so quietly she wondered a moment if she'd imagined it.

"Yes, August."

"Just so we're clear." He cleared his throat. She pressed her ear against his chest and he was sure she could hear the erratic beat of his heart, no stethoscope required. He was that nervous.

"I, er, hired a dance teacher. For the wedding. So I wouldn't embarrass you on the dance floor."

"Beth?"

"Yeah." He blushed. "The hour she charges for is dancing only. I swear on my life."

She relaxed a bit, and felt her face soften.

"You're taking dance lessons? Don't tell me—burlesque?" She looked up, eyes wide, and managed a grin.

It didn't matter. Didn't matter who she was. There was no way he could kiss her like he had, and it not mean anything. She wasn't a sexpert, but she was a woman and a woman's intuition had to stand for something.

So she kissed him. One last hit, she figured. If he could pull a 'love her and leave her' move, then so could she. One last time.

They were still a sweaty, wet mess in the hall when she reached for her wet jeans. Her body felt like a spaghetti noodle. It was as if she couldn't move, couldn't walk away, even if she wanted to. As they'd had sex, every muscle she had had tensed and then released at the same time, and she'd never felt anything like it, never even imagined anything like it, before in her life.

"That's makeup sex, I guess?" she mused aloud.

"What, did it not meet your sexpectations?"

"Did it meet yours?" she snapped back.

He didn't answer, just pulled her against him. His chest was warm and hard. Summoning beyond-human strength, she mustered the energy to trace one hand across the plane of his stomach, marveling at the thin scatter of tawny hair that trailed down the V of his hip.

"You should know. That was the best sex I've ever had," he said.

She kept touching him. Not because she wanted a re-peat performance, which she definitely did, but because she couldn't stop.

Suspending her hand a moment, she gathered her breath. "Aug?"

"Mmm-hmm?"

"I thought it was pretty good, too."

His hand found hers and squeezed.

"Can you sleep over?" he asked.

"No," she said. Because her decision had been made. There was no going back now. Not even when every burning fiber of her body wanted to stay, consequences be damned. She had to leave. Had to end things. She'd rather it was her, ending things now, than him, dumping her because she was pregnant. At least, now, she could leave him wanting more.

"I got the part," she said. Awkward, maybe, but she wanted to tell him. It didn't feel real, not without him saying wow. That he was proud of her.

He pressed a kiss into her hair. "I figured."

Who had told him? Mia?

"You were always going to get that part, Evie. You're a fabulous actress, and you're going to get whatever you want. I'm sure of it.

What if the thing she wanted the most in the world was him?

She didn't say anything, just let her hand slip onto his chest. If she was quiet and very still, she could feel his heartbeat. *Or was it hers?*

"I got the part, and I'm moving back. To LA."

She felt his chin nod against her, and she gathered the courage to speak past the lump in her throat. "I'm glad we had tonight. It's the perfect way to say goodbye." She tried to pull away. At first, his arms trapped her against his chest, but when she tried a second time, she knew what she had to say to get free.

"It was always going to end, August. Let's at least let it end well."

"I hate to see you cry." Mia put her hand on Evie's arm.

"I know you helped him." Evie choked back tears.

"I'd do it again. He's not a bad guy."

Her twin's approval just made Evie cry harder. "Yeah. But he doesn't want kids." Evie let her head fall heavily into her hands.

"Kids? You're twenty-eight. You've got nothing but time to help him change his mind." Her sister patted her back in warm concentric circles, but the comfort just made her feel worse.

"That's the thing, Mia. I don't."

Mia's hand froze on her back.

"It's okay. There's only one option for me now." Evie stood, pushing her shoulders back. It was time to live the life she'd been born into. It was time to grow up.

"Pregnant?" Ben repeated.

It had been easy to tell Ben. She'd spelled out the truth like a doctor. Totally devoid of emotion. If this was going to work, she had to come clean about everything. She owed her friend that. That, and so much more.

"Well, there's no avoiding the truth. I was stupid to think this would go another way." Evie hated making August out to be the bad guy. For blaming him for a decision he hadn't made consciously. But this rejection was easier to bear.

"I'm sure you didn't count on being pregnant and alone. I could kill—"

"It's not his fault," Evie interjected. She couldn't bear the thought of Ben, much less someone else, thinking ill of August. "I always knew he didn't want children."

"Sometimes a man decides things despite of what they might want. A man makes decisions he can be proud of, regardless of how he might have thought his life would turn out."

Ben's arm was heavy on her elbow, and Evie raised her eyes to look at him.

"You know how important you are to me, right?" She choked on the words. Somehow, it felt necessary for him to know that she *did* love him, however platonically that might be. "You're an epically good guy."

"Too good a guy to *let* you ruin your life."

As if there were any good options. "Nobody *let* me do anything. I decided this. Time for me to put my big-girl panties on and assume my responsibilities—"

"Let me assume them with you. Problems are always easier to bear together."

"Not sure what you can do to help, Ben. That's the thing—this is a mess of my own making."

She'd called him to have someone to talk to. Ben wouldn't judge her. He'd listen and be a vault with regards to the Hartmann rumor mill. If she could count on one thing, it was that.

"I could marry you." He made the statement quietly but with certainty. It wasn't a question.

She hated herself for considering it. For not denying him outright. But damn. Talk about big-girl panties.

"I know you don't have feelings for me, but Evie, I love you. For real. It might not be the toe-curling love you've always dreamed of, but it's real deep and I know if you give me a chance, I know this could turn into something good." His free hand gripped her other elbow, and his shoulders were squared to hers.

Her heart was breaking. For herself. For August. For Ben. For her baby. How could anyone make smart decisions with this kind of pressure?

Ben swiped his hands up and down her arms. "We could make our own family. I'm confident. In myself and in us. I'm confident enough for both of us."

She felt herself waver. This would be easy. Everyone would be happy. Everyone except August. And her.

She suddenly felt sick. "I'm going to faint."

"Don't do that," he whispered, then he released her arms and dropped to one knee.

"Evie Hartmann," he started.

It was happening.

She pressed her eyes shut and nodded. "That's my name." *What a stupid thing to say.*

She heard a fabric box click open. *He had a ring. She couldn't open her eyes. Couldn't look into his face and say no to the kindest offer she'd ever had.*

"It was my mother's." He made the statement to her closed eyes. "And I want you to have it."

She opened her eyes.

The ring was beautiful. A delicate solitaire with fine metal scrollwork on either side of the diamond. It was absolutely beautiful.

But not for her.

"Ben."

"Don't answer me right now. This isn't an ultimatum. Just think about it. You owe me that. You owe your baby that." He dropped the velvet ring box into the pocket of her trench coat. She felt the weight hang in the bottom of the pocket like a ton of bricks.

"I can answer you—" she started weakly.

"No. Sleep on it. Think about it. Nothing has to happen at a pace you're not comfortable with. I'll raise your kid as my own. I'll love that little baby on the sole virtue of his parentage. Of his family."

"Ben—" she started again.

"Just think about it. It's not the worst offer you're gonna get."

And just like that, he turned and walked away.

She looked down at her hands. She was holding the box. Had his mother's ring in her hands.

"Ben," she called after him.

"Tomorrow," he called over his shoulder. "Let's talk tomorrow. Everything is always better in the morning."

* * *

AUGUST: We need to talk. I don't want it to be one last time. I don't want us to be over Evie. Hell, we can make LA work. Please.

EVIE: Okay. Before the wedding. Let's chat.

AUGUST: Or now? I'll make you steak.

Maybe he was wrong. Maybe she wasn't ready to move on. Maybe she had changed her mind about the move to LA...

EVIE: Tomorrow. A chat before the wedding. If that's okay?

It wasn't.

AUGUST: Sure.

He hadn't expected the rush of emotion he'd felt when she'd stepped out from behind Nick Hartmann to answer his knock. Her hair pulled off her face in the classic Evie chignon. A white V-neck T-shirt that clung to her with a fit that left him oddly jealous of the scrap of fabric, and blue jeans, tapered into heeled boots.

Nick stepped aside. *Perfect. A family affair.* The presence of the eldest brother did nothing but feed his belief that he didn't belong. Couldn't belong. But it was a belief he was there to challenge.

"You look beautiful, Evie," he said, wishing his words were adequate. She was striking. He'd face a thousand dragons, a thousand Nicks, to be with her.

"Wanna go for a little walk?" She took a few steps toward him, and he offered an arm.

"Sure."

She nodded, but her lips were thin again. No smiles today. That was okay. He had some tricks up his sleeve.

Once they'd cleared the ranch, she loosened up a bit. But there was something about her face. A tightness that made him uneasy.

"August. We need to talk."

"About tomorrow, you mean?" He'd been thinking about it all day. She was wrong. They could go public at the wedding. Their relationship deserved an honest effort. A chance.

"I don't know if we want the same things." She was going for stoic, but her veneer was beginning to crack.

He laughed, but it was a hollow.

"My family is really important to me. Family in general." She twisted her hands, wringing them anxiously.

It was happening. She was ending things. *He'd expected more from her. Her roll in the hay was over. Virginity sorted, she was ready for the major leagues.*

"I see."

She pushed her shoulders back, her T-shirt straining against her chest. "I just think the fact that you don't want kids, that you don't value, er, heritage—"

"Well, not in the same way you do." His voice was clipped. Short. He fought for control.

He reached for her hand. "Evie," he started. Then he felt it.

A ring. On her finger.

"He proposed this morning." She didn't look at him when she made the admission.

"He" was Ben. Ben Kingsley.

"It was always gonna be him." He'd said it. Pronounced their death sentence.

She just nodded. Each nod a damning slice to his heart.

"August."

"Don't. Just… I need a minute." He turned away from her. Away from the ring, if you could even call the anchor on her hand a ring. He stared out at the landscape. Beautiful. Wild. He always thought of her when he was in the wild.

"I always knew you were too good for me." He spoke into the wind, but his words carried.

Stupid dance lessons. Stupid fantasy. Stupid him, thinking he'd be enough. Thinking there would ever be a situation in which the brothers, the Hartmanns, would accept him.

He should marry his own kind. Or better, never marry at all.

"I'm not too good for you, August. We just want different things."

"I know. I can't give you what you want. No matter what I did, it would never be enough. I mean, I get that."

"I'm going to take the ring off. For the wedding. I don't want to take any attention away from Jackson and Hannah. And I haven't told anyone. Not my brothers. Not even Mia. But I thought you should know now."

That was something. If she hadn't told anyone, maybe he could change her mind.

"When Ben asked me, he didn't press for an answer. I wanted you to know first. It was easier to show you than tell you. But I'm going to take it off now. For the wedding."

"It's just a ring, Evie." He turned toward her, and reached for her hand, taking it in both of his. "Damn it. Evie, it's a ring. You can take it off. Say no."

"This doesn't change what we shared, or how much that

meant to me." Her voice caught, but she tightened her mouth in resolve.

"That isn't a ring, it's a promise. It's your heart. Your future. And you're promising it to him."

"You have no idea how sorry I am."

Her words cut him. Even if he'd been expecting them on some level. She was the sun. The center of his world. And she had burned him.

"I get it, Evie. I just want you to be happy."

She didn't say anything. Just turned and walked away.

He listened hard. Didn't turn until he was sure she'd put enough space between them.

His eyes burned. It would be a large wedding. He could hide. He could avoid everyone. Then disappear. He'd done it before. At least, this time, he'd leave behind a state treasure. The largest single installation of solar power in the West. He'd done it. Made something of himself.

It was just too little.

Too late.

Fourteen

The Wedding

Paperwork was the worst. And it was unending when you were the boss. Quaid Corp had been selling interests in fracking for eight months, liquidating its shares in the abhorrent practice, but when he wrapped up the last contract, they would be fully finished. Divorced from oil, and all in on green energy. It was the dawn of a new era for the Quaids.

He'd flirted with the idea of visiting his dad. Visiting his brother. Updating them on the business, and the future of Quaid Corp. But he didn't. As he stared out the window of the renovated ranch, he felt calm. He knew exactly what he needed to do. Exactly who he needed to be. Sometimes the people in your family weren't the ones who mattered most. He knew it. He just needed Evie to realize it, too.

He leaned back in his chair, spinning back to his desk to assess the last round of paperwork. It was early, but he had the day off. There was a wedding to attend after all. He'd signed the contract yesterday. Toyota was investing. Being interested in pretty much anything related to green energy, they'd outbid Capital One, and thirty thousand acres of his land was about to be designated for a new wind farm. His part of the bill? A cool $180 million, but half of it would come from the state of Montana. His grant had been approved and the Clean Energy Grant allotment was made, and Quaid Corp had won, project fully funded to budget. Yes, the balance he owed was nearly all the money he'd made in ten years, plus the proceeds of the ranch severance and sale, but with the Tesla battery technology, he'd be able to power 200,000 homes with green energy, and that was just in year one. If he'd done the cash flow projection correctly, he'd be in a position to double down in six years.

The contract was printed. Signed and sorted.

The "Goldberg Variations" were playing," Bach's masterpiece as far as August was concerned. A simple aria, then thirty different variations, each of them epic.

Like Evie.

She was gonna be excited. Maybe even proud of him. This wind farm was a different variation of him. The variation she could be proud of. The Quaid variation he wanted to be. She'd loved his green energy idea, and now it was gonna become true. *If you can dream it, you can be it.*

Making his way to the kitchen, August flipped on the Bezzera espresso machine he'd had delivered. He'd ordered it three weeks ago, when he'd still labored under the delusion that Evie might spend another night with him. The white machine with oiled wooden accents lit up. At least it made a damn good latte.

The smell of coffee was delicate and delicious. And complex. Like someone he knew. He looked out the window of his kitchen and decided, *Today was the day he got her back.*

Was it clichéd to fight for a girl at someone else's wed-

ding? Maybe. But truth was truth, and August wasn't prepared to go one more day without the world knowing how he
felt about Evie Hartmann. It had been fourteen hours since
her admission, and already that felt like too long. He didn't
care whom she told. Didn't care how hard it was gonna be
to fight for her. He was ready to do anything. Be anything,
as long as it meant being with her.

His intentions were interrupted by a knock at the door,
and he had to will himself to bite back the thought that
maybe it was her. *No. That would be too easy.*

His phone display showed 7 a.m. Only people who hated
him would come this early.

Running a hand through his hair, he made his way to
the door.

"Hey."

Dressed in a suit, topped with a cream-colored cowboy
hat, stood Mia.

They weren't friends. Mostly because August struggled
with crippling pain at looking at Evie's mirror image. But 7
a.m.? She must *really* hate him. "Hey," he answered.

"Can I come in?" Mia shifted from foot to foot. She took
the cowboy hat and spun it in her hands. Fidgeting like a
four-year-old.

"You look like you need a coffee." August opened the
door fully, then led the way to the kitchen.

Mia took a seat on a varnished barstool, but she twitched
the entire seven minutes it took August to prepare the latte,
her foot hitting the bottom bar of the stool in a staccato
rhythm.

"What can I do ya for?" August asked.

Mia stared at the latte that was being handed to her.

"I didn't expect your place to be like…this," she answered, dodging his question.

That annoyed August. "Like this?"

"You know." Mia blushed, suddenly aware of her condescension. "Modern." She gestured around the kitchen.

August shrugged. Mia wasn't a bad sort, she was just ridiculously privileged. And it was fine. August didn't mind the shock anymore, or the assumptions and surprise that followed, when people bore witness to the two-million-dollar facelift he'd given the family home.

The kitchen was his favorite part of the update, an unexpected marriage of industrial chic and farmhouse charm. But he hadn't commissioned the work to impress anyone, he'd just wanted to feel at home. Right now, though, he felt seen, and by entirely the wrong person.

"Something I can help you with, Mia?"

She blushed. Cheeks pink. Not what August had expected.

"I shouldn't be here." Her foot tapped harder on the footstool.

"Why are you here?" He was still on his first coffee of the day. He had no filter, but honestly, the woman had come at 7 a.m. on a Saturday. She deserved the worst of whatever August could dish out. Except that she didn't. August was the baddie. "Actually I'm glad you came. We need to talk."

Mia didn't say anything. Just continued with her manic tapping.

"I know Ben asked her to marry him."

The tapping stopped.

Drawing on a calm he didn't know he had, August put the latte cup back on the countertop. Evie had been honest about that at least. It was a small shred of decency from an otherwise disappointing revelation.

"You know you're not right for her." Mia said simply, trying to quiet the insane jealousy that brewed within him.

August cleared his throat. "I don't know that at all, actually."

Do not antagonize her. She's been your only ally. Find out why she's come.

"I guess you're here because you know we've been…dating." *Sure. Dating was a stretch, but a good salesperson always overstated their position with confidence to intimidate the competition.*

"If that's what you want to call it," Mia answered quietly.

"I'd call it a hell of a lot more than that, actually. I've been in love with Evie for the better part of a decade."

She looked up, making a searing eye contact, her eyes a warm, piercing hazel. "Yeah, well, Ben's been in love with Evie as long as I can remember—"

"Evie? Or some construction of her? I don't think you even know her, or you would have figured out that she's meant to be with me. That she doesn't see Ben as a target to marry. She's doing it to make you lot happy." August gripped the countertop until his knuckles were white with the pressure.

"Know her? I can assure you, I know her, I'm her freaking twin."

"Yeah, well, I know her, too." August knew every inch of her. *Loved* every inch of her.

"You know what I meant, Quaid."

"Yeah, I know what you meant." That he wasn't good enough for Evie. Which might be true, but he loved her enough to accept her. To not want her to change. Not for a minute. "Look, I've got a hell of a day ahead of me…" Was there another way to get a ferociously protective twin to leave?

"She wants a family," Mia reminded him, making eye contact, face unreadable.

The words hit August in the gut. He'd known, but hearing them amplified the feeling he was gonna lose her. They echoed in his head. Prince Charming was precisely the kind of man Evie deserved. A better man wouldn't stand in the way.

"She's pregnant. I thought you should know."

It should occur to him that Mia made the statement to infer, perhaps, that Ben was the father. But August knew. Knew immediately that if there was a baby, it was his. He'd eat his own hat before he believed for a second Evie had given herself to Ben, and even if she had, he didn't want her any less, just blamed himself for creating whatever space that had allowed that to happen.

He pressed his eyes shut and thought about their whirlwind coupling in his hallway. The highlight of his life. He'd never been so irresponsible. They'd been careful. *Except once.*

"I guess you're the one who needs to know. Trying to talk your sister—my girl—into marrying another man." He reached into his pocket and withdrew the ring he'd bought her, six years ago. The day he signed his first fracking lease. "I've known for years she was the woman for me Mia, and I'll be damned if some other man raises my baby."

"I guess you're the one who needs to know. Trying to talk your sister—my girl—into marrying another man." August managed to direct the statement with as little attitude as his commitment to gentlemanly behavior would permit.

"Is she? Your girl? Then why is it me telling you about the baby and not her? Damn it, August, I was on your side. I helped you with the stupid dance lessons, the hotel room key. And my sister gets pregnant and doesn't even tell you?"

It hurt.

"That's my fault. But it's nothing I can't fix." He imbued

as much confidence as he could into his statement, willing it to be true.

Mia's face was tight, and August watched as her head bobbed. "Right. That's what I'd hoped to hear."

Mia got up and nodded, putting her hat back on her head. *Hoped to hear? Did he have a chance after all? August felt his throat tighten.*

"Best of luck to you, August. I always did like rooting for the underdog." She left his coffee untouched on the polished cement countertop. "You need to fight for her if you ever want to feel you deserve her."

August watched as Mia let herself out.

August stared at the cup a long time. Fourteen hours, and he hadn't stopped thinking about her. About the ring she wore on her finger. But fourteen hours wasn't long enough to understand why she hadn't come to him about the baby. Or how he was going to get her back. Or how his whole world was about to change.

He picked up Mia's coffee cup and held it, still warm with the coffee. *You need to fight for her if you ever want to feel you deserve her.*

Ben wasn't a bad guy. He was a good guy. A perfect guy, maybe. But for Evie, the only perfect guy was him.

The ceremony was beautiful. Beautiful and torturous. Somewhere between the walk down the aisle, clutching Prince Charming, and the altar, where she had a prime ticket to a romantic ceremony, she lost the plot. Evie was crying. And not just a single, graceful tear. It was a full-on runny-nose situation.

"Isn't it just so romantic?" Emily, Hannah's maid of honor, cooed in her ear, offering up a hankie.

"And do you, Jackson Hartman, take Hannah Bean to be

your lawfully wedded wife?" The priest's voice was strong and echoed through the small chapel.

"I do." There wasn't a moment of hesitation. Evie stared at her brother as he vowed to love Hannah, for better or for worse, for the rest of his days. It was true. It was love. It was pure. It was everything she wanted. Everything she'd ever dreamed of.

"And do you, Hannah Bean, take Jackson Hartmann to be your lawfully wedded husband?" the priest asked.

She searched for August in the crowd. He had to be there. She regretted letting him think she'd left him for Ben. She had given Ben back his ring before the ceremony. Her security blanket was gone, but she was a big girl now.

"I do," Hannah promised.

Several people in the audience murmured, and a few from the back row let out a clap. It was tentative at first, but soon all the invitees were hooting and clamoring.

"I now pronounce you man and wife."

Should she have come clean about the baby to August? Maybe she'd decided too fast? No. It would be worse to force him into a child he was clear about not wanting. And if he'd suggested, er, taking care of it? She'd lose the perfect way she remembered him.

It was worth something. Her memory of the past eight weeks.

It was worth a lot.

It was worth the pain.

It was even worth the lie.

Then she saw him. Staring at her. His eyes, a shocking blue, wide. He looked at her and her heart stopped. She felt dizzy. Weak. Unsure of everything she'd ever done. His eyes were wet. He'd been moved by the ceremony, too. Then, in the heat of August, Evie Hartmann fainted.

* * *

"Give her some space," a Bostonian voice ordered. *Emily, the maid of honor, her subconscious advised.*

"Someone, get some water." *Hannah, the only other Bostonian, whom Evie could identify with her eyes closed.*

"Is she all right?" *Nick.*

"Get some toast," Jackson suggested.

Voices were everywhere. Noise. Stifling heat. This dress was too tight. She was too hot. She couldn't breathe. Didn't want to open her eyes. Didn't want to face it all, without him.

Even if she had to.

"I'll call the ambulance," Josephine suggested.

"Relax, Mom, she's in good hands," Mia said. "We have two ER doctors as guests. Hannah and Emily can hold down a fainting spell."

"She's pregnant, tell Hannah." It was Ben. Ben, telling her secret. It was quiet, but she heard it. Judging from Mia's gasp, she'd heard it, too.

Her eyes flew open. "Ben!" He backed off, and her eyes closed again in a merciful curtain to shade her embarrassment.

"Evie, you're okay. It's gonna be okay." It was Mia again, this time her voice close to her head.

"Please get him," she said. "I want to talk to him."

She opened her eyes long enough to make contact with her sister. Mia nodded.

"Everybody, I think this is a wrap for the ceremony. Let's get into the courtyard for some drinks and leave Evie with the docs, *mmm'kay*?" Mia started ushering people out, and slowly, the room emptied. Mia could be pretty insistent when she wanted to be. Her brothers and their wives had kept up a nice fence around her. At least she didn't have to live with the extreme shame of public fainting.

"Can I have a moment?"

It was August. She knew the voice. Would know it anywhere.

"Yes," she answered, finding a strength she didn't know she had.

"I don't think now's the time—" Nick started.

"I think you should let them talk." It was Ben. The golden boy.

Josephine gasped, but Ben was instantly at her side. "Let's find you some champagne, to get through a wedding entirely sober would be a damn shame, if you ask me."

"You're a very bad man." Josephine was giggling. Ben had a way of bringing out the best in Josephine. None of the others had been able to do that.

Mia was back, having successfully emptied the chapel. It took about ten minutes. Long enough for her heart to move up her chest to her throat, but not long enough for her to gather herself together.

"Emily? Hannah?" August interrupted. "I think she's fine now. Let's get the bride and groom and the rest of y'all out in front of the photographer, what do you think?"

"Evie. I know. About the baby." He was direct. To the point.

Mia and Ben were the only people she'd told. August must have gotten the news from her twin.

"Yeah, well. I don't want you to be with me because I'm pregnant." She looked away. "It's damn hot in here, don't you think? Can you open a window?"

August didn't move, just reached for her hand. "You're saying there is another circumstance in which you might want me to be with you?"

Evie just rolled her eyes. "Fine. I'll do it." She got up and walked toward the windows. Anything to put some space between them. It was tough to breathe around August.

"You were wearing his ring." His voice was thick.

"It's a nice ring." *What else could she say?*

"You need to wear mine." He was behind her again. Talking over her shoulder. His body close enough to hers that she could feel the heat radiate from his muscles.

How she wanted to lean back into him. "Need to wear it?" she managed to say.

"Yeah," he said gruffly. "I need you to wear my ring. Be my wife."

"You haven't offered it to me."

"I'm offering now." He stuck his hand out. The ring he held was beautiful. Simple. Sparkling with promise and hope. Dare she start to hope? "I bought this ring for you six years ago."

"Six years ago?" she parroted like an idiot, her head reeling. *Was she gonna faint again?* She spun, turning from the window to look at him directly.

"Look. I know I should do this different. Write 'Marry me' on a cheese pizza or a cookie."

"I don't even like pizza." She was smiling now.

"Truth is, I've wanted to marry you since I met you. And I don't care what your brothers will say. I don't care what anyone says. I love you, Evie, and I think you know that."

She didn't answer. *I love you, Evie, and I think you know that.*

"I know I'm not good enough for you—" he started, stiffening his shoulders. He was putting his armor back on, and with that, her heart fell from her throat back into place.

"How can you say that?" She reached out a hand, pressed it, palm flat against his chest. Right over his heart. She could feel his heart beating, in perfect synchronicity to her own pulse. She felt calm. For the first time since she'd tried on Ben's ring, she didn't feel like fainting. Her world made sense. With August, everything made sense.

"I mean, I know I've had some luck. Gambling. Betting big on oil. Now, with the wind farm."

"August. What you do...that's not what makes you good." She felt his heartbeat speed up. She was making him nervous. Her own heart clenched.

He reached his hand out to settle over hers, interlocking their fingers. She was anchored again. She felt right again.

"Who you are makes you good. Your drive. Your heart. And it's not even about being good. It's about being right. It's about how you make people feel. How you make me feel."

"And how's that?" he asked.

"I feel more myself with you. I feel enough."

"Evie. You are so enough it's not even funny," he said, his voice choked with emotion.

"But now I'm a little more than just Evie. And I want this baby. I didn't plan it. Didn't trick you or anything. You have an out if you want it. I swear."

He tightened his grip on her fingers, then pulled her hand off his chest and to his mouth.

"I never thought for a second that you tricked me," he clarified.

"I know you don't want kids. I remember because when you said it, I thought to myself, it's okay. I don't have to have them, not if it means being with you. You will always be enough for me. But now? Now it's too late. I'm pregnant and I can't imagine not carrying your baby." She was rambling, and she knew it. "The last thing I want to do is trap you. You don't owe me a proposal, August. I don't want to change you."

He squeezed her hand. "Evie. You have changed me."

"I didn't want to."

"But you did, Evie. I love you."

She felt her eyes widen. She was speechless. "I love you more than coffee," he said, trying again. "More than breathing. I wake up and think of you. I go to sleep and I think of you. Hell, I dream of you. I left to the farthest corner of America, and was still a man consumed. There is no other woman for me. There is only you. You, and our baby."

Her eyes stung with tears. "I'm mad, you know."

"You're a dichotomy. So mad doesn't surprise me in the least." But he was smiling.

"I'm mad you took so long." She blinked in rapid succession. Happy tears.

"Yeah, well, I'm happy enough for both of us." He pressed a kiss on her lips. Soft. Quick. Possessive. *August.*

"I love you, Evie."

So she tried out two more truths and a lie:

She was still mad.

She felt at home with him.

She loved him.

The truth had never been clearer, but she kissed him anyway, just to make sure he got it.

* * * * *

COMING SOON!

We really hope you enjoyed reading this book. If you're looking for more romance be sure to head to the shops when new books are available on

Thursday 3rd August

MILLS & BOON

OUT NOW!

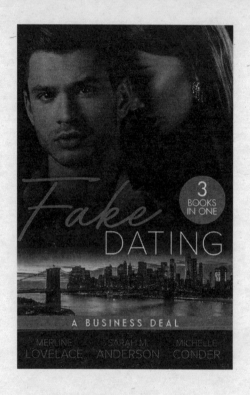

Available at
millsandboon.co.uk

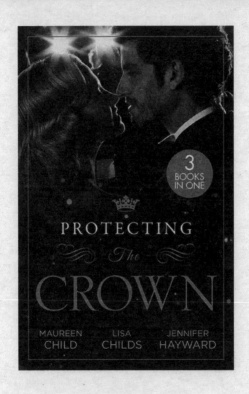

LET'S TALK
Romance

For exclusive extracts, competitions and special offers, find us online:

f MillsandBoon

🐦 @MillsandBoon

📷 @MillsandBoonUK

♪ @MillsandBoonUK

Get in touch on 01413 063 232

MILLS & BOON

THE HEART OF ROMANCE

A ROMANCE FOR EVERY READER

MODERN

Prepare to be swept off your feet by sophisticated, sexy and seductive heroes, in some of the world's most glamourous and romantic locations, where power and passion collide.

HISTORICAL

Escape with historical heroes from time gone by. Whether your passion is for wicked Regency Rakes, muscled Vikings or rugged Highlanders, awaken the romance of the past.

MEDICAL

Set your pulse racing with dedicated, delectable doctors in the high-pressure world of medicine, where emotions run high and passion, comfort and love are the best medicine.

True Love

Celebrate true love with tender stories of heartfelt romance, from the rush of falling in love to the joy a new baby can bring, and a focus on the emotional heart of a relationship.

Desire

Indulge in secrets and scandal, intense drama and sizzling hot action with heroes who have it all: wealth, status, good looks…everything but the right woman.

HEROES

The excitement of a gripping thriller, with intense romance at its heart. Resourceful, true-to-life women and strong, fearless men face danger and desire - a killer combination!

To see which titles are coming soon, please visit

millsandboon.co.uk/nextmonth